The Participants Trilogy

Brian Blose

CONTENTS

The Participants

Book 1 of the

Participants Trilogy

CHAPTER ONE
Zack
Iteration 144

Only a few customers dotted the convenience store after the morning rush. From behind the deli counter, Zack observed them. Two men in neon yellow t-shirts and old jeans perused the not-so-fresh meats on display; the first chewed the dirt-encrusted nails of one hand while the second debated whether he preferred greasy ham or dry turkey. Based on their clothing, Zack decided they must work for an excavation company.

The nail-biting first man had dull eyes and a verbal tic that caused him to mumble an affirmation to everything the second man said. The second man had the rugged looks women found attractive and held himself as if he were well aware of the fact.

"It's grease versus saw-dust," the handsome one said.

"Yep," said the nail-biter.

"Either way it'll be on stale-ass bread."

"Yep."

"Gotta love gas station food."

"Yep."

The handsome man rolled his eyes at the continued agreement of the nail-biter. *He doesn't like the guy,* thought Zack, *so why is he putting up with him?* He had a theory, but there was no way to be certain without asking a question.

"Does your father own the company?" Zack asked the nail-biter.

"Yep. Err, no. I mean no. I work with my brother."

"Works *for* his brother," the handsome man said. "Handles a shovel while I run the equipment. I'll take the ham. Put it on the least stale bread you got."

Zack fulfilled the order while he turned his attention to a kid buying a carton of smokes from Maggie at the register. The leather jacket, name-brand sneakers, and self-satisfied smirk provided Zack everything he needed to make his call: a high-school student skipping school. Maggie rang up the order without asking to see his identification.

A woman who looked about fifty entered the store sporting purse, shoes, and clothing worth more than Zack made in a month. The proud manner with which she displayed her articles suggested she was far less affluent than she appeared. Zack doubted she could afford her shopping habit.

In the back of the store, a young couple pawed at each other in a public display. Both were less than average in appearance. Zack imagined that fact contributed to the ardor in their display of affection. For some, the only thing better than being desired was having witnesses to the fact.

As Zack's gaze roved to the wall of windows facing the parking lot and gas pumps, he noticed a rusted Fiat with a missing license plate back into the handicap parking spot by the doors. Inside the car, two occupants pulled masks over their faces. His heart began to beat faster.

Maggie looked at him when he approached the register. She was a nineteen-year-old high-school dropout and still thought she was going places in life. For some reason, Zack liked her irrational optimism. "Kelly wants to see you in back. Said it was serious."

Maggie threw her head like a stallion. "What now? So help me God if she says I'm stealing again. I will flip on her. Seriously, I'm gonna flip." She stalked to Kelly's small office at the rear of the store.

Zack stepped up to the register and smiled at the fifty-year-old woman decked out in clothes she couldn't afford. "Kids these days," he said.

"I can't even remember that age." She handed him cash. "Pump two."

"The two of you might be closer in age than you think."

The woman laughed. "How old do you think I am, kid?"

Two men entered the store behind the woman, ski masks concealing their faces and hands deep inside pockets. They looked at one another before stepping into line behind the old woman. *These two are awful polite for robbers. They must be new to their profession,* he thought.

"I think you're five years old," Zack said as he returned the old woman's change.

She frowned at him, obviously unsure how to take him. "Funny," she finally deadpanned before turning to leave the store.

The men in ski masks pressed forward to lean ominously over the counter. "Give us all your money," the one wearing a camouflage hunting jacket growled.

The past five years had been an eternity to Zack. Five years observing creatures too simple to grasp the pointlessness of their lives. Five years wishing he had never been created. Five years waiting for the sky to open.

Zack smiled. "Are you trying to rob a gas station?"

The one in camo leaned closer, giving Zack a clear look into wild, bloodshot eyes. *Drugs*, Zack thought. The second robber leaned in, looked at Zack with tilted head, and smiled with feral intent. The second robber looked like he wanted to shoot someone.

"Hey, idiots, there's this thing called a cash drop box. We put large bills into a slot and the only way to get the money out is for the owner to use his key. At most you can get a few hundred dollars from a gas station. Hell, there's probably less than that in this drawer because it's been a light morning and we've had a lot of people use credit cards."

"Open the register or I'll blow your brains out," camo growled at him.

"All I have to do is push the silent alarm and the police will be here in minutes. You might as well start running now, cause I'm not giving you deadbeats a single dime. Got it?"

The second robber pulled a gun from his jacket pocket and pointed it at Zack's face. Obscenities began to pour from camo. Zack stared into the eyes of the man with the gun, ignoring the barrel six inches from his nose. "You don't have the balls."

"Last chance, shithead." The man pulled back on the slide action, cocking the pistol. "Open the register or die."

Zack couldn't force a laugh, but he managed to bring his smile back. "You didn't even have a round in the chamber when you put that in my face? Do you think this is a movie where people crap their pants whenever they hear someone load a round? I'm not impressed. If you and your boyfriend run now, you might have time for one last circle-jerk before the cops bust you."

The decision to kill registered in the gunman's eyes. Zack just had time to notice the shift of intent before a tidal wave of thunder hit him. He felt himself hit the floor. His vision was gone, leaving a claustrophobic darkness in its place. Fear and confusion struggled in vain against the encroaching tide of oblivion. Thoughts dimmed and Zack was free.

CHAPTER TWO
Elza
Iteration 1

She shuffled her feet with the other women as the brutes who had murdered their men herded them forward. Abduction was a new experience for Elza. The world had grown increasingly violent over the centuries to the point that its absence was more remarkable than its presence. Elza thought that particular observation would be useful to the Creator.

One of the women found the energy to sob. Elza moved away from the noise, sure one of the brutes would charge in to restore silence with more violence. A man shouted for quiet and the woman swallowed her grief. They trudged in stillness once more.

Elza studied the landscape. Trees, hills, and streams dominated. She had determined long ago that the intended subject of her observation was the people rather than the environment. She only noticed her surroundings when she had nothing better to observe or when she had trouble with her nerves.

The brutes had attacked her tribe's camp without warning that morning, murdered men and children, then gathered the surviving women together for their sport. Elza's constant handicap, the apathy men felt towards her, had saved her from all but a little roughness. She didn't know how long they would continue to ignore her. Eventually, they would hold her down and take their pleasure. Elza crossed her arms tightly across her chest. As an Observer, it was her duty to bear whatever happened in the service of the Creator.

It might be easier if she didn't struggle. Elza banished the worries from her mind. She should be grateful for the new experiences. The Creator needed to experience everything possible through Elza's senses so that She could have input for the design of the next Iteration of the world. *Still,* thought Elza, *it would be nice if the sky opened before these brutes put their hands on me.*

They stumbled to a stop at the edge of a camp. The leader of the brutes, a man called Kallig, raised his gray-bearded face skyward to roar in triumph. "Come look at my trophies! I bring ten women for the tribe!"

Thirteen women, Elza silently corrected him. She suspected Kallig was much better at spearing men in their sleep than he was at counting.

"Who brought the other three?" asked a man from the camp.

"I brought all of them, coward," Kallig said.

The man who had spoken walked towards the captive women until Kallig barred his way with a spear. "You don't get any of the women because you are a coward."

The man smiled up at the taller Kallig. "I'm not afraid of your spear and I already have a woman. Let me pass or I will send you to meet your uncle."

Kallig lifted his spear. "We'll have a feast to celebrate my victory!"

Elza ignored the women's restless movements as the man approached. While neither tall nor muscular, he strode confidently, sizing up the situation with a steady gaze. Elza froze for a second when his eyes met hers.

"My name is Hess," the man said. "I know this is probably the worst day of your life." His brilliant blue eyes met each of theirs in turn. "You will have time to grieve later, but for now you need to be smart. Resisting these men will only make them crueler. Try to please them as best as you can."

A woman held out a hand to him. "Protect me," she said. "I will do everything to please you if you protect me from them."

Hess sighed. "Sorry. I don't involve myself in these things." His gaze caught Elza's for a third time. He frowned. "What is wrong with your eyes?"

Elza's face flushed hot. "Nothing."

"Only one points at me." Hess scrutinized her.

"Perhaps the other objects to your looks."

Hess stepped close and pitched his voice low for her ears only. "Watch yourself in this tribe. You speak too boldly and watch too openly. The men here like to break stubborn women."

Downy chest hair peeked free of Hess's furs, different from the smooth chests of the other men of the tribe. Combined with his uncommonly pale eyes, it suggested he was an outsider by blood as well as temperament. "Why do you care what happens to us?"

"Wrong question, woman."

"And what is the right question?"

7

"The right question is why no one else cares." Hess stepped away, then hesitated. "If you aren't noticed, the men may forget you and tire themselves out on the others. You are smart. Do whatever it takes."

Elza watched Hess cross the camp, collect an attractive woman, and disappear into a tent. In spite of her situation, she found herself intrigued. Hess was, without a doubt, the most fascinating man she had ever met.

CHAPTER THREE
Zack
Iteration 144

The sirens were the first thing to reach him. Their strident wails pierced the haze of his mind, drawing him back towards full awareness. Zack opened his eyes to find himself in darkness. Immediately, he began to thrash his arms, striking at the space above him, wordlessly snarling in a kaleidoscope of emotions. Rage, fear, and weariness swirled within him in a corrosive solution, burning away the veneer of sanity.

"Oh my God, he's moving!"

Zack's movements dislodged a jacket from his face and the return of light banished the shadows within him. "He's moving, Kelly! Do something!"

He sat up. And then Zack remembered the robbers, the gun, and the thunder that pronounced the end of his life. But death had rejected him. Or, more accurately, his nature had rejected death just as it rejected every other harm inflicted upon his body.

Maggie was trying to climb Kelly like a pole, staring and pointing at him in horror. Zack momentarily pondered the psychology of her response. He decided the sense of revulsion had its origin in the proof that an essential assumption was false. Horror was the panicked realization of ignorance. Realizing a stick was in fact a snake forced an individual to recognize that they were not able to identify the threats in their environment. Seeing a dead body revive introduced a much greater uncertainty and therefore a correspondingly greater revulsion.

The intense curiosity which had seized him upon witnessing Maggie's reaction released him when he realized the spectacle he had made of himself. He was interfering with the events he was supposed to watch; violating the sanctity of his observations. The repercussions of his actions could ripple out to taint every aspect of his interactions in this world.

Kelly backed towards the door. "Shit, he's alive."

Zack said the only thing that came to mind. "I can't believe that guy missed me at that range. He must have been smoking something."

"No way he missed. Your brains are all over the cigarette display," Kelly said.

Zack glanced over his shoulder. As expected, no bodily fluids stained the merchandise. They had returned to where the Creator intended them to be, just as they did when he got a paper-cut or nicked himself shaving. "It's not there, Kelly. Maybe you girls just had a little too much excitement today and imagined things."

Maggie shook her head. "I swear to God I saw you dead. I threw the jacket from the lost and found on top of you it was so nasty."

"Then why are my brains inside my head right now?"

Paramedics loped into the store with medical kits, shouting questions about who was in charge and where the body was. Kelly glanced back and forth between the medics and Zack, then threw her hands in the air. "I need some fresh air."

One of the men approached him. "You hurt, kid?"

"No, sir," Zack said.

"Is anyone here hurt?"

Zack shrugged. "The women went crazy for a bit. Does that count?"

Not long after the ambulance departed, a state trooper arrived to gather evidence. Zack re-enacted the scene for the female officer, claiming to slip and fall whenever the gunman cocked his gun. The officer took each of their reports, then asked to see the surveillance video.

Zack's stomach dropped. There were three cameras inside the store. One pointed directly down at the register to prevent employee theft, another sat where it caught the face of every customer walking through the door, and the third was pointed at the deli counter. Zack turned to look at the third camera. He was almost certain that the background of the shot would show a perfect side profile of the person at the register.

They crowded into the manager's office while Kelly brought the camera feed up on the computer screen. At the officer's direction, Kelly showed the door camera from earlier. The rusty Fiat backed into the spot directly before the door and two men got out. There was no license plate. The two men had their masks on before they came into view to enter the store, then retreated to their car empty-handed a minute later. The officer made notes of everything, then asked to see the other cameras.

Kelly brought up the register camera and they watched events unfold. The front of Zack's face bobbed in and out of the picture from one side of the screen throughout the conversation. The officer muttered something about stupid macho men. When the gun came out, Zack wasn't in frame. They saw the gun fire without learning anything.

Zack held his breath as the feed from the third camera came onto the screen. In perfect clarity, it showed Zack abandon customers at the deli counter to kick Maggie off the register, taunt a gunman, and take a bullet to the head. The stream from the exit wound sprayed matter onto the cigarettes and the body collapsed.

At the same moment, Kelly, Maggie, and the police officer turned to look at him. Zack presented his best scowl. "Is this some kind of hoax?" He pointed a finger at his coworkers. "Are the two of you trying to mess with me?"

They stared at him until the officer cleared her throat. "I can't write this up as a homicide when the victim is still walking around. My report will say Mr. Vernon fell to the ground before the gun went off. I'll let the three of you decide for yourselves if this was a miracle or what not."

Zack returned to register duty once things were settled. There was a line of customers waiting to pay for gas and hear some gossip about events in the store. Zack downplayed his involvement and took cash as quickly as possible. Ideally he would leave after making himself so conspicuous. Unfortunately, he had made commitments which would keep him in western Pennsylvania for a while.

When a customer mentioned he heard from the radio that some guy died in a shooting, Zack pulled out his cell phone. There were no missed calls, but it would only be a matter of time before one of Lacey's coworkers told her the news. If he didn't contact her soon, she would call him in a panic. No matter what he did or said at that point, there would be a fight tonight.

Getting involved had been a mistake. He should have remained at the deli counter and observed. Zack's glanced to the corner of the store where Maggie was texting her friends. He knew her well enough to be certain she would have complied with any request of the gunman, but he couldn't be sure how a sociopath jonesing for his drug would react. The ambulance might have been necessary if Zack hadn't interfered.

Zack felt a flash of guilt at the thought. The divine command, a wordless understanding instilled within him by the Creator, demanded observation. It was open to some level of interpretation, but any dictionary ever compiled would list participation as the antonym of observation. Sometimes Zack found himself sympathizing with these creatures too much. They were nothing more than figments of the Creator's imagination, temporarily granted existence for a purpose Zack did not know.

When he finished with the last customer, Zack walked over to Maggie. "I have to make a phone call. You're on register."

Maggie kept a safe distance from him. "Lacey's gonna flip when she hears what you did. I went to school with her, remember, and Lacey's one mean bitch."

"It would be nice if Lacey heard my version of the story first."

Maggie smirked at him. "Too late. I texted her a pic before I tossed the jacket on your head."

I didn't think she had the guts to do that, Zack thought. "Let me see your phone," he said.

"No way. You just want to delete the evidence. You're too late, anyway. I sent it to like a hundred people. My friend Jess knows people. She's going to get it on the news for me."

She must really hate Lacey. And my spooky revival did nothing to endear me to her. How did I miss the fact that she was so cold-blooded? Zack resisted the curiosity that rose up within him. He needed to perform damage control right now. There was no time to study Maggie's psychology. Maybe he could remind her of the reason she was still alive. "Did Kelly have anything to say to you this morning?"

"I don't know what that was about. When I got to her office, I told her that if she tried getting me fired she would be sorry, then she got up in my face asking what I did. After that, you went and got your brains blown out."

No good deed goes unpunished, Zack thought. That kind of perverse incentive seemed a flaw in any sane world, but who was he to judge the Creator?

"Did you ever think that you were supposed to be on that register?"

Maggie nodded towards the door. "Your wifey just showed up."

Lacey stood there, mascara running down her face, frizzy straw-colored hair a ragged mess from raking her fingers through it as she did when nervous, one hand cradling a protruding abdomen wrapped in stretchy maternity clothes, staring at him in shock. Then she had the worst reaction Zack thought possible. Lacey ran forward and seized him with both arms, burying her face in his chest.

"I thought you were dead!"

Zack looked down at the mess of Lacey's hair and pondered the impulse that made this woman love him. They barely spoke except to argue. Physical chemistry was nonexistent. There wasn't even respect between them. Lacey's previous boyfriend knocked her up right before a judge sent him to jail for burning down a co-worker's house. Lacey hooked up with Zack at a bar and claimed to be pregnant with his child two days later. All these months later, Lacey still continued the charade. After every checkup, she dropped hints that her baby was growing fast and might come early. Lacey believed him to be an idiot, which he thought only fair as he had the same opinion of her. The only reason he could imagine for her devotion to him was desperation.

Zack patted Lacey's back and cleared his throat. "Let's talk outside." Where Maggie couldn't contradict his story.

"There's video of it all," Maggie volunteered. "Want to see it?"

"Stop this," Zack said.

"Zack got his brains blown out, then ten minutes later they grew back. When he started moving, I freaked out. I think Kelly might have shit in her Depends."

Lacey released him. "I want to see it."

"You don't want to watch the video." A flash of inspiration struck Zack. "Too much excitement isn't good for the baby. We should get you home to rest."

Lacey's eyes narrowed in suspicion. "I need to know what happened."

"I thought the guy was bluffing and he shot at me, but he missed."

While less than intelligent, Lacey's limited powers of deduction were bolstered by intimate familiarity. "You were asking for it. You wanted to die."

"Come on, Lacey, you don't believe that."

Her skin began to flush bright red until Zack could imagine steam shooting from her ears like a cartoon character. "I am pregnant with your baby! How dare you do something like this? You're an asshole, Zack, a fucking asshole! What would I do if you died? Move back into my mom's place? You know I can't stand her."

"You could move into section eight housing. There are programs to help people in your situation. It wouldn't be the end of the world."

Lacey threw up her hands. "I ain't living in some welfare apartment so my neighbors can give my kid drugs."

"Actually, they drug screen applicants for the housing assistance program, so your neighbors would be clean. But go ahead and assume people you never met are going to slip crack into your baby's bottle."

"Oh, I forgot how damn smart you are. Well guess what. You just admitted you were trying to get yourself killed!"

Zack glared at her. "I never said that. I just want you to stop the drama."

"Drama? You don't know shit about drama, honey. I lived with drama for eighteen years so don't talk to me about drama."

"So screaming at me in public doesn't count as drama?"

Lacey folded her arms. "We'll talk about it later. I need to go back to work now because we can't live on your paycheck. Just do me a favor and don't kill yourself when I'm eight months pregnant."

"I thought you were only at seven months." Zack regretted the words the moment he said them. Lacey's face went white. "Seven months and change. I'm just rounding up," she said. As she waddled past the door, Lacey raised both hands to her face.

Proposing to her had been a mistake. Not because of the frustration it caused him – Zack suspected he somehow deserved that. It had been a mistake because Lacey expected things from a husband he couldn't provide. She wanted love and Zack wasn't even sure such a thing existed. The best he could offer was pity.

"You should've stayed dead, Zack," Maggie said.

I wish it was that easy, he thought. Aloud he said, "I'm on break. You handle the register." Zack went outside to the employee break pavilion and sat on a picnic table, watching his wife cry in her car and wondering why the Creator needed an Observer. He did nothing about the former and came to no conclusion on the latter.

CHAPTER FOUR
Elza
Iteration 1

Half of the women abducted with Elza were claimed on the first day. Kallig, the leader of the brutes, granted each claim after a dramatic pause. His men seemed to have a good sense of their place in the social order and none made a selection before his betters were done. The division of spoils was handled in a solemn fashion by the brutes. The women all wept quietly in acceptance of their fate except for one who chose to struggle. That one was held down while her new man claimed her before everyone. The others were too numb to resist.

Hess watched the proceedings from a distance, scowling his disapproval. Kallig shouted for Hess to leave several times, but the other men pretended not to notice their witness. Elza already had a good feel for the group dynamic of this tribe, but Hess did not fit into the system. The tribe was ruled by fear and intimidation. The strongest and fiercest men commanded great respect. The weaker men endured the abuse of their betters. The women born into the tribe presented a meek face to the men but had a parallel power structure among themselves. The only person who didn't fit was Hess.

She didn't understand why Kallig constantly berated Hess, nor why Hess ignored the insults and commands. Kallig would not tolerate disobedience from someone he could kill. Affection obviously did not exist between Hess and him, so fear must hold his hand. But if Hess was superior in battle, why did he restrain himself? Did his status as an outsider mean that the other men would not follow him? Or did he object to the brutality of the others? If so, then why did he stay?

The puzzle of Hess was a welcome distraction from speculating on her fate. When the selections were done that first night, the un-chosen women slept fitfully on the bare earth while their relatives and friends were taken into the tents of the men. Elza noted the condition of her unwanted companions that night: gray hair, rotted teeth, unsightly blemishes, and sickly frames. Despite her apparent youth and health, in terms of attractiveness men grouped Elza with the old and disabled. She liked to think it made her more objective, but tonight she worried that the rejection of the men would come to cause her greater pain in the morning.

All of the women knew their future was grim. Being taken tonight would be bad, but being taken tomorrow would be worse. They had no future in this tribe of brutality but to suffer. If Elza could not slip away soon, the men would discover that her wounds vanished in moments. Given their sadistic streak, that could lead to a rather long torture session.

Elza spotted a sentry the moment she sat up. His outline turned towards her movement. She lay back on the ground. They were waiting for someone to attempt an escape. Throughout the night, she periodically checked to see if the sentries were awake. They always were. Morning dawned without her sleeping a single moment.

The camp came awake slowly, first children bringing the embers of the previous night's fires back to life, then women grinding acorns into meal for bread cooked on hot stones. The men ate smoked meat and bread before separating into hunting parties and guards. The unwanted women huddled together as the camp went about its normal activities. They remained unmolested unless they tried to move beyond the circle of earth where they had been left.

When Hess approached at midmorning, the women were grateful to receive a visitor. The guards averted their eyes when Hess passed. One of the old women asked what would happen to them. Hess knelt in their center. "Do you have a skill? You may be able to save yourself if you can tan hides or braid rope or mix medicines." Hess's normally firm gaze darted to the scenery as he spoke, and Elza knew his words were lies.

The women began to throw out useful skills they knew. Hess deliberated on each offering before agreeing it would be nice to have someone in their tribe who could weave fish traps and knap flint and work clay. The mood rose as the women latched onto the hope Hess provided them.

Elza pondered the question Hess had posed the previous day. Why did no one besides Hess care about the condition of the women? It was the question of a child too young to understand that concepts such as fairness and justice were a fiction created by doting parents. People always did what provided them the most benefit in their circumstances. They raised children with affection to ensure care in their old age. They cooperated to maximize food and safety for all. They fought strangers to preserve their own lives. In some tribes, like this one, they brutalized one another to avoid being the victim.

But Hess did not fit into this tribe. He violated the natural order and survived. She waited until his gaze crossed hers and spoke. "Do you have an answer to your own question? Why is it that no one else cares what happens to us?"

"I've been thinking about you, woman. What is your name?"

Her cheeks burned as she answered. "Elza."

"You don't fit in with your people, Elza. You are smart. You notice things." His eyes darted to the other women. "Don't you think things are better now than before? Imagine if every person tried to make the world better. Life does not have to be the way it is."

Elza noted the firmness of his voice contrasted with his hunched posture. There was some conflict within him. "You didn't answer the question."

"I guess I didn't. This probably won't mean anything to you, but the answer to my question is that He made this world wrong." Hess placed a hand on her shoulder and spoke softly. "I'm sorry, but the only help I can give is false hope. You would make a fascinating study under better conditions."

After he departed, one of the women spoke to her. "I think he may choose you as his woman." Another nodded. "This is a good time for a man to like you, Elza. He can protect you from the others."

She tried to support their delusions with a hopeful smile. They didn't know how to watch people. Hess didn't see a woman. He saw a subject to study, the same as when she looked at people. Elza had never expected to see it from one of them. What caused such a thing to develop in a man? If she survived, maybe she would have a chance to ask him. Of course, her observations would be contaminated once she survived her execution.

One of the guards came over to them. "What did Hess say? Is he going to kill Kallig with his powers?"

A woman hastily responded that Hess only wanted to know if they had useful skills for the tribe. The guard pondered that. "No one knows what Hess will do. The men are frightened."

Elza frowned. "What powers does Hess have?" This was something she had never encountered before.

"Hess is older than my father's father and cannot be hurt by weapons. They say he knows your thoughts just by looking at you."

Elza stood slowly and faced the direction Hess had gone. He sat on a rock nearby, looking in her direction. His last words echoed in her ears. *You would make a fascinating study under better conditions.* Everything turned surreal as she realized something completely unexpected. Other Observers existed —she was looking right at one.

CHAPTER FIVE
Zack
Iteration 144

Zack turned off his cell-phone when reporters discovered his number, which was towards the end of his shift. By the time Zack got home, the news had run not only the picture Maggie snapped with her phone, but also the damning video from the store camera, which someone had uploaded to the internet. The confrontation with Lacey began the moment he walked through the door and lasted for over an hour, only ending when Lacey began to cry. Zack uttered false assurances that he was happy, did love her, and thought life was great.

They ate a dinner of tater tots and chicken nuggets microwaved to a soggy mess while they watched the local news. Zack listened to a segment on road construction around Pittsburgh while Lacey pushed food around on her plate. "One of us needs to learn how to cook before the baby gets here."

"I know how to cook," Zack said.

"Microwaves don't count, hon."

"I cook food at work every day."

"That thing at your work is just a big toaster. I'm talkin' about real food."

The news anchors began discussing a recent crime spree targeting hubcaps. "Real food, huh? Don't you think it's hard to define real food when no one is certain what is real in the first place?"

"Real is when you can see and touch something. It's not complicated, Hon."

"It's not just seeing and touching. It's perceiving and remembering, which are unreliable mental processes. Let's give a hypothetical situation where the world began five years ago."

Lacey snorted. "World's lot older than that."

"How can anyone really know the age of the world? If the world sprang into existence five years ago, fully formed with a complete but false history, no one would know. Fake memories would match fake records."

"And Santa Clause has a magic sleigh too," Lacey said.

Zack smiled. "Who knows, right?"

"Pretty sure I know."

"You *think* you know."

"I know what you do at work ain't real cooking."

"How about making candy bar milkshakes? Is that real cooking?"

"Hell no. And you still owe me a new blender for that."

"It tasted good, though."

"Not as good as Dairy Queen."

The news returned to the story of the shooting. "Today in Sarver, a robbery goes bad and an employee loses his life. Except he's completely unharmed. Watch the security footage and decide if this is a miracle or a hoax." Zack turned off the television. Seeing himself on the news drove home the realization of how bad he had screwed up.

"Wow," Lacey said, "I didn't think anything could make you skip the news."

"Just make sure the baby comes at a convenient time."

"You watch the news in the delivery room and I'll put the remote where you don't want it."

After they finished dinner, Zack washed the mismatched dishes in the sink and replaced them in the cupboard while Lacey painted her nails at the table, filling their cramped trailer with fumes that couldn't be healthy. Zack grabbed a Penn Dark from the fridge and sat across from his wife. *Cue a comment about the cost of microbrews.*

"Y'know, if you didn't have to buy fancy Penn Brewery beer, we could get cable."

"Cable costs a bit more than that, Lacey." *Next she'll mention texting.*

"We could at least get texting on our plan. I'm the only person at work without it."

Zack began to peel the label, watching Lacey from the corner of his eye, waiting for her to mention Kelly Green, a former friend and compulsive label peeler whom Lacey despised.

"You know that annoys the hell out of me," she said.

Zack grunted. Usually he could direct her side of the conversation for at least five exchanges. Once he got twelve in a row, but he hadn't managed a roll like that in over a month. Instead of becoming more predictable with familiarity, Lacey grew increasingly temperamental. Zack thought that was his fault. His intimate influence rendered Lacey a contaminated subject. Instead of observing her behavior, he was observing her reactions to him.

He turned his attention to the bottle in his hands. The brewery was half an hour south, on the north side of Pittsburgh. It produced a range of beer varieties, but Penn Dark, their version of a German Dunkel, was his favorite. He thought it might be nice to visit the place one day, but his daily routine already demanded too much energy from him.

Zack wondered if he would have been happier under different circumstances. When this world sprang into existence, he was given the identity of Zack Vernon, twenty-year-old heir to a recently deceased business executive and owner of an investment portfolio worth seven million dollars. In his first day of life, Zack had contemplated his options. The money afforded him the ability to travel, live an extravagant lifestyle, pursue an education, or walk the world without the requirement of working.

In the terrifying darkness of his first night, Zack resolved to get rid of the money. The rash decision survived into the light of day and Zack arranged for everything he possessed to be donated to helping orphans. Zack had been surprised by how little transgressing the Divine Command bothered him.

Faced with the requirement to work, Zack took the first opening he could find that would allow him to observe people. Five years later, he still worked at the same gas station convenience store. The only significant change to his life had been the appearance of Lacey.

Zack threw the empty bottle in the trash and prepared for bed. He changed clothes, washed his face, brushed his teeth, checked the nightlight was plugged into the outlet, and climbed under the covers. He stared at the cheap glow-in-the-dark star stickers he had plastered to the ceiling and imagined the aftermath of his death. People screaming, robbers running, Maggie snapping her photo, Lacey crying, paramedics racing, and him in a puddle of blood and brains, feeling nothing. Tears slipped free of his eyes. He had almost escaped.

CHAPTER SIX
Elza
Iteration 1

I'm not the only one. I'm not the only one. I'm not the only one. The mantra ran through Elza's mind on a constant loop. She stared at Hess, unable to order her chaotic thoughts. For seven hundred years, she observed creation under the assumption that she was the only agent of the Creator. Suddenly, she wasn't alone. It made her a hell of a lot less important.

Another thought came to her. *How many are there? Just the two of us? Ten? A hundred?* There was no way to answer that question. Elza didn't understand why this knowledge had been withheld from her. At the moment of creation, Elza knew her purpose, understood the memories implanted in her mind were fabrications, and recalled the knowledge that one day the sky would open so she could leave existence to make her report. There had been no indication that other Observers walked the Earth.

"Look at her. She likes the idea of having a man."

The whispers of the women bothered her. "I don't care for Hess," she said. The women chuckled and went about their gossip. Elza scowled at their levity. Hess had done this to them, exchanged their terror for hope. He should not have interfered. His actions were inexcusable. The Creator was greater than all of creation. How could an Observer ever justify placing some tiny bit of creation above the Creator?

Elza felt a fire grow in her chest. She had endured beatings and humiliations in service to the Creator, while this *man* set himself up to live in comfort and indiscriminately altered events to his fancy. He didn't even switch tribes to avoid revealing his unnatural lifespan. Hess leveraged his nature into personal power.

She opened her mouth to tell the women that Hess had lied to them, then hesitated. Harsh words would not return them to a state of ignorance.

One interference would not cancel out another – they were already contaminated. Anything she said would only inflict distress upon the women for no cause.

They do not deserve my anger. He does. Elza folded her arms and glared at Hess, willing him to come speak with her again. She intended to make him regret his interference. That he tainted his own observations was bad, but compromising her work was unforgivable. Elza was about to have the worst experience of her life and it would be useless to the Creator because this man had contaminated the entire tribe.

Noon came and went. The brutes, their women, and Hess ate smoked meat, figs, and pine nuts. The captive women had nothing to eat but dandelions they picked from the same ground that they relieved themselves on. Elza ignored the hunger pangs. Her body was prone to fatigue, but she could ignore that infirmity when necessary. What she could not ignore was the fact that these men were going to brutalize and violate her in front of that man. Elza ground her teeth until her jaw sent stabs of pain all the way to her temple. Because he was an Observer for the creator, she couldn't even bring herself to request he not watch.

Glaring at the impassive Observer did no good. Elza finally plopped her rear to the ground. The good spirit of the other women had departed. They could fool themselves for only so long. That their captors denied them food and water and shade proved a lack of regard. These women were accustomed to hardship, but their resilience did not include trusting the brutes who had murdered their men and their children. Elza wasn't sure just when the change of mood had happened. She had been too busy trying to bring Hess back.

"You are a very odd woman, Elza."

She spun at *his* voice. He had waited until her attention was elsewhere to sneak up on her. "You are participating," she said.

Hess raised one brow on his handsome face. *Why is one such as him given an attractive form and made a man while I must be ugly and endure the touch of brutes?* Her best glare brought only an amused smile in response.

"I have nothing to do with what the men of this tribe do. You can blame me if it makes you feel better, but I am not involved."

"You are *participating.*" She emphasized the word.

Hess narrowed his eyes. "What are you saying?"

"The Creator did not send you here to bed beautiful women and tease Kallig."

The man sucked in one cheek as he pondered her words, but gave no other clues to his mental state. Finally, he spoke softly. "How many of us are there?"

"It doesn't matter. You are violating the Divine Command. This entire tribe is contaminated because of you. My observations are ruined." She spoke firmly, but kept her volume low to avoid a spectacle.

Hess sucked in his cheek again. "We participate just by existing. You can claim that I participate more than you think right, but you can't say I am wrong to do it. The Creator made us in this form. He obviously intended us to interact with people to make our observations."

She climbed to her feet. "These people fear you. That is manipulating, not observing. You said this world is wrong. That is judging, not observing. You comforted these women. That is interfering, not observing. She didn't place you in this world for your own enjoyment."

"*She?*" Hess flashed a smug grin. "You think the Creator is a woman?"

"Do you really think a man would create a world?"

Hess gestured around them. "Does this look like a world created for the benefit of women? Clearly the Creator must be a man."

This conversation is ridiculous. The Creator doesn't have flesh. Gender doesn't apply to Her. Then Elza saw the conviction in his eyes and stiffened her resolve. "What do men make? Nothing. On the other hand, women make everything people need. Clothes. Tents. Rope. Pottery. Children." Her legs wobbled beneath her.

"I have yet to observe a woman who could make a child by herself." Hess looped his arm through hers just before she dropped to the ground from exhaustion. "We can argue some more after you eat." He pulled her arm over his shoulder.

"Let go of me," she hissed.

Hess hesitated. "I don't know what good you think you're doing here, but I know what will happen to these women. You want no part in it."

"I don't interfere in events like you," Elza said.

"Don't make this about your pride. The Creator doesn't require this of you."

"Let me go."

"You said that I contaminated this entire tribe. If you believe that, then there is no reason for you to observe anything further here."

"Let me go."

Hess released her. "If you think enduring pain proves something, then go ahead and flatter your pride. All I see is stupidity."

Elza knelt to relieve her shaky legs. "As for me, I see a coward." The pity in his eyes burned her. "Get away from me. You are interfering with my observations."

Hess returned to his rock on the other side of the camp. She intended to glare at him for the remainder of the daylight, but hunger and lack of sleep conspired against her. Her eyes drifted closed.

CHAPTER SEVEN
Zack
Iteration 144

One day after the incident, a reporter from a Pittsburgh station came to the convenience store. Zack spoke to her briefly, explaining the video was a prank by some of his coworkers. The reporter asked him if he believed in miracles, Zack told her he wasn't religious, and she went on her way.

That same day, Kelly called him into her office so the store's owner could yell at him over the phone for escalating the situation with the robbers. Zack insisted he didn't think the man would shoot, apologized for making the gas station look bad, and begged to keep his job. The owner berated him for fifteen minutes before conceding Zack could keep his job.

Maggie didn't show for her shift and Zack learned later that she had quit. Kelly, never close to him, now spoke to him only when necessary. The other employees watched him constantly when they shared shifts. Many of the customers recognized him from the news and had questions or wanted to make comments. It tainted his observations and distracted him at the same time.

Zack decided he would give things two weeks to settle down. If he was still being scrutinized at the end of that time, he would get a job somewhere else. Provided he could find the energy.

For three days following the shooting, Zack went nowhere but work and home, skipping his customary trips to the library for internet access. He skipped the nightly news as well. He spent the time freed up from those activities laying in bed, staring at the ceiling and forcing his mind to stillness.

The fourth day, a Saturday, he wasn't scheduled to work. Zack spent the day with his wife, preparing the second bedroom of his trailer for a baby that was not his. The jobs Lacey assigned him were assembling a crib and changing table while she organized baby clothes, baby toys, and two hospital bags – one for her and one for the baby.

She prattled about the prices of everything until Zack made a throw-away comment about the cost of paying for college some day. That idea took hold in Lacey's mind and she insisted they immediately stock up on children's books. When they finished book shopping, Zack listened to Lacey's plans for the delivery. He rewarded Lacey for her productivity by ordering a pizza that stretched their budget more than was prudent, then was receptive to her advances later that night.

The fifth day, Sunday, his shift started at five in the morning. Zack worked the deli counter and watched the customers without any great interest, pondering happiness. Not the fleeting happiness that briefly accompanied success. The other kind. The kind that appeared when it shouldn't. In an elderly man whose every proud step brought pain. In a shy, obese woman who gambled away two dollars every morning at the lottery machine only to declare tomorrow must be her lucky day. In a long-haul trucker who announced he was single after catching his wife in the act.

As tempting as it was to diagnose these individuals with stupidity, Zack resisted the urge. They were functioning adults. They understood the circumstances of their own lives. Were they delusional? Did they intentionally lie to themselves in exchange for the taste of happiness? Zack gained no insight into the enigma despite devoting the entire morning to its consideration.

The arrival of a voluptuous blonde interrupted Zack's thoughts. Something caught his attention the moment she crossed the threshold. He studied her appearance and her mannerisms as she perused the shelves. The woman wore fashionable off-brand clothing, a conservative black blouse whose contours subtly suggested things to every man in the room and tan skirt that emphasized the movements of her hips. Her calm, curious inspection of her environment suggested intelligence, self-confidence, purpose, and situational awareness. Her appearance was a remarkable coordination of an outfit, a body, and an attitude.

He had no idea how to categorize this woman. If she were better dressed, he would say she was wealthy. If her movements were less seductive, he would guess she worked in law enforcement. He dismissed roles in rapid succession. Criminal? No; too relaxed. Celebrity? No; too natural.

She looked directly at him when her path through the store came closest to his counter. Her rapid assessment of him was obvious from the manner in which her eyes leaped from one feature to the next, pausing for brief inspections. Zack leaned forward. *Who is she?*

The woman smiled and swayed up to his counter. A tilt to her head told him she was about to slip into a less-than-honest role. He lifted his chin a hair and narrowed his eyes for an instant. The woman's demure shrug said she knew he could see through her and apologized for the act. Zack let out a slow breath. *We just had a whole conversation without a single word. Who the hell is this woman?*

"I saw you on the news the other day," she said.

Zack cleared his throat. "That was a hoax."

The woman's eyes darted towards the camera mounted to the wall beside him – the same camera that had caught the damning video. "You were sloppy."

She knows. "Who are you?"

"Call me Bridgette. I believe you go by Zack?"

"That's my name," he said.

She waved her hand in dismissal. "Names don't matter."

"Who are you?"

"Who do you think I am, Zack?" She leaned forward in anticipation.

Zack's eyes traced the outline of her face. "A model? Maybe a reporter?"

She shook her head. "My job is a lot more important than that."

Job. That suggested she was an employee and not an employer. "Professional manager, secret agent, scientist, preacher . . . . No? None of those? I give up."

Bridgette blinked and stepped back. "You're serious. You really don't know what I am."

"Why would you expect a complete stranger to be able to guess your job?"

Bridgette looked into his eyes as she spoke. "Hess, it's me."

Zack glanced down at the counter before responding. "I think you have me confused with someone else."

"No, Zack, I don't. I know exactly who you are. Who you have been for a hundred and forty-four iterations."

He cleared his throat. "Why don't you tell me who you think I am and I'll let you know if you're right or wrong?"

"You're an immortal Observer for the Creator."

Zack took a deep breath. *How does she know that? It's an impossible guess. There's no way anyone could know about me. Not unless . . . .* "I'm not the only one." He blinked, then spoke in a rush. "You're an Observer. Are there any others?"

Bridgette stared at him. "You're not this convincing of an actor."

"What do you mean?"

She shook her head. "Never mind. Can we talk outside?"

"Sure. There's a pavilion off to the side."

"I spotted it on my way in."

Zack laughed. "Of course you noticed it. I would have." He abandoned his post at the deli counter, trying to suppress the giddy excitement within him. Other Observers existed. It lessened the guilt he felt over his deficits to know that he didn't bear the entire burden of witnessing creation. It meant there were others who understood his problems. Others who might know how to deal with things. It meant there was hope for him.

He asked his first question before they reached the pavilion. "Do you have any idea how many of us there are?"

"Eleven," she said.

"That's awful specific. How do you know?"

Bridgette sat on the picnic table. "Because in a hundred and forty-four iterations, I have only met ten others. In case you hadn't noticed, it's pretty easy to spot our own kind. Even easier if they get themselves on the national news."

"Why eleven? It seems an odd number."

"Well, Zack, that's a very old question. Everyone has their own theory. Personally, I think the Creator is messing with us. People always have ten fingers. Twelve is almost always a holy number. But It makes eleven of us because numerology is a joke."

Zack frowned. "It? I always thought of the Creator as a He."

Bridgette smacked her knee. "Right. Well, I say the Creator is a woman."

He shrugged. "I guess it doesn't matter either way. Do you really think the Creator jokes with us? Doesn't that seem a little . . . irreverent?"

Bridgette shrugged. "Why not? We don't actually know anything about the Creator. For so many worlds, everyone thought there was a twelfth Observer in hiding. But some worlds are much smaller than this one. It would be impossible to avoid detection by all of us for this long."

"You talk as if this isn't the first world."

"This is number one-four-four, Zack."

"And all of you are the same age?"

"All of us."

Zack shook his head. "Not me, Bridgette. I only go back five years."

She took his hand in hers. "Hess, it's Elza. You're safe."

He retracted his hand as gently as possible. "I'm telling the truth. Maybe the Creator needed a twelfth Observer. Maybe I'm supposed to be a joke: a clumsy Observer who gets caught."

Bridgette sighed. "If this is your first life, then we should probably have a long talk. I'm sure you have a ton of questions. I rented a house just ten minutes from here." She pulled out a set of keys.

"I can't go now," Zack said. "But my shift ends at two. Does that work?"

She smiled. "Sure thing, honey. I'll be here."

INTERLUDE ONE
Hess
Iteration 143

The darkness was everything. Hess lay as if dead, listening to the heartbeat that would not cease counting eternity. Ragged breaths sawed through his parched throat at irregular intervals. Hunger gnawed at his middle and weakness wrapped him like a blanket. A tenuous peace existed in those moments of passivity. The weary emptiness was the state of least pain and he embraced its refuge. Hess forced down the memories struggling to rise within him. There was nothing but the darkness.

Time passed. Whether it passed quickly or slowly he did not know. Such concepts didn't exist in the darkness. There was only *now*, one torturous moment stretching to infinity. Hess did not contemplate time. He did not contemplate anything. He simply existed in the darkness.

He existed in the darkness until the echo of his gasping breath in the tiny space sparked a constellation of recollections. The violence of the memories triggered a physical response. Hess swung his fists at the darkness, striking stone surfaces above his face and to each side. "Elza!" Some part of him recognized the hoarse voice as his own. Another part reacted to the sound, imagining rescuers spoke to him. "Help me! Let me out of here! Please help me!"

Yet another part of him observed everything from a distance, chronicling events even though nothing new happened, even though nothing new would ever happen. *Panic attack triggered by perceived noise.* "Elza? Can you hear me, Elza? I'm sorry! So sorry! Please forgive me!" *Fragmented thought processes.* "Someone help me! Get me out of here! I will do anything!"

His fists, invisible in the dark, were made of pain. He struck harder and harder at surfaces he could not see, ratcheting the pain higher. Blood began to spatter, raining down on his face. Hess licked the tangy liquid from his lips, desperate for moisture. *Animal responses remain strong, instinctually seeking sources of comfort.*

"Why?" he demanded of the darkness. That question was everything, but no part of Hess was sure what it referenced. Why did the others do this to him? Why would the Creator allow his suffering to continue? Why had he violated the divine command in such a drastic fashion? Why would the Creator make a world where such suffering was possible? The question could be any one of those, or all of them together, or maybe something beyond words and logic, something born of the darkness that could only be sensed and never defined.

As Hess continued to pound his mangled fists, the objective portion of him continued its narration, repeating a story he told himself often. *The healing response restores as much moisture and calories to the body as necessary to support life for a short length of time. It appears likely that the atmosphere is being scrubbed free of carbon dioxide, but this is impossible to verify. Likely the products of respiration are reclaimed in the same way as blood.* Hess snarled wordlessly at the part of him observing his plight.

The rage that boiled up dwarfed everything that came before. Hess coiled his entire body and launched himself forward the eight inches to the stone ceiling, driving his forehead into it. The rebound struck the back of his head against the stone floor of his crypt. Hess struck upwards again. The impassive narrator vanished with the other aspects of his personality, all of them absorbed into the all-consuming emotion of the moment. Hess struck again and again with as much force as he could generate in his tiny prison until he died.

When Hess woke once more in the darkness, he began to weep, eyes burning but too dry for tears. His body was whole and undamaged save for a touch of dehydration. "Let me die! I don't want to live! Please, Creator, unmake me! I don't want to live! I don't want to live!"

He wept for a time he could not determine but which felt significant. Then emotional exhaustion brought a blessed return to the living coma that was the state of least pain. Memories bubbled beneath the surface, but Hess ignored them.

CHAPTER EIGHT
Zack
Iteration 144

The rest of his shift flowed as slow as molasses. Zack hardly noticed when an inebriated man dropped a gallon of milk onto the floor, sending a white flood out to wash away the dust. His mind buzzed with the knowledge that he wasn't alone. He wasn't sure why he hadn't gone with Bridgette. Lacey needed his paycheck, but Zack had never let that fact influence his choices in the past. Otherwise, he would have upgraded to a more profitable career months ago.

As the day passed, a vague uneasiness began to bother him. He couldn't eat anything on his lunch break. *What am I worried about? That she won't come back? That she won't like me? That I won't like her answers?* The more Zack probed at his uneasiness, the worse it became. The slight shadows throughout the room seemed to grow deeper as he dug into his suspicions, pooling together and flowing towards him.

Zack squeezed his eyes shut and emptied his mind. When he looked again, the shadows were gone. The darkness rarely threatened him during the day – only when he let himself become emotional did it become a problem. *Should I mention the darkness to Bridgette? Does she see it too or is something wrong with me? Am I insane?*

Several years previously, Zack considered admitting himself into a psychiatric ward on the hope that he was delusional and doctors could cure him. The prospect of becoming a medical experiment if he wasn't crazy hadn't been enough to deter him. In the end, the only reason he decided against it was because he couldn't be sure the staff of a crazy house would let him have a nightlight.

When two o'clock arrived, Zack updated his handwritten timecard and went to the parking lot. He looked around, but couldn't see Bridgette anywhere. Zack let out a breath. Maybe he could just go home and worry about the other Observers another day.

An African-American man with hair in cornrows stepped out of a pickup truck and walked towards him. "You want to see Bridgette?" the man asked him. Zack backed away from the man in the direction of the store. The man raised his hands to show he wasn't a threat. "I'm just here to give you a ride, friend. Let's go see Bridgette now."

Someone clamped a hand on his shoulder from behind and pressed something into his back. A deep woman's voice whispered in his ear. "Just walk forward, Hess. We have the girl. If you don't come talk to us, she's going to spend some more time underground. You don't want that, do you?"

"I'm not who you think I am," he said.

"We'll talk later. Now walk." When the woman prodded him in the back, Zack moved forward. The black man grabbed his arm and the two escorted him to the pickup. When they opened the passenger door, the woman jabbed something into his neck and Zack's entire body convulsed. When he stopped shaking, his arms were already twisted behind his back and shackled. They loaded him inside and were on the road before Zack managed to speak.

"Why are you doing this to me?"

The black man shook his head. "Playing stupid won't help you, Hess. We're going to do a replay of last Iteration. Two hundred years in a stone box just wasn't enough punishment for the stunt you pulled. And you didn't learn a damned thing. I turn on the news and see an Observer flaunting the Divine Command and you know what I think? I think we didn't do Hess good enough last time. That's what I think."

"I'm not Hess."

Zack jumped when the taser crackled in the woman's hand. She waved it in front of his face. "Might want to keep your mouth shut. Once we get to the farm, the fun is going to last for a long time. Just sit back and enjoy your last moments without pain."

"Put the taser away while I'm driving, Laura," the black man said.

"I have had enough of your paranoia."

"Have you noticed I'm a black man in a white country? People notice minorities. If anyone gets busted when Hess disappears, it will be me. So put the damn taser away."

"I'm a woman and I still have bigger balls than you, Drake."

The man slammed his fist on the steering wheel. "I'm going by Weston!"

"Sorry, chica, but Hess will know who did this to him. He's Drake; I'm Erik. Griff and Ingrid are waiting for us at the farmhouse."

Drake shook his head. "We should lock you up with him, Erik."

The woman named Erik snickered at that. "Don't let the tits fool you, Drake. I'm still more than you can handle. Even if you found the balls to make a move against me, the others wouldn't back you. No one wants me as an enemy."

"You are a psychopath," Drake said.

Erik laughed. "We're all psychopaths. When one of us starts caring for people is when the trouble starts. Just ask our bleeding heart here about how he wants to change the world."

"What I meant to say was serial killer," Drake said.

"You have no idea what kinds of things I discover for the Creator," Erik said. "The way people react to extreme situations reveals a lot about them. You wouldn't believe the things they will do to avoid a little pain. I can break the strongest in forty-eight hours. Some people crack without a single touch." Erik scraped her nails over Zack's face hard enough to draw blood. "I didn't get enough time with this one last Iteration. We had to be quick that time. But you're a nobody in this world. I can have all the time I want."

Drake shook his head. "You get twenty-four hours and then he goes in the ground. That's it."

"I'm calling the shots, Mr. Minority."

"We've been considering an intervention for you. Murder counts as participation if anything does."

Erik leaned forward to look across Zack's body. "You want to make this personal?"

"None of this is personal."

"Oh no, Drake, this is nothing but personal."

Drake didn't respond. After a minute, Erik grunted. "Just remember what I'm capable of and you won't be tempted to do something stupid."

The truck pulled off the road onto a long dirt drive. Drake spoke quietly. "For the record, Hess, this isn't personal for me. This is just driving your lesson home."

Zack stared out the window without thinking, forcing his mind to stillness. Whatever was about to happen to him was going to be bad.

CHAPTER NINE

Elza
Iteration 1

Rough hands startled her awake. An old woman knelt beside Elza. "The hunters are back."

Elza sat up to assess her situation. The captives huddled together while the returned brutes harassed the assimilated women and wrestled with one another. A chill crawled across her flesh as she watched them stir one another towards violence. Suddenly, she understood the purpose of the captives. The bonding ritual of the brutes required victims.

She instinctively sought the refuge of the herd, grasping at the other women, seeking a sanctuary from the wolves circling their perimeter. The barbarity of the tribe made sense to her now. Their culture reinforced violence through the deliberate dehumanization of the weak. The words of Hess came to her. *I know what will happen to these women. You want no part in it.*

Elza hardened her heart. Pain was fleeting and there was no injury her body would not heal. She would endure whatever the brutes did to her. Experiencing creation first-hand was her purpose.

The rowdiness of the camp increased as the sun's angle descended. Meat roasted on spits until hungry men carved charred, bloody slivers free. Women cooked squash and made fresh bread from acorns while in their midst captives starved. The tribe was like a fire escaped from its pit, consuming everything in its path as it spread death.

A woman assimilated the previous night screamed in the distance. Throughout the camp, the brutes released a chorus of laughter at her distress. Elza buried her face in the back of another captive. *I just need a moment to compose myself. Just a moment of peace. I can face this.*

Kallig's voice boomed from nearby. "Tonight we have our way!"

She flinched when the brutes roared in anticipation.

"Why do you do this, Kallig? Are you so afraid of helpless women?"

The roar died out, leaving an eerie silence in its wake. Kallig's deep voice responded to the challenge. "Go away, coward! *You* are afraid of the women! I deal with them like a man!"

"I fear nothing, Kallig. Nothing. Everyone knows I am no coward. I let deadly snakes live when they cross my path. You fear women more than I fear vipers!"

"We fear nothing, coward! We want our fun!"

Elza held her breath, waiting for Hess to respond.

After a moment, Kallig spoke again. "Sit on your rock and watch real men, coward!"

Elza looked up as the men surrounded them. There was over an hour left in the day for their ordeal, assuming sunset marked its end. If not, then she could only imagine how long it would last. All night, maybe. Longer if they discovered she did not stay dead.

Rough hands seized one of the captives, a woman covered with pox scars but possessing a shapely figure. She squealed and tried to slip free. A man with a pronounced limp slammed his fist into pox-scar's belly, then pushed her face-first to the ground. Before the prostrate woman could recover enough to scream, the limping man drove his spear through the back of her hand into the ground.

Hands seized Elza's hair. She found herself forced onto her back with a man's knee pressing on her middle so that she could not take a breath. The man on top of her spit directly into her face, then slapped her without warning. As Elza struggled for air, more hands began to rip at her clothing.

Screams and dark laughter came from all around. Elza swung her arms and legs. In that moment, all that mattered was escape. The man above her shifted his weight, letting her fill her lungs with a gasp, then a fist smashed her nose flat. Her arms and legs were pinned in rapid succession. Elza released the precious air into a raw scream. Meaty fingers grasped her jaw and shook her head.

The ordeal was more real than she had believed possible. It was happening and she had no control over it. She didn't even have enough air for a second scream. Every touch of the brutes inspired fresh revulsion. Her every sense became raw, highlighting the experience.

And then the weight was gone from her. Elza rolled into a ball, covering as much of herself as possible and hiding from them. The volume of the jeers dropped. "Touch her again and I kill you!" Elza flinched at the hands on her, then recognized the gentle touch of compassion and latched onto them. Her chest heaved rapidly and she couldn't see through her tears.

"You can't take her," one of the brutes said. "You didn't go to fight."

"I will kill you, coward, " Kallig roared.

The voice that responded snapped with an authority beyond the bravado of the others. "Don't you dare touch me. When I die, I come back angry. If I decide to kill you, *no one* can stop me. Not your whole tribe together."

"Fight him, Kallig!"

"He can't take a second woman! He didn't fight!"

"Quiet," shouted Kallig, silencing the other men. His tone was milder when he spoke again. "You know the rules. You only get one woman. That one is ugly and fat. Go see Dalana."

Elza squeezed his arm tighter. Hess sighed. "I will give up Dalana."

"You trade Dalana for this one? No. You will take Dalana back and have two women."

"Yes. I give up Dalana forever and you let me have this woman."

"Do you trick me, Hess?"

"I give up Dalana. I promise."

"Take the ugly one, then! You are a stupid one, coward!"

Hess squatted and transferred Elza onto his shoulders in a rapid movement. They were away from the brutes in twenty steps. Hess paused to tell Dalana she had to go see Kallig, which sent the beauty into a panic. Elza rode passively on his shoulder until they reached his rock, where Hess dropped her to the ground.

She took a moment to compose herself. "I told you not to interfere."

"You're lucky I don't follow your orders."

"You ruined my observations."

"You're welcome."

"This isn't a game! I have a sacred duty!"

Hess pointed to the gruesome scene. "I will let the Creator know all He needs to about what happens here. Those men don't have to touch you."

"I could have endured it without your interference."

Hess spun to face her. "Stop it! I don't care what you can or can't endure! The purpose of an Observer is not to endure torments. You think my participation interferes with my observations, but what value does the viewpoint of a victim hold for the Creator?"

"You are a horrible Observer."

"Stop talking to me, woman."

"I don't follow the orders of a coward."

"In this tribe, a woman obeys her man."

"You are *not* my man."

"I just traded Dalana for you. The least you can do is shut your mouth."

Elza glared at him. "I don't like you."

"I never asked you to like me. I just want you to stop making noise."

"You are going to regret interfering."

Hess stood up. "I hope you're quiet when you eat."

"Where are you going?" She scrambled to his side before he made five paces.

"Someone was *interfering* with my observations on the rock, so I'm done watching for the night. I'm going to eat and sleep and pretend you're not beside me."

Elza ignored the screams as she shadowed him to the cooking fires. "I really don't like you."

"I miss Dalana already."

CHAPTER TEN
Zack
Iteration 144

Zack struggled as he was forced face-first into the tub of water. His hands were cuffed behind his back and rope bound and lifted his feet into the air. There was no way to prevent the inevitable, but Zack struggled with instinctive passion to avoid inhaling the water.

The woman named Erik pressed her knee onto his shoulder blades, forcing his nose beneath the water. With a herculean effort, Zack managed to arch his back and neck enough to pant through his nose. Then a playful tap to the back of his head made him suck down a shot of water.

Involuntarily, Zack's lungs spasmed in a cough. The cough was followed by a gasping breath of water. His body spasmed in a wild attempt to find air, accompanied by laughter from Erik. His exertions triggered the impulse to inhale and Zack obliged his reflexes despite the fact that he was submerged.

Inhalations become an autonomic function once a certain point is reached. Uncertain whether the trigger is determined by lack of oxygen in blood or carbon dioxide levels. Zack recorded everything as an Observer without intending to do anything of the sort. He didn't know if the impulse to observe was another autonomic function or if he was trying to escape the experience through depersonalization. If the purpose was escape, Zack didn't think it was very effective.

He gasped several breaths of liquid and relaxed into the cold water. Death slowly enfolded him, allowing the welcoming warmth of nothingness to engulf him. Zack let it take him away, wishing his death would last this time.

Zack woke wet and shivering on the bathroom floor.

"How did you like that one?"

He turned his head to look at Erik. She appeared pudgy and weak, but possessed a maniacal strength. "I prefer the chainsaw."

Erik laughed and clapped her hands. "Me too! I think we really bonded over that one." Her false cheer faded, leaving only the predatory aura behind. "Death doesn't bother you. I need to focus more on the torture."

Zack shivered. So far, Erik had stabbed him to death, beaten him to death with a golf club, sliced him to death with a chainsaw, and crushed his skull with the blunt end of an axe. The dying really didn't bother him. Time and again, it was a welcome release from circumstances he would give anything to escape.

The other Observers had lectured him, each in turn, when he arrived. They didn't participate in any of the festivities. Erik had been disappointed by her colleagues' restraint, insulting their dedication to the Creator's work.

Erik dragged him from the cramped bathroom of the farmhouse using the rope binding his feet. They made it to the front porch before they encountered anyone. The man named Ingrid waited on the porch swing. "I think you're enjoying this too much, Erik."

"Watch yourself, Ingrid, or I'll put you on the naughty list."

"No you won't," Ingrid said. He studied her over his steepled fingers. "You are loyal to the Creator in your own perverse way. Hunting, tormenting, and murdering people is work to you, no matter how much you enjoy it. Doing the same with an Observer is just playing and you know it."

"Do you really want to risk being wrong?"

"I'm not wrong," Ingrid said. "You despised the relationship between Hess and Elza. If you focus your particular fetish on other Observers, then you would be committing the same sin as them."

"For what Hess did in the last Iteration, he deserves the worst I can do to him. Don't interfere with that, Ingrid. I will make you my enemy."

"And deprive the Creator of another Observer?"

Erik pointed at Zack. "This and the other have been useless as Observers from the first. The Creator won't miss their input."

"I think you're wrong, Erik. I've been man and woman, tall and short, dark and fair, thin and heavy, weak and strong. Every variation of human possible. We all have. Every Iteration sees us inserted into random identities. Except *them*. Hess always a man. Elza always a woman. The Creator must have a reason for that."

"And I have the urge to torture this man for eternity. Maybe the Creator has a reason for making me like that." Erik dragged Zack by the rope, sending him tumbling down the front steps. "Nice talk, Ingrid, but I got lots of torturing to do. We're going to play with electric next. Ciao."

CHAPTER ELEVEN
Elza
Iteration 1

Despite her anger, lingering fear, and the horrible cries of the women in the distance, Elza dropped into a sound sleep once wrapped in the warm blankets formerly used by Dalana. She didn't wake until midmorning, by which time Hess was gone.

She found him peeling a vine on top of his rock. "What are you doing?"

"Making rope," he said.

"Why?"

Hess shrugged. "I thought the Creator would like to know what different kinds of work feel like. I never imagined there were women Observers, so I learned how to do women's work after mastering the men's."

Elza looked towards where the women had been held.

"They're dead," Hess said. "I saved some breakfast for you."

The bodies were gone. "I won't cook for you," she said. "No matter what you said to this tribe, I am not your woman."

"I'm starting to think you don't like me," Hess said.

She picked up the bread and meat resting beside Hess on the rock. "You are a horrible Observer."

"No I'm not." Hess began weaving the strands of vine together.

"You participate!"

"So do you."

"How do I participate?"

"I saw you talking to the other women yesterday."

Elza glared at him. "It's not the same as what you do."

"It *is* the same. I just do a little more of it than you." Hess met her glare with a curious expression. "Can you see better or worse with your eyes pointing different ways?"

"How am I supposed to know?" She turned away from him to eat.

Hess kept his mouth shut until she finished her meal. "I am serving the Creator in the way I think best," he said. "You think my long presence in this tribe is for selfish reasons, but I hate what these people are. I stay because this is the best example of what is wrong with the world. The Creator sent us here to observe for Him. I think He means to use our input to make a better world." His next words were almost too soft to hear. "I hope He does."

"You care about them too much," Elza said.

"I'm sure the Creator cares too. He made them, after all."

They watched in silence from on top of the rock for most of the day. Elza thought the distance weakened their observations, but at least the contamination caused by Hess was limited. The tribe was lazy after the previous night's ritual. Men lounged about, receiving food from their women.

When Hess cooked bread, the other women laughed. Elza positioned herself to overhear their conversation. "Hess traded Dalana for that one. She doesn't even cook for him. Chase says Hess grows weak. He wants to challenge Kallig."

Hess contaminates everything I observe here, Elza thought. Still, she couldn't help but be fascinated by the circumstances. *I'll stay until they kill Kallig. Then I'll leave this tribe.*

The remainder of that day was uneventful. Hess completed his length of rope and used it to replace a worn one on his tent. Elza studied the elaborate construction of the shelter. It had a boxy frame of poles bound together with rope. Rushes padded the floor. Deer hides draped over the frame, then tucked under where they met the ground. Inside, heavy rocks held the hides tight, sealing the tent against drafts. The design was unique in her experience.

She slept soundly for a second night, then followed Hess through the woods while he attempted to hunt. "Chase is planning to kill Kallig," she said.

"Kallig is the father of Chase."

"They don't seem to like each other very much."

"That's because Kallig killed the uncle who raised him. Kallig knows how the tribe works. The same thing he did when he was young will be done to him."

"I have this idea," Elza said, "that groups of people are a system. Like how mountains have different kinds of trees than valleys." She struggled to find words to explain the concept. "You know, like how you can predict the moon and the tides."

"What are tides?"

"If you spent less time in one place, you would know about the sea."

"I know about the sea. It is a large lake," Hess said.

"Bigger than any lake. It has so much water that the moon affects it."

Hess laughed. "Is that what the people told you?"

"No," she said. "I reasoned it myself. The moon pulls on water like the ground pulls on us."

"I never saw the moon pull the water."

"Because you never move somewhere new."

"I have been all over the world. The place where I was born became so cold that water turned hard and fell to the ground. No one around here has ever heard of such a thing."

"I've heard about snow. But it's not real. The tides are."

Hess laughed. "Walk north as far as you can, Elza. When the first snow comes, you will know that I've traveled more than you ever claimed."

"And you can try finding the end of the world," Elza said.

"Walk north, Elza. You lose nothing if I am wrong."

She stumbled when stepping from one rock to another and landed in the stream. Hess sighed. "We might as well return to camp. The men will think I've gone simple-minded. First I trade Dalana for you and now I fail at hunting."

Elza ignored his hand and extracted herself from the stream. "You spend too much time learning skills. You should be observing."

"Let's get you back to the tent."

"Your tent is too fancy. It draws attention to you," she said.

"You'll wish you had a tent like mine when you learn that snow is real."

They trudged through the woods back the way they had come. The fact that Hess returned without success did draw attention. *Of course he's the best hunter of the tribe. He probably makes the best rope, too! The only thing he can't do right is the one thing he should be doing.*

Before they reached their tent, one of the men, Chase, called out to them. "Are you afraid to hurt a deer now, Hess? I think your man parts fell off when you got your new woman!"

This is the first time a man other than Kallig has insulted Hess since I've been here. Chase is announcing his intentions. Elza glanced to Hess, curious how he would react. Hess shook his head. "The challenge will come today or tomorrow," he whispered.

Inside the tent, Elza wrapped herself in the bedding while Hess hung her pants to dry. "Why do you care if someone challenges Kallig?" Her question grew in volume with every word. "That man is a monster! He deserves to die the same as his victims!"

"I know!" Hess turned his back to her. "I . . . took care of Kallig for a year when he was just a child, until his uncle took offense at an outsider raising his blood."

"*Why?*"

"He was a child, Elza."

"Children learn from the people who raise them!" *Though Hess didn't make much of an impact on Kallig. Still, this guilt should be exploited.*

"You know the part that bothers me? I made things worse. Kallig murdered his uncle and became the most brutal leader in the history of the tribe."

Elza collapsed back into her covers. "For a moment there, I thought there might be hope for you."

He forced a laugh. "If there's one thing I know for sure, it's that the two of us will never agree on anything."

"You're not one of them. They're not even real, Hess."

"Real enough." Hess settled into his blankets, face away from her.

They didn't speak again until the following morning. Elza woke hungry from missing dinner and shook him awake. "I want breakfast," she said.

"My woman used to bring me breakfast. Now I bring my woman breakfast."

"I'm not your woman. I'm an Observer."

"By the tradition of the tribe, you're my woman."

"I am not your woman."

"I'm pretty sure you are."

"I want breakfast."

"You know where the fires are."

"I'm not going out there by myself."

Hess smiled without opening his eyes. "Never thought you'd admit that."

"If I presented a convenient target now it would be interfering," she said.

"Well, we can't let that happen." Hess rolled out of his cocoon of furs. The camp was eerily silent for midmorning as they walked to the fires. None of the men had left to hunt. Everyone was waiting for something to happen.

Their appearance was the catalyst.

Kallig called to them. "Cook food for your woman, coward!"

"Quiet, old man!" Chase stood, spear in hand.

Kallig had his spear ready. Something in his stance told Elza that the man had known this challenge was coming. He knew his time was at an end – either today or some day soon.

The two combatants approached each other, crouched with spears held in one hand by the ear, and proceeded to shout insults. Elza watched the encounter, analyzing their bravado, trying to determine how much of the show was for their audience and how much was for themselves.

When it seemed like no real conflict would happen, Chase charged straight at the older man. Kallig threw his spear and missed by a hair.

Then Chase drove his spear home. Kallig turned the fire-hardened tip aside with his ribs, then roared in rage and punched Chase.

Chase reversed the motion of his spear and slammed the butt into Kallig's face. Kallig shook off the strike and tackled Chase. Only when the maneuver was complete did it become obvious that Chase had gotten his spear tip in place so that Kallig's lunge drove the point into his soft abdomen.

The younger man rolled free and punched the air in exultation. Kallig clutched at the spear impaling him. "I am the strongest man," Chase roared. He reached down and pulled his spear free. Kallig groaned. "I kill you, old man!"

And then Hess was there. "Stop!"

Chase turned to face the new threat, raising his spear again. "I don't fear you, Hess! I am in charge now!"

Elza shook her head, mouthing the word *no* at Hess. This was bad. So very, very bad. Worse than she ever imagined.

Hess kicked Kallig's spear into the air and caught it. Standing upright, spear held casually, Hess bared his chest. "You throw first, Chase." The larger man backed away two quick steps and kicked at the vegetation in a fit. "This isn't fair! You never challenged Kallig!"

I might as well get involved. Nothing I do can make this situation any worse. Her voice projected in the expectant quiet. "Hess, even you have to admit this is wrong. You can't stay with this tribe. We need to leave today. *Now.*"

Hess looked down at the wounded Kallig. "We'll wait until Kallig can travel."

"He can't come with us," she said.

"No," Kallig growled. "I don't need you to save me, coward. I don't fear death. I am a man! *This* is how a man dies, coward! Show him, Chase! Show the coward how men live and die!"

Chase hefted his spear, then hesitated.

"Get out of his way," Elza said. The moment Hess stood aside, Chase moved in for the kill, driving his spear into Kallig, pulling it free and stabbing in rapid succession, leaving a bloody, gasping mess of a man.

Elza seized the arm of Hess. "We're leaving now." He didn't resist. While Kallig died a violent death, they prepared two travel packs. "You know that was wrong," she said to him again and again.

Finally, Hess snapped. "I know!"

"You can't participate."

"What's stopping me?" Hess hefted his spear. "The Creator made sure we knew our duty, but He never bound us. I can act however I wish until the day the sky opens. Then the Creator can unmake me if I am unfit to observe. But until then, what stops me? What stops me from destroying this tribe? What stops me from forming one that works the way it should? What stops me, Elza?"

She took the spear from his hands. "I stop you, Hess."

"How can you be sure that I'm wrong? Do you think the Creator would do nothing if He were here?"

"She would never be here, Hess. The Creator creates. We observe. When this world ends, the Creator will create again and we will observe again."

Hess lifted his pack and settled it on his shoulders. "Maybe. Maybe not. The Creator might not want me in His flawed creations."

"We'll leave that decision to Her. Until then, you're an Observer. Now walk."

"Do you prefer a particular direction, woman?"

"Away from here."

"North it is."

CHAPTER TWELVE
Zack
Iteration 144

Flames licked the soles of his bare feet. The pain it brought struck in waves, alternating between excruciating and unbearable. Zack struggled against the duct tape binding his legs in place to the metallic frame, but his struggles did no good. His screams were equally futile. He continued both anyway.

The heating ring of a water heater provided the fire. In a twisted way, he appreciated the technical skill necessary to construct the torture device. The woman named Erik had converted the ring to run on propane, which burned hotter than natural gas. She had welded a heavy-duty weight bench to the fire ring and braced everything with steel bars. The roll of duct tape trapping him in place held him better than rope.

Erik watched him throughout like a master technician at her craft. She leaned forward to apply the welding torch in her hands to his big toe, causing the nail to snap in half from the incredible heat. The pain struck a split-second later, flaring out to consume his entire leg, so intense Zack wouldn't have known it originated in his toe if he hadn't seen it.

"Remember I promised you something special, Hess? It should be here soon. You haven't forgotten that we took Elza first, have you?" Erik tightened the knob on the propane tank, killing the flames. She waited until his flesh returned to perfect health. "I will torture Elza for a long time after you are buried. I will twist her mind until she hates you. The cute little love story ends in tragedy, Hess."

"I'm not Hess." Zack's voice broke.

"You wish you weren't." Erik took out her phone and began to type. "Every few Iterations the Creator comes up with something that just blows my mind. I thought the texting craze was ridiculous at first, but now I'm hooked. You want to ask a question but don't want to get sucked into a conversation? Send a text. If we go back to the stone age next Iteration, I don't know how I'll deal."

A bleep came from her phone. "They're bringing her out, lover-boy."

Zack remained silent. With a detached rationality, he knew he could not escape. The other Observers had every advantage — superior numbers, lifetimes of skills, weapons, *mobility*. Convincing them he was not the renegade Observer they sought seemed the only way out of the situation, but they responded to his protests with anger when they responded at all. Bearing their punishments until they buried him alive was the only other option.

The thought of being trapped in the dark for years, possibly centuries, sent a chill to his core. He didn't think he could survive such a thing. Yet, deep down, he wondered if he deserved what they did. He had given seven million dollars to charity. He had married a woman. He had forced a man to murder him and landed on the national news. It was a long list for just five years of life. The Creator might be best served with Zack interred in an unmarked grave.

Why would He create someone like me?

The barn door squealed as it opened. The black man called Drake and the man called Ingrid dragged Bridgette into the barn before securing the door once more. Bridgette moved forward in a daze, arms bound behind her back.

"I've had some time to work with both of you," Erik said. "But now comes the real test. I want the two of you to decide which one deserves to sit in the electric chair overnight. I'll begin accepting nominations . . . now."

Bridgette looked to the ground. The silence stretched.

"Really? No one wants to volunteer a name? I thought there would be a race to self-sacrifice. What do you think, Elza? Should it be you? If no one can give me a name, then I'll have to work out some form of couple therapy."

Bridgette looked at him suddenly. "This is your fault."

I don't want it to be me, Zack thought. "Take her," he said aloud.

The flash of anger on Erik's face disappeared behind a mild smile. "So much for true love. What do you think, Elza?"

Bridgette shook her head. "Take Hess instead."

The woman named Erik pulled her tazer and blasted Bridgette. "The chair is in the basement of the house. Get her strapped in. I'll be right behind you."

When the others were gone, Erik seized his face and stared into his eyes. "Why did you do it?"

"I'm not who you think I am. I don't care what you do to that woman."

Erik considered him for a long moment. "I could almost believe you. But I don't. You're not going to escape me. Not in this life and not in the next one. I have a new calling, Hess. I'm going to be the Creator's enforcer."

CHAPTER THIRTEEN
Elza
Iteration 1

Elza stumbled forward at the side of Hess as he shouted at her. "Faster!" He looked over his shoulder every few steps to judge their lead over their pursuers. Elza's rasping breath didn't provide enough air for her to object. Hess ran easily, carrying both their packs and looking like he was just hitting his stride.

The hunters behind them howled like animals. They *were* animals. They decorated their territory with hideous displays made from human corpses as warnings to intruders. Unfortunately, once you trespassed, leaving the area as quickly as possible wasn't enough. Hunters had found their trail.

It was only twenty days since they left the tribe of Kallig. Twenty long days filled with heated arguments and cold silences. The only thing they could agree on was the fact that the two of them would never agree on anything.

The exertion was too much for her. Elza's vision began to dim and she staggered to a halt. *Did he bring me here on purpose to be rid of me? I shouldn't have told him he deserved to be unmade by the Creator.* Sight returned to normal and Elza saw Hess by her side still. "I can't run anymore," she panted. "If I stay still after they kill me, it might trick them."

"When they cut you into pieces for one of their displays, they'll notice that your body parts vanish and come back together." Hess looked around as he spoke. "I want you to go deep into that thicket, lay down, and try to make your breathing sound less like a bear's."

Elza stared at him. "You're leaving me?"

"Worse, according to you. Now go." Hess ran to the crest of a hill as she tripped through the dense undergrowth in the direction he had pointed.

Their pursuers appeared before she could hide herself. Three charged after Hess while two turned in her direction. Elza mentally prepared herself

49

for what would come. She had been killed once for trespassing. It wasn't one of her more cherished experiences, but she hadn't had nightmares about the incident in close to a century.

The fastest of their pursuers let out a whoop as he closed on Hess, who faced the charge with stoic resolve. *I wish I'd let Hess take his spear when we left his tribe.* Hess spread his arms and the hunter drove the spear home.

Quick as a flash of lightning, Hess seized the spear with one hand and pulled it further into his body, at the same time bringing his other fist up to the opposite shoulder and then viciously chopping the throat of his attacker. That man stumbled back holding his neck.

The second hunter closed on him. Hess pulled the spear free of his body. With casual elegance, Hess twisted to the side and used the body of the spear in his hands to deflect that of his enemy, then drove his own spear home. A second man fell to the ground.

Once more weaponless, Hess charged the third hunter, dodging a thrown spear. When Hess hit the man, he did so in a low dive, forcing his target's knees to bend in an unnatural direction. Both of them disappeared from view as they rolled upon the ground.

Hess rose and staggered into an unsteady sprint towards where Elza watched, holding his bleeding abdomen closed with his hands. One of the two hunters pursuing her sprinted away, fleeing into the forest. The second crashed through the dense foliage of the thicket, struggling to reach her. Elza tried to judge the speed and position of the two men. Hess was moving faster, but she didn't think he could close the distance in time.

The hunter reached her first. He seized Elza by the hair and rested the point of his spear beneath her jaw. When Hess reached them, the hunter spoke. "Stop or I will kill your woman!"

"That would make me very angry," Hess said. "I would have to kill your entire tribe. But if you release my woman, I will let you go."

The point of the hunter's spear drew blood as the man trembled. "Are you an evil spirit?"

"Yes," Hess whispered. "I am the body of a man killed by your tribe. You should not keep us above the ground where we can wake up. We get angry, sometimes."

The hunter threw Elza to the ground and fled in the opposite direction, hindered by the thick vegetation. Hess pulled Elza to her feet.

"We need to leave," he said. "We'll walk until my bleeding stops, then run again."

CHAPTER FOURTEEN
Zack
Iteration 144

The Observers placed him face down for the night, left hand cuffed behind his back to right ankle, right hand to left ankle. They had moved him to the house, where a cramped family room had been cleared to serve as a holding area. The room's single exit led directly into the kitchen area, where two of his captors drank tea.

The man called Ingrid spoke. "We should bury him immediately."

Another voice responded. "Erik wants her fun."

"This isn't about playing games. We serve the Creator," Ingrid said. "Hess needs to be removed from events quickly so we can return to our observations."

"Just give Erik a few days with him."

Zack had twisted around to face the light that shone from the kitchen. In the night, fear of his immanent burial lurked closer to the surface. He concentrated on the soreness his unnatural position caused his shoulders. Pain was a safe thought.

What does Lacey think happened to me? She probably assumes I abandoned her. Zack hoped that in time she found someone who could love her. It was such a simple thing for a person to want. He had thought he could fake the emotion for her, but Zack knew better now. He would make an even worse person than he did an Observer.

The shadows from the kitchen moved from time to time. Even if Zack could free himself, the windows were boarded up and two armed guards prevented his escape through the kitchen. Still, he watched. After a few hours, the shadows stopped moving. If he knew a way to escape, this would be the time to do so. The darkness rose within and Zack had to suppress it. The darkness had been active ever since the shooting, threatening him day and night.

One of the shadows from the kitchen shifted. Zack watched it move silently, growing larger. The form of the man called Ingrid appeared in the doorway. He placed a finger over his lips, bidding Zack to remain silent. Then Ingrid slipped over to kneel at his side. Ingrid seized Zack's restraints. "When I free you, leave the house silently. The keys to the truck that brought you here are on the counter. Move somewhere far from here and don't draw attention to yourself." In rapid motions, Ingrid freed Zack, feet first, then seized Zack's chin. "The woman downstairs is not who she claims to be. She's Kerzon, trying to wound you in the way she thinks worst. Elza is still out there somewhere."

Zack crouched silently, cradling his arms close while strained shoulders healed. "I don't know who Elza is. I am not Hess."

"I don't have time to argue. You can't go anywhere associated with your Zack identity. Drive to somewhere with public transportation and disappear. The truck has several thousand dollars stashed beneath the seat. Be quiet. Erik didn't drink any tea."

Zack followed Ingrid out to the kitchen, where Ingrid settled back into his seat and slouched forward onto the table as if asleep. With swift motions, Zack swiped the keys from the counter and went out the kitchen door. He ran to the truck, clawed the door open, leaped inside, jammed the key into the ignition, twisted hard, shifted into drive, and hit the gas.

The truck bounced the entire length of the dirt driveway, then shot into motion when it reached the road. Zack's heart raced faster than the truck as he split his attention between the road ahead and the rear-view mirror. He took route twenty-eight south towards Pittsburgh, slowing to five over the speed limit. *Can't get pulled over now. I have to find a bus station or something.* Zack punched the seat. He didn't know where to find a bus station in Pittsburgh or anywhere else. He didn't know where to find anything. In the past five years, he had rarely traveled more than ten miles from rural Sarver.

He tensed every time he saw headlights behind him, until he was hunched over the steering wheel. *I don't know where I'm going. I am tired and confused and emotional. I need a map and some rest.* One of the false memories that came with the identity of Zack Vernon recalled itself suddenly. It was of a road trip taken with his parents. They had stopped at a hotel. While his parents went through the process of checking in, Zack had perused a display on the local attractions, paying particular attention to a map of the area.

Now where is a hotel? The answer to that was easy. Along route 28, just south of Tarentum, was a shopping complex known as the Pittsburgh Mills Mall, a beautiful facility full of retail locations suffering from lack of business. A hotel sat behind the mall. Hopefully he could discover the location of a bus terminal there.

INTERLUDE TWO
Hess
Iteration 143

Hess paced while Elza read the document. They were inside their private sanctum, the central chamber of their palace. Outside, bells called out the hour. Elza's eyes rose from the parchment.

"They want to surrender," she said. "Sidon is sailing at us with an army, but his administrators write to request our aid."

"It's a hedging tactic," Hess said. "Their King is away, the people are restless, and we keep winning battles. So far, at least . . . ."

Elza compressed her lips. "You want to introduce liquid fire."

"King Sidon has a superior navy."

"Using a weapon like that undermines the principles of our Empire. How can we preach humanitarianism while introducing this world to chemical weapons?"

Hess crossed his arms. "It was never going to be perfect."

"The Empire might fall short of its ideals, but we don't. You agreed that we would walk away before we violated the rules. No technological breakthroughs allowed. Sorry." Elza crossed the room to wrap her arms around him. This world saw her in a body most kindly described as mature, while he was perpetually stuck in the final days of puberty. He sometimes suspected the Creator had a sense of humor. The age difference bothered Elza more than him. She always worried when his form was more attractive than hers.

"Then we'll have to move our ships into the harbor and prepare for a siege. King Sidon can't beat us on land and we can't match his fleet." Hess planted a kiss on Elza's nose. "I ever tell you I have a thing for bossy noblewomen?"

"I smell mead. Did you open a fresh jug while I was meeting with the federal reserve chairmen?"

"I thought you might need a drink after manipulating the currency."

"Math doesn't give *me* headaches."

"It doesn't cause me pain, Elza. I just don't think those types of studies are something an Observer needs to know."

"I thought you were an Emperor."

"That's more of a hobby," Hess said.

"You couldn't do this without me. Conducting wars and giving speeches are very nice, but this Empire keeps running out of money. Your welfare state doesn't have the resources to fight wars. Fortunately, our trading partners are as bad at math as you are. Reserve banking and derivative options have turned this world upside down."

Hess poured two goblets of mead. "You know what else I can't do myself?"

Elza took a sip. "So help me if you say this decrepit body is your favorite."

The mead stung his mouth. "Wow. This is strong."

"Do you remember Iteration twenty-six?" Elza swirled the contents of her cup and took a gulp. "You were such a beer snob."

Beer? What is Beer? Hess sent a query into the abyss of his memory, seeking for beer and Iteration twenty-six. He took another drink, feeling the liquid burn like fire down his throat. "This is my favorite body of yours," he said.

Elza rolled her eyes. "You say that about every body I wear."

"I mean it every time."

"You may love me every time, Hess, but not my body. I have been morbidly obese, disturbingly frail, cross-eyed, and now elderly."

"In their time, they were all my favorite."

"You just like to humor me. To be honest, it gets tiring."

The returning recollection bubbled up from the endless eternity of his memory. Hess recalled dragging Elza to the local brewery of every town they traveled through. They wore matching middle-aged, dark-skinned bodies in that world. Elza had rolled her eyes every time he asked the locals where the town brewer lived. An associated recollection burst into his primary memory, of Iteration ninety-five, when Elza produced the most vitriolic substance ever called a wine. She had been a breathtakingly beautiful blonde in that life, drawing the eyes of every man who passed.

"At least I had the decency to give you something drinkable in twenty-six. Do you remember when you had a winery? That hellish liquid was not fit for human consumption. When it didn't sell, I had to help drink the entire inventory."

Elza blinked in surprise. "A winery?"

"In a minute you'll remember why you don't recall it more often."

They drank more of the mead, which had subtle apple notes buried beneath its harshness. Playing *remember when* over a glass of whatever poured was a tradition longer than the entire recorded history of the current world. They remembered every moment of their endless lives with perfect clarity, though only a minute fraction of it fit into primary memory at any moment. The time required to pull forth the seldom-accessed memories grew longer as they continued to accumulate more experiences.

Some Iterations lasted much longer than others, but a good approximation was a thousand years each, which meant he had close to a hundred and forty-three thousand years of life stored inside his eternal skull. Sometimes he felt ancient. But never a hundred and forty-three thousand years ancient.

"You didn't drink more than a few bottles of my wine," Elza said. "We sold the bulk of it to be distilled into grape liquor."

"Really? Well, you can't deny it was bad."

Elza laughed. "It was terrible. You tried so hard not to make a face when I let you do the first tasting after it aged. I knew it wouldn't win any awards when it was still in oak, but I didn't want to give up."

"I really mean it," Hess said. "This body of yours is my favorite."

"You must be trying to annoy me."

"I'm serious."

"Which is your second favorite?"

"The first," he said.

"Lazy eye and all?"

"You know, I never knew I was lonely till the day I wasn't."

"Different question. Which body was the best for a cozy?"

Hess swirled his mead. "You've asked this before. Iteration six, no question about it."

"I never understood your obsession with curves," she said.

"To be quite honest, Elza, neither do I. It just is."

They sat in silence. Hess slouched into his chair. "I'm tired," he said.

Elza put a hand to her forehead and spoke with slurred words. "I think we've been poisoned again. Annoying. Hope wears off fast."

Crap. Hope it kills us — effects will be shorter that way. If it's just inconvenient, it could take hours for our bodies to purge the poison. Hess tried to stand, but his legs couldn't support him. He eyed the bell on the table by Elza's elbow. "Call servants," he said.

Elza rang the bell and they waited.

When the door opened, a servant and two guards entered. "Help us to bed," Elza said. The servant ignored her and turned to face Hess. "Was your mead poisoned?"

An inside job. Great. This will start all sorts of zombie rumors.

The servant's eyes followed every twitch of his face in a familiar manner. "Observer," he said. The servant, a plain young woman, nodded. "It's Ingrid, Hess. And your sick game of Empires ends now. We've debated among ourselves and decided that your disobedience has to be punished."

His tongue became too numb for speech. Hess sought Elza with his eyes as the other Observers placed him on the bed and wrapped him in linens. A frustrated anger boiled within him. *I will make them regret this.*

CHAPTER FIFTEEN

Hess
Iteration 143

His plan was to rent a room, clean himself up, buy clean clothes, sleep for a few hours, and make his way into Pittsburgh to catch a bus early in the morning. What happened was Zack lay on his bed and fell asleep before he dredged up the motivation to move.

He woke midmorning to the sound of talking in the room next to his. Zack checked the clock, saw it was after nine, and rolled out of the bed. In the bathroom mirror, he appeared normal enough save for his clothing, which was sliced and faded from repeatedly soaking in his blood. While the blood may have vanished from his shirt and pants, the damage it had caused remained.

Studying his appearance, Zack decided a change of clothes would be worth the delay. Anything that made him harder to spot could potentially save him. Which was why he needed to abandon the truck as soon as possible. *Why didn't I learn anything about the closest city that didn't come from a television? I really am a terrible Observer.*

Zack tore the wrapper from the tiny hotel soap and turned on the water. He thoroughly washed his face and hands. While he was toweling dry, Zack glanced at the wedding band perched on his ring finger. He imagined Lacey at home, clutching her phone, unsure if he lived or not. *She deserves to know. Well, maybe not know the truth, but to have some sort of closure. If I tell her I know the baby isn't mine, then she can move on with her life.*

The hotel room phone felt heavy in his hands as he dialed Lacey's number. He took a breath and prepared himself for the accusation that would be in her voice. The phone rang twice and picked up. "Hello?" The voice was Erik's. "Is that you, Zack Vernon? *Hess?*"

What is she doing with Lacey's phone? Shit, this is so wrong. "What do you want?" he said.

"Hiya Hess! Seems like just yesterday you were on the farm. So anyway, I was thinking you could stop over for another visit. Lacey's here right now and we were just talking about how much happier she would be if you joined us."

Zack had to clear his throat to speak. "Why take her? She doesn't know anything."

"Same reason I abduct anyone. Cause I wanna play. Now I want two things from you in exchange for the little darling's life, Hess. First, come back to the farm. Second, tell me which one of these shitheads helped you escape."

He squeezed his eyes shut. *Am I supposed to just abandon her? There has to be another way.* The solution struck him. "I'll call back with my decision in an hour."

"I don't think so," Erik said. "You call the authorities and things go very, very bad. Things look squeaky clean at the farm right now. Ingrid's got the legal right to be here. Cops won't find shit if they show. This ain't my first rodeo."

"I'm not coming back to the farm," Zack said.

"That's a shame. Well, you called to talk to Lacey. Here she is."

"Zack?" Lacey's voice climbed octaves as she spoke. "Why are they doing this? I'm afraid for the baby. Oh, God, Zack, I am so afraid. She smashed my fucking hand with a hammer. Please, Zack, please . . . I don't know what I'm asking. Just, it's the baby. I don't want the baby to die."

Erik's voice returned. "I can do a lot worse than a hammer, Hess. I can cut her unborn child out of her and slice the thing into pieces while she watches. By the standard of these creatures, I'm pretty deranged, Hess. This woman would die a death more horrifying than you can imagine. Mutilation means something to a mortal that it never could to us. We see a mangled limb and wait for the thing to fix itself, but they see a piece of themselves irreversibly destroyed. You can't imagine how easy it is to terrorize them."

There was silence on the line as Zack thought. Finally, Erik spoke again. "How about a compromise?"

"You want to catch me. I don't want caught. Not much room for compromise."

"We've just got to be a little creative, Hess. Stop treating things all binary-like. Instead of caught and not-caught, let's deal in degrees of risk. I'm willing to release Lacey to you in a time and location you choose. You can make it as public or as remote as your soft heart desires. The only stipulation is that you show alone."

Zack sighed. "Deal. We'll meet at the parking lot of buffalo plaza."

"Less than a mile from a police station. Well played, Hess. Just make sure you show alone. The professionals haven't been playing these games for nearly as long as I have. How long will it take you to get there from the . . . Tarentum Hyatt?"

Caller ID. He grabbed the room key. "I'll be there at ten." The moment he slammed the phone home, Zack was running through the door. *They are always two steps ahead of me.*

CHAPTER SIXTEEN
Elza
Iteration 1

She watched Hess haggle with an elderly man. They spoke a different way in this region and Elza could understand only one word in four. Hess didn't seem to have any trouble communicating with the locals, which he often claimed proved him better traveled than her.

The elderly man pointed at her and Elza felt her cheeks heat. Her body had grown stronger during the three months they traveled at the maddening pace Hess set for them. Hess shook his head *no*. When they weren't hiking at a reckless pace, they were either procuring food or sleeping like the dead. While hiking, she thought they carried too many supplies. While making camp, she thought they carried far too few. Though the lifestyle was far from comfortable, she could not deny it had done her body some good. Hess looked back at her and mouthed *this one offered a whole tent for you.*

Elza pointedly ignored the rest of the negotiations. In the distance, there were tall mountains with white rock caps Hess claimed were snow. They had walked for the remainder of the spring season and through the entire summer. The two of them had settled into a daily routine almost devoid of words. There seemed no point to speaking when they could understand each other's intentions so well through observation and words added only arguments.

As Hess returned, she saw the small smile on his face and decided they would argue that day. "I've discovered that the secret to selling a woman," he announced, "is telling people she can't talk. That's the third offer."

"You don't own me," Elza said.

"I'm pretty sure I do. I traded Dalana for you." His eyes sparkled in the daylight. Elza looked away. She had dreamed of him saving her again the previous night. She wished that had been where the dream ended.

"We're both Observers. That means we're equal."

"Men own women in this world. Probably because the Creator is a man."

He could tell I planned to pick a fight and beat me to it. Elza glared at Hess. "Have I ever mentioned that I don't like you?"

"Regularly, but it doesn't bother me."

"Then I'll find something else to say."

"You know, if you were one of them, you would be the most interesting thing I've ever observed," Hess said.

Elza held out her hand. "What did you buy?"

"Not a tent. Those things cost an entire woman this far north."

"You don't have a woman to trade."

"A lot of the people we meet think otherwise."

"What did you buy?"

"Nothing."

"That will make a wonderful dinner tonight. Or perhaps we will eat those skins you insist we carry everywhere."

Hess shrugged. "He offered a bundle of apples for a deer pelt. We need the material to build a tent."

"Do you intend to starve to death?"

"We're going to set up camp for a few days so we can hunt," Hess said.

"So I have to spend all night making traps?"

"I thought we might try something different this time. I want you to come with me. You can have one of my extra spears."

Elza raised a brow. "You say I scare away the animals when I go with you."

"Animals are a lot like men. Too much talking keeps them away."

"And they both smell," Elza added.

Hess stopped walking and pulled his three spears free of his pack. The things broke faster than the fire-hardened variety used by settled tribes, but otherwise served them well. He selected one and handed it to her. Elza hefted it overhand.

"No, no, no," Hess said. He dropped everything to the ground except one spear and demonstrated the proper stance. Elza mimicked him as best she could. When he shook his head, she fixed him with a warning look. "What am I doing wrong?"

Hess put his last spear down. "Try again."

She bent slightly at the knees and lifted the spear up to her ear. Hess stepped close and placed one hand on her shoulder. "Lean forward." His other hand touched the hip closest him. "Center yourself."

"I'm not very good at this," she said.

The breath of his laugh tickled her cheek. "It might take some time."

"I suppose I'm not getting any older," she said.

CHAPTER SEVENTEEN
Zack
Iteration 144

Zack looked every direction as he turned from route 356 into the plaza's back entrance. None of the cars appeared occupied as he passed them. His heart beat out a steady rhythm. Zack drove slowly around the outer perimeter of the parking lot, then parked close to the entrance of the grocery store.

I'm ten minutes early. Maybe they're not here yet. Zack kept the truck running in case he needed to escape fast. As the minutes ticked by, he imagined the various ways the Observers could best him. *Well, they could taze me and drag me away before anyone objected. They could show up dressed like cops and shoot me. They could call the real cops on me, then wait for me to be released from questioning. They could release Lacey in bad condition and ambush me at the hospital.*

At ten o'clock, Zack tensed when a man approached his truck. *I should have stopped to buy a weapon. Even a knife would be better than nothing.* The man unlocked the door of a car parked next to Zack's borrowed truck, got inside, and drove away. Zack glanced to the clock. It was a minute past ten.

Zack twisted around in his seat, looking in every direction. The only people he saw were carrying bags of groceries to their vehicles. None of them looked suspicious. He sank back into his seat and glanced at the clock. It was five after. *They're not releasing Lacey. They just wanted me to come back.*

He threw the truck into drive. There were five of them. It was probably safe to assume that one of them would still be at the farm watching Lacey. The man called Ingrid had released him without revealing himself. That left only three of them to worry about.

I don't know the first thing about espionage, Zack thought. He slowly circled the lot a final time and moved to the back entrance, expecting someone to pull out and block him. His truck returned to route 356 without incident. Zack watched his rearview mirror as he drove, but no one followed him.

He decided his course on the fly. He would return to the trailer park, pack a bag, and get lost. The others might release Lacey when he didn't return. Zack tried not to consider the other possibility.

Zack parked beside Lacey's car at their trailer. His keys were with his phone, somewhere on the hellish farm of the Observers, which meant he would need to break a window to get into his own home. He was halfway to his door when a car parked at the back of his driveway, blocking in both vehicles.

Bridgette stepped out of the car. "Get in the car, Hess."

"Get away from me," he said as she walked forward.

"It's me – Elza."

"I don't even know who that is."

Bridgette reached behind her and pulled out a tiny handgun. "We really messed you up, didn't we? And here I thought we wouldn't be able to leave a mark. Doesn't matter what you remember, Hess. You're getting in my car. Whether I put a hole in your skull first is your decision."

"You're going to shoot me in public?" Zack backed away from her.

"Doesn't look like too many of your neighbors are home at the moment. Plus, you would be surprised how many people mistake the sound of a gunshot for something else."

As he backed up, the heel of his foot struck the first of two wobbly steps leading up to his trailer's front door. His best plan was to break down the door and bludgeon Bridgette to death with a frying pan while taking shots from her handgun.

Zack bent his knees, preparing to leap for the door. Bridgette raised her gun, lining the sites up on him. The front door of his trailer opened.

A form swung out onto the top step, large handgun cradled in two steady hands, paused, and fired past Zack. He turned in time to see Bridgette hit the ground, one eye crying a stream of blood. From behind, he heard the sound of a hammer cocking. "Grab her body," said the woman.

Zack swallowed. "Who are you?"

The woman, short, petite, with black hair, brown eyes, and a distinctive nose, analyzed him briefly before answering. "I'm a girl with a gun. Now grab her body, Zack Vernon."

The way her gun unerringly moved to center on his face every time he shifted convinced Zack he wouldn't gain much by arguing. He went to where Bridgette lay and bent down. There wasn't much of a mess in the front, but his fingers encountered a disturbing amount of moisture when they slid beneath the body. He stood with it in his arms. "Where am I taking it?"

"Her car."

"And then what?"

"Then Kerzon gets what she deserves. I'm going to dig a hole, put her in a casket, and pile dirt on top. She's going to spend a few hundred years tearing her nails out on the walls of her shiny metal box."

Zack dropped the body.

"Pick her back up."

Zack bent to retrieve Bridgette, then stopped. The woman squatted across from him, the muzzle of her weapon still pointed directly at him. "Pick. Her. Up."

"You can't bury her alive," he said. "You can't do that to someone. No one deserves to be trapped in the dark forever."

The tip of the handgun, so steady, sank towards the ground. "Who are you?"

"Just promise me you won't bury her."

"Who are you?"

"Zack. I've never been anyone else. I swear."

The muzzle shook when she raised her gun. "Get in the car."

"You're not going to take the body?"

"No," she said. "Just get in the car."

He glanced around the trailer court. No one had emerged to investigate the sound of gunfire. No one was coming to help him. There was nowhere to run. Zack got into the passenger side of the running vehicle. The woman entered from the driver side.

As she drove around and back towards the exit, Zack studied the blood on his hands. It would vanish when Bridgette revived, but for the moment he was covered. "What are you going to do with me?"

The woman let out a deep breath. "I don't know."

"Who are you?"

"I'm using the name Quebec Wallace."

"Quebec like the province?"

"That's right."

"Are you Canadian?"

"No," she said.

"Are you Elza?"

She didn't answer.

"I'm not Hess."

"Tell me something, *Zack*. Why pull the trick with that robber?"

"It was an accident, *Quebec*."

She shook her head. "Let's assume I'm not stupid. Why did you challenge that man? Were you trying to draw other Observers?"

"I didn't know I could come back from a bullet to the brain."

Quebec watched him from the corner of her eye as she stopped at a light. "We don't die, *Zack*. Not ever. Not even when it's the only thing we want. Which is why you don't want the others to get their hands on you. Back there, Kerzon wasn't abducting you to bake cookies."

"I know."

"You're lucky I was there."

Zack glanced to the gun resting in her lap. "So you're not going to shoot me?"

"I never promised that, *Zack*."

"Quit saying my name like that. You might as well be using the other one."

Quebec reached into her purse and tossed him a set of handcuffs. "Put those on and be quiet. I need to figure out what I'm going to do."

CHAPTER EIGHTEEN
Elza
Iteration 1

She huddled within the pile of furs at the center of their small tent. Two days ago, the snow had come, whiting out the sky and covering everything with its coldness on the same day Hess disappeared, abandoning her in the snow she had denied existed. Elza still didn't know why he had left.

Maybe he finally came to his senses. We shouldn't be traveling together. The Creator didn't send us here to Observe each other. Elza shivered deeper in the furs, wondering how cold it could get. *At least I don't have to listen to Hess gloat about the snow.* Outside, the wind howled its anger.

The tent shook around her, sending down showers of fine snow. Elza flinched, waiting for the tent to collapse. Instead, the door flap peeled back to reveal a pale figure. With wooden motions, Hess crawled into the tent, turned to refasten the door, and dropped to the ground beside her.

He didn't abandon me. Elza touched his shoulder, then yanked her hand back. He was as cold as the snow. "Where did you go?" she asked.

"Got lost in the whiteout," he said. "Stupid. Should have stayed closer to tent. Died ten times, at least. Now I remember why I never returned north."

"You're cold," she accused.

"Do me a favor? Kill me. Rock to my head. I'll come back warm." Hess lay in the same place he had collapsed, body twitching but not shivering, radiating coldness.

"I can't kill you," she said.

"Won't last."

"Doesn't matter," Elza said. She placed half of the furs from her pile onto him. "You'll warm up."

"Hope not. Dying is less painful."

She burrowed deep into her furs, feeling the cold more than ever from the door's opening and then losing half her covers. "I guess you were right about snow."

"Thought being right would feel a little better," he said. "Next we can find the sea. Only fair."

Elza watched him for a time. "We can't stay together, Hess. We have a purpose."

"Sure you want to leave me alone? Might do something wrong."

"I know you will. But She didn't send me here to watch you." Elza tested his temperature with a finger. She couldn't tell if there was any improvement. "I still don't understand why you interfere."

"I was close to here when the world started. Just a mountain over." Hess spoke slowly, voice rasping. "Had a tribe, a mother, and a sister. Lots of memories that weren't real. Started observing. Things seemed fine at first. Men did their work, women did theirs. Everyone helped out. Sister grew into a woman. Beautiful. So kind. I loved her as much as I could one of them, knowing she wasn't real.

"Best hunter of the tribe decided he wanted her. Got rid of his old woman. Seemed wrong, but I wasn't there to judge. My sister . . . Cora . . . she was scared, but went when he came for her. Cora stayed with the hunter, with Ron. Cora was a good woman to her man. She fed him and lay with him and made clothes for him. Wasn't enough for Ron. He liked when people feared him. He fought with the other men. Hurt them for fun. Started hitting Cora too.

"But I didn't do anything. I wasn't there to judge. I was just an Observer. I stayed in my own tent and watched the people ruin their lives. After Ron broke Cora's nose, she wasn't so beautiful. He hit her more and harder after that. He was better when she held his child in her. I hoped it would stay like that. Cora stopped speaking to anyone except Ron. She wouldn't even look at me.

"She had her baby when Ron was out hunting. Cora was so happy. She held her baby all that day, smiled at everyone. She thought Ron would be happy, too. But Ron wanted a son. He took the baby and threw her in the cooking fires."

Elza watched Hess, reading the rage in his features. His voice grew stronger suddenly.

"I couldn't do nothing that time. Ron was bigger than me and much stronger. When I hit him, he hit back until I couldn't stand. Then he held my hand in the fire so it would be useless for hunting. I tried to push him into the fire later that night. He was too strong and instead he broke my neck.

"I kept coming back, Elza. I kept trying to hurt this man. He kept killing me and I kept returning. The other people were frightened, but Ron didn't care. He thought it was a joke that he could kill me so many times. While Ron and I were fighting, Cora left the camp. They found her body at the bottom of a cliff. Ron took another woman and I left the tribe."

Hess met her eyes. "The world is not right, Elza."

She placed her hand on his neck, feeling the returned warmth. "If you were a man, you would be a good one," she said.

"But I'm not."

"No. Instead you're a terrible Observer."

"Do you ever wish you were just a woman?"

She pulled her hand away from him. "I wouldn't like that. The Creator didn't give me an appealing form. If my purpose was to find a man, I don't think I would do well at it."

"You might do better than you think."

"No, Hess. I have tried to play the part of a woman for a long time. Men only want me when a better woman isn't around. I would rather be an Observer than one of them." She rolled to her other side, away from him. He was the same as other men, exclaiming over the beauty of his sister and reminding her constantly of his last woman, the beautiful Dalana.

The cold didn't relent as they lay in silence.

"How long does it stay like this?"

"Three months," Hess said.

"I don't like snow. It's too cold."

Hess shifted closer to her. "In the north, you have to share warmth if you want to sleep comfortably." Elza didn't protest as he rearranged the furs around them.

"I never asked to see the snow," she said.

Hess slid close until they were touching and wrapped an arm around her. "Maybe if we hate the snow enough, the Creator will make the next world without it."

"Your clothes are wet," she said. Hess began to shift around beneath the covers, then tossed his clothes onto the top of their covers. With fewer layers between them, she could feel the heat of his body. "Do you really think the Creator cares about our preferences?"

His warm breath tickled her neck. "He wouldn't need Observers if He didn't want our input."

Elza shifted closer to his warmth. "She wants our experiences, not our opinions."

The hand around her shifted. "Then why aren't we supposed to participate?"

"I don't know, Hess."

His lips brushed her neck. She leaned into it. "Hess, I'm still cold."

CHAPTER NINETEEN
Zack
Iteration 144

Quebec escorted him into her room at the Butler Days Inn, then released one of his hands to cuff him to the bed. When she finished securing him, Quebec went to the room's table, placed her gun down, and retrieved implements from a suitcase already in the room. All without saying a word. She hadn't spoken except to silence him since the car.

With the assistance of a tiny screwdriver, the handgun came apart in her hands. Quebec drizzled oil onto a rag and several Q-tips, then began to thoroughly scrub the weapon. Her every movement was deliberate in the extreme, almost inhumanly economical.

"What kind of gun is it?"

His other questions had only tightened the skin around her eyes, but she answered this one. "It's a Ruger Security Six. I'm firing three fifty-seven hollow points through it."

"Do you have to clean it very often?"

"I clean it after every trip to the range. And sometimes just to help me think."

Zack looked around the hotel room. Besides two suitcases and the cleaning kit on the table, Quebec had left no mark on the place. "Do you go to the range a lot?"

"Most people would say so."

"How often do you go?"

Quebec dropped the rag and began to rapidly reassemble her pistol. "I try to put three hundred rounds downrange every week."

"Is it expensive?"

"Doesn't matter. I can get as much money as I need."

"How?"

"Casinos," Quebec said.

"What, you count cards?"

"I count cards, read expressions, do probability analyses. And when I win big, I make sure it is statistically likely so I avoid notice. Casinos are like ATM's to me." Quebec tightened a final screw, loaded six rounds into the cylinder, and snapped it closed with a flick of her wrist.

Now that she's talking . . . . "So what are we going to do?"

Quebec dug into a suitcase and brought out a slim laptop. "I haven't decided yet. We should leave the area, change identities, and lay low. That's what we should do."

"Then why aren't we doing that?"

Her fingers drummed on the table. "Because I don't think I can walk away from them. They deserve the very worst I can do to them."

"I know." Zack thought of Lacey, begging him to save her and the baby. "I know they do."

"But not the darkness," Quebec said, voice soft. She looked towards him, making eye contact for the first time since the car.

He dropped his eyes. "I don't know what they did to you, but you can't do *that* to them."

"That's what they did to me, Zack. Locked me away in the dark. Me and the man I loved. It's impossible to know how long I was there before the world ended. All I can say is it was too long. Did you know I can't even ride an elevator? Every time I think of stepping inside, I imagine the thing breaking down and trapping me inside. Try dealing with that in New York City."

Zack cleared his throat. "Does night bother you?"

"I'm not a big fan of the dark." Quebec stood and walked to stand beside where he lay on the bed. She held out her wrist to display an analog watch with neon hands and hour markers. "My watch is made with tritium. The hands and hour markers will glow day and night for over ten years." She undid the clasp and removed the watch. Quebec leaned over him to wrap it around the wrist of his free hand. Her dark hair tickled his face as she fastened it.

"Now you don't have to worry about the dark," she said.

When Quebec stood, Zack released a breath he didn't realize he had been holding. The scent of her, floral fabric softener and fruit body lotion mingled with gunpowder and oil, lingered over him. "Won't you need the watch?"

Her eyes were steady on him. "I think it's enough not being alone."

"I'm not him," Zack said.

Quebec turned her back on him and went to her laptop. "I'm trying to find their base of operations. It will be somewhere close, but remote enough that no one will interfere with them. They haven't had much time to set up in the area, so they're probably squatting in an unoccupied hunting lodge or abandoned building. Do you know of anywhere they could hole up? It would have to be out of screaming range of neighbors."

"I know where they are."

Her back stiffened. "You were there? How did you escape?"

"Someone named Ingrid helped me out."

"Ingrid? Are you sure it was her? Maybe I'll go easy on her for that."

"Ingrid was a man."

"Well, she was a woman the first time we met her," Quebec said.

"I am not Hess."

In a sudden motion, Quebec swiped her laptop from the table, sending it crashing to the floor. "You're not Hess? Then why does everyone think you are? Do you think we're stupid?" Her voice grew shriller. "There are a million different ways for us to identify each other. We know. So please stop the act. *Please.*"

"I'm sorry, Quebec." Zack closed his eyes to block out her pain. "Was he your husband?"

"*Husband?*" She shook her head. "Never my husband. Never. Marriage is what these people do to ease their insecurities. They try to bind love in a contract. We never needed that. You chose me world by world, moment by moment, again and again. We've spent lifetimes together. I don't even know who I am without you." Quebec wrestled herself back under control. "Who else is with them?"

"Erik. A guy named Drake. I heard them mention someone named Griff, but I never met him."

"So Erik, Drake, Griff, Ingrid, and Kerzon. I might be able to handle the five of them."

"I don't think that's a good idea," he said. "You're not exactly Rambo."

"I have enough muscles to pull a trigger. It takes over five minutes to regenerate after a death. If I can surprise them, then my only trouble will be restraining the bodies before they wake up."

"They were going to bury me in the ground. What if they do that to you? It would be a lot worse than getting on an elevator. And Erik has a few kinks that almost make you want to go underground." Zack raised his chin. "I won't tell you where they are unless you promise not to go after them."

She bent to retrieve her laptop. "I can find them without you."

"They're not where you think they are."

"Then I go back to your trailer and wait for them to pick up their truck."

"Enough people have been hurt already," Zack said.

"Your wife?"

"Her name's Lacey. Erik threatened to cut the baby out of her."

Quebec looked at him. "Do you love her?"

"I like her most of the time."

"The baby isn't yours. Observers are sterile."

Zack shrugged. "She was pregnant before I met her. What does it matter which body made the baby? Lacey needed someone. Her baby will need someone. Why shouldn't I do something useful while I'm stuck here?"

The hint of a smile played at the corner of her lips. "What do you see when you look at these people? Do you dream of a better world for them?"

"They make such a mess of their lives," Zack said. "But they're happy with it. I don't understand that. I wish I could, but I can't."

Quebec nodded, serious again. "Sometimes happiness seems impossible."

"Promise me you won't go after them."

"Show me where they are and I promise to stay away."

CHAPTER TWENTY

Elza
Iteration 1

The late winter snow was beautiful as it twirled to the ground. Elza watched the frosted landscape around their tent, breathing in the chill air. It was almost time for them to leave the north, but not quite yet. The world promised more days of snow, more long, cold nights.

Hess emerged from the tent with a long, thin spear in his hands. "I'll be quick." He bent to kiss her, wrapping her tightly in his arms.

"The fire will be ready to light when you get back," she said.

They stood there a moment, eyes locked. Since the day they agreed to separate once they traveled south of the mountains, their partings had grown longer. Hess bent to kiss her once more. When he straightened, she rested her forehead on his chest. *This needs to end.*

"I better go now if we want to eat," Hess said.

"Hurry back."

The way he looked at her in the moment before turning away . . . . Elza watched him disappear through the frosty trees. They still had weeks before they could begin their journey. Maybe a month to cross the mountains. Then their paths parted. They would stop whatever it was they were doing and return to Observing.

Trying not to think, Elza swept their stone hearth free of snow with the branch of a nearby shrub, then set out in search of firewood. The area around their tent was picked clean, so she made a large circle to gather fallen branches. Their existence in the frozen land had become routine.

Maybe we should visit the sea before we go our own ways. What is a few more months compared to the hundreds of years we have lived? She shook her head. It had to end soon. Before one of them said something to make things serious. Though their conversations touched on every other topic under the sun, they managed to avoid that one subject. Whatever was between them had to remain unsaid.

She stacked the wood in a dry spot on each trip back to their camp. When she had enough to cook several fish, Elza arranged the sticks and used a flint knife to create a pile of kindling. Then she filled a wooden bowl with snow and placed it where the heat of the fire could melt it later. There were few edible plants available and no palatable ones, so their diet consisted almost entirely of meat and fish. When she had tried collecting acorns in the fall, Hess had informed her that the ones this far north were too bitter to eat. She had quickly realized he understated the case against their edibility.

She sat to wait for Hess. As she did often lately, Elza reflected on her long life. The moment creation sprang into motion had been glorious, coming awake full of righteous purpose. Everything had fascinated her. The false memories of the identity provided her by the Creator were dim shadows incomparable to the experiences she accumulated every moment.

In the early days, nothing could perturb her. Elza had walked through life knowing everything was a temporary illusion, the Creator's grand dream. People lived their transient lives and died without ever grasping the truth of their existence. She had felt so privileged.

Over the years, something had stolen the joy of her calling. Perhaps it had been enduring the constant rejections of the creatures she was sent to observe. Perhaps it had been the tedious monotony of centuries. Perhaps it had been the gravitation of the world towards brutality. Or maybe all of it together was to blame. There had been no single dramatic event to change her, only lifetimes of hollow memories. Despite enduring beatings and deaths over the years, it wasn't until recently that she had truly experienced drama.

What if Hess hadn't been there to stop the men? The men would have done what they wanted to her, of course. She could endure anything, but not without consequences. *Would that have been the dramatic event that changed me? Like Hess had with his sister's death? If I live long enough, isn't it inevitable that something will happen that I can't handle?*

The wind picked up and Elza moved to avoid the snow-filled gusts, going inside the tent where their mingled scents took her mind in a different direction. Though few enough men showed interest in her, there had been many owing to the sheer number of years she lived on the world. Most treated her with apathy, happy to part ways when the time came. Several had regarded her as property. A small few had genuinely liked her. But none of them had looked at her the way Hess did.

If I was just a woman and he was just a man . . . . She didn't finish the thought. The wind outside howled its loneliness while Elza waited inside the tent. Hours passed.

Then the entire world began to thrum in an impossibly deep pitch. With every second that passed, the sensation grew stronger, as if existence itself were about to shred into a million slivers. Without knowing how, Elza recognized what happened. From the moment of Creation, she had known this world was only the first Iteration of many and that it would end when the sky opened.

A counterpoint to the deep thrumming began, a wailing shriek emanating from everything and nothing. The volume of both increased with every moment, triggering an expectation deep within her. The ultimate moment of her existence was about to arrive. It was time to return to the Creator.

The sky opened. To all outward senses, nothing changed, but to Elza it seemed that the restraints of the mundane world vanished, ripped away by an unknown force. Nothing held her to creation. The rumbling and shrieking became louder still, warning her to leave or be consumed with a world marked for destruction.

Elza hesitated for just a second, eyes going to the door of the tent. Then she slipped free of the world to join the Creator.

CHAPTER TWENTY-ONE
Zack
Iteration 144

He picked at the lock on his cuffs with the tip of a pen. Quebec had left an hour ago to retrieve the rental car she'd abandoned near his trailer. The pen made a terrible lock-picking tool. Zack didn't think he would do better with anything short of the actual key. If there were real people who could open a lock with nothing but a hairpin or a paperclip, Zack wasn't one of them.

The door ended his halfhearted efforts by opening. Quebec entered bearing plastic bags.

"Did you go shopping while I was stuck to the bed?"

Quebec cocked her head and looked at him. "I abandoned a car along a back road, walked a mile to retrieve another, and bought you a change of clothes. Be happy it didn't take longer."

"Well, I have to use the bathroom."

She pulled the key out of her pocket and unlocked the handcuffs. "You should take a shower while you're in there."

He took her advice. Fifteen minutes later, he emerged clean from the bathroom wearing new clothes. Quebec gestured at the array of vending machine food arranged on the table. Something in her mannerism made him smile. "Did you spend all your casino winnings on this?"

"Travel with me and you eat nothing but the best," she said.

A twinge of his stomach reminded him he hadn't eaten in close to a day. Zack sat across the table from Quebec and opened a bag of mini-donuts. "Want to hear something funny?"

Quebec's brown eyes fixed on him as he ate. "Always."

"I am a great cook." Zack gestured at the junk food. "But I eat like this all the time. Up until the past year, I used to make all sorts of things I found in cookbooks. I stopped because right after we got married, Lacey told me I had to learn how to cook because she wasn't doing housework. I tossed out everything in my kitchen that wasn't nailed down and Lacey never noticed. We've been eating freezer meals ever since. Tater tots are the closest thing to a vegetable I've had in months."

"You do realize Observers can get fat, don't you?"

"What about teeth? Will those go bad?"

"They'll fix themselves before you notice a cavity exists. Bad breath is something else. So either brush or chew gum or eat parsley."

"Parsley? Seriously?"

"It works. Remember Iteration five?" The light in Quebec's eyes dimmed. "No. Of course you don't. You don't remember anything."

Zack's smile faded. "Sorry." It always came back to Hess. "What was he like?"

"Hess," Quebec said, "was the best man and the worst Observer. Out of all of us, he was the best at *doing things*. It didn't matter what body he had, Hess could always take care of himself. But he didn't do abstract. He hated higher mathematics and never got the hang of counting cards despite having a perfect memory. He was always stepping in to interfere because behind all his disapproval, he really cared for the people."

She wiped her eyes with a sleeve. "Every Iteration, he would tell me that *this* body of mine was his favorite. There were times when it drove me crazy, but he never stopped saying it. And he always found me. Even if it took centuries, he would search every moment until we met. In worlds with computers it took only days. Except this one. I did everything I was supposed to."

Quebec looked directly at him. "How could you forget me? I need you, Hess."

Zack looked down at his hands.

INTERLUDE THREE
Hess
Iteration 142

Hess sipped his tea as he read the news by the early morning light shining through the bay window of their squat house. Alan ran into the room wearing his gray school uniform to stand attentively at his side. Hess shuffled the paper, pretending not to notice the boy.

Across the table, Elza hid a smile in her tea, watching the people pass by their window. They had bought the house for that window. Impractical as hell in the middle of a city noted for its crime, the thing nevertheless provided a perfect picture of the world for their enjoyment.

"Good morning, sir," Alan said in the high-pitched voice of a nine-year-old.

Hess moved as if startled. "Good morning, Alan. How did you sleep?"

"Very good, sir."

"Would you like me to grab you a cup of tea and some toast?"

Alan's shoulders slumped. "Uh, yes, sir. That would be nice."

"Quit teasing him," Elza said.

Hess reached into the pocket of his vest and pulled out two coins. "Almost forgot our deal. I owe you something from the bakery for getting good marks at the academy." He placed the coins on the table.

"Thank you, sir."

"Enjoy it, Alan. You worked hard for it."

Alan scooped up the coins. "I don't mind studying, sir. I like going to school."

"Keep it up and you'll land a nice job that'll allow you as many sweets from the bakery as you can eat."

Alan turned to go and hesitated. "Sir, when I am older, if I do well in my studies and land a nice job like you say, then I want to adopt an orphan off the streets like you and the madam. Maybe a couple of them."

"You're going to make a good man," Elza said.

"Thank you, madam."

"Spend every cent, Alan," Hess said.

When the child scampered from the room, Elza turned back from the window. In this world the body she wore was plain and plump. "If one of our fosters ever took after you, it's this one."

Hess returned his attention to the paper. "Thirteen people died in a fire yesterday."

She returned her attention to the window. "Third fire this month. That should motivate the city council to pass stricter building codes."

"Everything they do is reactive. All it would take is a little foresight to prevent these tragedies." Hess crumpled the paper and threw it into the fireplace. "They can't look more than a few days into the future."

"What do you expect from them, Hess? We've seen the consequence of every action a thousand times, but the brightest of them are little more than children. Besides, you don't really want a world without conflict. Do you?"

"Definitely not. The second Iteration was a disaster."

"Not entirely," Elza said. "There are a few moments from that Iteration I always hold in my memory."

Hess moved his seat next to hers. Outside, people rushed to and fro, off to work or running chores. Alan would probably be at the bakery by now. The boy had been starving to death a year ago. The turning point in his life had been when a sudden blizzard prevented him from returning to the slums after a day spent begging. Alan should have frozen to death that night. Instead, two Observers saw him from their bay window and let him stay the night in their spare room. He waited out the snow a few days, then agreed to stay on as a serving boy in exchange for room and board. After a while, Hess had insisted Alan get an education.

He leaned towards Elza. "Did you know Alan calls us his parents?"

"I haven't heard it," she said.

"Just to his friends."

"Have you been spying on him?"

"Elza, I am an Observer. What do you expect?"

"An Observer doesn't take in strays."

"You didn't object."

"Hess, I stopped objecting long ago. It never did any good."

As he opened his mouth, creation began to rumble and scream, announcing the end of the world. Elza turned to him, wincing at sirens audible only to Observers. "I guess that's it for this one. The timing is a bit inconvenient. I was hoping to see how Alan turned out."

Hess looked out the window, at the world in motion, ignorant that its end was seconds away. Alan was probably biting into a pastry or sucking on a hard candy. He reached out for Elza's hand. "Do you really want to see how he will turn out?" The sky opened. It was as if the Creator had torn away a wall, exposing them to whatever existed beyond the world. Just a thought would send them free of the world. "Because I think we can."

She smiled at him. "Find me fast." Elza vanished.

As the rumbling and screaming grew in volume, he stared out the window. *At least Alan dies happy.* Hess stepped out of existence.

CHAPTER TWENTY-TWO
Hess
Iteration 142

It took close to an hour of awkward silence for Quebec to regain her equilibrium. Zack used the time to reflect on his failures. When Quebec informed him they were leaving for New York that night and started a shower, he found the pen that had failed to pick his lock and wrote a quick letter.

The hours I have spent with you have been the best of my life. I wish I was Hess, but I'm not. Maybe he is still out there somewhere, lost in a rainforest or trapped in the arctic. I need to leave now. If I stay with you, I will only cause you more pain. Remember your promise to stay away from the others.

Zack took the car keys and slipped out of the room. In the parking lot, the key fob identified her rental car for him. He had her Prius on the road before anyone could exit the hotel. Zack forced his mind to stillness as he drove past familiar sights. It wasn't until he parked at the gas station where he had worked the past five years that his stomach began to churn.

His manager Kelly scowled at him the moment he entered the store. "The hell have you been?"

Zack ignored her, depending on the line of customers at the register to keep her occupied. He punched the digits to Lacey's cell phone number into the store's phone and listened to it ring. When it picked up on the fourth ring, just before the voicemail would kick in, there was only breathing on the other side.

"Do you still have Lacey?"

Erik's voice replied. "She's been whining about that hand of hers."

"Are you still willing to release her in exchange for me?"

"Deal's still on, lover-boy."

"Then come pick me up. I'm at the gas station."

"No tricks?"

"No tricks. I'm turning myself in." He hung up the receiver and went outside to sit at the employee's break pavilion. His hands shook as he sat on the picnic table. *Lacey wants to live and I don't. Maybe this will make up for the love I could never give her.*

Kelly stormed out of the store before Erik arrived. "You better be quitting, because I don't need the trouble you cause. You miss your shift. You don't even call. You don't even answer when I call."

"I quit, Kelly."

"Thank God," she said. "Now get the hell off company property. Check's in the mail."

"Just waiting on my ride. This will be the last time you have to see my face."

Kelly started back towards the store. "There's something wrong with you."

The truck he had driven only that morning pulled up before the pavilion. Erik waved him over, eyes steady as an eagle's. "Hop in, Hess." A quiet expectation had replaced the levity.

Zack circled the truck and climbed into the passenger seat. "All by yourself?"

"The others don't have the stomach for this. I think next Iteration I'll be hunting you solo." She glanced towards him often as she drove. "I prefer it that way. Might take longer to find you, but I won't have to deal with their rules."

He remained silent, unable to think of a safe response.

"They think I'm as bad as you," Erik said. "But all of us have our quirks. Things that draw us world after world. Drake with the science and tech crap. Ingrid and religions. Griff does the migrant worker shtick every time. Serial murders are just another quirk. A useful one. You wouldn't believe how much people reveal about themselves in extreme situations. The rest of you think you learn human nature watching them putz about their routines, but only I discover the truth.

"There is something magical in the moment an individual chooses annihilation over continuation. You can bring them back to the side of sanity, but if they cross the line too many times they are broken forever. This is what I show the Creator. The true reaction of life to its existence. You would be surprised how weak the will to live is in the most fortunate. The downtrodden have so much more fight in them. I think that says something about the nature of these creatures."

She pulled into the long driveway of the farm, slowing the truck to a crawl. "Why did you return, Hess? What pushed you across that magic line?"

Zack swallowed. "I've always been broken, Erik."

"We're not like them. Wounds vanish. Even experiences fade into the background. We have too many of them to fixate on any one for long. So what tipped the scales from life to death?"

The game with Bridgette posing as Elza was supposed to hurt me. Maybe I can convinced her to stop hunting Quebec. "Elza doesn't want me anymore. She blames me for what happened to her."

Erik considered his words. "Did she steal you away from Kerzon just to return your mix tape? I don't believe that, Hess. I think you would do anything to save your woman."

She laughed. "I used to think I had more in common with you than any of the others. Sure, you saved the people and I killed them, but at heart the two of us were men of action – even when I was a woman. I know better now. Your sympathy with the people turned you against the Creator. I am loyal, Hess. Absolutely and completely loyal. I will never forgive you for your stunt last Iteration."

The truck pulled to a stop before the barn. Zack nearly collapsed to the ground on his shaky legs when he stepped out of the vehicle. Erik crooked her finger to move him forward. "Now that you are separated from the other woman, the two of us can get on with our relationship. It will be a bit different from what you're used to. More kink, less kissing. And more time in the dark. Lacey told me about your nightlight."

Zack's pace slowed to a crawl as they neared the barn. Each step forward moved slower and covered less distance. His breath came quickly. "Where is she? You promised to let Lacey go."

"She's waiting inside the barn, Hess. I'll release her soon as you willingly sit down in your chair and let me tie you up. You're the one dragging things out. Take big boy steps if you want to speed things up."

Zack gathered his nerve and quickened his pace. They stepped inside the barn, where Lacey sat bound to a sturdy wooden chair, looking ragged. Her face was puffy from dark emotion and retained water. Her pregnant belly rose and fell with her rapid breathing. She started crying when he appeared.

"Things will be better now," he said, unable to stop the quiver in his voice. "I couldn't figure out a way to save both of us, but you get to go home now. You need to take care of the baby. Understand?" Zack collapsed into the chair beside her.

The other Observers were present, silent in the background. Erik slipped up behind him, pulled one arm over the solid central rung of the ladder-back chair and the other below, then cuffed them together. *I'm the only one who doesn't carry handcuffs,* he thought, then laughed hysterically.

"Good boy, Hess. Now let's release Lacey." Erik stepped around to the front of Zack's wife, picked up a large knife that looked suitable for hacking through a rainforest, and stabbed it through the base of Lacey's jaw up into her head. As Lacey spasmed, the woman named Erik twisted the knife with a savage motion of her wrist and elbow.

Sudden rage seized Zack. "We had a deal!"

Erik pulled the knife free and spit in his face. "You dragged her into this when you escaped. Did you really think I would let her run free after witnessing everything? Be happy I gave her a quick death, Hess. I had a lot worse planned for her. I'll have to find someone else to torture. Maybe Elza. Everyone knows I never cared for the clever little bitch."

The woman loomed over him with her knife, then jabbed it forward into his face. Zack flinched away a hair too slow. "It doesn't get any darker than not having eyeballs, Hess. I can slice these things out all fucking day."

CHAPTER TWENTY-THREE
Elza
Iteration 2

For a fleeting instant there was a flicker of nothingness. Then the world crashed into existence about her. Information poured into her: facts, skills, experiences; all the false memories she would need to fake the identity of the body she wore. The new memories were dull gray in comparison to the stunning recollection of a tent set in the middle of a frozen wilderness.

The world sprang into motion around Elza. While a moment ago she had waited for Hess in overpowering cold, now she baked beneath a fiery sun in a lush field of Taro lined by plantain trees. The brown-skinned women and men working the fields cut greens with bronze knives and dug into the ground for the starchy fruit. They would work at the harvest all day, then feast that night, just as they would every day until the crop was harvested and stored for the coming year.

Elza turned to the woman beside her, a cousin named Lana who was also her best friend. Each recalled fact pushed the tent further back in her memory, diminishing the lingering sense of coldness. Lana put out a hand. "Are you well, Nora?"

She looked down at the brown skin of her hand, then to her shapely figure. Elza recalled that she was the most beautiful woman in the village. Many of the boys hoped she would ask them to be her man, but so far she had not chosen one.

Elza placed her hands to her temples. One moment she had been waiting for Hess and the next she was here. There had been no transcendental union with the Creator. There hadn't been *any* experience from beyond. And now she was surrounded by strangers she knew intimately. Fake memories of fake people filled her head.

"No, Lana, I am not well." Even the language she spoke was different.

"Go in from the fields, child," said one of the older men. "No one will think bad of you if you need a break. We will manage without you for a time."

Elza nodded and ran to the village, a collection of thatched huts where she had grown up surrounded by a close-knit agricultural community. *No, I never lived here. I was with Hess this morning. He promised he would be quick, but he didn't make it back in time.*

The village was small and her long legs were swift, so she was soon at the far side of the village. Rolling hills stretched into the distance, dotted with small settlements much like hers. Elza stopped running and sank to her knees.

Was he out there somewhere? She refused to believe the Creator would discard Hess, no matter how poor of an Observer he might be. He had to be out there. As her eyes scanned the horizon, she remembered more false memories, of people telling her that the land went on forever in each direction and that there were as many villages as stars in the sky.

The Creator had separated them. Elza squeezed her eyes shut, dwelling in the last moment they had shared, visualizing the way he had looked at her. She sighed. All the brutality and tenderness of that world was gone forever. A new one stood in its place and it was her purpose to observe it.

"What is wrong, Nora?"

Elza turned to look at her cousin Lana. She stood up. "Nothing. I just felt odd for a moment."

Lana stroked her hair. "They will think we're lazy if we stay away too long."

"Let's go back to the fields, then," Elza said. As she rejoined the rest of her village, they smiled encouragement at her. She returned to where she had stood when the world began and bent to her task. It seemed a good world to her. She thought even Hess would approve of this one.

CHAPTER TWENTY-FOUR
Zack
Iteration 144

He slumped in the chair, making himself forget his circumstances. Erik had gone with Drake and Bridgette to bury Lacey, grumbling that the others didn't know how to make a body disappear. Griff stood outside the barn, looking uncomfortable, leaving only the man named Ingrid to watch him.

Ingrid moved closer. "Why did you come back?"

Zack shook his head, not sure he knew the answer anymore.

Ingrid leaned closer. "Can you endure the torture and the dark? I will return to free you in a few weeks if you can."

Zack shook his head again. He could not bear it. Not for a moment longer.

Ingrid came still closer, until his lips were by Zack's ear. "There is something else I can do. Something that will stop all of this." He heard Ingrid lick his lips. "I have the power to open the sky."

Zack twisted around to look at Ingrid. "The Creator opens the sky."

"No, Hess," Ingrid whispered. "*I* open the sky in world after world. The Creator isn't out there waiting for our reports. The Creator sacrifices Itself to bring a world into existence and sustain every particle of matter. Until I open the sky, there is no Creator. There is only the world and us."

He swallowed. "You can end the world."

"If I had known what was done to you last Iteration, I would have opened the sky sooner. If you cannot bear what is done to you, I will stop this Iteration now."

Seven billion people live on this world. Even if only one in a hundred is truly happy, that is seventy million lives that want to live. Zack shook his head. "You can't do that. You can't just kill every person in existence."

"They will never know a moment of pain. Between one moment and the next, they will simply cease to exist. It is the fate of everything that is made to one day be unmade, Hess."

"You can't kill creation to save me."

"They're not real. You are."

Zack shook his head. "Everyone keeps saying that. But what makes us any different from them? Just because we don't die? That's not enough."

"No, Hess. We are so much more than these creatures. Every particle of their matter is sustained by the Creator's essence. But we are more than that. We're not sent here to observe for the Creator, Hess. We *are* the Creator. Tiny slivers of the Creator embedded within the world to experience *Our* creation."

"Don't do it, Ingrid," Zack said. "No matter what they do to me. No matter what I say. I don't want you to do it because of me."

Erik's voice boomed from the barn door. "Why all the whispering, Ingrid? Do you have secret business with Hess?" She strode inside, hard eyes skewering Ingrid. "Here I was thinking Griff must be our rotten apple. Never considered the possibility that you organized this whole operation just to make sure we failed. Is that how things stand here?"

Ingrid sneered at Erik. "Your mind is twisted from your hobbies. Remember the role I played last time. Ask yourself if it makes sense for me to betray the cause I started and championed. I still think *you* released Hess so that you wouldn't have to follow the rules we established. The reason I am whispering with Hess is I want him to tell me the truth of his escape."

Erik looked back and forth between the two of them before settling her gaze on Zack. "I'll get the truth out of him."

"No," Ingrid said, "you will make him say the words you plant in him."

Erik's hand drifted to the holster at her waist.

"Car coming," Griff shouted.

"Get rid of them," Erik said.

From outside, the sound of the approaching car grew louder. Erik scowled at him. "Be very quiet, Hess. Things can always get worse. Always."

The car's engine grew louder. Zack heard Griff's shouts for the vehicle to get off private property. The car door opened. Griff repeated his demand. A shot rang out. "Shit," Erik said. She pulled free her handgun and ran to crouch at the side of the open barn door. Ingrid ran to the other side.

From where he sat, Zack saw Bridgette emerge from the house, take a hit to her shoulder, and duck back inside. Quebec strode into view, handgun held at the ready, swiveling to point first towards the house, then towards the barn, then back again. Erik took aim.

CHAPTER TWENTY-FIVE
Elza
Iteration 2

Elza walked into the guest pavilion of the village and settled her travel pack to the ground. The local men ogled her as she moved to the communal well. Gaining acceptance in a new community was never a challenge for her. The greatest trouble she had was escaping the men who proclaimed their undying love for her. Even after more than one hundred years and four name changes, she still wasn't accustomed to the attention.

They wouldn't chase me if I looked the same as last Iteration. Infatuation is so shallow.

Some of the other women frowned in her direction. According to the tradition in these parts, a woman could ask any man to be hers. If he had previously accepted another woman's offer, he then had the choice to trade if he wished. Men went to all sorts of trouble to impress women.

One of her men over the years had practiced running and lifting heavy objects to make his form more appealing. Most of them strived to gain a reputation throughout the village as a hard worker so that they could bring respect to a woman. Without exception, they all bathed and groomed themselves to an extent she found laughable.

This world was very different from the previous one. She thought it better in many ways, but the carefree existence of the brown-skinned villagers lacked a certain gravitas. People were too polite, conflict too rare, food too plentiful, wants too trivial. *This cannot be the world Hess demanded of the Creator. It is so boring!*

She drank from the well, watching the people around her, trying to decide if she wanted to settle in the area. There were too many young men and not enough beautiful women. It was counterproductive for an Observer to draw attention the way she did.

When she finished her drink, one of the older women approached. "Hello, friend. Are you looking for a new home? I have a grandson about your age."

You think *you have a grandson my age.* "Sorry, friend, but I am passing through."

"So sad. My grandson is a very good worker." The woman paused for a response that didn't come, then continued. "Will you at least accept our hospitality for the night?"

"I would be honored, friend," Elza said.

"Excellent. Could you help us pound the Taro into dough?"

Elza gave a slight bow. "I would be honored to help feed the people."

The old woman led her to a small pavilion across from the well where a number of young women gathered. In their midst was a single man who lifted and dropped one of the large paddles into the wooden bowl holding the boiled Taro root. Each of the women around him worked in teams, one pounding with the paddle while the other moved the doughy mass between strikes. The man worked solo, varying the angle of his paddle to spin and flip the dough in an impressive display.

Elza's feet froze to the ground as she watched the man's mastery of a woman's task. He smirked as if he knew she watched him. Her heart began to skip. Elza stepped up to the man. "Why is it you do the work of women?" she asked.

"I like to do all the work," he said. "Also, there are pretty women here."

Her eyes darted over him, taking in every feature. "You are very good at this."

"I am a good worker." He looked at her and smiled. The vacuous pride in his eyes revealed to Elza that this man was a good-natured, proud, hardworking man and nothing more. His eyes slid past her to the old woman. "Hello, grandmother. Do you see how fast I am getting?"

She moved to help some of the other women. *I definitely will not settle in this village. I need somewhere small. Somewhere quiet. A place where I can take a break from shallow men. Somewhere I can be alone.*

CHAPTER TWENTY-SIX
Zack
Iteration 144

"Quebec! Get down!" His warning came just in time. Quebec threw herself back just as Erik fired. The shot missed.

Quebec rushed forward once more, cradling her gun with an insane intensity. *What is she doing here? She can't expect to win against all five of them.* The answer was obvious. *She thinks I'm Hess. She will do anything to save me.*

"Get out of here!" he shouted. "Quebec, leave!"

Erik fired. Quebec swore and shifted her weight off of one leg. She hobbled forward, hands steady on her weapon. From the house, Bridgette emerged with Drake at her side. Both of them were armed.

No. Zack struggled against his bonds. *No.* All around, the shadows began to grow. *No!* Helpless rage and frustration boiled higher. This was his fault. He landed on the national news. He returned to his trailer. He told Quebec where the farm was. He gave her a reason to come here. Anything that happened to her would be his fault.

The shadows pooled together, emerging from the corners of the barn and from beneath objects to coalesce into the darkness. "Go away, Quebec! Run!" His throat burned from the force of his shout.

Drake shot at Quebec, hitting her in the side. Erik squeezed off another shot, striking the gun from Quebec's hands, leaving her defenseless, enemies on all sides. *No!* The darkness boiled, climbing the walls, consuming the ceiling, dripping over everything.

He stopped breathing. In broad daylight, the darkness rose up to claim Zack. It surrounded him, strangling him with the numb terror that lurked wherever light wasn't.

Zack struggled to escape, to return to the light. He knew it still shone somewhere. *Not again!* The voice thundered in his mind. On its echoes came another. *I don't want to live!*

Zack silenced the voices. He could sense the light out there, knew the way back existed if only he could find it. He had to escape the darkness, leave it behind and forget it ever existed. Return to the state of least pain.

The darkness boiled about him. Zack pushed back at it, forcing everything to stop. He remembered how he had done it before. How he could do it again. Make it all go away. Forget everything.

The force of his will pushed at the darkness, forcing it to the corners of his mind. The darkness fought back, struggling to resist its banishment. *How could you forget me?* Her voice rose from the depths and struck him. His struggle ceased, the darkness and his terror abandoning their battle as one, leaving a sudden peace in their wake.

She needs me. Things stirred within the depths, eager to rise. Zack knew part of what was there. A night stretching to infinity, filled with terror and self-hatred. But there was more. So much more. *I have to. She needs me.*

Zack embraced the darkness.

CHAPTER TWENTY-SEVEN
Elza
Iteration 2

She ran the entire way from her village to the somewhat larger village the locals called a city, drenching her wool dress with sweat and bruising her bare feet on stones hidden within the hard-packed dirt. Her race began in the Taro fields the moment she heard the news and ended when she reached the guest pavilion at the outskirts of the settlement. Her top concern had been that the visitor would leave before she arrived, but judging by the crowd, this was not the case.

Elza straightened her dress as she studied the people assembled to wish the stranger good travel. The group was disproportionately female. They had come from miles away to see a man with pale skin claiming to search the entire world for a lover from a previous life, each wearing her best dress, no doubt secretly hoping the stranger would recognize his true love in her.

The stranger was easy to spot. His skin was even paler than Elza's had been in the previous world and contrasted with the dark hues of everyone else. Elza seized the elbow of a woman she knew. "What is the stranger's name?"

The woman smiled. "We have taken to calling him Mister White, but he gives his proper name as Wren."

Elza's lips compressed to a determined line. Names meant nothing. Among these people, she answered to Tessa, the name of a village on the other side of the mountains. Observers had to change identities often to prevent others from noticing they did not age or retain injuries.

"What is the name of the woman he searches for?" Elza asked.

The woman chuckled. "Mister White! Come here now and meet a beautiful young woman! She would like to know about your search! And maybe ask you to be her man!"

Mister White turned at the shouting and approached. He was plain in his looks, remarkable only because of his uncommon coloration. But the way he studied every face and every gesture confirmed to her in an instant that this man was an Observer. Unaccountably, Elza found she couldn't speak.

She stared as the man spread his hands wide and nodded his head in the local manner of greeting. "Greetings, friends. I don't have time to tell stories now. The world is very large and I can't stay any place more than a few days. All I can tell you is that I am searching for a woman."

The village woman threw her arm around Elza's neck. "Tessa here is a woman. She came here three summers ago and hasn't picked a man yet, though many have let her know they would say yes."

Mister White bowed deeply towards Elza. "My apologies, Tessa. You are very beautiful, but I already have a woman."

"What's her name?" she squeezed the question through the tightness at her throat.

"Her name," Mister White said, "is Elza. Tell everyone you know a man walks the world looking for Elza." Mister White – Hess – returned to his preparations, rolling up his bedding and packing his bags.

Embedded within Elza was the certainty that she existed for a single purpose: to observe creation on behalf of the Creator. The core of her identity rested upon that fact. Nothing mattered but her sacred duty. Nothing could be allowed to interfere with her work. The days she had spent with Hess would always live within her dreams, but they had been a mistake she could never repeat. Her existence had a purpose far nobler than that of a mortal woman languishing in the arms of a lover. She was an Observer.

Elza dabbed at her eyes as each of the village elders bowed to Hess, treating him like a man on a sacred mission, never realizing Hess had turned his back on his true purpose. She walked with the others as they escorted Hess to the turn in the road, where by tradition people would part. Hess never looked back as he passed the turn.

The women congregated before the collection of thatch huts they called a city, joking with one another that eventually some pretty face would catch Mister White. The one who had spoken on her behalf earlier patted her shoulder. "Don't be sad to see him go, Tessa. He's no different than any other man. Some day, he will realize his woman does not exist and forget about her."

Elza jerked away from the hand on her shoulder. "What do you know of men?" she snapped. "What do you know about anything?"

The woman's shocked expression clouded with anger. "I know more than a girl without a man. You think you are special, girl. Some day you will settle with a normal man and realize different."

Hess grew smaller with distance and the women began to disperse.

Elza ignored the woman at her side, studying the dwindling form of her man and recalling all the times she had wondered where he was . . . wondered in what way he was violating the sacred command of the Observers. Now she knew the answer to that question. He had been seeking her.

Letting him find her would only encourage his obsession. Their dalliance would taint the work of two Observers, depriving the Creator of precious input into the experience of Her world. The only solution was to remain hidden. Hess would eventually tire of his search and resume his duties. Given enough time, it might even be as the woman claimed. Hess might forget her.

Her feet moved before she could restrain them. In a moment, Elza was running again. The abuse to her feet had healed and her form in this world was light and swift. She caught up to Hess in moments.

He spoke without looking at her. "Go home, woman."

Elza clasped her hands together. "I just need to know one thing. Please."

Hess stopped walking. "What?"

"Do you love her?"

For a moment, it seemed he wouldn't speak. "I couldn't hate everything He made." He pointed back to the village. "Go home. Choose a man and be happy with your life."

Elza stared back towards the village, where the people went about their daily activities. That was where she belonged, among the subjects, among the participants of this world. She turned again to see Hess striding away from her.

This was where it should end. She had all the answers she had ever sought from Hess. She knew how he had spent his time in this world. She knew that those days together had meant as much to him as they had to her. She knew he loved her. Anything more would be a dereliction of duty.

"Wait," she called. He continued walking. "Hess, wait!"

He froze, then turned to face her. Elza took his hands in hers and pressed them to her face. Though every feature was changed, the way he looked at her remained the same. And that was all that mattered. She kissed his hands. "If you would walk the world for me, then I would go with you. I cannot believe She would disapprove of that."

CHAPTER TWENTY-EIGHT
Hess
Iteration 144

It was like waking from a dream. Only the nightmare was real. Hess twisted to look at his bindings. The cuffs were of professional quality and would require time and effort to break or pick. But the chair was something else. While solid in appearance, the thick rungs of the ladder-back were held in their tongue-and-groove placement by wood glue more than anything.

Hess seized the slat with both hands behind his back and simultaneously twisted and drove back on one side. The glue snapped and the rung came free along one side, wood splintering along the edge. Hess seized the rung in both hands and pulled it out from the opposite side.

He stood quickly, brought his cuffed hands below his glutes, sat and lifted both legs, and brought his hands up the front of his body, still bearing the splintered rung from the chair. He launched forward into a run, crashing into Erik and slamming his makeshift spear into her throat, severing one of her carotid arteries and piercing her trachea. His hands, still bound together, seized the gun from her hands. He glanced at the weapon. It said *Glock* along the side and beneath that *9mm*. The Creator tended to recycle things from one world to the next. Ammunition types were much like languages and measurement systems in that they never varied much.

Hess raised the gun and fired off three rounds rapidly into the back of Drake, who squatted over the downed Elza. Bridgette – no, Kerzon – raised her weapon and fired at him. Hess fired his last round, missed, and felt the trigger go soft under his finger.

At that moment, the entirety of creation began to scream its destruction in a terrible duet, high screech and deep rumble announcing the end of the world. *No!* Hess ran from the barn, pointing the empty Glock at Kerzon, driving her back.

Invisible to all but them, the force binding Observers to the world evaporated, torn aside to reveal another direction available to them. The sky was open. Kerzon puffed out of existence. Hess crashed to his knees beside Elza. Her eyes met his. Broken and bleeding, she recognized him and smiled. "Find me fast," she said.

"You have to wait," he said. "We can't leave yet."

To the side, Drake vanished.

"I'm sorry, Hess," Ingrid shouted. "The situation escalated too far. I want them to think the Creator objected to the fighting."

Hess picked up Elza's dropped Ruger Security Six, stood, and aimed at Ingrid, hoping there was an unfired round inside it. "You are no friend of mine, Ingrid. You led the others against us last Iteration."

"I am not Ingrid."

He pulled back the hammer of the gun. While the double-action revolver would fire without the help, Hess knew cocking the pistol would create a shorter trigger pull and increase his marksmanship by a small amount. At the twenty yards between him and Ingrid, he could put a piece of lead directly between her eyes provided Elza had maintained her weapon as he'd taught her. Provided there was a live round left to fire. "You convinced a lot of people that you were Ingrid."

"I know enough to play the part."

"Who are you?"

"My driver's license says Jerome Whittaker."

Hess narrowed his eyes. "Who are you?"

"I'm the twelfth Observer, Hess. The rest of you took the name of the identity you wore when you first met another, so I guess that makes me Jerome."

Hess glanced down to Elza. Her wounds were closing quickly. All about them, Creation continued to scream its two-toned swan note, rumbling and screeching as if it were tearing itself apart. "I don't believe you. How could an Observer hide from us all this time?"

"Because my job is to prevent situations like the one you had last Iteration. I get the executive summary of your lives planted in my head every Iteration. I know the twists and turns of every Observer's long life. I know where each one of you is inserted at the moment of Creation. Avoiding your attention is easy. I stay hidden because mingling doesn't serve my purpose."

Hess hesitated, then lowered the gun. "What happens if we stay here?"

"The twelve of us are pieces of the Creator. The Creator cannot awaken and draw back Its essence from creation without all of us. I imagine the world would continue to turn so long as one of us remains in it."

Elza pushed to her feet. "We can't stay here, Hess."

"It's my fault he ended the world."

"You hate all the worlds, Hess."

"But *they* don't. They screw up everything again and again because they are stupid and selfish, but they love their lives, Elza."

She turned to the twelfth Observer. "Does this noise ever stop?"

"I don't know," Jerome said. He pointed at Hess. "But he might."

"Hess? How would Hess know?"

Jerome smiled. "You never told her, Hess?"

"Told me what?"

"That he stayed behind on that first world," Jerome said.

Elza met his eyes. "You went back to the tent."

"I had to. We left things unsaid."

Jerome spread his hands. "And does the sound ever stop? I only get a summary, Hess, not the actual memories."

"It ends after five minutes or so," Hess said.

"Then I wish the two of you the best." Jerome vanished.

All around them, the horrible sound reached a crescendo and ceased. "I like him," Elza said.

Hess took her hands in his. "Elza, I am so, so, so sorry for turning them against you. I never meant for you to be hurt."

She placed a finger over his lips. "I will face imprisonment a hundred times, Hess, but you can *never forget me*."

"Never. I swear."

Elza looked around the empty farm. "So what are we going to do with this world? There's no one around to stop us from any insanity you can conceive."

"This might sound crazy, but I just want to watch them."

"Before we get to that, I have a stolen car with my prints all over it."

Hess held her handgun out to her. "How does this sound for a plan? Find a key for these handcuffs. Meanwhile I berate you for carrying a revolver instead of something with a clip. Then we wipe the car for prints and abandon it in a bad neighborhood with the doors unlocked."

"You know that clips jam." Elza pulled a universal handcuff key out of her pocket and released him as she talked. "Usually at the worst possible moment."

"That happened once in a hundred and forty-four Iterations."

"It happened the first time I needed to shoot someone," Elza said. "And it wasn't my fault I had to charge into a gunfight today. So drop the issue. We need to take care of some things and then I want to eat real food. I've been eating out of vending machines for days now."

Hess looked in the direction the others had carried Lacey's body. "We're not doing any good here." As they walked towards the car, Hess placed an arm around her shoulder. "Considering Jerome's revelation, I think it's time to tell you something."

"Let me guess." Elza waved at her figure. "This body is your favorite."

He nodded. "I was going to say that. But I want you to know *why* this time."

"Because it's flexible?"

"Because this body is the one that's with me."

Elza raised up on her toes to place a soft kiss on his lips. "Are you sure that's the only reason? I know you are partial to curves, but this body is *flexible*."

"How flexible?"

She flashed a smile. "I'll show you later, Hess. We have to dump a stolen car and get some food and maybe a drink or two or ten."

Hess snapped his fingers. "I know just the place to eat. The Penn Brewery is just half an hour away. Their food is supposed to be good and I know their beer is amazing."

"Is that a microbrewery? You're a beer snob, aren't you? It's Iteration twenty-six all over again."

Agents of the Demiurge

Book 2 of the Participants Trilogy

CHAPTER ONE
Erik
Iteration 2

He took the name Mezzin as he entered the village. Mezzin. The name of a man from the previous world. A man who never properly existed, given the fact that the only remnant of his existence was an unflattering memory of the Creator's Observer. But then, none of these creatures could be said to properly exist. They would all vanish when the Creator ended this world.

Mezzin smiled when he greeted an old man at the village's guest pavilion. The elderly should be more perceptive with the benefit of experience, but they rarely achieved that potential. This one chose to ramble about the weather instead of inquiring about the business of a stranger. Foolish. But then, this world didn't inspire the same paranoia as the previous one.

Was this a better world for the people to inhabit? Probably. These pathetic creatures didn't have the requisite resilience to survive a brush with true brutality. The previous world saw them cowering in constant fear, striking out before they could become victims. This one saw them utterly dependent upon their community, terrified of what they saw as untamed wilderness beyond their settlements.

The village elder granted Mezzin guest status after a while, promising that if he worked hard the village would vote to adopt him as a new member. Mezzin made the appropriate gratitude-heavy response to the offer. The old man then introduced him to the work leader, a man named Rek.

"Why do you come to our village?" Rek spoke bluntly.

"I spent all my life with the same woman. She always wanted to be a mother, but for many years nothing happened. When she was almost too old for children, it finally happened. We were so happy." Mezzin turned his face to the ground as if fighting emotion. "But she was not meant to be a mother. I could not stay after losing her and the baby, so I had to find a new home."

Rek's voice grew gentler. "I am sorry, friend. You can pick what work you wish to do today, whether you wish it to be easy or hard. The people will not think any less of you whatever your choice."

Dead woman was a great back story. People gave him space to grieve, he could ask sensitive questions without raising suspicions, and none of the other men assumed he had come to tempt away their women. Embellishing the tale with the death of a long anticipated baby only sweetened the deal. The problem was, people assumed grief had rendered him fragile.

"I don't ask for pity," Mezzin said. "Give me the hardest work you have."

The hardest work the village had that day was digging irrigation ditches. Mezzin used the shoulder blade of an antelope to dig the soil. The other men on ditch duty wore disgruntlement openly. Even in a society where men competed for reputations as hard workers, nobody truly wanted the hardest work. They were weak, all of them. They didn't even eat the meat of land animals. The bones they used for tools came from corpses they found on the land around their villages.

Mezzin deepened the irrigation ditch with steady movements of his arms and back. Sweat poured from him in the ever-present heat. Blisters formed on the brown skin of his hands, then burst and bled before vanishing as if they had never existed. Mezzin continued to work at a maniacal rate until daylight began to fade. Then he stood to survey their progress.

The ditch licked a shallow river at one end, then snaked back and forth among the raised beds where Taro would grow. Irrigation was one hell of an idea. Thought up by the Creator, of course. These creatures only thought those ideas they were told to think and did actions they were shown to do. If this world hadn't been born with a fake history of agriculture, then it would be hunt and gather all over again.

Roughly half the ditch had been completed. Mezzin could see the faint outline drawn in the dirt, marking where the water should flow. Even without the benefit of the markings, the proper location was obvious. The people of this village rotated their fields, like all the others. There had once been another irrigation ditch in the same spot they now dug. River silt, human refuse, foot traffic, and time had nearly erased the traces before the village rotated back to the same piece of land.

The other men brought Mezzin back to the center of the village, where everyone sat together to drink water before the women served dinner. He had to hear Rek tell everyone the sad history he had invented for himself. Had to hear the sympathies of the pathetic creatures directed at him. Had to react all depressed. Perhaps it was time for him to switch cover stories. Next village he would pose as a man being pursued by a pack of vicious man-eating tigers. That tale always stirred things up in a satisfying manner.

Women distributed banana leaves, then passed bowls of food around. Mezzin scooped some sticky Taro dough from one bowl and placed it on his leaf, pulled several plantains free from a bundle, took a few berries, added liberal amounts of green vegetables, and accepted a few nuts. He watched the people go about their nightly meal. They seemed to revel in their existence.

The old man who had welcomed Mezzin into the village stood up before everyone, placed a finger from each hand into his mouth, and whistled for attention. "Who wants to hear the story of the White Traveler?"

Mezzin sat slightly straighter. Stories were excellent material for the Creator. They cut through all the daily minutiae of life to get to the important things. Stories told you what people wanted, what they valued, and how they wished they could be. And, of course, stories were so much more interesting than watching a village of idiots put food into their mouths while swapping inane gossip.

The women of the village began to clap. The old man appeared disappointed. "None of the men want to hear this story? I cannot believe such a thing! Women, you must get the men excited for my story!"

The men groaned so nearly in unison that it appeared staged. Mezzin wiped the sneer from his mouth before anyone noticed. This was going to be one of *those* stories. Something about a fantastical figure teaching the men a lesson, no doubt. Mezzin didn't care for such stories, not even when he suspected he might have inspired a few such stories himself.

Women and men alike were soon calling for the story of the White Traveler to be told. When the village had demonstrated its enthusiasm with a particularly annoying cacophony, the old man placed both hands over his heart and the crowd grew quiet.

"Near ten seasons ago, the White Traveler came through our village. He came from the North Road at sunset, and even in the dark we knew this stranger to be unusual in his looks. His skin was pale. Paler even than the skin of the Rhino. It wasn't until the next day that we saw him in proper light and knew his skin to be so white and clear that the veins of his arms and hands showed *blue*.

"This was a most unusual man in appearance. That first night, we asked who he was and what he wanted with us. I admit I was frightened of him. His oddness came from more than his looks. This man walked with big steps and talked in a strange manner and watched from pale eyes that held no fear of anything. He stood at the entrance of our guest pavilion and asked to be received as a friend.

"He said 'You may call me Wren, but my true name is a secret.' Now, friends, this seemed most unusual to me. So I asked what he wanted with us. 'I am walking the entire world,' the White Traveler told me. He had come from a place so far away that the people had pale skin. So I asked 'why do you travel the world?'

"The White Traveler looked at me and said 'I seek a woman.' I told him that he was welcome to stay in the guest pavilion, but that I didn't think any of our women would ask him to be their man. He told me 'I do not want to steal anyone from your village. I walk the world for a particular woman.'"

The old man shook his head in wonder. "He said these words, and every woman in the entire village instantly wanted him. I have never seen so much fuss over one man in my long life. But the White Traveler, he would not say yes to any woman who asked him to be her man. He said he wanted only the woman Elza.

"So we asked 'Who is this woman Elza? What does she look like?' But the man did not know! He said that he had known her in another life, another world. A frightening world, he told us, where no one was ever safe. He did not know if she was young or old, beautiful or homely. All the White Traveler knew was he wanted back his woman.

"Now, we all thought this man was crazy. Surely his tall tale could not be true, we said to one another. The man stayed with us three days, telling everyone his story and begging us to spread word to everyone we knew. I wanted to fix the man's crooked thoughts, so I began to ask him questions. I said 'How will you know Elza when you find her? You don't even know what she looks like!'

"But the White Traveler only smiled. He said 'She will know my true name.' So all the women began trying to guess the White Traveler's name. And of course no one guessed right. So on the day he left, I asked him 'Do you really think you'll find your woman?'

"The man looked at the horizon and said 'This world is larger than it has any right to be. But even if the maker of the world placed oceans and desserts between us, I will find her.'"

Mezzin's breath caught. *Maker of the world?* Impossible. These creatures knew nothing of the Creator. They talked nonsense about mythical ancestors and people descending from animals, never suspecting the truth.

All around, the women sat straighter in anticipation. The story was not over. The old man pointed to a corner of the village square. "In my young days, I loved being around the beautiful women of this tribe so much that I used to pound the Taro into dough with them. One day, the most beautiful woman I had ever seen passed through our village. She was so stunning that my heart hurt and I could not stand to look upon her for more than a single glance at a time. This woman stayed only a single night, but I never forgot the look of her. Nor did the other men my age, though much time passed.

"Last summer, that woman returned to pass through our village. She had not aged a single day, though forty years were passed. Escorting her was the White Traveler. He also remained young. This woman went by the name of Elza. And she called her man Hess."

The old man raised his shoulders in an awkward shrug. "We know so little about our world. Everyone knows that the road south has people with darker skin than ours, but until the White Traveler came, we never knew the road north would reach lands where people have paler skin. Perhaps the stories of the man are true. Perhaps the maker of the world exists. I do not know, friends. But I do know that the White Traveler went on a very long journey. And at its end, he did find the woman he sought."

The old man sat for a drink of water and some rest while the village went back to its gossip. Mezzin left the remains of his meal to move closer to the old man. "Is every word of your story true?"

"Dear friend, surely a man your age has heard the story of the White Traveler! His path took him to all the villages I know of."

Mezzin licked his lips. "What did this man say of the Creator?"

"*That* was the word he used for his maker of the world! Creator."

He placed a hand to his head to fight a sudden vertigo. "Old man, did the White Traveler say if he worked for the Creator? Did he say if his purpose was to watch you? Did he use the word Observer?"

The old man's brow wrinkled. "No. He never said any of those things."

Mezzin picked at his meal until the women came by to collect the banana leaves. As darkness descended, the people moved to their homes. The old man approached him. "Are you ready for sleep, friend?"

"This Hess and Elza went north when they left here?"

"Yes. I walked with them to the edge of the village when they left."

Mezzin licked his lips. "This was one year ago?"

"Last summer."

Without another word, Mezzin walked towards the north road, ignoring questions from the old man. There was no time to waste lounging around this village. He had Observers to find.

CHAPTER TWO
Hess
Iteration 145

The new world erupted into existence around Hess, a riot of sensory input following the nothingness between Iterations. He stood in the loading bay of an industrial warehouse, surrounded by the frozen forms of people not yet animated. Bright light streamed in from the open bay doors. To one side, stacks of palletized product waited beside a computer terminal. The scent of exhaust filled the air.

It presented a stark contrast to the world he had left. Perpetually gray skies were replaced by sunshine. Cracked mortar and rusting metal swapped with clean and new construction. Permafrost traded for green grass visible through the doors. The dying corpse of a world was gone, and a new one full of promise stood ready for him to observe.

Memories flooded into Hess, hazy impressions of a life within this world. A set of false recollections to match the fake history of the newly born universe. Black-and-white memories of snowball fights and prom dates and college courses and business trips flowed into him, meticulous in detail but oddly flat in tone so he could never mistake these memories for ones he had actually lived.

The name of his identity was Jed Orlin and he was the Director of Logistics for TFK Motors. He was one of the dark-skinned upper class, unlike the pale working class men around him posed about their tasks, created mid-motion. One man bent forward at the waist, dust pan held for another to sweep up glass fragments. Hess's new memories told him a forklift operator had smashed a fluorescent light several minutes past.

Three men he recalled as slackers congregated together, one of them with hands raised to emphasize whatever point he was making. Several others were using pallet jacks to move heavy steel components onto a waiting trailer. The truck driver stood beside the woman at the computer

108

workstation, complaining to her that the bill of lading had not been e-filed prior to his arrival.

Hess lived in a gated community, drove a luxury car, and held season tickets to the symphony orchestra. He had just escaped a relationship with a half-pale gold-digger and a friend had set him up on a date with an attractive neighbor woman that evening.

Every Iteration of the world began *in media res*, only no one knew of the joke except him and eleven other Observers. People never noticed a difference between their present realities and their staged memories. They lacked the capacity to identify any inconsistencies within themselves.

The world crashed into motion around him. One moment there was the eerie silence of a world not yet alive and the next people continued actions they only thought they had begun – walking, talking, loading product, pushing a broom.

Hess pulled his smart phone out of his pocket. This world had an internet, which meant finding Elza would take a matter of days instead of decades or centuries. He fiddled with the touch screen interface until he found an app to connect him to public message boards.

The content of the messages he posted and where he chose to post them were part of an elaborate, organic code – the result of lifetimes of shared experiences. On a travel blog he reviewed a restaurant from the nineteenth Iteration that they had owned together. He placed a free advertisement on a classified site, "man looking for woman with lazy eye, will pay up to one tent." On a message board for personal finance, Hess left an anecdote about selling pig bladders for profit.

On a less technological world, he would travel to the world's largest city and frequent its largest park every morning. When things became truly primitive, he simply covered as much ground as possible. But a world like this made things simple. They would both scatter electronic breadcrumbs to lead the other to their online presence, then establish contact and decide where to locate themselves.

Dear Jed Orlin, Hess's identity, had achieved financial independence at forty years of age, which gave him the opportunity to move anywhere Elza desired. And he had precious little in the way of family to wonder where he had gone. Very convenient.

"Mr. Orlin? Do you still want to meet? The architecture firm sent over the preliminary plans for the warehouse expansion." The speaker was Gwen Furman, with a job title his identity could never remember, whose nebulous role included serving as an efficiency expert. The misremembering bugged him. Hess never forgot anything he consciously experienced, but the memories he inherited at the start of a world were as fallible as anyone else's, as if at the moment of creation he had been plugged into an established role in place of the true actor.

Apparently, among the details Jed Orlin had forgotten before Hess inherited his memories was a warehouse expansion meeting. He frowned. He didn't remember *anything* about plans to expand the warehouse. "Sure," he said. "We'll meet in my office."

While they relocated, Hess probed at his memories, trying to determine if his identity regularly forgot meetings. Every recollection presented evidence to the contrary. Jed had been a master multitasker largely because he didn't miss the little things.

Gwen sat after him, the movement causing a religious pendant on her necklace to slip free of her shirt. Hess stared. Emblazoned on the surface of the pendant was a raised fist instead of the sacred eagle emblem he expected. Based on his memories, it should have been a sacred eagle.

Is the Creator messing with me, he wondered. But that made no sense. Jerome had revealed to him last Iteration that the Observers were pieces of the Creator. Why would anyone turn against a part of himself? Of course, another piece of the Creator was Erik, who wanted only the worst for Hess. Did their desires balance out to a net zero? Did the Creator even care about the rivalry among its components?

"Are you OK, Mr. Orlin?"

"Oh, sorry, Gwen. I just noticed your pendant."

She squinted at him. "What about it?"

"It just occurred to me that I don't know much about it."

Gwen sat up straighter, losing the submissive slouch. Her eyes darted to the door. Lips lifted every so subtly towards the suggestion of a sneer. Hess knew he had said something wrong. Very wrong. If he wasn't mistaken, Gwen planned to sell him out.

He soon learned that the Church had contracted with TFK Motors to use its logistics network and warehouse facilities – a fact that should be well known by the Director of Logistics. Following their meeting, Gwen scampered off and he brought up a facilities map on his monitor.

Fully a quarter of the warehouse was dedicated to the Church's use. The inventory list looked better suited to an arms dealer than a religious institution. Nine millimeter handguns, five point seven millimeter rifles, flashbangs, canisters of CS gas, tasers, body armor, and tons of ammunition.

Hess switched back to the facilities map. The section used by the Church had reinforced walls. An armory occupied a quarter of his warehouse and he remembered nothing about it. Hess sent a message to his assistant letting her know he was taking off early, then snuck out to his car.

He kept one eye on his rear view mirror until the campus of TFK Motors disappeared into the distance, then hit the gas. His neighborhood sat atop a bluff overlooking the city, which gave it a nice view but made commuting annoying as hell. Hess drove the winding switchback at twice the speed limit, racing around the tight bends that led up the gentler incline at the far side of the bluff. His wheels screeched as he came around the final corner and he pulled off the main road to enter his housing plan.

The gate opened when it recognized the electronic tag on his dashboard, then closed behind him. Rows of townhouses stretched to either side of the road. Further on, the houses became larger and sat on large lawns. Somewhere in the center was a community center complete with rec room, gym, swimming pool, and a convenience store dedicated to price gouging locals unwilling to drive twenty minutes to the next grocery.

Hess blew past the community center in his rush, eyes catching on the immense Church building sitting on a site he distinctly recalled being soccer fields and horseshoe pits. "Not funny, Creator," he said. "Not funny at all."

He parked on the curb in front of his townhouse and ran inside. There were two suitcases in the back of his bedroom closet. After locating them, Hess set about the task of packing. Undergarments, pants, shirts, shoes, coat, tablet computer, every bit of spare cash in the house, granola bars, crackers, and a giant tin of almonds went inside.

A siren from immediately outside interrupted any further packing. A quick glance out the window revealed two SUV's with official Church detailing on the doors. The tension that had built in him ever since he saw the fist on Gwen's pendant faded. Hess studied the people getting out of the vehicles. Paramilitary by dress. Civilian by posture. Only one of them carried himself like he knew his way around a fight.

Hess seized a broom from the closet, set his hands on the improvised weapon, and opened the door just before the men got there. He stepped out and froze as if in shock, giving himself a moment to fix everyone's position in his mind. Four men, the confident one in front, followed by two weekend warriors eager for some action, and a lone pale man bringing up the rear. Housewives in all directions were poking their heads out of windows and doors to see the excitement.

Witnesses. He would need to run as soon as the goons were dead. Hess squeezed the broom handle hard, letting every other muscle go slack so that when he struck it would be with the speed of a viper.

"Jed!"

Everyone turned to look at the source of the shout. A woman whom Hess recognized as his date for that evening jogged down the street towards the scene. The moment of distraction her arrival provided would have been the perfect time to erupt into violence and destroy his adversaries.

Instead, Hess watched the woman lope towards them at a pace faster than her curvaceous form looked built to sustain. One of the men mumbled, "Girl's got bounce in all the right places."

Everyone waited until the woman arrived and leaned against the house beside Hess, panting. The leader of the Church men cleared his throat. "Jed Orlin, your name has been submitted to the Church of Opposition as a suspicious person. We are here to investigate you."

Hess lowered the broom, lining up the head of its shaft for his first strike, which would take the leader directly in the throat. The woman's foot pressed down on the broom's bristles, pinning it to the ground. She shot a fierce frown at him.

"Really? I'll bet I know who reported me," he said. "Her name is Gwen Furman and she works for me at TFK Motors. Earlier today, I gave her an informal reprimand that she didn't appreciate. She told me I wouldn't have the opportunity to put my complaint on her record."

The lead man stared at him without blinking, maintaining unflinching eye contact. "I can't reveal the identity of the person who submitted your name. If we suspect someone of making false reports, we will handle that ourselves. Right now, we have to follow procedure and check you out. If you cooperate, this won't take much of your time. If not, we will have to escalate our investigation to the next level."

The woman spoke up. "Investigator, Jed isn't a suspicious person. He just told me last night about how being successful at work was how he sought dignity. We were discussing the Church and how neither of us were very active in the local congregation. Jed and I thought we might start attending together."

Hess managed to keep his face impassive. The lead Church man studied the woman with his unblinking gaze. "What is your name?"

"Theora Winfield. And you, Investigator?"

"Investigator Monterey."

"Pleased to meet you, Investigator."

He swiveled back to Hess, steely eyes locked onto his target. "You have been living in this community for seven years. Why haven't you joined the congregation?"

Hess spun the story the woman had started, hoping he wouldn't say anything to contradict her memory. "I intended to join. But I've been busy with work. It's like Theora said – I find a lot of dignity in my work." The significance of dignity was lost on him, so he decided not to elaborate further on that topic. "I became Director of Logistics this past year. That is a huge achievement for someone my age. TFK Motors is the third largest employer in the city, you know."

The man's eyes shifted to the door behind Hess. A search of the house would reveal hastily packed luggage, which would undoubtedly take this conversation in a less friendly direction. Though if they did go inside, he could kill them without the neighbors witnessing the fact. He might get a fifteen minute head start.

Theora spoke again, bringing everyone's attention back to her. "I can't believe you forgot about our date, Jed! You promised to meet me at the community center at four sharp. I showed up five minutes early and saw you drive past like a maniac. I know you obsess about your job, but this was supposed to be a big date."

Something in her expression rang false. There was a hint too much tightness around the eyes. Combined with the tilt to her head, it suggested she was sending him a subtle message of some sort. Whatever it was, Hess didn't get it. Hopefully Theora's words about him being a loyal citizen were accurate. With all the holes in his memory this Iteration, Hess couldn't assume anything.

He put on his most convincing wince. "I didn't forget. Honest, Theora. Things were happening at work and I stayed a little later than I intended."

"Your date has been delayed," Inspector Monterey said.

Theora sighed. "I understand, Inspector. We probably missed our match with the Keegers already."

The Inspector blinked. "Are you acquainted with the Keeger family?"

"Yes. Never met the judge, but the kids are into broom hockey."

"So I hear," the Inspector said. "Mr. Orlin, it is somewhat suspicious we don't see you at Church meetings. How about you make yourself less suspicious in the future?"

"I will, Inspector," Hess said.

"Have a good day, then." The four Church men went to their SUV's, climbed inside, and drove away.

Theora folded her arms across her chest and fixed him with a look. "Well?" she asked.

"Well what?"

"Seriously?"

Hess tried to think of something to say, but he didn't have any memories of a relationship with this woman to guide him. As far as he recalled, they had never spoken. "I'm not sure what you want me to say."

"Maybe you should thank me for intervening before you could make a bigger mess of the situation." In addition to her voluptuous figure, Theora was a beautiful woman, with deep black skin and kinky hair dangling halfway to her shoulders. Her chocolate eyes were calculating and critical above pouty lips. Something in the way she held herself . . . .

Elza glared at him. "Do you recognize me now?"

He cleared his throat. "Of course. I was . . . preoccupied before."

"That would be a polite way to put it. Unfortunately, I'm not feeling particularly polite at the moment."

Hess glanced at the street. "What do you know of the Church?"

"Only what I've read in the past two hours." Her eyes narrowed. "Which no doubt makes me the expert here. If, on the other hand, instead of carefully researching the gaps in my knowledge, I had decided to gallivant around and act suspicious, then I would be as ignorant as you."

"I think I deserve a pass on this one, considering the woman I was *appreciating* was you."

"I don't care how attractive you find the female figure. There is an appropriate time and place to appreciate it. The middle of an investigation was not an appropriate time. You're not an animal, Hess. You're not even a person. You're an Observer. There is no excuse for your failure to compartmentalize."

Hess folded his arms. "Is this really about me looking at you? Or is something else bothering you?"

"Knowledge was withheld from us, Hess. That bothers me. You managed to draw the Church to you within hours of this world's start. That bothers me. You nearly proclaimed yourself an Agent of the Demiurge by attacking representatives of the Church of Opposition. That bothers me. The fact that you can't take your eyes off my chest is the tip of a very large iceberg."

"Sorry," he said. "But you know that when I feel threatened, I act."

She shook her head. "What if I hadn't been walking to the Church building when you flew past? What if I hadn't recognized your driving style? You would be public enemy number one right now. Every scion of a perverse religion would be hunting you down."

"It's fine, Elza. No one is hunting me. We're together and ready to handle whatever mischief this world can throw at us." He smiled. "The Creator actually set us up on a date. I don't think we've ever started out in the same city, let alone on the same block."

Elza didn't relent her steely gaze. "The Creator also edited important facts out of our memories."

"He's definitely giving us mixed signals this Iteration."

She folded her arms.

"You can relax now," he said softly. "This is a new world. One without stockpiles of nukes poised to bring about Hell on Earth. I'm sure we'll see the people ruin their lives in countless ways, but we don't have to worry about witnessing that kind of misery again. If the Creator values my opinion, there will never be another world with the knowledge to crack an atom."

Elza stared at him a moment, face blank, before turning away. "We need to research the Church in detail before tomorrow."

"Any particular reason for the deadline?"

"Yes. We're going to Church."

CHAPTER THREE
Erik
Iteration 145

The Church of Opposition embraced the shameful truth at the heart of the pathetic creatures with a blunt aplomb he appreciated. Erik sauntered towards the local worship center, noting the clean lines and arches of the classical architecture on display. They took pride in their little rebellion.

His current body was that of a muscular, middle-aged man with a history of tanning his pale skin to pass as one of the upper class. He always appreciated a strong body, though he sometimes missed the challenge of making do with a less capable form. Also, people tended to suspect big men when people started to disappear.

Erik sauntered into the Church like he owned the building. The place of non-worship looked like the bastard offspring of temple and office space. Entering through the front door brought him face to face with a sour receptionist. To her left were doors leading to public restrooms and the gathering hall. To her right was a hall leading to the offices of the various Church officials.

"Can I help you?"

He leaned against the counter and glanced at the computer screen. The card game there looked to be going poorly, which no doubt fueled her disagreeable attitude. "I would like to report suspicious persons."

The receptionist sat up, bringing her hands together in a silent clap. "I'll have to ask a few questions first. People are always filing false reports on neighbors they don't like."

"Certainly," Erik said. "I trust the Church knows best how to handle this kind of situation."

She smiled, which transformed her plain features in an unflattering manner. No doubt she subscribed to the fallacy that everyone looked better with the corners of their mouths turned up. "First question. How do you know the party in question?"

"They are my mother and father," he said.

The receptionist blinked. "Your parents?"

"That's right. Though of course I will disown them if the Church investigation confirms my suspicions."

"Question two. Why do you suspect them?"

"Because when I was a child they forbade me from visiting the Church or reading the Book of Grievances. As an adult, I decided to explore the religion myself. I've attended a few gatherings and read the entire Book. Naturally I became suspicious of my parent's attitude towards the Church. So I set a test for them. I told them I was planning to join the congregation to see what their response would be." He paused dramatically. "And they tried to forbid it. What possible reason could two people have to prevent an adult from joining a local congregation?"

The receptionist searched around on her desk before bringing up a standardized form. She placed it and a pen on top of the counter. "Question three. Do you have any disagreements with the suspects we should know about?"

"My relationship with my parents has only ever had one conflict. They don't want me involved with the Church."

The receptionist handed the paperwork to him. "Please fill this out. I'll let the Investigator know someone is here for him."

Erik maintained his charade of righteous indignation while the receptionist was gone, working on the assumption that he was under surveillance. He would have to live the lie from now until he changed identities. The Church was an instrument perfectly suited to locate and handle a rogue Observer – no doubt why the Creator had dreamed it up – but it could catch the wrong prey if he got sloppy.

His parents in this world were private people with few hobbies outside their home. They avoided the Church due to an innocent misunderstanding in their youths which would doubtless be on file somewhere. That, combined with testimony from their son, anecdotes from acquaintances eager for a few moments in the limelight, and circumstantial evidence put together by a zealous investigation team, should be more than enough to convict them of the crime of worshiping.

The receptionist returned to take the paperwork, then disappeared again. Erik did his best to look conflicted, in case there were cameras watching him. Half an hour passed before the Investigator came to collect Erik and bring him into an impressive office where the man slowly read through the papers.

"You love your parents?"

Erik had to think about that one. How would one of these pathetic creatures react to that question? A normal person would be angry at the betrayal. But probably not enough to write a parent out of their life. Indecision would be best. "I'm still working that out. They're my parents, but now I have to question everything."

The investigator grunted. "How do I know you're not lying?"

"I memorized the Book of Grievances. Do you think I did that in a single night?" He had, actually. "My parents need to explain why they don't support the Opposition. Maybe they are just Atheists."

"*Just* Atheists?"

"Better than being Worshipers. Or Agents. Chapter two, paragraph twelve: 'The Opposition has four enemies. First are the Apathetic, those who accept the Mission but lack zeal. Inspire them through exhortation or communal pressure or fear. Second are the Atheists, those who refuse to believe the Demiurge exists. Force their conversion at all costs. Third are the Worshipers, those who serve the Demiurge. Kill them. Fourth are the Agents of the Demiurge. They are the greatest enemy of the Opposition. Torture them day and night for the crime of serving the source of evil.'"

The Investigator smirked. "Are you trying to impress me? Every twelve-year-old can quote that passage."

"Name another as a test."

"Chapter seven, paragraph four. A personal favorite."

His perfect memory supplied the exact words, but Erik thought that level of aptitude might be a bit suspicious. "Paragraph four? Let me think a minute. That whole chapter is about personal conduct. Paragraph two covers proper grooming. Three is about clothes. So four is the one about proper language. 'Let the words you speak convey your dignity. Coarse language is the recourse of a weak and low mind. Members of the Opposition aspire to be greater than our default nature.'"

The Investigator sat back in his chair. "Close. It actually starts with 'Let every word.' But not terrible."

"I would like to join your congregation this week."

"Talk to the Deacon. She handles the mundane work of the parish."

Erik wanted to ask to join the investigation team, but it was too soon for that. It would look suspicious. No. First his parents would be found guilty. He would join the congregation. Over a few months, he would gain respect here as a scholar of the Book. Then he would ask to be a deputy investigator.

From there, he could work his way up the hierarchy of the Church's militant arm. Before long, Erik would be in the perfect spot to resume his search for Hess and Elza. Last Iteration, it had taken five years and a careless stunt for him to find Hess.

Then the Creator ended that world before Erik had the chance to do more than warm Hess up. The timing had seemed ominous. But then came the most wonderful surprise. A Church organization existed that was perfectly designed to aid him in apprehending and punishing Hess. It was as if the Creator wanted to help him. Even better, the Church was a surprise. Erik's identity, Fran Wilson, had no memory of it. Presumably the same was true of Hess.

Erik wiped the smile from his face. He wasn't supposed to be happy. He was, after all, setting his parents up to die horrible deaths.

CHAPTER FOUR
Hess
Iteration 145

Inspector Monterey studied their every move as they navigated the cavernous interior of the Church building. At Elza's urging, Hess had spent the previous evening looking through hundreds of online photos of weddings and funerals that had taken place within this building so that he was superficially familiar with the layout. Hopefully familiar enough to fake years of casual church attendance.

Hess and Elza chatted with neighbors they recognized on their way to the meeting room. Hess shook hands with fellow executives at TFK Motors and introduced Elza as a special friend. For her part, Elza dragged him around to meet numerous people a decade younger than his apparent age. None of their social interactions lasted long. Under the guise of smitten lovers going public, they managed to escape each conversation without exchanging more than the most basic pleasantries.

After researching the Church of Opposition overnight, they knew enough of its theology and traditions to participate in a meeting. What they lacked was knowledge of how their identities had participated in the Church previously. They knew they were not members of the local congregation, but it would be odd for their identities to have *never* had any interactions with the dominant religion of the world.

Getting those details wrong would be suspicious. Thus the new love charade. Hess thought they sold the act convincingly enough, given the wistful expressions cast their way by the elderly and the annoyed eyerolls of the young. In fact, Hess thought he himself was the only person in the room not sold on their mutual devotion. Every touch of his brought an unwelcome tension to Elza's shoulders.

She never held grudges long. Yesterday's events should be forgiven. Yet they still had not made love in their new bodies. Usually the novelty of becoming intimately familiar with their latest forms kept them occupied for quite some time.

It continued to surprise Hess how much difference there was between bodies. In one like his current, a formidable libido lurked in the background, subtly sexualizing every situation so that a bit lip appeared an erotic invitation. Other bodies seemed keyed to quiet contemplation and required serious stimulation to elicit any reaction.

And those were only the differences in *his* bodies. Elza could range from nymph to asexual depending upon the body. Demographics didn't seem to matter much. They had each been elders with appetites and young adults lacking passion. Body composition, skin color, and relative attractiveness all proved unreliable forecasts.

Even the fake history of their identities failed to predict their responses. Jed Orlin had been far more interested in salary than sex. But give Hess the body of Jed Orlin and suddenly he couldn't keep his eyes from wandering all over the place. Of course, part of his problem may be due to the fact that a frigid Elza had been inserted into the body of the curvaceous Theora Winfield.

While people began taking their seats inside the meeting room, Hess studied his woman. She touched her lips a lot. Elza tended to do that when her body was wired for pleasure. But she had dressed in a separate room that morning.

They sat towards the back of the meeting room in hard pews. Up front, the Deacon of the congregation stood in front of the podium and raised his right fist into the air. "Damn the Demiurge!"

Everyone erupted to their feet, punched a fist into the air, and shouted the profanity back at the Deacon loud enough that their combined roar echoed in the cavernous space. "Damn the Demiurge!"

The Deacon was an old, distinguished man with a hawkish appearance. He glared at his audience. "This world is flawed!"

"Damn the Demiurge!"

The Deacon slammed a fist on the podium. "Full of pain!"

"Damn the Demiurge!"

"Our bodies are made to fail!"

"Damn the Demiurge!"

"The nations doomed to war!"

"Damn the Demiurge!"

"Our children can never have the happiness we want for them!"

"Damn the Demiurge!"

The Deacon paused dramatically, looked around the room, smiled. "We have been created to suffer and die. Existence itself is a punishment decreed for us before we ever became flesh. Pain and humiliation is what the Demiurge gave us."

Hess almost shouted out the refrain, but held back, noticing the crowd waited for something. They held still and the Deacon's voice became softer. "People of the Opposition, what we have been given is worse than nothing. But we know the truth. We know of the world's flaws. We know of the Demiurge's spite. And we choose to meet spite with spite."

The Deacon's voice rose. "We will fix the flaws!"

"Damn the Demiurge!"

"We will overcome the enemies!"

"Damn the Demiurge!"

"We will take the dignity that has been denied us!"

"Damn the Demiurge!"

After the final, roaring exclamation, militant music blared from speakers throughout the room. The members of the local Investigation Team marched up the aisles to about face and stare at the congregation. Their leader, Investigator Monterey, stepped to the podium.

"I am pleased to report that this parish remains clear of all suspicious individuals. This community is a model of virtue for the entire nation to follow. I want to express my sincere admiration to each of you for your steadfast Opposition. You live your lives with true dignity." Investigator Monterey brought his hands together in a steady clap that was taken up by the congregation.

When the Deacon returned to the podium, the Investigation Team took their seats in the front pew. "As I am sure everyone is aware, Investigator Monterey has been nominated for another Medal of Piety. His service to our community has been exemplary, and we all look forward to the award ceremony."

There was more clapping, then the Deacon asked everyone to take a seat. Collection plates were passed around. Hess and Elza each contributed a generous amount. Next on the meeting agenda was a musical performance from the children.

As they sat there, listening to young boys and girls sing their hatred of the Creator, Elza reached one hand over surreptitiously to tap his elbow. Hess directed a quizzical expression at her, but at a shake of her head he dutifully returned his attention to the front of the room.

The tapping and caressing of his elbow continued. Hess tried to pay attention to the words sung by the children, but the mystery of Elza's behavior proved more interesting by far. Was she initiating something *now*? Hess felt himself reacting to the possibility.

It made no sense for her to become amorous at the moment. No matter the chemistry of her body, Elza was rational to a fault. She would not jeopardize their identities for a cheap thrill. Unfortunately, there was no way to have a frank conversation with her while surrounded by people . . . .

A memory rose from the depths. An Observer's perfect recall had limitations. First, they only remembered what they had consciously experienced. They couldn't flip through a book and instantly know its contents. They had to read the words one at a time to permanently capture them. Second, they couldn't remember all of it at once. Much as a normal person could only hold so much in short term memory, an Observer could only hold so much in long term memory. After that, things faded into deep memory.

Some experiences never left his primary memory – the moments that defined him refused to fade into the background. The memories that did fade wound up in the depths and could take some time to rise back to the surface when something triggered their recall.

Now, Hess remembered the lover's language of Iteration thirty-two. It had been invented as a means of private communication between aristocratic couples. After enjoying a few generations of popularity, the language had gone out of vogue and been forgotten by everyone except two Observers.

The fact that he had misinterpreted Elza's communications as foreplay meant he couldn't recall the exact sequence to translate. He tapped on the back of Elza's hand. *Start again.*

Her fingers stopped, then began anew. *The rituals match the typical profile of those used by popular religions. They are all based around building communal identity and reinforcing cognitive biases.*

Hess gave two gentle pinches in rapid succession with his thumb and index finger, the signal for agreement. *I forgot all about this language.*

The children's music ended and a lecturer pulled from the elders of the congregation went up front to speak about the threats to human dignity. Apparently, the threats were religion, atheism, homosexuality, and violent video games.

Elza's fingers tapped at his arm. *Ridiculous. Obvious theological flaws. They oppose the Creator and any imposed natural order. So why oppose homosexuality? Non compliance with biology should be a virtue.*

Hess waited until her fingers stopped to reply. *All religions are the same. They pick things they approve and disapprove and worry about fitting things together later. It's just people using a platform to get power.*

Her fingers pounded a response into his elbow. *Not all the same. Some allow people to question assumptions and fix flaws. This one is incompatible with free thought.*

Up front, the Deacon took the pulpit again to read a series of stories from the news. Each story highlighted people overcoming challenges in their lives. Throughout the congregation, people nodded in earnest approval of every word they heard. Elza's fingers remained still throughout his talk.

Then everyone stood to sing a few hymns of Opposition. When that was done, the Deacon delivered a benediction about seizing dignity from the mess of everyday life. Everyone raised a fist in the air, cursed the Creator a final time, and filed out of the meeting room to chat in the hallway and make their way home.

As Hess worked his way outside with Elza, Inspector Monterey appeared beside them. "I hope the two of you plan to attend regularly. I've been following up on our conversation yesterday, and both of you have spotless reputations in the community."

Hess plastered a smile to his face. "We already agreed to attend again next week. Congratulations on your nomination, Investigator."

The Investigator gave the slightest inclination of his head, then slipped away. Elza took his arm, tapping as they walked out the door together. *He is career man, not interested in risking his reputation on someone who might not be found guilty.*

As they strolled towards his house, Hess tapped back. *When are you going to tell me what is bothering you?*

Elza pulled her arm free. "Just give me some space, Hess."

CHAPTER FIVE
Erik
Iteration 2

He took the name Cazzel on his way into the village. Cazzel. A man from the previous world who liked to torment and force himself on those weaker than himself – typically women and young boys. A man who had the misfortune to turn his attentions upon the Creator's Observer.

A smile wormed its way onto his face as he recalled his retribution against the original Cazzel. That man had not enjoyed having a tent stake driven up his rectum one bit. Judging by how he had begged and threatened and screamed, having his tent burnt down on top of him hadn't been a pleasant experience either. Even as a woman in a man's world, the Creator's Observer had been superior.

Though if there were more than one Observer, then he wouldn't truly be *the* Creator's Observer. He would be *one of* the Observers. The evidence that others existed was thin, just stories of a man seeking his woman from another world. But knowledge of the Creator had come from somewhere. If one of these creatures had puzzled out the world's origins, then that was a development the Creator would need to know. On the other hand, if other Observers *were* out there, then he thought it only right to get familiar.

At the guest pavilion of this village, a man sat on the ground and tended a small fire in the hearth. Cazzel squatted beside the man. "Are you the one who greets visitors around here?"

The man shrugged as he poked at the fire. "Women's crafts and talking to guests is the only work fit for me anymore."

Cazzel frowned. "Why do you say that? You look young and strong."

The man's lips twisted into a sneer. "Tens of days ago I was young and strong. Today I am broken and worthless."

"Well," Cazzel said, "at least you are good at welcoming visitors."

The man tossed his fire stick aside. "Welcome to our village, stranger. Have you come so late in the day to eat our food without sharing in our work? Will you leave early tomorrow before anyone can ask you to help us dig a new well? Are you one of those men who walks from village to village for free meals and brags of your brave travels? Or do you search for a home with many beautiful women and little work to go around? Tell me, stranger, what manner of wanderer are you?"

Cazzel cackled at the outburst. "I like you. Shame you're broken. We could get into all sorts of mischief otherwise."

"I am no friend to you."

"Oh, I never named you friend. I just enjoy a little hostility here and there." Cazzel leaned forward to study the man. "Why is it you can't work?"

The man spat on the ground between them. "Entertain yourself."

"Are there worms in your leavings? Does blood fill your phlegm? Or are you wrong in your head? What makes you broken, angry man?"

The man threw a wild punch. Cazzel shifted his weight to let it pass, then reached for his walking stick. Its end had a decorative knob carved to look like the face of a smiling bald man. When he gave that knob a strong pull, it would come off to reveal the walking stick had a sharpened point. It wasn't a spear by any means, but it was a weapon. No one harassed the Creator's Observer without punishment.

His hand on the knob, Cazzel hesitated. His opponent rolled back on his hips, face red with anger and humiliation, moving awkwardly. Where his legs should have been, there were only stumps. The man's deficit had been hidden by blankets before, but now that his hasty attack had exposed flesh, his deformity was unmasked for all to see.

Cazzel dropped his walking stick and bent to study the man. The flesh where his legs ended was covered with horrid scars. Clearly this was not a defect of birth. The man's legs had been removed. Recently.

"What happened to your legs?" he asked.

"Leave my village," the man hissed. "Or I will say you hit me."

Cazzel reached for his walking stick, pulled off its cap, and pressed the sharpened point to the cripple's chin. "Answer my question or I will do a lot worse than hitting you."

"Go ahead. Kill me. You will be doing me a favor."

Cazzel tilted his head to the side. "Then I won't kill you. I will do something you want less. The loss of your legs bothers you. If you don't give me the answers I want, then I will break more parts of your body." He poked at the closer of the man's hands. "I will smash the bones at the back of your hand so you can never use your fingers again. If that doesn't motivate you, then I will knock out your teeth so that you can't chew food properly or sound out all your words. I could take your eyes and leave you in eternal darkness, or scar your face so that your family feels horror every time they look on you."

He smiled at the man. "I want simple answers. And you want me to go away. To be fair, I will answer your question first. You asked what manner of wanderer I am. The answer is a very dangerous one. I am willing to do more violence than anyone you have ever met. And I don't care if people hate me. I don't even care if they try to kill me.

"Your turn now. What happened to your legs?"

The man met Cazzel's gaze with fire in his eyes. "They were crushed between the stones of the old well."

"The old well? Did it collapse with you inside it?"

"It collapsed when we pulled free one of the blocks lining the shaft. We needed the stones to hold up the walls of the new well."

Cazzel nodded, filling in the blanks in his mind. "Your old well went dry. Because the soil around here is sandy, you need stone to keep the new well from collapsing. But there isn't a lot of suitable stone to be found, so you scavenged from the old well. Somebody – probably you – pulled a stone free in the wrong order and caused an accident. Is all of that right?"

"Yes, stranger," the man spat. "All of that is right."

"The pain was terrible?"

"Yes."

"When your people pulled you free, your legs were useless?"

"Yes."

"They knew you would die from the wounds inside, so they cut off your legs and stopped the bleeding with fire?"

The man shook his head. "No. My people wept and held me and said their goodbyes. I was ready for death. But then the strangers came. The White Man said he could save me, and my mother begged for his help.

The cripple spat on the ground again. "The strangers took my legs and said I was healed. The life they gave me is worse than death. I was a hard worker. My village respected me. Women looked at me. Now every eye that turns my way shows pity."

"What were the names of these strangers?"

"The White Man gave the name Tyro, but his woman called him Hess. The woman was Mara."

Cazzel smiled. Mara was the name of a village ten days' travel south. Not a proper woman's name at all, just a convenient moniker for an Observer. "Her real name was Elza." He spoke before he thought through the words. *Real name.* The concept seemed odd to him. Names were for the pathetic creatures they observed. Names were things he used and discarded without a second thought.

But the Observers he followed had names. Hess and Elza. Labels of convenience, maybe. Maybe something more. Real name. The name used by people who knew the truth about you. Soon he would need to choose a name for himself. A name that would follow him through eternity, persisting in world after world, one known to the others like him.

"Which way did the strangers go when they left?"

The man shrugged. "I didn't walk them to the end of the village."

Cazzel placed the knob on the end of his walking stick, hiding his weapon once more. "You don't have to worry that I will eat the food of your village without working in return. I am leaving tonight to follow those strangers."

"Are they your friends?" the cripple asked.

"I'll figure that out when I meet them."

CHAPTER SIX
Hess
Iteration 145

He fired Gwen Furman after setting her up to fail on what should have been a simple project. Her disgraceful exit from TFK Motors made it unlikely anyone would ever take her claims about him seriously. Not long after he took care of Gwen, the company president gave him a promotion to vice president of logistics, a title created specifically for him.

Hess suspected the promotion had less to do with his performance than it did with the fact that he was a member of the same Church congregation as most of TFK Motor's executives. Dating Elza had benefits as well. As Theora Winfield, she had an uncle who was a judge presiding over Customs violation cases in TFK Motor's jurisdiction and a cousin on the board of Jones Automotive, their biggest customer. Also, Theora's father lived a life of leisure, on occasion attending charity events with important people.

Elza's trust fund managed to make the wealth Hess had at his disposal appear laughable in comparison. The two of them rarely had access to so much money. Usually they lived as migrant workers in the worlds, drifting from place to place, taking odd jobs and going where whimsy led them. Those were his favorite times, when they lived by their wits and never knew what would happen next. In comparison, the steady grind of regular life wore on him.

As he had for the past two months, Hess left work early. He had decided that since his performance had far less of an impact on his job than the quality of his connections, there was little incentive to put forth effort.

The logistics department essentially ran itself, anyway. Connections ensured that the Church continued to use TFK Motors to warehouse and ship its weapons. Connections prevented any problems with Customs. Connections kept the people on top where they wanted to be. Meanwhile, those without connections worked their asses off to feed their families.

Hess reflected on the mess of a world he inhabited as he drove home. A world he had created, however indirectly. *Why,* he wondered, *do I create such worlds?* When the consciousnesses of the twelve Observers merged to form the Creator, was equal weight given to Erik's desire to inflict pain as to Hess's opinions on how the world could be improved to benefit the people? Did the Creator engineer misery into His blueprints?

If that was the case, then maybe the religion of Deispite had a point. Maybe the Creator *was* evil. Hess ground his teeth. Could everything wrong with the succession of sorry worlds be placed at the feet of a twisted Observer's obsession with spite and hatred?

Erik had tormented him the previous Iteration. Threatened to hunt him through eternity. Two Iterations ago, Ingrid had led the group of Observers that buried him and Elza alive, leaving them to beat their fists against the insides of stone sarcophagi for centuries.

The other Observers were a problem for more than just him. Their apathy and self-righteous hatred tainted every world they created, bringing billions of individuals into lives purposefully filled with pain. For that, they deserved the hatred directed at them by the Church of Opposition.

When he arrived home, Hess began preparing an elaborate meal. He removed a flank steak from a vinegar-based marinade he had improvised and preheated the oven. With economical motions, he went about cutting sweet potatoes into fries. Cooking was a calming ritual for him. It combined simple tasks with the freedom for nearly unlimited variability. When the fries were cut, Hess pulled a tub of rendered duck fat from the fridge and tossed a portion of it into a skillet to heat up.

Elza's parents were coming over for a late dinner. She had suggested eating out, but Hess needed the outlet cooking provided. Despite what everyone in the community assumed about Elza's frequent overnight stays, precious little happened that Hess would consider an outlet.

Whatever consumed Elza left no room for the two of them. It was worse than the stretch in Iteration one hundred and four when she had despaired that they had already witnessed all the variety that humanity had to offer. Everything he had said to comfort her then had driven her further from him until it culminated in a year-long separation. When she had finally returned, Elza had told him that even if the people never did anything new, she thought there were further insights they could discover.

This time, he didn't know what problem haunted Elza. She wasn't sharing and he knew better than to push.

Hess pulled a bag of fresh green beans from the fridge and drizzled walnut oil onto a pan. While the oil heated, he pulled a pomegranate from the fridge and prepared it with deft strokes of a paring knife. The meal he had devised consisted of a salad topped with pomegranate and a balsamic vinaigrette, then a medium rare flank steak with a side of sweet potato fries and sauteed green beans, with a dessert created from frozen banana slices.

Before he could start cooking the green beans, a knock at the door interrupted him. Hess wiped his hands before going to the door and peeking through the eye hole. On the other side, a waif-thin white woman waited. Her faded eyes flashed to the eye hole, no doubt noticing movement there, then rapidly moved on, taking in detail after detail in a meticulous fashion.

Hess felt his lip curl into a snarl. *Observer.* He yanked the door open, seized the waif by an arm, and pulled her into his house. As she swung past him, Hess looped his other arm around her neck. A combination of her momentum and his rapid shoulder roll snapped the woman's spine.

Hess closed his front door and dragged the Observer's body to his basement before she could resurrect.

CHAPTER SEVEN
Erik
Iteration 145

People took one look at him and melted into the background. His stocky build didn't have much to do with it. The somber cap of the Investigator's Corps scared people all by itself. In theory, Investigators couldn't violate the rights of a citizen without the prior approval of an elected judge. The restrictions were even greater for Deputy Investigators like him. But the power of his office made the rules nice and elastic.

Of course, it wasn't all rainbows. The world was four months old and he had yet to entice the ugly truth free of one of the pathetic creatures. He liked to start every Iteration with a creative interrogation. Last time he had combined two of his favorite methods: silence and chemistry.

The silence really messed with the people. Turned the torture up a notch. His first victim last Iteration had been a sinewy biker with steely eyes and a chiseled face. A tough bastard. For the first hour, at least. Then the threats and manly curses gave way to pleading and questions. *Why are you doing this? What did I do to you? Why won't you say anything?* That man had not particularly enjoyed having pepper spray squirted into his eyes.

Erik's lips twitched towards a smile. He had broken that man by dribbling a solution of water and lye over one of his feet until the skin melted off of him into a gory puddle. Lye always ended the game quicker than Erik liked, but watching the *horrified* reactions of the people to their liquefied flesh never got old.

Four months. Every day, at least one of the people did something to draw his attention. Acted tough on a street corner. Dressed fancy. Talked too loud. Littered. Tried to use expired coupons at the checkout line. Walked alone at night. Smiled at him.

Unfortunately, he was too busy playing choir boy to take care of business. The religion of Deispite somehow managed to intertwine his favorite things with the biggest flaws of the people. Torture and murder were permitted; scrutiny and intimidation outright encouraged. But then there were the *rules*. Arbitrary ordinances for everything.

Of course, that was hardly a surprise when the religion itself was built on hatred of the Creator and all existence. Erik thought it was the first religion of the people to embrace their deepest secret. He had known for a long time what these pathetic creatures thought of their lives. They hated themselves, their world, and the grand entity who had made it all. At least the people of the Church admitted they hated existence. Their nihilistic attempts to rise above their self-hatred were more amusing than annoying. For now. Once he no longer needed them to hunt Hess, that might change.

Erik wore an army surplus jacket with his current last name, Wilson, embroidered onto the fabric above his chest pocket. The uniform, plus the high rate of Investigators with a military background, caused a lot of people to assume he had served. Some of his fellow deputies didn't care for his presumption, but none of them had bothered him since the first called him out. Apparently, even the toughest guys on the investigation team didn't like someone stalking their family members.

People from soft societies never pushed him far. At some level, they sensed that he was willing to go much further in pursuit of vengeance than they would dare dream. It freaked them out a little when their posturing failed to impact him.

He met up with another deputy investigator on his way into the Church building. The woman nodded to him. "Any idea what this meeting is about?"

"I heard someone from the regional office was here," Erik said.

"Great. Another lecture on proper behavior."

The two of them entered the gathering hall and sat in separate pews. Other deputies filed into the room. Then, in order of seniority, they were called from the room. Erik settled in to wait, displaying the dignified mannerisms expected from a member of the Opposition.

The fifteen deputies in front of him left one by one until he was the only person in the room. Then the secretary appeared to summon him. Erik followed her down the hall. "They doing staff reviews or something?"

"Something," the secretary said, cradling one hand.

"You injured?" he asked.

"Just a scratch. Don't worry about it." She opened the door to the conference room and waited for him to enter. The door closed behind him.

Erik walked forward and extended his hand towards the man he didn't recognize. "Hello, sir. My name is Fran Wilson."

"A pleasure, deputy. I am Lieutenant Investigator Edwin. I see from your record that you've been here a few months."

"Yes, sir."

Edwin was thirty at most, but held himself erect with rigid professionalism. "You reported your parents as suspicious individuals and they were later executed for the crime of worship. Since then, you have become a cornerstone of the congregation. If I was uncharitable, I might wonder if you sold your parents out for your own gain."

"Their betrayal deeply hurt me, sir. I choose to honor their memory by hunting down those who perverted them."

"You *honor* their memory, deputy?"

"Chapter five, paragraph forty six: 'There is good in all people commensurate with the level that they reject the Demiurge.' My parents never indoctrinated me in their faith. I owe them my purity of spirit."

"Quoting the Book impresses simple people, deputy. I am intelligent enough to know that anyone sufficiently motivated can twist isolated passages to support any course of action."

Erik fought down a snarl before it could reach his face. "Yes, sir."

"Hold out your hand, deputy."

When Erik complied, the Lieutenant Investigator pulled his belt knife and sliced Erik's hand open. Startled, Erik pulled his hand to his chest and turned to the door. The Investigator and one of the senior deputies stood there, tasers in hand. Erik licked his lips. "Are you going to kill me?"

The Lieutenant Investigator gestured impatiently at Erik's hand. "Show it to me."

"What?"

"Your hand. Show it to me."

"Why?"

"Because the Church has an Agent of the Demiurge in custody. We learned a fascinating lesson from him. Agents don't retain injury. Now show me your hand, deputy."

Erik spun to the door. He lifted his hands into a boxer's pose, distracting the eyes of his adversaries, then kicked the Investigator's groin, pivoted, and kicked again at the other deputy's knee.

He danced back to give himself space. Using the pause in action, Erik ripped a network cable free and wrapped it in each hand to create a rudimentary garrote.

The thunderous report reached his ears at the same time a stab of pain struck his chest. Erik's eyes registered the Lieutenant Inspector holding a handgun, then darted down to behold the bloody patch sitting center left on his chest. Based on the rapid growth of the red shirt stain, either his pulmonary, aorta, or heart itself had a giant hole in it.

Erik tried to charge his adversary, but his body refused to work right. While he liked to think himself immune to psychological shock, the rapid drop in blood pressure had done the deed. He collapsed to the ground.

The Lieutenant Inspector's face radiated zeal like an oven. "I got you, hated one. And you are going to suffer for what your master has done. I will make sure of it."

CHAPTER EIGHT
Hess
Iteration 145

Hess bound the Observer's body to a support pole in his basement using his belt collection. One belt looped around her waist to hold her snug against the pole. Another did the same for her feet. Hess used the cloth belt of a bathrobe to tie her bony wrists together behind her back.

When the Observer's neck mended, her pale eyes blinked and her emaciated form tugged against the restraints. Hess studied the figure, watching for any telltale quirks. Who was it? He wasn't sure what he would do if this was Ingrid or Erik. Torture wasn't something he had ever done. He preferred to keep that particular activity on the never ever list. But killing an Observer wasn't possible. Maybe torture was the only way to deal with his opponents. It might even force a touch of empathy into them. Maybe some torture now would make the next world a better place.

The waif stared back at him, then blew out a breath. "Hess."

He still had no idea who this was. "And you are?"

"Jerome," said the woman.

He had known Jerome for less than an hour, during a time when he was operating at less than his optimum. "Prove it."

"I opened the sky for you last Iteration, then you and Elza stayed behind." The waif raised a brow. "How about letting me go now?"

Hess removed the bindings. "Didn't it occur to you that I might not react well to an Observer knocking on my door?"

Jerome sighed. "I didn't even know for sure an Observer lived here."

"I thought the Creator gave you a cheat sheet telling you where the rest of us start off every Iteration."

"Oh, the Creator did," Jerome said. "Only those memories are about as reliable as any others this Iteration."

"Well, it's nice to know the Creator isn't playing favorites." Hess gestured towards the stairs. "As much as I'm enjoying your visit, I need to prepare for an important dinner. Could you come back tomorrow?"

Jerome shook her head. "We have an emergency situation."

"Is the Church after you?"

Her eyes grew distant. "Worse. I think we've splintered the Creator."

CHAPTER NINE
Erik
Iteration 2

He took the name Torrik as he entered the village. Torrik. The name of a man who died in the previous world when he tripped over his own feet and smacked his head into a rock. That Torrik had become a joke in his tribe for suffering such an ignominious death. It was a good joke, though the people of this world didn't have the proper constitution to appreciate it.

Torrik ignored the guest pavilion to first walk to the edge of the water. This was not a sea like he had encountered in the previous world. This water was known to be both traversable and safe to drink. It lapped at the shoreline with regular waves, but the people stared at him in perplexion when he asked if it rose and fell in tides.

Still, such a large body of water drew his eyes as surely as the ground pulled his feet to it. Torrik breathed the pungent air and stared at the distant horizon. It appeared to go on forever, a little slice of eternity carved from water, changing every moment with swift movements, blues and grays and greens mingling with the reds and yellows of a setting sun in a stunning tableau. The world was undeniably beautiful. A true masterpiece. If no one else could appreciate that fact, he could.

And he served the Creator who had made all of it.

When the light faded, Torrik strolled back towards the guest pavilion. The villagers had already gathered for their evening meal in the open square at its side, and they smiled as he joined them. A woman approached with a bowl of soup that bore the unmistakable scent of fish, which Torrik had encountered far too rarely in this plant-eating world.

He accepted the bowl with a genuine smile. "Thank you, friend."

The woman bowed graciously. All around him, people watched with bright eyes. "You are very welcome to food and shelter while you stay among us. We are a curious folk, however, and you must be prepared for us to harass you for what stories you have."

Torrik slurped his soup; closed his eyes to savor the richness of it. He hunted from time to time when his appetite for hearty fare overcame his desire to blend with the locals. But the meat of land animals was one flavor and the flesh of sea animals a completely different one.

"I have many stories, friend. But first, could you tell me if a White Man passed through here recently? I am seeking a friend of mine, and I believe he came this way."

The woman bobbed her head. "He is here with us now. Abner, come here now and sit with your friend!"

When the white man appeared from the crowd of brown-skinned people, Torrik licked his lips. He had hoped their meeting would occur away from the eyes of people, somewhere they could speak freely. But they would be able to talk around their secrets without revealing themselves to the villagers. Unless the meeting turned out less friendly than he hoped. In which case, he had other concerns.

The man was balding, overweight, and squinted at everything in the manner of those with weak eyes. When the man had an opportunity to properly assess Torrik, he folded his arms. "I don't know this man."

Torrik hesitated. "I think we are watching things for the same person."

"Watching things? What are you talking about? I spend all my time fishing. Walked nearly the whole way around the lake, I reckon. Stop a few days every village I come to. Maybe you met me in some village, but I meet lots of people. I don't know you."

Everything about the white man was wrong. His irritable nature, his ignorance, the way he appeared oblivious to everything happening around him. Torrik's eyes assessed the man before him with the clinical efficiency of an Observer. This man Abner was not Hess.

In one of the villages he had passed through, he had begun to follow the trail of the wrong White Man. To the mindless creatures of the villages, there might not be much difference between one pale stranger and another. But the gulf could not have been larger.

"This is not the white man I am seeking," Torrik said. "My friend is . . . more distinguished than this fisherman."

Abner screwed his face up. "What do you mean by that?"

"I mean my words to be an insult. You have wasted my time." Torrik placed one hand on the knob of his walking stick and waited for the pale stranger to make a move.

Fool he may have been, but the white man had a functional sense of self preservation. After an awkward pause, he vanished back into the crowd without another word. Torrik finished his bowl of fish soup and left the village. He had lost the trail of the other Observers.

But not for long. Now that he knew they existed, the world was not large enough to prevent him from finding them.

CHAPTER TEN
Hess
Iteration 145

Elza hadn't answered his calls, so when she arrived with her parents, she froze at the sight of Jerome. "Who is this?"

Hess snapped his fingers impatiently at Jerome. "I hired Lilly to prepare dinner. Her father is *Jerome*. You remember Jerome, right?"

The two women exchanged the slightest of nods. "Of course I remember Jerome," Elza said.

"I admire your charity," Elza's father said, "but perhaps you should have the woman mow your lawn instead of letting her around food."

"Walter!"

"Oh, don't lecture me, Yolanda. I have given plenty to the pale community. And my point is valid. Even if you trust this woman not to eat the food she's paid to serve, she hardly looks the type to know fine dining."

Hess forced a smile. "I understand your concerns, Walter," he said. "But I know her father to be a tireless worker. Lilly's appearance is due to a genetic condition."

Walter chuckled. "Would that happen to be a predilection for heroin?"

"Her body doesn't produce an enzyme required to digest starches." Hess flashed a big smile. "But some people have a predilection for mischaracterizing others based on appearance."

"I keep a reliable chef on retainer," Walter said. "I don't recall his name at the moment, but he works at the Iris. Excellent chef. If I'd known you were so desperate, I would have financed your dinner."

Yolanda shot a stern glare at her husband at the same moment that Elza fixed her level gaze on Hess. He cleared his throat. "Tell me, Walter, what is it you do with all your free time?"

"I'm a gentleman, Jed. In addition to helping unapologetic social climbers gain connections, I do quite a bit of charity work."

Yolanda nudged her husband with an elbow to the ribs, which managed to silence him. While Walter was old money, Yolanda came from ancient money and by all accounts could not abide boorish behavior. She smiled at Hess. "Everything smells delicious. We have been looking forward to sitting down with you for quite some time now. Dear Theora has never been so enamored of a man as she is of you."

The conversation veered off into the territory of who was marrying whom, who had recently born a child, and who was pursuing elected office. Jerome served them sparkling wine while they casually chatted about the people they knew, dropping names with careless abandon.

When they moved to the table a quarter of an hour later, Yolanda brought up the annual picnic sponsored by the congregation and suggested everyone present volunteer for the planning committee. The meal went down well, with Walter restraining himself to a single backhanded compliment, noting that hiring a pale-skinned woman to cook a poorer cut of meat was wise.

Hess leaned over to tap Elza's elbow. *Dessert special for you.*

Her quizzical expression morphed into delight when Jerome set their bowls before them. Walter frowned at the pudding. "What is it?"

"Dessert."

"What is it made from?"

"Bananas."

Walter poked his spoon at it. "What did your pale cook do with the bananas?"

"Actually," Hess said, "I made this course myself."

Yolanda lifted her spoon to him in salute. "Very impressive, Jed. I have always considered cooking akin to art."

"What did *you* do to the poor bananas?"

"I froze them, pureed them, then added vanilla and hazelnut milk."

Walter shook his head. "Sounds rather unappetizing."

Hess shrugged. "If you don't care to try it, you could pass your bowl to Theora. She seems to like it."

Elza gave him the first unguarded smile he had seen from her since the world began. Hess settled back into his seat and savored the moment.

Her parents stayed another fifteen minutes, then departed for home after Elza indicated she intended to stay. The moment the door closed behind them, Elza spun on him. "What is the fourth ingredient?"

"Elza, I don't know what you're talking about."

She advanced on him. "Bananas, vanilla extract, hazelnut milk, and what else? Don't tell me there isn't another ingredient. I've tried replicating your recipe a hundred times at least."

"It's an eternal mystery," he said. "Only I know the secret."

"You had better tell me."

"I'm the only one who can make my banana pudding."

Elza spun to Jerome. "Do you know?"

The emaciated woman folded her arms. "I do not. There are more important things to discuss at the moment, at any rate."

"I'm sure your issue, whatever it is, can wait," she said on her way into the kitchen.

Jerome's deep-set eyes glowed with frustration. "Damn it, Hess. We can't afford to operate on our usual timelines. We're no longer dealing with eternity."

Hess patted Jerome's shoulder gently, feeling the sharp outlines of bird-like bones beneath parchment-thin skin. He couldn't imagine what inhabiting such a body would be like. "You told me your theory that our conflict gave the Creator a case of split personality. Even if that is possible, it isn't something we are in a position to immediately fix."

The sound of cupboards slamming came from the kitchen. Hess sighed. "She's going to tear apart the kitchen, upend my trash, and then refuse to clean up."

Jerome walked into the kitchen and raised her voice. "I'm conducting a vote. The Creator wants to know if the Observers should die at the end of this Iteration."

CHAPTER ELEVEN
Erik
Iteration 145

He screamed and wept, reacting to the pain and exhaustion and fear. The Punishers of the Church always went about their job with fervor, utterly convinced they were taking their vengeance upon the individual responsible for their brother's death in a car accident, their aunt's cancer prognosis, their girlfriend's infidelity, their bad credit rating, and the fact that they stubbed their toe getting out of bed that morning.

They came in teams of three, rotating often so that whoever worked on him was always fresh. The teams themselves switched out several times a day. The Punisher on duty now, a hulking brute complete with lopsided nose and knife scars, beat Erik with a length of cast iron pipe. Suspended from the ceiling by manacles clasped to his wrists and chained to the floor by his ankles, Erik hung taught as a piano wire. Each time the pipe struck, his body shifted the limited extent possible, causing his bindings to dig into the flesh of his extremities.

His ribs shattered time and again only to reform. The time span between damage and repair was often long enough that the brute could knock free fragments of bones and organs to litter the cold cement floor. When the egg timer rang to announce the end of another fifteen minute stretch, the brute tossed the pipe aside and paused to catch his breath.

Erik cried, unashamed, as the pain continued. Bit by bit, it lessened as injuries vanished. The team began to gather their implements, so they must be done with their shift. When the last of the damage done to his body evaporated, leaving him whole again, Erik began to laugh.

"You fuckers don't know what you're doing. Might as well be a group of school girls playing dolls."

The brute rushed forward and punched Erik in the face. After, Erik grinned through the blood pouring from his nose and mouth. He had bared his teeth at the last moment and, judging by the way the brute cradled his hand, damage had been done. Damage that wouldn't disappear in five minutes.

"Aw, does that hurt? Worse than your period, ain't it, princess? Your widdle hand got bit by a scawy Agent."

The brute firmed up his face and flashed the crazy eyes. "I'm gonna think up new ways to hurt you tonight. Tomorrow I will hear you begging and crying and screaming."

Erik spat his blood at the brute. "Oh, I react to things. I admit it with no shame. Difference is, I've been here two weeks and I'm still talking shit soon as you losers finish your best work. Put one of you in my place for just an hour and what happens then?

"One of these days, you dick-heads are going to slip up, and I will leave an impression on every one of you I cross that day. You will never be able to say the same to me. There ain't a mark on my body, girls, and my mind is fucking dandy. I'll bet this whole torture experience messes with you three more than it does with me.

"See, I am better than you pathetic creatures in every way. You think the Creator hates you? Don't flatter yourselves. Your whole world is an idle amusement. None of you deserve hatred. You should feel honored you get mild curiosity."

The brute came closer, wearing the crazy eyes again. "You'll pay."

"I know, cupcake. I just don't care." Erik felt his nose reform. "I once flayed the skin from a man's abdomen and made him look at his organs. Freaked. Him. Out. He begged me to kill him. I offered to stitch his skin back together and release him, but he insisted on immediate death. He was a big guy like you. Did the same bit with the clenched jaw and wide eyes. Thought because he showed *alpha male body language* that he was something special. He wasn't. Guy begged to die just from seeing his insides. Wasn't even in much pain.

"I did the same thing to a six year old girl. She begged for me to let her go. I didn't even offer to stitch her up. Blew my mind that she was braver than the tough guy. I had to actually start *pulling the organs out* before she requested the easy way out."

Erik studied the queasy expression on the face of the brute. "Does the torture of children bother you? It's not much different, really. Smaller cuts, so if anything it's easier. You have to be diligent for shock, though. Their systems just aren't as robust as ours."

The brute turned away.

"You got a daughter? Niece? Little sister?"

The brute whirled and punched in a fluid motion. Erik was ready and managed to open his jaw, twist his neck, and bite down as the fist made contact, effectively using his teeth to fillet the flesh of the fingers from bone. Spitting shattered teeth, Erik yelled at the brute who mutely stared at his mutilated hand. "Scared now? Imagine what I'll do when I'm free!"

After the team left the room, Erik closed his eyes. The sleep deprivation bothered him more than the torture. Physical damage and pain were transient. Sleep debt was constant. The round-the-clock torture made catching shut eye a bit problematic, so he did his best to catch a few minutes of rest whenever possible.

"That doesn't look terribly comfortable."

Erik opened his eyes to find an ugly woman in the room. Her square head sat atop a solid body. If a man had possessed the same build, Erik would have said he looked like a lumberjack. On a woman, the result was less flattering. "Neither does your face," he said. "Where's the rest of your team? Or do you want to hit me all by yourself to take out all the rage you feel at the Creator for making you so damn ugly?"

The woman studied him. Not with the inhuman efficiency of an Observer with thousands of lifetimes' worth of experience, but with the slow studiousness of a woman who wanted to understand something. "You're very different from the other Observer."

"Oh, I'm unique, all right." Erik shook his head to clear it. She hadn't called him an Agent, but an Observer. This woman wasn't one of the Punishers. "You the good cop to their bad cop? I suppose the deal is I talk to you and things get better for me?"

"You might consider it a deal of sorts. Talk to me for an hour every day and that will be an hour less for them to hurt you. That is the only thing I can offer."

Erik grunted. "Do I have to tell the truth?"

"You have to convince me our sessions provide value."

"So I have to make you *think* I tell the truth?"

"We both know you will lie as much as you think possible. I don't want to play games with you. I'm a theologian, not an interrogator. My name is Simone Killian. Have you heard of me?"

Simone Killian was famous. Descended from the First Opposer. Aunt of the current Premier. Professor Emeritus of Theology at the national seminary. Author of the Angolan translation of the Book of Grievances. Writer of half a dozen bestsellers describing how words and traditions from hundreds of years in the past applied perfectly to the modern age.

"Anything you remember prior to four months ago never happened," Erik said. "You're famous for a back story the Creator gave you. Kinda ironic if you think about it. Your whole deal is opposing the Creator, but you owe the Creator everything you are — even your opposition."

"That's an ancient argument," she said. "The apologetics of antiquity responded by noting that if the Demiurge caused the Opposition, then that proves the thing hates itself."

Erik recoiled as far as his bindings would allow. "What? That's ridiculous! Look around you. This world is glorious. Every complaint you creatures make can be summed up as 'I want everything my way all the time or the world ain't fair.' Guess what, sister. There are over three billion of you turds wishing to be king of this world. That's something that can't ever work out for more than one person. The only conceivable world that your religion could accept has a population of uno. Sounds fucking boring to me."

Simone placed a hand to her cheek. "By my dignity, you're right! Humans owe everything to the Creator and need to start worshiping immediately! What fools we have been!"

Erik glared at her. "Is that how the country's leading theologian answers a question about a logical fallacy?"

"I was answering your childish outburst on the same level. I always respond in kind to any argument. Logic meets logic. Emotion meets emotion. Authority meets authority. I feel that doing otherwise puts me at a disadvantage." Simone squinted at him. "Do you truly believe we demand some form of paradise? I mistook that as a straw man argument meant to belittle me, but now I think you were serious."

She folded her massive arms across her chest. "You claim that the world began four months ago. Let's accept that assertion for the purpose of our discussion. At the moment of creation, there were tens of millions of people dying of terminal diseases. And millions more in jail for crimes that never truly happened. I know men crippled in the service of this country and children born with defects. None of this had to be. The Creator chose to make those people suffer."

Erik smirked. "People start wars all the time. They die of drug overdoses and car accidents and all sorts of self-inflicted fates. Why wouldn't the Creator give the world a matching back story?"

"There's a very simple counter example. Disease. Why create a world filled with so many harmful microbes? There can be no benevolent purpose to it."

"*Benevolent?*" Erik laughed. "So that's where your major malfunction happened. I thought we already established it's impossible for everyone to live a magically fulfilled life."

"Not creating dysentery doesn't qualify as magic wish fulfillment."

"Bacteria evolve rapidly," Erik said. "Sooner or later a bug would come along that did horrible things. Would be awful suspicious if that event was unique in the history of the world. The Creator kept the back story realistic."

"And why are bacteria necessary at all? Couldn't your Creator build a world without microbes?"

Erik rolled his eyes. "Let's cut through the bullshit. You still think the world should be built to make you happy."

"Of course not. Just better suited to us."

"Right. To make all of you collectively happier."

"I don't care to argue the semantics."

"Been there, done that."

Simone's heavy brow drew down. "Excuse me?"

"This ain't the first world, tubby. There were plenty before this one. A couple of those matched your pretty little picture of paradise. No war, hardly any disease, never any starvation."

"Then your Creator chose to make this one to spite us."

"Shit, sister, the Creator did you a kindness." Erik used his chin to gesture at a couple of torture implements the previous team hadn't taken with them. "You may have heard that I'm in the business myself."

"I've read that you claim to be superior at inflicting pain."

"I'm a fucking artist. In comparison, your boys are nothing more than monkeys smearing their shit on the wall."

"Your point?"

"I use torture to gauge how strongly people wish to live. The quicker they ask for death, the less they value their lives. With me so far?"

Simone squinted again, silently studying him.

"I'll assume I haven't lost you yet. My point in explaining my test method is that the empirical evidence ain't in your favor. People living in a paradise will embrace death to avoid a hang-nail. But take some miserable smuck from a world like this and you need to put in a bit of effort to get the same result. And then there are the crazy worlds. The people from one of those require serious convincing.

"You seeing my point yet? Your thought experiment don't match the data. People aren't happiest in worlds full of roses and bubblegum. They need contrast. A little tragedy to bring out the sweetness."

She shook her head. "I reject your 'test'."

"Well, you would know best, considering you have hundreds of thousands of years of life experience. Wait a minute. That's me. You're only four months old."

"Did it ever occur to you that people from better worlds might not have the coping mechanisms to deal with your hideous experiments?"

"What the hell is a coping mechanism in the first place? A way to survive trauma. Why don't supposedly happy people develop these wonderful coping skills when they have need of them? You know, like all the other people do all the time?"

"Coping skills are developed over time. You can't throw someone who has never been challenged into a trial and expect a miracle."

Erik sighed. "You have no idea what you're talking about."

"Belittling me doesn't make my argument wrong."

"Coping mechanisms pop up fully formed. A mind pushed past its limits invents something to keep the urge for self-destruction at bay. I've played with enough people to know the process more intimately than you know the contours of your vibrator. People subconsciously decide when their lives are worth protecting with psychological barriers. It's all choice."

Simone's eyes bored into him. "Do not insult me again."

"You gonna hit me if I do? Didn't work out too well for the last guy."

"I won't come back for tomorrow's conversation. You represent the antithesis of everything I stand for, yet I am willing to treat you with dignity. All I ask in return is for a modicum of respect. I can ignore your base language, but the crude jokes at my expense end or our association ends."

"Mutual respect? I'm hanging naked from the ceiling after weeks of excruciating torture and you take issue with colorful language? This is exactly the kind of attitude I expect from you people. Everything has to be your way all the time or the world ain't fair."

Simone folded her arms. "I have nothing to do with your circumstances. I can and do choose to speak to you civilly. In return, I expect the same."

"Do you blame the Creator for making you an unattractive woman? Is that the source of your personal opposition? You are rich, famous, and powerful, but you hate the Creator cause you ain't pretty enough?"

"Respect," Simon said.

"Fine. I won't insult your looks or your sex life. If you feel like returning the respect, you could adjust my bindings."

"Out of the question."

"Why? Afraid to come closer?"

"I believe your boasts to the Punishers that you will eventually escape. You are far more cunning than I."

Erik grunted. His eyes drifted closed.

"Do you really plan to sleep through the rest of our interview?"

"Ssssh. I'm mutual respecting."

"We have another Observer in custody."

"So I hear."

"Don't you want to know who it is?"

"Unless his name is Hess, I don't care."

"This Hess character comes up a lot when I talk to your kind. He's a rebel of sorts, as I understand."

"He would eat up your blasphemous religion."

"So one of your own kind hates the Demiurge?"

"Don't flatter yourself, chica. Hess doesn't hate the Creator. He suffers from a messiah complex that interferes with our mission."

"He tried to improve a world for the benefit of its people and you buried him alive in punishment."

Erik opened his eyes. "That world didn't need any improving."

"What about this one?"

"Watch the next sunset. Really watch it. Consider the phenomenon. Hydrogen atoms fuse into helium atoms millions of miles away, release photons to rush through space, diffract in the atmosphere, pass through the lens of your eye to strike your retina, where a series of chemical reactions passes the message to a network of neurons that perceives a fucking sunset. Think about the complexity of that. Marvel at it. Recognize that every moment you exist is unique and will never happen again. Feel the significance of a universe capable of hosting billions just like you, all of them walking around having their own unique moments. You do that, then come tell me you think the Creator shouldn't have brought this world into existence. Explain how much better an empty, unobserved void would be. Try to convince me."

Simone frowned, then dismissed whatever thought troubled her with a firm shake of her head. "Nothing you say can justify the state of this world."

"Do you see me cursing the Creator? I've been tortured for two weeks by a religion perfectly designed to catch and torment Observers. A religion made by the Creator, mind you. Likely it will be years of the same before I get my chance to escape. I got legitimate reasons to get pissy. But I'm not crying foul. Why is that?"

"You tell me."

"No. You figure out the answer for yourself."

"Do you want to know the name of the other Observer?"

"Who is it?"

Simone raised her chin. "I want your name first."

"Erik."

"I thought as much."

"Who is it?"

"A man by the name of Ingrid."

Erik grunted. "Do me a favor? Pass a message along to my good friend. Tell him 'I know it was you who released the prisoner last Iteration'."

Simone nodded. "I'll let him know that."

CHAPTER TWELVE
Hess
Iteration 145

Hess stared at Jerome. "Die?"

"Well, have our memories erased. It's the same as dying. The Creator will abide by the majority decision of our vote."

Elza brushed her hair back out of her eyes. "Are we the first ones you've approached?"

"About that," Jerome said. "I barely found the two of you. If Hess hadn't left messages all over the internet from a device owned by Jed Orlin, I would still be out there looking for you."

"I thought you knew our identities at the start of every iteration," Elza said.

Jerome nodded her head so vigorously that her spindly neck looked in danger of snapping. "My head is full of all the usual details. Names, locations, appearances. All of it. But according to my memories, Hess is a white man named Carl Lindenburg and Elza is on the other side of the planet.

"When the Creator added the Church to the history of this world, your identities must have changed. For the first time in my existence, I have a reason to find the eleven of you. And for the first time in my existence, I don't have the means to do so.

"Something is wrong with the Creator. The war between you two and the others has had serious consequences."

"Wait a minute," Hess said. "How much of this is knowledge supplied by the Creator and how much is guesses?"

Jerome grimaced. "All I know for sure is my mission and the fact that everything I knew about this world at the moment of creation is wrong." She stared at Hess with her deep-set eyes. "I think that's enough to know something is wrong."

Hess crossed his arms. "What is wrong is the fact that Erik gets his rocks off by torturing the people. And the fact that Ingrid feels entitled to punish us. Those two deserve the very worst this world has to offer. I hope the Church of Opposition gets its hands on those two Agents."

Jerome's jaw dropped. "Why?"

"Because," Hess snapped, "*they* are what is wrong with every world. They want suffering to exist. Erik just for the fun of it. Ingrid because of her obsession with consequences. Their spite has sabotaged every world I have ever walked, Jerome. They deserve the enmity of the people."

For a moment, Jerome was silent. "If that is how you feel, then I don't think the current batch of Observers can be effective any longer. I vote to wipe our memories and end us."

"What?"

Jerome sagged against the kitchen counter. "The rules provided by the Creator are simple. Everyone gets to vote. There is no changing a vote once cast. A refusal to vote counts in favor of wiping. I must conduct the vote as quickly as possible and open the sky once I have the final vote."

"And you think we are unfit to Observe because I don't approve of my coworkers?"

Jerome shook her head. "Because you hate them. And they probably hate you. We serve something greater than ourselves, Hess."

"No," Hess said, "we serve ourselves."

"Our consciousnesses join together to form the Creator's. Our memories inform the Creator. But we aren't the Creator any more than your hand is the sum total of you."

Hess forced a smile. "Thanks for your opinion, Jerome. But we like our lives just fine, so we'll be voting against proposition suicide."

"I get to make my own choice, Hess." Elza met his eyes. "And I'm tired." She looked away. "I vote in favor of ending the Observers."

Hess stared. He opened his mouth, then shut it when no words came to him. Finally, he stumbled forward to collapse into one of the bar stools in his kitchen. Hess shook his head emphatically and avoided eye contact with the two women.

Jerome cleared her throat. "You despise Erik. Voting to wipe our memories would destroy him. It would let the Observers start over with fresh personalities. Likely the worlds would improve as a result."

Hess ran a hand through his hair. "So you want to forget *us*? Forget we ever happened? That doesn't make sense, Elza. Last Iteration you made me promise to never forget you. Now you vote to erase everything we are from existence. Everything we ever were."

"I am *tired*, Hess. Eternity is too long."

"Too long to spend with me?"

Elza turned to look out the window. "You know I love you."

"Really? Because I just heard you give up on us."

"I tired of life before we ever met, Hess. Way back in Iteration one. Back then, the only thing that kept me going was a sense of duty. When we ran into each other in Kallig's tribe, you hated the world, but I hated my life.

"It's funny to look back on, but I actually thought I'd seen everything existence had to offer. Then we met and I forgot how miserable I was. For a while. But love can't fix everything."

Hess struck a fist on the table. "Where the hell is this coming from? Are you still upset about the nuclear war last Iteration?"

Elza grimaced. "No, Hess, that has nothing to do with anything."

He stabbed a finger at her. "You made me swear to never forget you!"

"Because I couldn't live without you. That's the difference here, Hess. I'm not asking you to live without me. What I want is the same mercy the people are granted every world. I want to cease being."

"Why?"

Elza stared at him.

"Why, Elza? What possible reason could you have for wanting to die?"

"Didn't you want to die when you were Zack?"

"I wasn't myself."

"But you remember it. That's how I feel, Hess. Don't you remember what I told you after I abducted you last Iteration?"

Hess hated remembering the five years he had spent suppressing his deep memories, the time he had lived under the identity of Zack Vernon. After he had escaped from Erik, he had gone back to his trailer and encountered Elza. During their initial conversation, after he revealed he wanted to die, she had responded by saying "We don't die, Zack. Not ever. Not even when it's the only thing we want."

"We were happy," he said.

Elza's eyes misted. "Happier than I thought possible."

"I suppose I should thank you for pretending I was more than a distraction." Hess got to his feet. "On second thought, never mind. None of it matters because we're being killed."

He slammed the door on his way out of the house.

CHAPTER THIRTEEN
Erik
Iteration 2

He took the name Mott as he entered the village. Mott. The name of a man who had been mauled by a lion and survived . . . for a time. It had been an entertaining, if short, show. He had watched the man named Mott beg for help, then try to drag his mangled body to safety when he realized the only witness intended to do no more than watch.

Mott readied his usual questions. Had they seen a pale man traveling with a beautiful woman? Which of the nearby villages was largest? Had anyone heard talk of someone creating the world?

While trying to find someone to answer his questions, Mott stumbled upon an interesting scene. A dozen women swarmed over one of their number, shrieking a strident chorus of "no, Beeta, no!" as they restrained her. Even as the events unfolded, the village elders emerged from the guest pavilion to make ineffective soothing motions with their hands.

His questions died unasked. Something much more interesting than following cold trails was happening here. Dark memories stirred. A world ago, he had been a shapely woman in the midst of a swarm of men, beaten and taken with wild force. He had taken his vengeance upon each of those men after, striking from the dark and planting evidence to frame their own brothers of the deed.

Even without the benefit of perfect recall, Mott would always remember the feel of those restraining hands stealing his autonomy, turning him into a helpless victim. That had been a poignant lesson in the virtue of strength. Lacking it, your world was one of limitations. The only way to be free of the trappings of weakness was to seize power.

And the easiest power to possess was freedom from morality. Even the most twisted men of the first world had respected some boundaries. Feeding poison berries to a child and posing the corpse in a strong man's tent had caused him to shriek like a young girl. Many times Mott had started forest fires during droughts to destroy entire tribes, though truthfully that had been more for his amusement than a play for power.

Studying the woman at the center of everyone's attention, Mott wondered what she had done. Every village of the second world was similar to a depressing degree. The same traditions and mannerisms and beliefs existed everywhere. It was a pacifist's wet dream. What would cause the villagers to restrain a woman?

Mott leaned against a support beam of the guest pavilion to watch events unfold. The women crowded the one at their center until one of them emerged carrying a bronze knife. Then the level of agitation dropped dramatically.

One of the older women spoke in a clear voice, silencing the rest. "Beeta, you must be strong, girl. Fight this madness. You don't want to bring grief on your mother and your father. Too many people care for you, child."

The old woman paused after each sentence so that the others could chime in with words of agreement. The object of their attention slowly transitioned from crazed intensity to mellow passivity. Beeta looked defeated. He couldn't tell who she had intended as the target of the knife – herself or one of the others. It was all but impossible to predict what someone under the spell of madness would do, where they might turn their destructive impulses.

"I wish you had not seen that," a man said from beside him.

Mott startled, then forced his features to stillness. "Does the woman want to harm someone or is she seeking attention?"

"Beeta harms no one but herself."

"My name is Mott."

"Welcome to our village, Mott. We will have food and company tonight. Tomorrow, if you are able, you can help the men thatch roofs."

Mott's eyes drifted back to the crazy woman. It had been years since he traveled with his last companion. Keeno had been that man's name. He was a man with the face of a child and the heart of a snake. Until he turned on the Creator's Observer. Then Keeno had been a man without a face and the heart of a terrified child.

Perhaps it was time for a new companion.

"My sister was like Beeta," Mott said.

There was a sharp intake of breath. "What happened to her?"

"I was always able to talk sense into her. First when we were children and then later when she chose a man. But I wasn't around all the time. The women knew not to let her have a knife, but one day she took a shard of pottery and used that instead. If I had been there that day, I could have stopped her. No one knew the right words to use. Everyone thought they needed to convince her that everything was good, but she knew in her heart that wasn't true."

"What else would you tell someone burdened with a heavy heart but that things are better than they seem?"

"I always asked my sister about her thoughts and let her tell me the truth she knew instead of forcing my truth on her. Because I had never argued with her, she trusted me to understand. Everyone else in her life tried to make her better. She could never trust them again because of that. Everyone in our entire village became her enemy except for me."

"But why did you never try to talk sense to your sister?"

"Because she was my older sister and *I* trusted *her*. She confided in me and by the time I was old enough to wish her better I knew the ways of mental illnesses intimately and didn't make the same mistakes as everyone else. Only I knew how to talk to her. Only I had never betrayed her trust."

The man was silent for a long time. Mott glanced over from time to time, noting the play of thoughts on the man's face. Finally, the man spoke. "We never knew. We wanted to comfort her, make her feel better."

"Of course you meant well," Mott said. "It is no one's fault that you didn't know the things I know."

The man sighed. "You are wise, my friend. No one is to blame for not knowing the best way to support dear Beeta."

"You couldn't have known that your kind words would make it impossible for her to trust everyone in the village," Mott added.

"Not everyone in the village. My friend, you have never spoken to Beeta. Surely she would not think you are against her. You know the right way to calm madness. Would you be willing to speak with her? I promise you that everyone would think you a hard worker indeed if your labor tomorrow was words with Beeta instead of laying thatch."

Mott bowed deeply. "I would be honored to help that young woman. After the loss of my sister, I could never walk away from someone who needed help in the fight against madness."

CHAPTER FOURTEEN
Hess
Iteration 145

He stalked the neighborhood on foot for two hours before returning home. Elza and Jerome sat in the living room, eyes glued to the television. They fidgeted as he entered the house.

Hess shook his head. "I'm not interested in whatever you have to say. Elza — I don't even want to see you right now. And Jerome — I want you gone from my life forever."

Elza pointed at the television.

"I don't care," Hess began.

Then the video caught his attention. An older man with a bulbous nose flinched as a red-hot poker contacted his chest, mouth open in a scream as flesh discolored and bled. The poker pulled away. The man on the screen wept while they watched.

"What are you watching?"

Jerome answered. "Ingrid."

Other marks began to fade, blackened flesh reverting to flawless skin. The poker descended again, once more glowing an angry red. As Hess flinched in sympathy, Jerome un-muted the television set, filling the room with hoarse moans and heavy sobs.

"The man seen here, one Forrest Clark, has been positively identified by the Church as an Agent of the Demiurge," a voice-over narrated. Ingrid's screams faded into desperate pleading as the poker pulled away.

"Turn it off," Hess said.

Jerome turned her deep-set eyes on Hess, emaciated face looking like a skull in the flickering light of the television. "Why? This is what you wanted, Hess. The people are punishing Ingrid for you. You ought to watch the entire episode to take your pleasure in what you've done."

"This has nothing to do with me," he said.

"You blame Ingrid and Erik for everything you think wrong with the worlds. How is it any different when your darkest wishes are brought to life? You can't have it both ways, Hess. Either Ingrid is innocent or you are guilty."

Hess glared at Jerome. "Then open the sky. We'll vote next Iteration."

"No."

"Why not? Your job is to prevent situations."

"Not this time. I collect votes. That is my only mission. Though I sure as hell don't know how I'm going to get Ingrid's vote."

"Hess is right," Elza interrupted. "You have to open the sky. Even if you had a way to find the others and get in to see Ingrid, this world isn't safe. The people are looking for us and now they know that identifying us is as easy as performing a prick test."

Jerome's eyes moved between Hess and Elza. "My present form may not be suited to breaking into a prison, but if that's what I need to do, then that is what I am going to do."

Elza leaned forward. "Why bother? Considering what is happening to Ingrid, his decision should be obvious."

"You don't know that," Hess said.

"Like you care." Jerome nodded towards the television. "This is your revenge fantasy."

"You really believe I caused this?"

Jerome hesitated the barest fraction of a second. "Yes."

Hess lifted his chin. "What's your plan for getting him out?"

"I can't get him out. I'll have to save Ingrid for last, break in, get his vote, and end the world."

"No," Hess said. "That will take too long. The Church will be holding Ingrid at their headquarters in the city. I can get access to as many personal weapons as we need, and it shouldn't be hard to improvise some explosives."

Jerome raised a brow. "Seriously?"

"I thought you did research on my cover identity. Jed Orlin is VP of Logistics at TFK Motors. My organization moves weapons for the Church."

"I'm just surprised you want to help Ingrid."

"Then you don't know the first thing about me," Hess said. "I've wished for a lot of bad things to happen to Ingrid, but I didn't put him in that room to be tortured. And I'm not leaving him there."

Elza sighed. "Pipe bombs won't get you into a secure facility."

"I'll rig some propane tanks or something."

"You need to breach their security and create a diversion. That means heavy explosives." Elza clasped her hands together. "But heavy explosives are kept secured."

"We could brew a batch of plastic explosives," Hess said.

"You're not thinking big enough," Elza said. "This world never developed atomic theory. Consequently, it is possible to buy large amounts of radioactive material without alarming a government office."

"You want to set off a dirty bomb?"

"Still not big enough, Hess. I have enough money in my trust fund to buy over a hundred pounds of uranium. That should be sufficient to start a chain reaction without enrichment."

Jerome raised a hand to her mouth. "You know how to build a nuke?"

"Why wouldn't I? It's just physics and engineering."

CHAPTER FIFTEEN
Erik
Iteration 145

When Simone entered, Erik was still giggling from his latest stunt.

Instead of hanging him from the ceiling, his tormentors now bound him spread eagle to the cold concrete floor. Still naked, of course. The only times they placed coverings on him were when they started fires.

"You gouged a man's eye out," she said.

"He broke my hand enough for it to slip free. I'd say he was asking for a friendly poke. His buddies nearly shit their pants when I licked the eye juice off my thumb."

"I've seen videos of what they do to you."

"Hot, ain't it?"

Simone grimaced. "Distasteful at best. But what I find most disturbing is how rapidly you alternate between despair and lucidity. I am certain neither state is an act, which makes me wonder if you are sane."

"Come on, chica, use that big brain of yours. Why do normal people get fucked up from bad experiences? Cause they're children terrified of the future. Even your grandmas only got eighty years of memories to draw on. Shallow well, if you ask me. And you're all obsessed with the possibility that bad things will happen to you.

"Not me. Cut off my cock and it'll grow back before I need to piss. Light me on fire and everything's peachy in five. Pain's a bitch, but it doesn't last. Neither will this prison. I'll get out. And even if I don't, this world will end. You all fade away like you never were and I go on my merry way.

"You pathetic creatures are blips on the radar, honey. I'm real. You are not. Nothing you do to my body can stick. And despite your best efforts, there hasn't been a dent in my mind yet. Some day, all of this will be a memory I dust off every couple decades and say 'hey, I remember this one time when I got caught.' The problem with trying to torture a guy like me is you can't make me vulnerable."

"Ingrid hasn't been as resilient."

"Ingrid is a pussy," Erik said. "Did he send a message?"

Simone folded her arms. "Ingrid maintains he was a young woman last Iteration, living in a place called Kyrgyzstan."

"Fucking liar!"

"Watch your language, or I will stop carrying messages again."

Erik stopped struggling against his bindings and took a deep, slow breath. "He was a man in America. He bought a farm in Sarver when Hess broke cover. Then he went rogue on us. I *know* it was him. Kerzon was with me a hundred percent and Drake wouldn't mess with me. It was either Ingrid or Griff. And action ain't exactly Griff's thing.

"I know it was him. I fucking know. He referenced the time we set off the fire alarm at a movie theater, back in Iteration twenty. No one knew that story except the two of us. And he had that annoying tick where he licks his lips all the time." Erik paused. "He did it the first day, at least." He frowned in thought, rushing through memories of the previous Iteration. The man claiming to be Ingrid had never licked his lips after the first day their band met up to take down Hess.

"I have a new question for Ingrid. Ask him if he ever told one of the others about the movie theater." Erik frowned. Himself, Drake, Kerzon, Griff, Hess, and Elza were accounted for last Iteration. If he accepted Ingrid's assertion that he had been off posing as a child bride in some backwater country, then that meant seven Observers were accounted for. That left four suspects. Even if the dreamy Mariana left her study of animals, she couldn't act worth shit. Greg was a coward who hid within academia. Mel hated Hess and didn't do much besides obsess over art. Which left just San.

San? Could she pull off an almost flawless impersonation? The crazy bitch was a thrill seeker with no sense of danger. She was also a close friend of Elza. But if San had been there, why had she helped them catch Hess in the first place?

None of the Observers had the guts, the talent, and the motive to do it. Which left one other possibility. "Actually, Simone, forget that last message. Instead, I want you to tell Ingrid 'there is a twelfth'."

"A twelfth Observer?"

"That's right, sister. We got ourselves a sleeper agent. Guy aligned himself with the wrong side, cause I'm going to find him."

Simone nodded. "And what do I get in exchange for passing this message?"

"There's a postage stamp up my ass."

"Erik . . . ."

"Same deal as last time. Ask a question and I'll give you an answer."

"Then I want to know what Hess did that was so wrong."

"I told you before. He tried to change the world."

"I want specifics, Erik, or your message doesn't go."

He took a deep breath. "Dear old Hess has always had a bit of a soft heart, you see. Took in orphans and shit like that. Tracked down serial killers from time to time . . . . Anyway, I never cared about any of that. I do a fair amount of what the others deem *participation*.

"But then, in Iteration one four three, Hess makes himself king. He takes some tiny nation and conquers most of the known world. Sets up national academies and a welfare system. Gets his woman to do fancy accounting that bankrupts everyone except them. Turns the entire world upside down.

"He touched the entire world. Everyone was either under his rule, under the rule of someone allied with him, or under the rule of one of his enemies. I never had a problem with the orphans, but this was too far. He stopped observing. The Creator gave him a holy mission and he went rogue so pathetic creatures like you would have happier lives."

"Is that really so terrible?"

Erik laughed. "Hell yeah, it is. I don't expect you to ever understand the big picture, but the lot of you are ants living in the dirt. What would you think of a man who bulldozed your house for the benefit of an ant colony?"

"We are not ants."

"Oh, I know. Ants have better character."

Simone rolled her eyes. "Why did you take that man's eye? Did you do it in revenge for the pain he caused you? Or were you motivated by hatred?"

"There were a lot of reasons to get pokey with my thumb. I don't like you creatures to begin with, and your whole Church opposes existence."

"Not existence," Simone said. "The Creator."

"I thought we were done arguing about what you people want."

"So you put your thumb in a man's eye because you hate us?"

"And I like to see fear when my *punishers* look at me. Plus I'm stuck here. You know, the whole prison aspect. I managed to get a hand free, so I had to take advantage of it. Hess might have figured out a way to escape, but the only option I could see was doing some damage."

She leaned closer. "Whatever you feel for Hess borders on obsession. I can't figure out if it is hate or love or some combination of the two."

"Don't go analyzing me like a person again. I don't get into love or sex or even companionship. I'm not built that way. I don't need another person to *get me*. The Creator does that."

There was a knock on the door. Simone checked her watch. "Our session is up. I will talk to you again tomorrow." Before she put a hand on the door, she turned back. "I finally watched a sunset."

"Beautiful, right?"

Simone nodded. "Will this world really cease to exist?"

"Just like all the others. Some day everything you know will be just a memory in the head of some eye-poking asshole."

CHAPTER SIXTEEN
Hess
Iteration 145

Elza took the lead in their planning the moment she mentioned building a nuclear weapon. She turned off the television, herded them into the dining room, and began to outline their course of action.

"Our most immediate concern is hiding from the Church authorities. We will assume a nation-wide hunt is under way. Given that our obvious tell has been revealed to the world, we can expect at a minimum for every citizen to be tested once. Anyone who managed to avoid the mandatory testing would be identified as a suspicious person."

She fixed her eyes on Hess. "The most obvious way to avoid capture is to disappear, but if you intend to launch a rescue operation, we can't go into hiding. We will need the advantages provided by my wealth and your position if we intend to succeed."

Hess nodded.

"Then we need to pass their test. That means two things. First, we must appear to retain an injury inflicted on us. This shouldn't be too difficult if we can get reliable intelligence on which area of the body is most likely to be targeted. A shallow layer of latex will suffice to replicate a laceration or shallow puncture wound.

"The second thing we need to worry about is blood. Both the blood that remains on the wound and the blood that stains the testing implement. While our blood flows quite believably outside our bodies, its tendency to vanish within minutes of its exit will be their primary means of identifying us.

"Which is why we will require frequent, large blood transfusions." Elza pointed to her wrist. "I know from experience that our bodies will not only retain foreign blood, but subsequently shed it in a mundane manner."

In response to Jerome's expression, Hess whispered, "She likes to conduct experiments."

"I didn't realize her hobby extended to studying our nature."

"Why not?"

"Because our purpose is to study the people," Jerome said.

"No, I mean why didn't you know about her experiments? I thought you had the summary of our entire lives in your head."

Jerome rolled her eyes. "It's an executive summary. It's more of a highlight reel than a comprehensive history."

"We don't have time for these tangents," Elza said. "If you want to get Ingrid out of prison, then we need to begin our preparations." She pointed at Hess. "Get liquid latex and acrylic paints from a craft store. Black, red, blue, and yellow at a minimum. Pay with cash and get home quickly."

She pointed at Jerome next. "You're coming with me to the hospital to help pick up some type O. I can bankroll the purchase, but someone with pale skin needs to perform the transaction."

"You want me to buy blood on the black market?"

"They call it an underground market this Iteration, due to obvious reasons, but yes, I want you to buy something that the seller doesn't have the legal right to sell. They should agree to the transaction if you offer them a generous sum. Then they play around with their records to make the blood disappear from the system."

Jerome hesitated. "And if they refuse?"

"Then we visit another hospital. There are five within driving distance."

"And if they report me to the police?"

Hess slapped Jerome on her bony back. "Save some of your panic for when we're charging into a Church torture compound with a nuke."

With a sigh much too large for Jerome's slight frame, she stood. "Let's get this over with."

Hess made it back home hours before the others. To productively pass the time, he began mixing paint with latex in small batches, then comparing the dried product to his flesh. After some experimentation, he managed to achieve a reasonable match and moved on to the creation of false skin.

The task proved less difficult than he had expected, requiring little more than a steady hand and an eye for detail. Hess painted a layer onto his forearm, then cut himself with a knife. Blood welled upward through wound and artifice to pool, run, and drip onto the table surface.

When his injury erased itself from existence and his blood reverted to its proper location, Hess scrutinized the gash held in place by latex. Discounting the lack of blood, it appeared realistic enough.

Lights from outside caught his attention. Hess moved to the window, where he saw one of the Church SUV's opening its doors to release a swarm of Deputy Investigators. Hess ran back into the living room, plastered a small amount of premixed skin onto his index finger, hastily molded it while he moved to the fridge and retrieved a tray of thawing ground beef.

Hess sliced his finger, then dipped a kitchen towel in the puddle beneath the ground beef and wrapped that around the wounded appendage. Pounding at the door announced the arrival of the Investigators. Hess tossed the meat into the trash, threw a jacket over the evidence of his experimentation with latex, squeezed some beef juice from his makeshift bandage onto the knife blade, and walked to the door.

A second round of pounding began just as he yanked the door open. Before they could say a word, Hess waved his wrapped hand in front of them. "Whatever you want, it has to wait five damn minutes!"

He didn't give them time to process his words, but went about the business of locating his first aid kit and then cleaning and bandaging his fake injury while the Church Investigators watched. "Damn the Demiurge," he muttered loud enough for all to hear. "This is that woman's fault for not taking care of the leftovers."

Hess made eye contact with the dominant one of the group. "Honestly, I wish I could afford trained help. Do you know how hard it is to live on the bluff when you have to hire incompetent pales from the Boyce neighborhood? Theora's father certainly took notice of her inadequacies. And he very bluntly called me on them in front of everyone."

The Deputy opened his mouth and Hess resumed his rant, seizing the knife and tossing it into the sink. "Cutting my own leftovers. I'll bet Mr. Winfield would find it hilarious that I cut myself. Damn the Demiurge!"

All three of the Deputies exchanged awkward glances.

"I'm sorry for my outburst, gentlemen. I hired that woman to impress Mr. Winfield, but it backfired spectacularly. The plan was to request his permission to ask for Theora's hand." Hess sighed. "But instead of asking for *her* hand, I made a fool of myself and now I have cut *my own* hand. Or at least a finger."

"Mr. Orlin," the leader of the deputies said, "We need to test you."

"I've been drinking, but I never went anywhere near my car."

"Right, Mr. Orlin. We need to test that you aren't an Agent."

Hess snorted. "What do you want me to do? Curse the Demiurge? I've been doing that all night, buddies."

"We need to see your blood," the man said.

"Seriously? It's on the table, it's on the rag, it's all over the place."

"We're supposed to draw it ourselves."

Hess picked up the kitchen towel streaked with red. "Here is my blood. Honestly, why are you coming here in the middle of the night trying to draw my blood? Haven't I had a bad enough day as it is?"

Awkward silence. Then one of the other men, silent up until this point, spoke. "He did bleed all over the place while we watched. More blood than we saw from any of the people we did ourselves."

"Yeah." The leader nodded. "Yeah, you're right. Take it easy, Mr. Orlin. We'll get out of your way." He paused at the door. "Oh, there's something that might make you feel a bit better on the news."

"What's that?" Hess asked.

"They found an Agent of the Demiurge."

Hours later, Elza returned with Jerome and a duffel bag. She wasted no time hanging bags of blood from wire coat hangers suspended off of ceiling fans and jabbing needles into veins for all three of them.

Hess snapped his fingers at Jerome. "You have to keep moving the needle. Let it sit still for too long and your body will disintegrate the metal. An Observer taking a transfusion is pretty much constant poking."

Jerome clenched her jaw. "How much blood do we need?"

"Three units a day," Elza said, then, when Jerome made a face, continued, "Or you could risk a visit to the Church headquarters under less pleasant circumstances. Honestly, Jerome, this may be inconvenient, but it beats the alternative."

"Assuming latex and packed red blood cells fool anyone."

"It will," Hess said, nodding towards the band-aid on his finger. In response to their startled expressions, he detailed the events of that evening, causing Jerome to mutter imprecations.

Halfway through his first unit of blood, Hess let the needle linger in place for too long and its tip vanished, eliminated from existence where it intersected his body. He swapped in a fresh needle and went back to work. Their nature conspired to make receiving blood difficult, but fortunately their immunity to disease allowed them to reuse and swap needles with impunity.

As they finished their transfusions, Elza doled out further assignments. The duty of discovering the details of the Investigator's test fell to Hess. It would be his responsibility to learn where they needed to apply a layer of latex pseudo-skin. He also needed to pre-mix dye and latex to match their flesh tones.

To Jerome, Elza gave the job of computer research, the purpose of which was to create a report of the Church headquarters' facilities, personnel, traditions, and standard operating procedures. Elza informed them that she would begin sourcing the materials and components necessary for the construction of their nuclear weapon.

They managed a few hours of sleep before the light of dawn brought them awake to tackle their tasks. That first day, Hess colored latex before visiting his neighbors on various errands. He returned a borrowed garden hose, gifted a fifth of premium gin, asked for suggestions on planning the upcoming Church picnic, and complained about his disastrous dinner party the previous night.

The fruit of his frantic socializing was the knowledge that the Deputies performed their test by piercing the palm with a sterile lancet and then observing both the wound and a handkerchief dabbed in the resulting blood. Returning with this knowledge, Hess set about painting fake flesh onto all three of them in the specified region.

Jerome spent the day working on a laptop and filling a notepad with her findings, while Elza diagrammed her weapon complete with measurements in the margins. They all took an hour break to receive another blood transfusion, then went back to their various tasks.

His assigned labor complete, Hess turned his attentions to preparing a meal and acquiring small arms. The meal consisted of lamb tips basted in ginger soy dressing, wild rice, and sauteed vegetables. His weapon purchases included two nine millimeter semi-automatic handguns, a twelve gauge shotgun, and a tiny .22 caliber suitable as a backup weapon – all bought second hand through an anonymous online market.

When he returned that evening with all four weapons, Hess microwaved a quick dinner of mostly edible noodles in flavorless sauce, then sat down for another blood transfusion. He discovered that the Deputies had returned to the house while he was gone.

Jerome and Elza had passed the prick test, but the Deputies insisted that they needed to conduct the official test on Hess. Then Jerome informed them that she had managed to contact several of the other Observers online and, more than that, had invited San and Drake for a visit.

Which ignited the requisite argument over the fact that Jerome had invited people into their lives without even the courtesy of asking – though their main argument was the inclusion of Drake, who had assisted Ingrid in burying Hess and Elza alive during Iteration one forty three and then helped Erik hunt down Hess in one forty four. San had a standing invitation from Elza to visit whenever she wanted, which typically meant a month spent in her company every few Iterations.

Their conflict expired before anyone retracted a position, its heat smothered by needle induced frustration. In a conciliatory gesture, Jerome agreed to inform them before she contacted any of the others.

When they completed their infusion, Elza asked a question. "How did San react when you revealed your existence?"

Jerome cleared her throat. "That remains to be seen."

"Does that also remain to be seen with Drake?"

"Yes."

Elza's lips peeled apart in a snarl. "Then you must be posing as one of us. I expect a different answer the next time I ask that question."

When Jerome shot a look at him, Hess lifted one of the nine millimeters he had purchased free of a holster strapped below his armpit. "If Drake tries to pick things up where we left off last Iteration, I'm ready. He won't find me confused this time."

Jerome compressed her lips to a fine line. "They hurt you worse than I realized. Maybe they even deserve your hatred. But we serve the Creator."

"We are the Creator. You told me that."

"Hess, we are fragments of the Creator's consciousness. That makes us special as hell, but it doesn't mean we are equal to the One we serve. The needs of the Creator supersede all else."

Hess shoved his handgun home in its holster. "I never believed that. Not even when I thought I was the only Observer out there. Bringing a world into existence carries moral obligations. Creating worlds of brutality for our entertainment is wrong."

"Enough with the lectures already," Jerome said. "I will never accept that your morality applies to the Creator."

The next morning, when they met up for another session of needle work, Jerome informed them that she had revealed herself to San and Drake the previous evening over the phone and proved her identity as the twelfth Observer by revealing intimate details of their lives.

Hess endured a poke from visiting Deputies, then went with Elza to pick up a length of heavy steel pipe and finalize the lease on a dilapidated garage within the business district of the city. After, they separated with separate shopping lists. Explosives and blasting caps topped his list. On Elza's were all the various tools she would need to machine a length of pipe into the core of a nuclear device.

When they arrived back home in the afternoon, pulling in front of his house in their separate vehicles, a stout middle-aged woman met them in the driveway, dressed in a rumpled woman's suit and smoking a pungent cigar with such aplomb that she could only be one person.

Elza embraced San warmly the moment she exited her car. "I can't wait to hear what you've done since we last talked!"

"Please tell me you've gone male already," San said. "The Creator owes you some variety in your sex. And the rest of us would adore seeing Hess get familiar with a man."

Hess waved on his way to the house. "Always a pleasure, San."

Inside, Jerome stood with bony arms crossed and head tilted. "It seems I am not very popular among my own kind."

"We have no history with you," Hess said.

"Nor am I likely to have the time to develop one."

Hess glared out the window towards the reunion. "She voted already?"

"So far it's three to one in favor of annihilation."

After a moment, Hess nodded towards the kitchen. "Come help me hide the premium ingredients."

"If you are worried about the balsamic vinegar, you're too late. San emptied the entire bottle glazing odd items."

Hess grunted. "That bottle cost two hundred dollars. Knowing her, she wasted it on crackers and lemons."

"Canned tuna, mixed nuts, tea leaves, and chocolate chips. She reports it all tasted horrible."

"Just give me a hand with the wine," Hess said.

CHAPTER SEVENTEEN
Erik
Iteration 2

Beeta's family surrounded her all night. Mott spent the evening meal elaborating on his story of treating his fictional sister's madness. The village elders hung on every word. Before he retired to a pallet in the guest pavilion that night, Beeta's mother stopped by to beg for his help.

So it was that the villagers delivered a crazy woman into his care the next morning. Beeta sagged between her escorts, an expression of profound apathy on her face.

Mott schooled his features into the concerned smile he had practiced. "Hello, Beeta. My name is Mott. Did they tell you about me?"

Beeta's lips formed into an innocent pout. "Dead sister."

Her escorts froze in mortification until Mott's laughter rang out. "Dead sister indeed. You go right to the heart of things."

The crazy woman's cultivated detachment slipped enough that she openly studied him. "What do you want?"

Mott shrugged. "All sorts of things. Isn't that how it is with everyone? If we wanted only one thing, life would be boring."

"What do you want with me?"

"What do you think I want with you?"

Beeta looked away from him. "You think you can fix me."

"Is that what they told you?" Mott put enough amusement into his tone that Beeta's eyes came back to him. "That is what they wanted to hear and not what I told them."

"You're not trying to fix me?"

"Have you ever thought that maybe you aren't broken?"

She kicked over the chamber pot he had filled the previous night. "You don't know anything about me."

170

"Neither do the people of your village. They think you are broken, but so far I haven't seen anything to convince me of that. I see a woman with a strong spirit. You see, Beeta, the more tightly the rules bind us, the more we want our freedom. People say it is wrong to speak mean words. Wrong to think violent thoughts. Wrong to want unpopular things. But we have a choice, Beeta. We can believe the people and despise ourselves or we can reject everything they hold dear and take our freedom."

Mott stepped closer to Beeta and dropped his voice to a whisper. "You see, Beeta, when I told everyone that my sister had a touch of madness and I was able to speak sense to her, I may have reversed a few of the details."

He glanced to her concerned escorts and spoke loud enough to be heard by all. "Do you think that your troubles come from your own mind, Beeta? Or is there a chance that other people provoke the anger from you? What do you think?"

She furrowed her brow in thought. "I don't know. Sometimes my thoughts run fast and I know I am right no matter what anyone says. But other times I believe everything they say of me and I only want for the pain to go away."

"Yesterday you were sad."

"Yes."

"And what of today?"

"I don't know. I'm just tired. So tired."

Mott nodded to her escorts. "Too tired to escape?"

Beeta recoiled. "I can't do that!"

"Why not?"

"My mother would worry!"

"Just for a day, until you came back."

She shook her head. "I can't hurt her any more."

"Whose rule is that? Yours? Or theirs?"

A pause. Then a smile. "You're worse than me."

"Why do you say that?"

"You ran away, didn't you? So your sister couldn't make you behave anymore. Now you're free and you can do anything you want."

"I don't want your guards to know my story. So if you want to hear the truth about me, then we have to escape."

The corners of Beeta's lips twitched. "Promise me you will tell me the full truth of any question I ask you."

"The full truth?"

"You have to promise if you want me to come with you."

"Very well, Beeta. I promise to tell you the full truth."

"On three, then." Her eyes sparkled. "One." And then she was running, leaving him waiting for additional numbers that weren't coming.

Mott followed after a moment, barely ahead of the two villagers on guard duty.

Beeta never looked back, running straight for the edge of the village. Mott lagged behind, then spun when the first of the two escorts, a man, passed by. Mott locked his arms around the man's neck and used every iota of torque his legs, torso, and arms could generate to cause a delicious popping noise, followed by the collapse of a warm corpse.

Before the second guard, the woman, could decide how to react to the violence, Mott punched her in the throat hard enough to hurt his knuckles. As she stumbled back, her mouth open to release a scream that could not escape her crushed windpipe, Mott swept her legs out from under her.

The woman landed on her back and Mott knelt down to firmly grasp one of her ears. He pulled hard, fast, and it came free to hang by a thread of skin, the wound oddly bloodless at the instant of its appearance. The woman's eyes bulged, but still no sound escaped her. Mott shoved the severed ear into her open mouth, then resumed chasing his crazy woman.

CHAPTER EIGHTEEN
Hess
Iteration 145

He watched San dunk tater tots into maple syrup and place them on top of a thick layer of corned beef sandwiched between slices of french toast. "It works, in a weird way. But you have to use grade A syrup. None of the cheap stuff." She smirked at Hess as she spoke.

Hess turned away from the spectacle to face Jerome. "Looks like the two of us need to pursue an alternate dinner. Again."

Jerome nodded. "I'm not eating that."

"Jeeze, Jay, why you hating on my San-wich? This will be as big as the pretzel burger." San winked. "Besides, what you gonna eat? Pantry's bare as an Observer's womb, ya know?"

Hess dredged up the best smile he could manage. "We'll stop somewhere on our way to the shop."

"What's happening at the shop? You two shacking up?"

"We're guarding the device," Hess said.

Jerome folded her arms. "And being less suspicious. Two white women spending nights in this neighborhood will not go unnoticed."

"Well," San said, "if any midnight action happens, I want in on it."

Elza's voice boomed from the other room. "Wait fifteen minutes and we'll go with you."

"Elz, hon, you going to try my culinary delight?"

"Sure, San, bring me in a sample."

Hess jerked his thumb to the door. "Come on, Jerome. We'll leave now and get lamb wraps from a shop downtown. The ladies will beat us to the shop anyway."

"You know, I'm one of the ladies," Jerome said.

"Not if you want a lamb wrap."

They didn't speak again until Hess parked his car beside Elza's, outside the garage they had leased for the purpose of constructing their doomsday weapon. "Why does Elza like San?"

Jerome blinked at the question. "I don't have the slightest clue."

"Your executive summary left that out?"

"The mental stuff isn't covered. My only insights into your emotions and motivations are the result of assumptions."

Hess grunted. "That so? Well, assume something for me."

"Maybe because they are so different from each other? Elza is hyper rational and San is whimsical. Their interactions might provide some kind of balance to them."

"Opposites attracting? By that logic, Erik and I should be best buds."

Jerome raised an eyebrow. "While I don't think I can categorize whatever is between you and Erik as friendship, it is most definitely significant. Besides you, Erik never sustained much interest in the other Observers."

"He felt a special bond because me and Elza were the first he encountered," Hess said. "When you met him, he was busy punishing me. But he would have done just as bad to Elza."

"No," Jerome said. "Erik only spoke of Elza in connection with you. He wanted to use her to hurt you. Why do you think he talked Kerzon into posing as Elza? She was supposed to make you think Elza hated you. Erik wanted you all to himself, Hess."

"And he's out there looking for me," Hess said.

"Another reason to wipe our memories."

Instead of answering, Hess got out of the car. Jerome caught up to him and interjected her emaciated form between him and the entryway. "What happened last Iteration after I left? My cheat sheet only says you remained behind for a time."

Hess shook his head. "Nothing important."

"A nuclear war happened. I figured that much out," Jerome said.

"The people ruined their world. Business as usual."

Jerome squinted up at him. "What about you and Elza? The two of you seemed fine when I last saw you."

"I understand that you feel a special connection with all of us because you know so many of our secrets. But when we look at you, we see a stranger. I'm not going to confide in you, Jerome. Not now, not ever."

Drake arrived the next morning, wearing the body of a tall, skinny white man with an acne problem. He met Hess and Jerome at a grimy food court nestled between run-down office buildings and the campus of a fragrant distillery.

Jerome waited at a table wearing a tacky floral-themed hat so he could identify her. Drake noticed her the moment he entered, froze in the doorway until someone shoved him from behind, then moved off to the side. He scanned the room while chewing his cheek. Finally, Drake approached the table.

"You Jerome?"

She nodded. "Hello, Drake. It's a pleasure to meet you."

"Prove you are who you claim."

"I thought we did that online."

"Humor me," he said.

"During Iteration five, you tortured a man out of curiosity after meeting Erik. During Iteration seventeen, you became addicted to coca leaves. During Iteration one hundred and thirty four, you owned a brothel." Jerome leaned forward. "Those facts, combined with our previous conversations, should be more than enough to convince you. If not, you are free to leave after casting your vote."

Drake laughed, a harsh throaty grumble. "Really? You have to ask that with all you know about me? What you think I'll vote?"

"The Creator wants you to make your own decision, Drake."

Hess shifted slightly in his position at a nearby booth and Drake jumped. "Who is that?" He patted at his pockets, hastily seeking something. Hess shook his head slowly and Drake froze.

"That would be Hess," Jerome said.

"Oh, shit," Drake said. "Is he still sore about before? You said he was cool about me coming here."

Jerome cleared her throat. "Don't do anything to escalate the situation. Hess only wants to see for himself that you are not a threat."

Drake squeezed his eyes shut. "Look, Jerome, I'm two seconds from getting caught by this crazy Church. You got to make Hess help me. I know he and Elza figured out some way to outsmart the people. They'll probably wind up getting rich or taking over a continent or something. I don't care what they get up to. Just get them on my side."

Hess joined their table, sitting with his left arm draped over the back of his chair so that the upper half of his half-zipped jacket flared open enough that he could dart a hand in to retrieve his sidearm if necessary. He stared at Drake, barely blinking. His voice rumbled from his chest when he spoke. "If you ever try to hurt us again, I will do things to you that would shock Erik."

"It wasn't my idea. I was going along with the others. Both times. Ingrid and Griff and Erik and Kerzon are the ones you need to worry about."

"Shut up."

Drake's mouth snapped shut.

"I'm not interested in being friends again, if that word ever even applied to us. You need help because you can't handle this world. I can give you that help, but there's a condition. We are extracting Ingrid from the Church headquarters. You can help us or you can walk now."

"After casting your vote," Jerome added.

"You forgive Ingrid but not me? That ain't fair, man."

Hess slammed his fist on the table, causing both Jerome and Drake to jump. He took a calming breath before letting himself speak. "Ingrid is not forgiven. None of you are. This is about doing the right thing. Maybe I'm the only one who cares about right and wrong anymore. Maybe I'm the only one who ever did."

Jerome's hand patted his arm awkwardly. "I care. That's why I kept an eye on you last Iteration. I moved to live in the same community as you after millennia of avoiding every other Observer because the internet was full of secret codes from Elza and you never responded. When you starred on the national news and the others started to stir, I posed as Ingrid to sabotage their hunt. I helped you escape. When against all sense you came back, I opened the sky for you.

"I know you aren't fond of me, Hess, but I have never been anything other than your friend. When I knew you needed help, I was there for you. I would have done that for any of the Observers. That's why I invited Drake into your life – because now he needs help. And I am going to join you in attacking what is essentially a military base because Ingrid needs help."

"You're also trying to end me and the woman I love."

"Hess," Jerome sighed. "Look at the other Observers. Ingrid lived in misery long before the Church of Opposition existed. And Mel? No one can deny that death would be a mercy for Mel. Honestly, Hess, I think you're the only one who really wants to live. The others deserve a rest. Eternity is too much for them. Everything that is made must one day be unmade."

Hess had never moved his eyes from Drake. "Do you agree to my condition? Or are you leaving?"

"I'll help out with your rescue mission. Just don't get me caught."

On the ride back to the warehouse, Drake voted to die. Hess did his best not to dwell on the numbers. Four to one so far, with Mel's vote guaranteed to go the wrong way. Two more votes would constitute a majority in favor of annihilation. Did Ingrid really want to die? What about Mariana? Who knew what Erik would vote.

Still preoccupied with his thoughts, Hess hardly noticed Elza stride up to Drake and break his jaw with a savage swing of a wrench. By the time he realized what had happened, Elza had returned to work as if breaking someone's jaw was nothing out of the ordinary.

Within five minutes, Drake's mild paranoia was the only remnant of the altercation. Jerome began infusing blood into their newest member while Hess went to speak with his woman.

"What was the deal with the wrench?"

"It was the heaviest tool on my workbench at the time." Elza barely glanced up as she positioned lumps of metal inside of an aquarium.

"Ah," he said. "I guess that makes sense. Though I'm not sure why you hit him at all."

"The last time I saw him, he shot me."

Hess prodded her ribs with a finger. "Then you should have poked him with something pointy like a screwdriver or a jackhammer."

An almost-smile graced her lips. "There's never a jackhammer on my workbench when I need one."

"My fault," Hess said. "I borrowed it to teach San a lesson after she used a five hundred dollar bottle of wine to cook my favorite leather jacket."

Elza spun to face him. "You're joking."

"Unfortunately. We don't actually *have* a jackhammer, you know."

"Did she try to cook leather?"

Hess shrugged. "Not that I know of. But who can say for sure what insanity she has or hasn't done on her own time?" He pointed at the fish tank. "Are you planning to get pets? If you remember, the last time we owned fish they didn't live very long."

"Nothing is going to live for long in this tank," she said. "I'm afraid most of the uranium we've received so far is depleted. The people of this world have been using it for armor plating for over a century. That's long enough to make a sample useless for our purposes."

Hess stepped closer to her. "So plan B is killing fish? The Church will never suspect it."

Elza leaned into him the slightest bit. "Plan B is improvising. I'm lining the inside of the pipe with Tungsten Carbide like before, but now I am going to add a layer of Beryllium around the central uranium mass."

"I was just about to suggest that."

"I'm sure you were," she said. "The uranium will be surrounded by neutron reflectors and interleaved with layers of graphene to serve as neutron moderators. I'm also using more uranium than I planned."

"The fish will never see it coming."

Elza pecked a quick kiss on his cheek. "I submerged my samples to start a minor reaction. I'm going to time how fast the temperature rises and use that as a rough gauge of radioactivity.

"We don't have enough time to properly enrich our uranium. I don't even have time to design an implosion device. So my grand idea is to build a gun type bomb with the uranium mass split into three sub-critical masses. It will be a minor miracle if the thing doesn't go off early and a major miracle if the explosion rates in the kiloton range."

"How much time do you have?"

"None right now." Elza pulled away from him. "Maybe tonight."

"I miss you. I miss *us*."

"Tonight. If you promise not to talk about things."

"Sure. Why not?" Hess grimaced. "We always manage to not talk about important things."

CHAPTER NINETEEN
Erik
Iteration 145

After a week spent suspended in the air by his feet, Erik was finally back on the ground. Unfortunately, the room temperature had been set uncomfortably low. Cold made the torture less painful, so they might switch things up soon. But then again, the cold made him miserable and too weary to fight back against people who were increasingly uncomfortable being in the same room as him.

Simone didn't seem to mind the temperature when she arrived. No doubt her burly form was well suited to arctic environments. "Don't judge me, it's cold." His voice trembled from the constant shivering.

When she squinted at him in confusion, Erik sighed. "Dick joke."

"I can never understand your fascination with crudity."

"Just stupid rules," he shivered. "Who the fuck decides one word is good and one word is bad? You people make those rules. I'm above them."

She began to pace. "They are moving you to a new facility tonight. Church members will be able to make a pilgrimage to the site and torture you for their grievances. My request to continue our interviews after the move has been denied. I was told that any further visits with you would require me to pay a tribute to strike you for fifteen minutes."

Erik forced a smile. "What, you'll only visit me when it's free?"

"They are monetizing you. Whoring out the Church! Our whole religion is built on dignity and we are selling out." Simone knocked a tray free of a table, sending scalpels, pliers, belts, scissors, razors, hammer and nails, and a curling iron scattering across the floor. "Is this the Creator's plan? To undermine everything we believe by sending two Agents as sacrifices?"

Erik stared as the normally staid woman marched back and forth, hands shaking in rage. "Is that the Creator's plan? Tell me, Erik. Tell me the truth."

"The truth is the Creator doesn't care. Worship. Opposition. None of that matters. The only purpose that there has ever been is replacing nothing with something. You pathetic creatures don't have a fucking clue how honored you are just to exist."

Simone shook her head. "They're whoring out the Church. Like there isn't enough money in the coffers already. Sessions with the two of you are booked out three months in advance already. People can't wait to punish you for all the wrongs in their lives."

Erik cackled. "What do you think Deispite is?"

"I'm not sure anymore." She lowered her voice. "I am starting to wonder if blaming an external force is counter productive."

"It's a coping mechanism," Erik said through his shivers. "You direct your self hatred outward onto another target."

"We don't hate ourselves."

"Been around hundreds of thousands of years. Everybody I ever worked on asked to die. They ask to die. Then I ask my question. Then they die. I don't prompt them. Never even let them know death is an option. They have to ask. Has to be their own idea."

Simone stared at him. "Maybe you're right about us wanting our own deaths. Maybe. But if so, there's another part to us. A part that wants to live. Just because you only see one side of the coin doesn't mean it doesn't have another."

"Instincts tell you to live. Instincts put there by the Creator. You people decide between those instincts and embracing death. And you choose wrong. Every. Fucking. Time."

"We don't have time to argue about it."

"So sad."

"What was the question?"

"You mean *my* question? The one I ask my victims?" Erik smiled. "Only one way to hear that question, chica. If things work our for me, I'll be sure to let you know what it is."

After a minute of silence, Simone moved closer to him than she had ever before come. She spoke just above a whisper. "Could you deliver a message to the Creator for me?"

Erik cocked his head to the side. "You got me intrigued."

"Is it possible?"

"I couldn't withhold something from the Creator even if I wanted."

"Will the Creator know what I ask immediately?"

"I make my report after a world ends."

Simone sighed. "My message is for the Creator only. I want you to treat it as confidential. Agreed?"

"You got me dying of curiosity, cupcake."

"I need your assurance."

"Scout's honor."

She hesitated a moment, then looked him directly in the eye. "By the time you receive my message, it will be too late for my world. Create again."

Simone got to her feet. "Good luck, Erik."

"That was blasphemy," he whispered.

Her eyes narrowed. "You agreed to my terms."

"So I did."

She left the room and Erik smiled. If he managed to escape in time, he was going to look that woman up. And Simone *would* answer his question.

CHAPTER TWENTY
Hess
Iteration 145

Two events accelerated their preparations.

The first event was a Church announcement that not only would citizens be able to purchase fifteen minute sessions to punish an Agent for whatever they cared to blame on the Demiurge, but that there were in fact two captive Agents available for punishment. Hess and Elza joined Jerome, San, and Drake in front of a portable television set to study the footage.

The second Agent, a wiry white man, screamed as he writhed in pain. The video reel consisted of many segments spliced together like the trailer to a perverse movie. All five Observers stared at the screen, frowning with near identical expressions.

San gestured dramatically at the television. "Pure propaganda piece."

"No," Elza said. "They showed a single, uncut torture session to great effect when they unveiled Ingrid. This doesn't let the audience see spontaneous healing." She nodded with business-like finality. "They don't have a second Observer. This is a grand bluff."

Jerome put a finger on the screen, drawing their eyes to the face of one of the punishers. Subtle twitches riddled his otherwise stony features and his gaze moved too rapidly, morphing into a flinch whenever the body before him bucked against its restraints. "They're terrified," she said.

And they were. Once Hess turned his attention from the victim to the perpetrators, their nerves became obvious. He shuffled through his memory, trying to recall the bindings used on this Observer. Ingrid had been hardly restrained compared to the comprehensive job done to this one.

"Whoever it is has escaped before," Hess said, pointing to ankle strap, belt strap, arm strap, wrist strap, and neck strap. "He has obviously been a tough case for them."

His thoughts went to the six Observers still unaccounted for in this world. Mariana didn't possess sufficient ferocity to instill fear in a field mouse. Griff tended to defer to authority of any form. As well as Mel fought with condescension and witty words, he lacked whatever capacity made one a man of action. Greg didn't do well with anything physical. That only left two possibilities.

"Kerzon?"

For a moment, silence. Then a sigh from Elza. "Kerzon can be a magnificent bully, but only one of us could turn the psychological table like that."

Jerome turned her skull-like face on him. "Will you rescue *him*?"

"Can I bury him alive after he votes?"

"I would only dig him back up," Jerome said.

"You know," Hess said, "I'm not a fan of your morals."

San snickered suddenly and violently, making a sound like a stalling engine. "Sucks to be on the getting end of it, don't it, Hess?"

"In case you forgot, I spent centuries on the wrong end of moral outrage," Hess snapped.

San met his words with a smirk. "It's almost enough to make you question your fairy tale version of right and wrong, isn't it?"

"Stop it," Elza snapped.

"Did I find the line?"

"That's the line, San. Stop antagonizing Hess or get out of my life."

San folded her arms. "Fine. I'll take it easy on your *man*. Honestly, how did the Creator decide which of you two to make which sex?"

Elza's back straightened. Hess laid a hand on her shoulder. "Don't," he said. "I know you value San's friendship – though I doubt even the Creator understands the reason why."

His woman glanced back at him. "You're going to risk getting caught *again* so you can save the person you hate most. No one is allowed to ridicule you for your values. Especially not a woman who has none."

They shared a look for a moment before they returned their attention to San, whose expression had gone empty. She shrugged. "Sorry to set you off, Elza. I won't discuss ethics again."

Hess pinched the bridge of his nose. "We're going to bring Erik out of there. Because that's the right thing to do."

They began planning in earnest after that. Hess had been purchasing small arms and ammunition on the black market for months. He had constructed compartments in the gas tank and muffler of his car, stored several of the weapons, then aged the fresh welds with liberal applications of salt water.

Retrieving those weapons would require a bit of brute force, but until then his vehicle would pass any inspection conceived by security forces. Hess had never encountered a guard who was willing to disassemble the components of a luxury car in the name of thoroughness. Vehicle inspections tended to follow a remarkably standardized script, derived from universally practical considerations.

Typically, the occupants were removed from the vehicle for the duration of the search. While they were kept under surveillance, someone would perform an undercarriage inspection using a mirror on the end of a pole, looking for conspicuous evidence such as mysterious containers bolted or taped in place. Another person would investigate the contents of the cab. Often a third individual would search the engine compartment and the trunk. Given the right – or wrong – set of circumstances, someone *might* go so far as to dump suitcases, slice open upholstery, or take apart the air filter.

That cache of weapons was part of escape plan A. His car would await them in a parking lot located in the section of the Church headquarters closest to the new Interrogation Complex while being outside of the high security zone. They would enter the complex on all terrain vehicles with guns blazing in the immediate aftermath of their nuke's explosion. After retrieving Ingrid and Erik, they would intermix with people running to safety until they reached the car. If they could not reach the car, then they would leave Church property on foot and use motorcycles kept in a storage rental unit to escape the city.

Hess had constructed a number of improvised explosive devices using pipes, gun powder, buckshot, and circuitry from remote controlled toy cars. He also had copious amounts of chlorine gas made from reacting bleach and hydrochloric acid – the production of which twice resulted in painful accidents, one of which proved fatal to him while the other had him wheezing and coughing blood for a time.

The annoying gas leaks happened at every step of the process. When he mixed bleach and acid together in batches inside a glass jug from a water cooler, poisonous vapor would leak before he managed to fit his rigged valve into place to channel the gas into the immense natural gas tank he had prepared for that purpose. When he loaded the chlorine gas from the immense vessel into refrigerant tanks pumped to be functional vacuums, more gas slipped free to cause mischief. And any time he moved the collection of tanks from one place to another, the jostling caused the emission of painfully peppery scents.

Drake, due to boredom or a desire to be helpful or some base need, synthesized a significant quantity of methamphetamine. He tested a sample from each batch of his product, further calling his motives into question. Fortunately, the same space constraints that prevented Hess from making large batches of chlorine gas also prevented Drake from destroying their garage whenever his chemistry equipment eventually exploded. After that incident, Elza threatened Drake with the wrench until he promised to cease all chemistry.

Jerome and San contributed to the group's activities by keeping them supplied with blood for transfusions and performing most of the cooking. The meals provided by Jerome were plain fare such as beans and rice while San created a mix of eclectic masterpieces and inedible experiments. The other Observers raved about her chocolate and tea chicken planks for days, only for San to announce that not only would she never make it again, but she intended to guard the secret of its recipe for the rest of her life.

Throughout everything, Elza worked tirelessly. She melted and recast uranium in molds; created three-dimensional scaffolds of neutron moderators; constructed a mechanism to explosively fire a sub-critical ring from each end of the pipe to thread a sub-critical spike in the center, where a ring of tungsten carbide and beryllium would encircle the combined mass.

Per Elza's explanation of her construction, the wedges of uranium would generate neutrons through radioactive decay. The graphene matrix would bring the ejected neutrons down to speeds where they were more likely to react with the nuclei of other uranium atoms to continue a chain reaction. The ring of neutron reflectors would reflect a portion of the escaping neutrons back to ground zero to renew their efforts. And when the three sub-critical masses met one another, the rate of chain reactions would rapidly accelerate in fractions of a second until their homemade doomsday weapon blossomed into a mushroom cloud laden with radioactive fallout.

Meanwhile, Hess spent time training the others. He covered handgun and rifle marksmanship, deploying tanks of chlorine gas, setting off an IED, urban assault tactics, and gas mask usage. He forced them through drills wearing the masks, accustoming them to the extra effort required for each breath so they wouldn't panic when breathing became hard during their operation and rip off their mask to take a breath of poisonous green gas.

They packed army rucksacks with pipe bombs, bound tanks of chlorine gas to the ATV's with bungee straps, and prepared speed loaders to fill clips with rounds of ammunition at the last minute (because, as Hess stressed to the others, keeping the springs of a clip under constant pressure by storing them loaded was begging for a misfire).

Maps of the Church campus were long since memorized. The idea of using their prodigious stores of methamphetamine as part of their assault had long been ridiculed out of consideration. All that remained was for Elza to complete construction of their opening salvo, which would simultaneously shock and awe the enemy and cut all electronic communications in the region of operations.

Elza finished her work only five months after she began. They celebrated the completion of their weapon of mass destruction in the shop with an elaborate dinner and copious amounts of a Zinfandel chosen by San which tasted like turpentine on first encounter, but transformed into a beautiful, fiery taste sensation under the numbing influence of alcohol. At a later point in their evening of revelry, they christened their nuke, giving it the name *Demiurge's Dick* after a spirited debate.

"Opposition's bout to get slapped with *Demiurge's Dick*," Drake shouted, grabbing his crotch with one hand and throwing the other into the air. He gyrated his hips suggestively.

Jerome giggled until she fell off her seat, for what was at least the fifth time that evening. Drake tried to help her up but landed on the floor with her instead. San slouched forward to pass out on the table. Elza pouted, upset that the name she had put forth, *Triumph of Reason*, had not won.

She stage whispered to Hess "You'd think the woman who built the damn thing would get to name it."

When Hess attempted to play the part of the knight errant by spray-painting Elza's chosen moniker on the device's casing, he sprayed himself in the face with yellow paint and declared himself jailed on the charge of painting under the influence.

The next morning, Hess awoke to Elza's frantic curses. He staggered to his feet and ran for the nearest gun. Armed, Hess stumbled about, finger hovering beside the safety as he squinted in every direction.

"Put the gun away," Elza snapped. "We have an emergency situation here. *Demiurge's Dick* is on the verge of exploding prematurely."

Hess lowered his pistol. "I thought you didn't care for that name."

"That was before it pissed me off." Elza read the dial of her Geiger counter again. "We can take it apart or we can set it off. Either way, we need to get started right now."

Hess looked to the gun in his hand. "Then our plan is in motion. Tell the others they have five minutes to get stone cold sober."

"Hess, I don't want to see you do that."

His finger slipped the safety. Hess nestled the cold barrel into the tissue of his jaw. "It won't last."

"Doesn't matter," she said.

He pulled the trigger.

Once Hess woke up, life restored and hangover free, he put a bullet through the brains of Jerome and Drake, who hadn't followed his instructions to sober up by resurrection. Elza flew around the garage, moving equipment so they could move the mass of steel named *Demiurge's Dick* into the SUV without incident. As she passed him, she managed a glare. "All I ask is a little discretion when you do that. I don't want to see you die."

"You just want me to cease existing," he said.

Elza spun away. "We agreed not to speak about this."

"I just find it a little inconsistent that you don't want to see me take a nap for five minutes when you voted to erase us from existence." Hess rapped his knuckles on a work bench. "We lived lifetimes together, Elza. Thousands of lifetimes. The entire time I thought the two of us were happy. I looked forward to eternity together."

"My vote wasn't about you," Elza said, back still to him. "The monotony of existence hurts, Hess. It's a physical pain. You've been like a drug. You take away the worst of it and fill me with happy feelings. But in the final sum, I don't know when the Creator will give us another chance to quit. I had to take the opportunity when it was offered."

"How can this not be about me? About us? We have hardly been apart save for the odd century. Rejecting your life is rejecting us."

"No," Elza said. "This is about opening your eyes in the morning and wishing you still slept. About facing the dawn of a new world and wishing the Creator hadn't bothered. You know what I'm feeling. When you were Zack Vernon . . . ."

"Zack was not me!"

"Really?" Elza turned back to face him. "Why wouldn't *Zack* let me bury Kerzon alive? Why did *Zack* marry a woman out of pity? Why would *Zack* donate a fortune to an orphanage? Why did *Zack* try to trade his life for Lacey's? I see one hell of a resemblance, no matter what you say."

"Zack remembered nothing. The moment I came back to myself, I wanted to live as much as ever."

"For a time, you were Zack Vernon. You wanted to die so bad you manipulated a man into putting a piece of lead through your brain. That was with five years of memories. Try to imagine feeling that way with a hundred thousand plus years of monotonous existence under your belt."

San cleared her throat loudly. "Hey, awkward conversationalists, you've got an audience. Besides, I thought we were at DEFCON one, charging into battle with swords drawn and all that. The domestic drama can wait until after we take care of business."

Elza fixed Hess with a steady gaze. "We can discuss this later."

"As soon as I get back," he said.

"Just put a pin in it until then." And Elza was off, bouncing around the garage as if their conversation hadn't happened.

San stood shoulder to shoulder with him and dipped her head in his direction. "Look, hon, we both know relationships aren't my thing, but it's obvious even to me that you need to forget about the voting disagreement of Iteration one four five. The decision isn't going to go the way you want.

Sucks, I know. I'd be pissed if I wasn't getting my way. But try to be practical about things for a minute. We're getting our memories wiped after this world ends. That's how things are playing out. Do you really want your last days to be like this? Why don't you just pretend things are okey dokey until the clock runs out? You'll be happier. Elza'll be happier. Everyone's a winner."

Hess glanced down at San. "I'm not ready to give up."

"I think you're unique in that regard."

When Jerome and Drake revived with imprecations on their lips, Hess jumped into the role of leader, deflecting their complaints and directing their energies into loading *Demiurge's Dick* into the waiting SUV and attaching the two trailers, each loaded with two ATV's, to pickup trucks.

Hess checked every piece of equipment was in place and informed his team that because they didn't have time to drop off the getaway car, they would need to use escape plan B – use the motorcycles stashed outside of Church property. While conducting a last minute pep talk, Elza broke into their circle to interrupt him.

"Change of plans," she announced. "Moving *Demiurge's Dick* got it dangerously excited. Which is much worse than it sounds, though probably not in the way any of you expect."

San cocked her head the way she did before a punchline. "Patronize much?"

"Our nuke is going to go off prematurely."

"Should've called it by it's name that time," San said.

Elza pointed over her shoulder with a thumb. "If one of the sub-critical masses goes early, we're not talking megatons of explosive power. We're talking run-of-the-mill car bomb. That's one disturbing aspect of the problem. The other is that even if I get the weapon into position without a criticality accident, the firing of the explosive charges will likely cause a premature reaction. I can still try to set it off, but you cannot rely upon this weapon. You need to change your plans."

San leaned close to Jerome and whispered loud enough for everyone to hear, "She missed like ten perfect opportunities to deploy the ridiculously childish name right there."

"This is operation time," Hess said. "We're not telling jokes anymore. Everything is life and death starting now. All of you signed up for this, so it's time to make good on your commitments.

"We are going in now. Elza will take the nuke to its position as planned. Then she will set about creating an alternate diversion." Hess pointed at Drake. "Get your meth."

Elza frowned. "What do you expect me to do with it?"

"Taint the city water or something. Stir up trouble."

"Even if we had enough to contaminate an entire city's water supply, it would take too long to help us."

Hess waved his hand. "You'll think up something."

"I always do, don't I?"

He circled a finger over his head and pointed to the waiting pickup trucks. "Mount up. We're going now."

CHAPTER TWENTY-ONE
Erik
Iteration 2

At his insistence, they slept out under the stars that night instead of seeking shelter at a nearby village. When Beeta made advances towards him in the night, Mott performed the duties of a lover with as much passion as he could manage. Apparently, it was enough.

"We are amazing together," she said.

"Better than normal people."

"So much better. I think we should keep walking forever. We can stop at a new village at sunset each day, eat a free dinner, then leave after breakfast. If everyone we meet calls us lazy, it still won't matter, because every day we meet new people. Every day we *are* new people. Don't you think that will be amazing?"

Mott smiled. "We can do anything we want. *Anything.*"

"That's right. We never have to work. Never have to hold our tongues. If we don't like someone, we can tell them their flaws."

"Or hit them," Mott said.

"We can slap them right in the face when we leave in the morning. They won't be able to do anything to us. We can break every rule."

"We could kill them."

Beeta smacked his knee. "Don't tease me. We are together now. We are going to be free together. You can't tease me."

"Of course not."

She snuggled close to him. "You promised to answer my questions."

"With the full truth," he added.

"Tell me about your sister."

"I never had a sister. That was just a story I made up so the people of your village would trust me."

"You tricked them!" Her tone was halfway between outrage and awe.

"Wasn't very hard."

Beeta squeezed him tight. "Tell me about your mother, then."

For a moment, he hesitated. "Never had a mother."

"Did she die giving birth?"

He reached for his walking stick, then pulled off the cap to reveal its point. "I was not born. I am not a creature of blood and bone like your people. Watch."

The half-moon provided just enough light to make out the widening of her eyes when he pushed the weapon's point into a readily accessible surface vein of his arm. Blood flowed freely. "Touch it," he commanded.

When she hesitated, Mott seized one of her hands and forced it into the flow of warm, dark liquid. She stared at the moisture on her hands, face unreadable.

"Watch it vanish." Soon enough, it did. One moment his blood covered her hand and dripped from his arm. The next moment it did not. There was no wound on his arm. Not even a scar. As if the injury had never existed.

Beeta touched his healed arm. "How is this?"

"I will tell you a great secret, Beeta, because we are companions now."

"Please tell me."

"Someone made this world. A magnificent being. The Creator sent me into the world to watch it. I never had a mother. When the world was made, I looked the same as I do today."

She frowned in thought. "But why?"

"You got to be a bit more specific, Beeta. Why what?"

"Why make a world?"

"Because It could. Because *something* beats an eternity of *nothing*. Because this world is amazing, even if the people bore me to tears."

"Did the Creator make the people, too?"

"If something exists, then the Creator made it."

"Even me?"

"Sure." Though considering the world was over a hundred years old, the Creator hadn't made Beeta directly. But the creatures of this world wouldn't care about such fine details. "Would you believe there was another world before this one? It was very different. People didn't have villages and rules. Instead there were tribes and power.

"I don't think I have much influence over the Creator, but I would love to see the two kinds of worlds mixed together. Tribes would raid villages. Villages would have to fight back. And I have no idea what would happen from there. But I'm sure it would be a lot of fun."

Beeta remained silent so long that he thought she slept when suddenly she spoke again. "But why make anything? I don't get it."

"Because creation is more glorious than the most pleasing song or the most beautiful weaving. You should be grateful. You would never have existed otherwise. Think about that. Would you rather not exist?"

She drew in an unsteady breath. "I tried to make myself die."

"Don't believe your own lies, Beeta. You like the attention. Every time you threatened to harm yourself, you got to be special. You got to have power. People let you stay in from work. I know the games you play and I know the reasons behind them. You want to live as much as anyone else."

"I don't."

"Really?" He held out his walking stick. "If you want to end your life so bad, then go ahead and do it. I won't stop you."

Beeta took the walking stick and held it to her arm. Then with a dramatic gesture, she drew the sharp point across her flesh.

"Doesn't look very deep. Are you sure you're serious about this?"

She breathed rapidly several times, then drove the walking stick down into her leg. Mott closed his mouth. Slowly, she pulled the point free of her thigh. There didn't appear to be any blood at first, but then a spurt shot free of the wound.

Mott watched several more pulses escape the wound. "Do you realize your wounds won't go away like mine did?"

"I know," she said. "And my family isn't around to stop me this time."

"That's right. They're not here to stop you. That wound will kill you if it's not treated soon."

Beeta remained still.

"You have to ask for my help."

Several minutes passed in silence.

"I'm not the fools of your village, Beeta. I won't let you manipulate me. If you want to live, you're going to have to ask me to help you."

"I just wish I didn't have to hurt my mother," she whispered. "Better if I was never born than to hurt her like this. Your Creator never should have made me."

"Do not insult the Creator."

There was no response.

"Beg for your life, Beeta."

When he felt at her neck, there was still a faint heartbeat, but the wound on her leg now bled at the barest trickle. Her eyes blinked and then focused on him.

"Why create a world like this?"

Mott stared at her still form until morning, then returned to the village. He found Beeta's mother and killed her in front of the elders with his bare hands. Then he killed the elders.

The men of the village managed to wrestle him to the ground and smash his head with rocks before he could do much more, but he returned to life long before they could put him beneath the ground. More died. They managed to kill him again. When he came back to life next, the people of the village were gone, their homes abandoned.

Cowards, all of them.

Mott burnt down the village, then took his belongings and walked into the wilderness. She had despised existence itself. That was an important observation. Essential, even. The Creator needed to know the ugly truth of the pathetic creatures.

CHAPTER TWENTY-TWO
Hess
Iteration 145

Hess drove the lead truck with Jerome riding shotgun. Visible in the rear-view mirror was the truck carrying San and Drake. They went to the western edge of the Church's property, which was primarily parks, gardens, and playgrounds separated from the surrounding city by nothing more imposing than guard rails.

They parked the trucks in a side alley, strapped rucksacks firmly to themselves, pushed the quads to the edge of Church property, lifted them one at a time over the guard rail, then started the engines and drove off through the wooded nature reserve.

For thirty minutes, Hess led his crew on an off road adventure, navigating around thickets, through creeks, and past a dozen other obstacles until they arrived at the chain-link fence that separated the main campus of the Church from its park.

There, Hess had them cut their engines and went forward alone to cut an ATV-sized hole in the fence with a pair of bolt cutters. Then they waited for Elza's call, using the tree line as cover.

Drake spent the time muttering to himself. San practiced drawing her handgun. Jerome peered in every direction with her large eyes. Hess sat cross-legged on the ground, phone held in his lap.

It took half an hour for the phone to ring.

"The nuke is set," Elza said in greeting. "Speed dial one on your phone to detonate it. There is no way to predict how much of a bang we will get from it, so try not to rely on it too much. As far as distracting the authorities is concerned, I'm having mixed results.

"I have been vaporizing meth in the open air market. A few fights have broken out and at least one couple is having intercourse in public. Nothing that warrants serious attention from emergency responders. Fortunately, I managed to convince a few people that agents are lurking in the market."

Hess clenched his jaw. "You convinced the people *how*?"

"I severed my arm and threw it into a crowd of people," Elza said.

"So now you're running from a mob?"

"Hiding. And most of the mob is stoned."

"Elza . . . ."

"It was the best I could do under the circumstances. I brought an acetylene tank from our garage, so I will be able to burn down the warehouse I'm in if they find me. I'll be fine. You have to focus on your main objective for now."

"We'll discuss this back at the garage," Hess said.

"Back at the garage," Elza echoed, an odd catch to her voice.

"Tell me the truth. Do I need to scrub this mission to come after you?"

"No," Elza said. "I may be improvising, but things are under control."

Hess released his breath. "Good. See you soon."

"Goodbye." Elza hung up.

San cleared her throat. "Are we good to go?"

"It's on," Hess said, looking at the three Observers with him. "Do not open fire before I do. Riding ATV's on the secure part of the Church's campus is trespassing and rates sending a few patrols after us. The second we start shooting, orders will go out to lock everything down and outside reinforcements will be brought in to help neutralize us.

"When bullets start flying, keep your heads down. We don't have time to die and resurrect. Time is everything in this operation. If you have to run through covering fire, cover your head with your arms and sprint. Don't stop if you take hits. And when they start nailing us with cover fire, that's when we toss our bombs."

Every eye widened at his speech. Apparently, this was the moment his audience realized on a visceral level that they were going to war. Hess smiled. "If you start to panic, I want you to remember one thing. *This* is what I do best."

While the others were still mounting up on their ATV's, Hess rode down the hill and through the hole he had cut, then coasted towards the path he knew from maps, studying terrain he had committed to memory. The others were not an ideal team for this mission. Drake lived in constant fear. San lacked a functional sense of self-preservation. Jerome inhabited an emaciated form ill suited to conflict.

If he could have traded any of the three for Elza, he would have. But Elza was the only one he could trust to do her part unsupervised. Indeed, she would handle her particular task better than he could have.

He glanced over his shoulder to verify there were three ATV's tailing him, then shifted gears with a tap of his foot and twisted the throttle. They sailed past barracks housing and administrative buildings, drawing curious stares from the few Church employees outside at mid-morning.

Stares are fine, Hess thought. *Scowls are the dangerous reaction.*

Due to a combination of training and self-selection bias, soldiers as a group were more likely to report suspicious activity. However, most of the individuals they passed were off duty and busy with their own activities. And there was no such thing as an anonymous tip in the Church. If you called in a report, there *would* be paperwork. Hopefully inconvenience outweighed concern in the minds of their witnesses.

Hess led his group past an armory and glided to a stop beside the row of concrete jersey barriers forming a barrier between the secure region of the Church campus and the ultra-secure sanctum where rogue Agents were held in a punishment complex. He dismounted and waved Drake forward. The two of them lifted the front end of each ATV and fed the machines over the makeshift wall, moving with swift motions.

"What am I doing?" Drake muttered to himself. "Stupid, stupid!"

Hess herded his group over the jersey barriers, saw them remounted, then paused. "We go fast now. Remember, I fire the first shot."

When he looked over his shoulder, Hess saw concerned faces peeking out of the armory. If they hadn't already been reported as intruders, they would be now. No one had reason to suspect they carried weapons, but soon they would demonstrate otherwise.

Hess drove at the compound full throttle, crossing the immaculately groomed yard and heading straight for the side door of the classically architected building. There were shouts in the distance as they skidded to a stop near the outer row of white colonnades.

He pulled free one of his pipe bombs, flipped on a switch that had once belonged to a remote controlled car, used a roll of duct tape to secure the device to the heavy metal door between the door handle and the deadbolt, then dashed back to hide behind a column. Hess dragged Jerome behind cover before powering on the remote control in his hand and turning the toy's steering wheel.

There was a thump from the explosion and a squeal of twisting metal. Dark smoke drifted past the columns. Hess tucked away the remote control and pulled his nine millimeter. The others were still standing in place when Hess kicked open the remnants of the shattered door. He ducked to the side and surveyed the hall inside for two seconds.

"Get the gas," Hess said.

"We got to get out of here," Drake said.

Hess pushed Drake towards his ATV. "I told you to get the gas. The door leads to a tight side corridor. It's a perfect choke point." When Drake still hesitated, Hess put his finger in Drake's face. "You can grab the gas cylinders or you can discover how I handle deserters. *Move.*"

While Drake moved to detach the cylinders from their ATV's, Hess stationed San inside the building, instructing her to assume a prone position with a rifle. He directed Jerome to guard the approach from behind the colonnades, telling her to lay down cover fire if she saw anyone.

Meanwhile, Hess stood ready with handgun cradled in the palms of both hands, holding it low to conserve his arm strength. Marching around with your hands held at shoulder level like a movie character clearing a building was a good way to fatigue your muscles. And even if the strain wasn't noticeable, it would impact accuracy. The key was to hold low, stay relaxed, and be ready to snap the weapon into position.

Before Drake finished with the final tank, a security team consisting of three men on a golf cart arrived. Hess stepped out of cover, aligned his sights on the driver, breathed out halfway, and gently squeezed the trigger until the weapon jumped in his hands. He slipped behind cover, noting that the driver was no longer inside his vehicle and that the golf cart had stopped moving.

Now, while they are still gathering their wits, he thought. Hess peeked around the column he was using as cover and shot the man leaning over his downed comrade. The final man returned covering fire until Hess put two bullets into the golf cart. As he'd hoped, the sound of metal plinking convinced the man to seek better cover.

Drake was pulling the final tank through the door, so Hess followed him inside with Jerome. "Masks on," Hess said. When everyone had complied, he twisted open the valve on one of the tanks.

"Do you think the guards will have masks?" San asked.

"Doesn't matter," Hess said. "Standard filters don't remove chlorine."

He handed the twelve gauge shotgun to Drake. He'd set a modified choke on it and loaded buckshot. Drake didn't have the marksmanship to merit using slugs, so the compromise was sacrificing some kill power for a more forgiving spread. "Shoot for the head," he said. "Everyone else aim for center mass."

Hess opened the valve on a second tank, then toppled it onto its side and rolled it down the hall before them. With hand signals, he sent Jerome and Drake to opposite walls and moved San to the rear of their formation.

They jogged down the hall, kicking the canister ahead of them. At every door, they stopped to check the handle. If the door opened, they cleared the room. If not, they moved on. The first three open doors led to unoccupied rooms. They left the cylinder of chlorine to vent at the first intersection they passed.

The fourth door opened on panicked office staff. Jerome and Drake handled them with a volley of wild gunfire. Obedient to their training, they checked each body to verify no one had survived before returning to the hall. Hess scowled at the goofy exultation on Drake's face, but refrained from saying anything more than a command to reload.

Twice they caught someone in the halls and gunned them down. Three more times they cleared an occupied room. Hess let Jerome and Drake handle the rooms. Those two needed a boost to their confidence and he didn't care to kill civilians himself.

At the end of the hall a staircase led down to an underground level. They approached cautiously and peered into the open chamber beneath them. Hess recognized a wall of people and started to duck back.

The crack of a volley of gunfire reached him just before the space around him erupted with ricochets and shrapnel. Hess touched a hand to a sting on his scalp and it came away moist. Beside him, Jerome lay in a puddle of blood, ominously still. Drake scrambled back on all fours, shotgun abandoned.

San seized his shoulder. "Behind us, Hess! They're coming down the hall behind us! What do we do?"

As the seconds ticked by, the wound on his scalp became harder to ignore. It burned with a fierce intensity and drizzled blood down his forehead to run into his eyes. Hess shook his head, trying to bring things back into focus.

"Hess, hon, we need you now. Right now," San shouted.

Drake's voice cracked. "Shit, San, his skull's showing! Man's useless!"

Hess shook his head again. It would clear in a few minutes. He didn't think he had a few minutes. "Gas cylinders," Hess said.

"Right," San said. "Drake, open those cylinders up and roll them back the hall."

Hess ripped his protective mask from his face to empty his stomach.

"Mask back on, Hess! We're opening the gas."

"No, wait," Hess said. He shook his head again. "Stop, San!"

"We have to do it now," she said.

"Cylinders down the steps. Bombs behind us." He paused to vomit once more. When he managed to gasp a messy breath, he continued. "Gas will stay down there and stop pursuit."

"Right. Good thinking, Hess. Now put on your mask."

Hess collapsed onto his side. For moments, there was nothing but the nauseating sense of vertigo. Then someone pressed a mask to his face, making it harder to breathe. Hess floated in a daze, barely aware of explosions happening nearby. Gunshots followed.

Coughing came from next to him. "Did I die?"

"Jerome! Get your gun! Cover fire now!"

"How long has Hess been down?"

"Too long! Start shooting!"

They need me to take charge, he thought. Hess pushed himself to a seated position. He touched his scalp, winced at the pain, and squinted at the scene around him. The stairs before him were blurry for some reason. *Gas. They gassed the room below us.* Further from the steps, his comrades fired wild suppressing fire back the hall.

Hess stumbled to his feet. "Down the steps," he said.

For a moment, it seemed he was going by himself. Then boots pounded beside him. Hess seized the railing with one hand and held his nine millimeter in his other. He raised the handgun when he left the steps, turned in a slow arc, trying to find an opponent to target, then lowered his hands.

There were plenty of people in the room, all of them contorted in agonized death poses. Several stairways led back to the upper floor, but every door leading deeper into the compound stood sealed. The hazy room had signs everywhere instructing people on where to register and where to sit for mandatory briefings and where to wait for a proctor to escort them.

Hess fought off a wave of nausea. This was not a good time to fill his mask with vomit. He looked from one steel door to another, trying to guess which one he should blow. *Have to pick one fast. Our masks can't stand up to this much chlorine gas for long.*

"Now what?" San asked.

Hess pointed at the door closest to the designated waiting area.

San grasped the significance of the gesture and ripped off her rucksack to pull free a pipe bomb and its remote control detonator. As she worked, Hess winced at the pain of his scalp. He reached a gore-covered hand towards his wound.

And the pain evaporated. Before his eyes, the blood on his hand vanished. Hess relished the relief a second before he registered the events around him. Jerome sat to one side with her back against the wall, handgun in her holster. Drake had his shotgun hanging from his shoulder on its sling and his arms were crossed. Meanwhile, San prepared to blast a hole through a door most likely separating them from armed and ready opposition.

Hess had time to get his nine millimeter up before him, but his shout to form up got lost in the roar of the explosion. As the door rocked back and collapsed off of its hinges, bullets whizzed at them. Hess fired several times, then jumped to the side.

He pulled a bomb from his ruck, activated it, and lobbed it through the open doorway. A twist of the remote control's steering wheel brought a rumble and then silence.

Not more than three feet from him, Drake's mangled corpse leaked red ichor. Jerome shook as she patted her body, searching for damage. San stood frozen.

"San, you drag Drake! Jerome, you watch our tail! I'm on point." Hess pulled out another pipe bomb. His second to last. Judging by what little he remembered of the mess at the top of the stairs, the others were probably out of explosives. They had squandered their resources while he was out of commission with a concussion.

He spotted movement around a corner and deployed his bomb. After that, they moved forward unopposed. Hess followed convenient markings painted on the wall, moving towards *Punishment Center 1*.

Two men waited inside the designated room, watching the invaders approach through the reinforced glass wall. Behind them, a bound form hung suspended from the ceiling by chains affixed to a leather body harness. The soldiers held their handguns with tense expectation, waiting for someone to try the door.

Hess met their eyes through the windows.

"Does anyone have another bomb?" San asked.

"Not necessary." Hess gestured for the girls to stay to one side of the door, then moved opposite them before twisting the door knob and giving a swift kick to open it.

One of the soldiers squeezed off a few rounds before realizing no one was coming inside. Following a quiet moment, a soldier shot at the glass beside Hess, startling him. He smiled and shook his head at the two men, then positioned himself so that he could fire into the room without opening himself up to them.

Hess shot at the concrete wall. Inside the room, both men jumped at the sound of the strike and its ricochet. His next shot hit the metal sink in the corner. One of the soldiers shot into the hall, trying to use the same technique. Hess laughed. "Do you really think that angle works in your favor? Besides, I don't care if you shoot me. Haven't you realized by now that you can't keep a good Agent down?"

When he fired his third shot into the room, the soldiers abandoned their place facing the door, rushing to stand across the reinforced glass wall from Hess. From a closer vantage, they looked shaken. *Of course they're worried. They've met Erik. For all they know, we're all as monstrous.*

"The Demiurge has something special planned for the Church of Opposition!" Hess smiled at them through the glass.

He gestured at San. "Get closer to the door and lay down covering fire. Keep them in the corner they've put themselves in."

As she squeezed off shots in three second intervals, Hess crossed back to where a revived Drake squatted. Hess took the shotgun. "Use handguns to support San," he said.

When Drake and Jerome started to fire into the room, Hess went to the floor, held the shotgun past the door frame, and fired. Both soldiers retreated further into the corner, one of them bleeding from an indirect hit.

Hess pumped another shell into the chamber, got to his knees, ducked beneath the cover fire, and shuffled sideways into the room, firing at the men and pumping the shotgun in rapid succession until he emptied his weapon.

He pulled his nine millimeter and put a final round through the head of each soldier before turning to the captive Observer. The man's eyes streamed tears as they fixated on Hess.

"Take me out of here, Hess. *Please.* By the Creator, have pity on me."

Hess put a hand to Ingrid's face. "I've got you."

CHAPTER TWENTY-THREE
Erik
Iteration 145

On numerous occasions, Erik had observed the frequency of his torture to be sub-optimal. Pain existed as an intersection of the biological and the psychological, a mental phenomenon that required an active mind. The Church's unending torment robbed him of the capacity to truly suffer. Their constant application of pain made everything a surreal experience.

Which wasn't to say it didn't hurt. Or that he wasn't desperate for even a momentary respite. Time and again, he screamed, he wept, he begged, he threatened, he gasped, thrashed, flinched. His life was a torment to him. He no longer had the energy to taunt his attackers. Precious little remained of his former fire.

And yet . . . . And yet, Erik could not help noting during scattered instants of lucidity that they could do so much better. With a perverse pride, he worked through the problem of how to maximize his own suffering. They should allow him time to rest between sessions so that he could better appreciate what they did. And vary the length of the sessions. Maybe wire up some machines to inflict pain at random intervals.

As it was, he had no idea how long he had been tortured at the new compound. Time had grown elastic for him. Individual moments stretched long, but whenever he looked back in his memory, events squeezed together into a blurry mess of questionable duration. It could have been weeks or years. At this point, the difference in scale seemed vague.

Then the torture stopped. Erik watched the guards rush his latest tormentor from the room, send away the line of paying customers, and seal the door. They exchanged concerned glances and listened intently to whatever they heard over their ear radios.

For a time, Erik waited for something to happen. Then he slept. Sleep was hard to find in an unending torture marathon.

When the door opened, Erik startled awake with the panicked certainty that his torture was about to resume. He knew that his tormentors had finally worked out the method he had outlined to maximize his pain. Knew with absolute certainty that they had let him sleep to intensify the next session.

The crack of gunshots brought him out of his paranoia. Erik squinted at the scene before him, watching invaders fire through the open door. The two guards sought cover from the suppressing fire, which allowed the four invaders to rush inside. They spread out and flanked the guards.

Erik watched the movements of the invaders, subconsciously compiling the familiar motions of the forms until he realized Observers stood before him. Observers. The obvious explanation for their presence struck him when they finished off the guards and lined up to face him.

The stupid fucks came to rescue me. Erik started to giggle. He recognized them now. Hess stood closest to him. Hess. Could he handle Hess now? No. Definitely not. When the Church first incarcerated him, he had been a brawny fellow. Now he was a stick figure. Crazy how the body of an Observer could become fat or thin or muscular over time.

"Before I release you, I want your promise that you won't come after me again," Hess said.

Erik licked his lips. "Oh, Hessie, whatchya worried about? You're my hero. I'm practically president of the Hess fan club right now."

"Your promise."

His smile twisted into a sneer. Part of Erik froze at the words rising to his lips, knowing he could be damning himself. "Words are words, Hess. I'm gonna to do what I'm gonna to do. And I'm gonna do."

The Observer at Hess's side nudged him. "We don't have to take him out of here, Hess."

Erik's eyes snapped to her emaciated face. Other than the heightened awareness common to all Observers, there was no tell to give away her identity. "Ah," Erik said. "*Number Twelve.* So happy to make your acquaintance, you backstabbing little bitch. Did you have fun sabotaging my operation last Iteration?"

"We don't leave anyone behind." Hess sighed. "Not even him."

"Then I'd better speak to him privately," the girl said.

"No," Hess said.

"Don't worry, crackhead, I'm not afraid of whatever you have to say."

The twelfth Observer hesitated, then nodded. "Very well, Erik. I am the twelfth Observer. Much as the rest of you are the Creator's eyes and ears, I am the Creator's hand in the world. I open the sky. And I prevent conflicts between Observers from escalating."

Erik bared his teeth. "Fucking liar."

"To enable me to do my job, the Creator gives me the summary of every Observer's life. I know things about you that no one else does, Erik. I know what your father did to you on the first day. I know how you repaid Cazzel for his advances. I know that Mannin was the first of your understudies. And I know what Beeta did."

"Shut your mouth," Erik growled.

The woman nodded. "I won't speak any more in front of the others, but if you want we can talk in private."

Erik struggled against his bonds for a moment, then stopped. "You said you open the sky. You can't open the sky. The Creator does."

"No, Erik. This might be hard for you to accept, but the Creator sacrifices Its very existence to birth worlds. For the duration of every Iteration, the Creator does not exist. Until the world ends, there are only twelve slivers of the Creator's consciousness."

He stared at the woman.

"*We* are the Creator, Erik. That is why you cannot harm Hess or me or any of the Observers. Because the thing you serve with such loyalty is the sum of the twelve of us."

Erik twisted to gauge the reactions around him. The others believed it. Could she be lying? How could she know what happened on the first day? How could she know about Beeta?

Hess stepped close enough to touch him. "We don't have time for you to process this. How about we compromise? If I get you out of here, you leave me alone for the rest of this Iteration."

"Fine," Erik said. "The two of us can table our shit for an Iteration. I make no promises about number twelve here."

"He won't hurt me. And the name is Jerome," the woman said.

"Whatever, *twelve*. You gonna let me down?"

The others watched him warily once he stood free. Erik shuffled his feet to one of the fallen guards and stumbled into a kneeling position. His breath came quick from the small exertion. "Did anyone think to bring something to eat? The Church had me on one of those no food diets."

"Hurry it up with the clothes," Drake mumbled.

"You say something, coward?"

"He said to hurry," San said.

Erik fumbled at the buttons a moment, numb fingers slipping free. "In case the lot of you haven't noticed, I'm not exactly recovered."

Hess knelt down and began removing the blood-soaked garments from the corpse. "Drake and San, go make sure Ingrid isn't sleeping on over-watch duty. Jerome, collect any ammo you can find in this room."

While the others went about their assigned tasks, Hess dressed Erik with impersonal efficiency. "We can't afford to carry you out of here," he said.

"I know it's too much to expect you to run, but I need you walking under your own power and holding a weapon."

Erik grimaced. "I need fucking food, Hess. They never fed me once in all the years I've been here."

"Months," Hess said. "And we didn't have room to pack you a lunch."

Erik glanced at the corpse beside him. "Any idea which parts are best to eat raw?"

"I believe that would be the intestines," Hess said.

Erik cocked an eyebrow. "You're telling jokes now? How about you do something useful and pop this bastard's eyes out for me." He watched Hess bend over the body. "Then cut out some belly fat."

Hess pulled a knife. "Fine, but this is all we have time for."

"You better have one hell of an escape plan," Erik said.

"We have a nuke."

"Nuke as in nuclear bomb? Thought this world didn't have nuclear."

"The people don't. *We* do."

Erik took the gelatinous yellow mass offered him. "Bout time Elza used that big ol brain of hers on something worthwhile. Tell you what. You get your woman to build me one of those toys and all's forgiven."

"Don't threaten her." Hess spoke with cold precision. He sucked in one cheek, a tell that indicated he was contemplating something. *Dear ol Hess has never been too soft to take care of business.*

"Relax," Erik said. "I gave you a hall pass for the rest of this Iteration. That extends to your woman. But nothing warms up a friendship faster than the gift of thermonuclear weapons."

Hess reached to his side and brought out something. A phone. "I'll let you push the button." He didn't release the phone when Erik tried to take it. "Speed dial one. You don't detonate it until I tell you to."

"Deal." Erik pulled the phone close and studied its display. There was no reception inside the compound. He smiled. "The fuck we waiting on, Hess?"

"You."

"I'm ready to get my freak on right now. I can take tubby's tummy butter to go. Just give me a hand up and we can go find some cell service."

The first few steps proved to Erik that it would be a challenging escape. He gritted his teeth and pumped his feet as fast as he could while Hess led the team of Observers through the halls. Ingrid trembled like a leaf in the wind and lagged behind until one of the others prodded him.

Erik concentrated on putting one foot in front of the other. He swallowed raw fat at infrequent intervals, waiting until he thought his gag reflex under control before each bite. What he really needed was carbohydrates to raise his blood sugar.

Nevertheless, he managed. An unbreakable body could take infinite punishment. Over the Iterations, Erik had torn muscles, dislocated shoulders, broken bones, and received every type of injury imaginable at a prodigious rate. His work put him into some crazy situations. Over time, he had stopped caring about the temporary consequences of wounds. Pain was transient. Most damage only impaired performance if he let it. Pushing through was an ingrained part of who he was.

Erik slowed his pace as his vision darkened. There was only so much pushing he could do at the moment. He had always thought it odd that an Observer's body could throw off damage within minutes – could repair any form of death possible – yet remained vulnerable to lifestyle choices. Too much food made a heavy Observer. Too little food made the emaciated wreck that he was now.

They paused at the entrance to a large room with stairs leading up in various directions. Hess raced ahead with the functional members of their group, leaving Erik and Ingrid behind. "Told you there was a twelfth."

"You were right," Ingrid said.

"Did you get the names of any of our guards?"

"No." Ingrid's voice trembled.

"Oh, get over it already, cupcake. We're gonna get out of here, then I'm gonna go guard hunting. Right after I look up dear ol Simone. The good times are coming back. For me, of course. The Church people might disagree once I get started on them."

Erik licked his lips. "It's been forever since I've done spicy torture. If you combine menthol and capsaicin, you can trick the body's heat and cold receptors into firing at the same time. The sensation is *excruciating*. See, the only time both hot and cold senses fire together is when serious burning or frost-biting is happening. The brain interprets the combination as a big ol emergency. What I like best is so little damage is done that you can keep working for days on a person. Just abrade a patch of skin with sandpaper, apply spicy torture potion liberally, and observe."

Gunshots interrupted him. Erik glanced around, then took another bite of belly fat. He maneuvered it to the back of his throat and swallowed, then overrode the resultant urge to vomit by sheer force of will. "Tortured a group once with filth. Chained them in a pit and dumped sewage on them. Was fun at first, but not very productive. Most of them died of hypothermia. One died of an infection. Last guy begged to die so he wouldn't have to hang out with decomposing corpses. Kinda a failed experiment. Live and learn, right?"

San ran back to collect and chaperone them to the main staircase, giving terse orders for them to avoid getting too close to the smaller stairs to each side. Erik followed as quickly as possible, pleasantly surprised that his body appeared stronger after the short rest.

Then came the stairs. San had to haul both of her charges up the steps, which left her huffing nearly as much as them. Gunfire sounded from up ahead. As they hugged the walls of the corridor for the minimal cover found there, Erik ran through what he remembered of the compound's layout from the day he had been transported.

The main corridor they stood in stretched between the stairs leading down to the lower level and the lobby. Outside the glass doors of the lobby was the parking lot. Erik squinted down the hall. There were a shit ton of flashing lights outside.

"Erik! Does the phone have reception yet?"

He pulled the device from the pocket of his borrowed pants. "No."

"That's unfortunate. So here's the plan," Hess said. "San, Jerome, Drake, and Ingrid are going to run into the lobby with guns blazing. I follow right behind and take out anyone lurking in the corners. Erik, you are going to guard our rears. Everyone kill as many people as you can and try not to die."

"Screw that," Drake said. "Use the last pipe bomb."

"I'm saving it."

"For what? Don't you see the cops out there? We're screwed, Hess. Jerome needs to end the world before they string us up."

Hess shook his head. "We haven't lost until we've lost, Drake. We are going to take the lobby. Then we are going to toss a pipe bomb at the police cordon. That will give us some space. Then we set off the nuke. If it doesn't fizzle, then we use the distraction to get to the motorcycles we stashed. That's what we're going to do. Now let's do it."

Erik watched the others storm into the lobby. Drake pushed a protesting Ingrid before him as a human shield, firing wildly at the soldiers behind the reception desk. Jerome went at his side, thin arms thrown into the air with the recoil of each trigger pull. San jogged in the opposite direction, an insane bounce in her step.

A cacophony of gunfire erupted. Hess hefted a rifled to his shoulder and stepped into the room. He paused, put his cheek to the stock of his rifle, and fired twice. Then he pivoted and repeated the procedure. Time and again, Hess turned, acquired a target, shot, and turned again. There was no rush, only inhumanly efficient movement.

The pounding of boots on steps brought Erik back to his task of guarding the rear approach. He brought his handgun up and blew the face off the first man to appear in his line of sight. The next one got it in the chest. Target number three got lucky and managed to tumble back down the steps without injury.

From the direction of the lobby, the shooting stopped. Erik glanced over his shoulder, trying to determine who had finished whom. From the direction of the steps, another wave of soldiers appeared.

Erik took out three this time. The others retreated, but not before putting a piece of metal in his shoulder. He glanced back again, then spun and raised his weapon at the figure silhouetted at the entry to the lobby.

"Come on," Hess said.

Erik stumbled into a semi-jog until he reached the lobby. Bodies lay where they had fallen in pools of red. Most were Church soldiers. He did a quick assessment. Only Hess and Jerome had survived.

"Do you have reception now?"

Erik pulled out the phone again. There was a single bar of reception. He dialed one and put the phone to his ear. Hess watched expectantly. Seconds ticked by. Then a flat beep sounded. The phone display now showed zero bars of reception. "Dropped call," he said.

"We'll try again outside." Hess directed Jerome to guard their rear, then pulled free a pipe bomb. He handed a remote control to Erik. "Twist the wheel when I tell you, then run out and get behind one of the colonnades. Make the call as soon as you're in place."

He took the control offered to him. Hess pulled open the door and threw the pipe like a javelin, sending it into the front ranks of first responders. Before Hess could give the order, Erik spun the knob. A satisfying blast sounded, clearing its blast radius and sending everyone else dodging for cover.

Erik ran through the door and made it to the nearest column. Hess joined him. The phone once more showed a single bar. Erik punched the keys and put it to his ear. The sound of speed dialing greeted him, followed by ringing.

He glanced around wildly. Where was he supposed to watch for the explosion? "Where's the bomb?"

"On the bluff." Hess pointed ahead. "Ground zero is my house."

The phone continued to ring at his ear.

"Please don't fizzle," Hess whispered.

Light washed over them, bright as a camera flash to the eyes and as warming as the noonday sun. "It's brighter than it should be," Hess said.

Erik jumped out from behind the column and struck a dramatic pose. "BOOM, MOTHERFUCKERS!"

A split second later, the shock wave killed everyone present.

CHAPTER TWENTY-FOUR
Hess
Iteration 145

Escape was almost simple following the detonation. Anyone who might have attempted to stop them either lay motionless in death or had fled in the grip of unreasoning panic, no doubt convinced the Demiurge had chosen to smite the people. All six Observers walked free of the Church headquarters, resisted only by terrain rearranged by the explosion and continuing structural collapses.

Their disintegrated clothing proved their greatest inconvenience. While their bodies reformed unharmed, their coverings had a more mundane nature and hung on them in threads where it hung on them at all. They scavenged clothing from corpses farther from the epicenter and strutted free of the destruction.

In the immediate aftermath of the explosion, following their resurrections, Erik had slapped Hess heartily on the back and proclaimed everything forgiven. More, he promised that if the two of them ever had another disagreement, his magnanimity could always be purchased for the modest price of one doomsday weapon.

Jerome shepherded Ingrid along, sickly waif leading emaciated man to his emancipation. Drake and Erik pointed out interesting sights with glee, fascinated by twisted skyscrapers in the distance and split pavement and gushing water mains and hot rain falling from the expanding cap of the mushroom cloud. Due to the unexpected ferocity of their nuke and the resultant destruction of the storage space hosting their getaway motorcycles, Hess lead them in the direction of the garage on foot.

Fortunately, the garage had survived the devastation of the city. The damage suffered by their base of operations was limited in scope to fried electronics and shattered windows. They filed inside and collapsed onto the second-hand furniture.

Jerome stirred first, rising to collect unworn clothing and blankets from the office room. Hess noticed her hand linger against that of Drake when she passed him a bundle. He rolled his eyes, then glanced to the window. He saw only half-light unsuitable for estimating time there. "What time is it? Elza should be back by now."

San sat up. "Her car was parked at the end of the block when we got here, so she made it back. Is there any sign that she's been inside?"

"If she made it back already, then why isn't she here?" Hess went first to the door to verify Elza's car was not on the street. Back inside, he noticed that her bags were gone. Moving more quickly now, he searched the garage until he found a note penned in her hand on the rickety card table they had used for their feast the previous evening.

My Dearest Hess,

I wish I could say the right words to return our relationship to normal. Failing that, I wish I could persuade you to pretend everything is normal. Because I am unable to do either of those things, our future together is guaranteed to hold nothing but bitterness – and I do not want that for us.

The love between us has burned hot for longer than the shelf life of most civilizations. It was real, Hess, every moment of it. I know your nature makes it impossible for you to understand how I could value our time together and yet still choose to end our lives. I also know that my decision to walk away will be something you cannot reconcile with my most ardent professions. Nevertheless, I will try.

From a tent deep within a frozen wilderness to an anonymous village nestled within fields of Taro to innumerable instances stretched across our very own portion of eternity, I have loved you. I loved you before I had the strength to say the words. I loved you in helpless desperation when I believed our dalliance treason against the Creator. I loved you enough to help you raise orphans and found charitable organizations and introduce non-native technologies and take over the known world and even build a nuclear weapon.

I love your unflinching dedication to doing the right thing. I love your unending empathy for creatures whose pain is largely self-inflicted. I love your grand visions for a better world. I love how you are always fully present within the moment. I love how you take charge of circumstances which would cause anyone else to surrender. I love how you transform me from a cold, intellectual bitch into someone worth knowing.

Our love is more enduring than anything that has come before and anything likely to come after. It is more real than entire worlds – 144 have ceased to exist while we have persevered. But all things come to an end. Nothing lasts forever. Eventually our love would meet a trial it could not overcome.

I prefer to end our love at high tide, while it still is real, while we regret not a single moment of our time together. For the duration of this world, I will yearn for your presence, your conversation, your touch, for you. I have chosen to believe that you yearn for me in return. To me, this mutual yearning is far preferable to caustic arguments undermining our history.

I know this letter has been hard to read, and trust me, it was every bit as hard to write. Our love yet endures. It will end soon, when we cease to exist, but it will end in its glory.
With all my love,
Elza

Hess placed the letter back on the table, arranging it identical to the way he had found it. When Jerome approached, Hess shook his head. He tried to respond to the question on her face, but his throat refused to pass sound. The dawning realization on every face in the room brought the reality home, each expression of shock driving the fiery nail deeper into his soul.

No one interrupted the awkward silence until someone noticed Erik's absence. Jerome and Drake and Ingrid and San went about their business, eating and sleeping and packing bags and debating whether or not Erik would return.

Hess spent the hours in a twilight existence, re-reading a letter already imprinted upon his perfect memory. His thoughts moved at a glacial pace, frozen into virtual immobility. For most of that time, he reclined on a bed in the garage's office, the one he had last used in the company of Elza.

His memory ran a slide show on loop depicting Elza in all one hundred and forty-five bodies. They had all been his favorite in their time, simply by virtue of the fact that they had been the vessel to bring his woman back to him. The tensions of the present world had prevented their usual banter so that he never had the opportunity to tell Elza that her current form was his favorite. Now he would never get that chance. More, he could never mean those words now. Because this was the body that had walked away from him.

Within hours, San departed in a flurry of witty goodbyes. She broke form only for Hess. For him, she kissed his cheek and whispered words of commiseration. Then San was gone and the garage grew even quieter, even emptier.

CHAPTER TWENTY-FIVE
Erik
Iteration 2

He took the name Erik as he entered the village. Erik. The name of a victim several villages back. That man had fought for his life with admirable passion, though ultimately with little success. Everyone chose death at some point. The pathetic creatures valued their lives only so long as they basked in the warmth of pleasant experiences.

None of them appreciated the gift of existence granted them. They lived, they experienced, they thought, they ate and mated and played and did all the myriad activities that people did. None of that could happen without the Creator's endowment of *being*.

They didn't understand the enormity of *something* existing. No one did. They couldn't comprehend the concept of nothing. They couldn't grasp that the alternative to the Creator's world was eternal emptiness.

Instead, the people saw the world as a stage for their pathetic stories of domestic drudgery. Each one thought himself unique and worthy of some special place in the order of existence. They thought the world existed for their personal benefit and opted out of life the moment that benefit declined.

It was a tragedy only he could see. The Creator replaced emptiness with something-ness and the dumb creatures couldn't appreciate the majesty of what had been done. It was beyond ignorance. Beyond selfishness.

They thought the world flawed when it didn't cater to every momentary, contradictory whim. Never did it occur to them that the world might not be created for their benefit. That any one person's ideal might constitute a nightmare for every other person. They never questioned their ceaseless desires, only a world that didn't fulfill them.

Erik had asked dozens of people his question so far. None of them had provided a satisfactory answer. Each had experienced an agonizing death.

In some ways, the deaths provided more insight than the words. After all, whether intended to be great truths or self-serving lies, in the end words were just puffs of air. Death was pure.

He went through his normal routine, visiting the village's guest pavilion and meeting the locals. This village had about sixty people, and as usual, his victim chose himself. An obnoxiously social man moved about the square with an effervescent joy, flirting with any woman old enough to talk and young enough to walk, joking with the men and throwing balls with the boys. The name of this social addict was Geron.

Geron's constant motion looked at first glance to be an outlet for his youthful exuberance, but Erik saw something bleaker in the manic activity. Erik suspected that Geron in fact couldn't stand to be still. And not because of some deep love of life. No. Geron couldn't bear to truly exist in a moment because he despised his existence. His frantic dance around the people of his village served to distract him from the misery he felt in the odd moment of reflection.

This man would soon be robbed of all distractions. Instead of the mental noise of a haphazard existence, Geron would experience pure contemplation punctuated by excruciating agony, all of it permeated by overwhelming fear. How quickly would he give up hope and embrace annihilation? For most, a single night sufficed.

After his treatment of a victim named Yurin caused him to question the purity of his intentions, Erik had decided to hold himself to a simple rule: if a victim asked for death, he would grant the wish. That was the magic moment, after all, when they chose death over life. Their self-hatred was the ugly truth he sought to uncover. Once they chose annihilation, he granted their freedom.

Erik ate with the villagers and relaxed until night. He waited until Geron went inside a house, then retired to a hammock in the guest pavilion, feigning sleep. The village grew silent.

Without a sound, Erik left the hammock. He slung his bag on his back and moved to a house near the one Geron slept inside. Using dry kindling from his bag, he built a small structure. Then he brought out strips of cloth and placed them inside his construction.

Erik snuck to the remnants of the communal fires and blew life back into an ember. When it glowed a cheery red, he transferred its spark to a piece of kindling and carried it back to where he had made his preparations. The cloth blazed to life, then the kindling frame caught fire. Then the building it abutted began to burn.

He returned to the guest pavilion to wait. Minutes passed before anyone noticed the flames. By then, one wall of the house was consumed by fire and the thatched roof was sending smoke throughout the village. Screams for help shattered the night.

Erik emerged from the pavilion at the same time that most people were leaving their houses. He jogged up to Geron. "We need to get water! Come help me carry jugs from the spring!"

Without a moment's hesitation, Geron followed him out of the village. Of course, five other men were running in the same direction. Before Erik and Geron could reach the spring, the fastest man rushed back towards the village, shouting "someone shattered all the jugs!"

Geron stared at Erik, dumbfounded. "Someone broke the jugs. Why would someone do that? How are we going to put out the fire now?"

"We need to go to the nearest village. We will ask their men to bring jugs to help us put out the fire."

Geron nodded his head. "Yes, let's do that."

As easy as that, Erik got Geron alone. He waited until they were midway between villages before striking his target in the back of the head with the shaft of his walking stick. Geron went from running to rolling through the dust so fast the effect was positively comical.

Erik put his walking stick through a loop on his bag, then started to drag his unconscious victim into the bush. No one would think to look for Geron until it was too late. The people of the village were dealing with one emergency and couldn't comprehend that someone might use the confusion to cover a murder. What fools the people were.

"You always use the same method," a voice said from the darkness.

Erik looked up too late. A fist collided with his face, sending him to the ground with the taste of blood in his mouth. "That makes you predictable," the voice continued.

In a flash, Erik ripped the knob off of his walking stick and lurched back to his feet. He took a split second to regain his balance and then drove the sharpened point at his opponent with all the viciousness he could summon.

The man twisted aside, jabbed Erik's nose again, and then drove a heel into Erik's calf, collapsing him in an awkward sprawl. The man picked up the walking stick and inspected the sharpened point. "Been a while since I've seen a spear."

"Kill him already," said a woman he couldn't see.

The man rolled his eyes. "So *now* you want me to participate?"

"I want you to finish what you started so we can put this incident behind us."

"First I want to know why he kills."

Erik stared up at the man, squinting in the dark to make out distinguishing characteristics. Was the flesh he saw unusually pale? Erik began to laugh. "What's your name, stranger?"

"My name is Tzem. Now tell me why you kill people."

"That's not your name," Erik said. "You are Hess."

The startled twitch proved everything. Erik found he couldn't stop giggling. "I spent over a year following your path and now *you* find *me*."

"Careful," Elza said to her man.

"Something isn't right about him," Hess said.

"I expected you to be weak." Erik put a hand to his broken nose. "All those stories of love and helping the people. I'm so very happy you're not. It makes you much more interesting."

Hess hefted the walking stick. "Why were you following us?"

"Oh, Hess, I just wanted to meet someone like me."

For several heartbeats, no one moved. Then Hess tossed the walking stick aside. "We are nothing alike, *Observer*."

Erik stood slowly, eyes tracking the tension that never left Hess. "I believe Elza just accused you of participating. Sounds like the two of you have a disagreement. An old one, I'd say. Might even go back to the first world if I've put the clues together right. Way I see it, we have to do some participating if we're going to discover answers to the hard questions. Ain't that how you see things, Hess? Ain't we two plantains from the same bunch?"

"He doesn't kill for pleasure," Elza said.

"Neither do I. Though I do find pleasure in my work."

Hess folded his arms. "I won't let you kill this man."

"No worries. I've lost interest in Geron. I want to talk."

"Good. We have a camp a few miles from here. What is your name?"

Erik blinked. After losing their trail, he had stopped his efforts to select an appropriate moniker. He had assumed so many names over the years. Names he had worn and discarded in rapid succession. None of them meant anything to him.

"Maybe you shouldn't have started with such a difficult question," Elza muttered.

He glared at her. "Erik. My name is Erik."

"Sounds awful hard to remember," she said.

Hess grunted. "Follow me and we will have that talk."

CHAPTER TWENTY-SIX
Hess
Iteration 145

Erik returned approximately ten hours after his unannounced departure, whistling a jaunty tune as he kicked the locked door open. Once inside, he went straight to their food stores, seized a box of animal crackers, and proceeded to dump fist fulls into his mouth, sending crumbs cascading from the corners of his mouth as he chewed.

"Fucking city's an edible food vacuum," he said. "Would'a eaten me some survivors, but that shit's never good raw."

Drake's attempt to fade into the background resulted in a tin can crashing to the floor to scatter nuts in a riot of sound. Erik rolled his eyes. "So what's the dealio, Mr. Hess? Your woman ditch you for reals? Look at the bright side, she made you a big bomb first. If that ain't love, then nothing is."

Hess found his voice. "What do you want?"

"Food. Conversation. Some of your shop tools. I've got a friend waiting for me not far from here. We are going to have so much fun. I haven't had a single moment of me-time this whole fucking Iteration. Only time I got close to torture, it was from the wrong side. Amateurs didn't even know what they were doing. Iteration twenty-seven. Those boys were masters of the trade. Masters. They used belt sanders to strip away my skin. Made a fucking game of it. Competed to see which of them could remove the most flesh before it started to come back."

"You got caught before?" They were Ingrid's first words in days.

Erik shrugged. "This is time number three. You'd think I might learn a lesson or some shit, but that's not my style. And ya gotta respect my style. Ain't that right, Hess? I mean, *I* never had a woman leave *me*."

Jerome cleared her throat.

"The fuck? Don't tell me you got some contrary factoid in Encyclopedia Observia that says otherwise." Erik's easy smile faltered. He poked his finger hard at Jerome's flat chest. "And don't you go misconstruing that bitch Beeta and her suiciding ways."

"Easy," Hess growled.

"You got your replacement woman picked out already? Nice, Hess. Don't let your dipstick get dry."

"Enough. We have business." Jerome pointed one finger at Ingrid and another at Erik. "The Creator instructed me to conduct a vote. Choice one is all Observers have their memories wiped. Choice two is everything stays the same. Failure to answer in a timely fashion will be considered a vote in favor of the memory wipe."

Silence.

Erik looked around the room. "Are you fucking kidding me?"

Ingrid waited for Jerome's somber denial before responding. "Wipe us. Creator should have done it a long time since."

"Shit!" Erik glared at Jerome. "I say no. What's the vote at?"

"Five votes for. Two votes against."

Erik retrieved a screwdriver from the floor and moved to stand above Hess. "What did you vote, lover-boy?" He leaned forward. "Did you vote to put your sorry ass out of its misery?"

Hess sat back in his chair. "Get out of my face, Erik."

"What. Was. Your. Vote."

"I'm you're only ally in this, Erik."

"You voted for life?" Erik considered that. "What about now? You still feel that way without your lady friend?"

"I would vote to wipe *your* mind in an instant, Erik. But I'm not willing to sacrifice myself to get there."

Erik's dour expression flipped to sunshine instantly. "I hear ya, brother. To hell with everyone but numero uno. Well, I got lots of anti-therapy to conduct. Take it easy, Hess. I hope the rest of you come down with kidney stones and hemorrhoids."

On his saunter to the door, Erik broke into a frantic shuffle, slammed Drake into the wall, and drove his screwdriver into Drake's eye socket, pushing it deep until only the handle remained free. "Oh ya," Erik said, voice dripping honey, "almost forgot to tell you fuckers. Might be a good idea to watch yer backs. I'm a tad sore over this voting thing."

They watched Erik leave, then Drake pull a tool free of his head. Within two hours, Ingrid and Drake were gone, departing without words of farewell or even a backward glance.

Jerome sat across from Hess when the two of them were alone. Her sharp features seemed to radiate loneliness far more acutely than what he felt. "Don't feel bad that he left without a kiss," Hess said. "I'm sure you know better than me how many hookups there have been in the history of the Observers. It's a cheap thrill to them."

"Drake was an asshole," Jerome said. "I'm not going to miss him. For a while, though, while we were planning the operation, I felt like I was part of the team. I was finally one of you. I'm just realizing how much I'm going to miss that."

Hess looked down at his hands. "As you might be aware, I have not a thing to do with myself. And that body of yours remains the most pathetically useless shell to ever house an Observer. If you want a chaperone or a side kick or a traveling companion, just say the word."

"I'd like a friend."

"Then you have one."

CHAPTER TWENTY-SEVEN
Erik
Iteration 145

She waited just as he'd left her. Erik hummed a tune while he undid the convoluted trappings that kept her in place. First he removed the lock from the chain's links and unwrapped Simone's legs. Then he rolled the woman to extricate her from the tarp. After that, he cut the duct tape binding her legs together.

Erik pulled the hood from her head and flashed his brightest smile. "Simone! I've missed our visits!"

Tangled and knotted hair crowned her head like a drunken bird's nest. Snot and slobber foamed around her mouth like a slimy goatee. Her eyes squinted at the light. "I want you to kill me now," she said.

He snapped his fingers. "Well, gosh darnit, you outsmarted me! Now I don't get to torture you. I'm just shit out of luck, aren't I?" Erik smiled. "Actually, sweetie, since *you* broke the rules, now *I* get to break the rules."

Erik spent five minutes manhandling her into a seat. Even with her arms bound behind her back, Simone had plenty of muscle mass to resist him with. When he had her in place, they were both panting and covered in sweat.

"You're making me work for my reward," he said.

"Please don't do this to me, Erik. I never hurt you."

"Aw, did you think we were friends?" He used nylon rope to tie her legs to those of the chair. Overkill, considering he had already secured her to the back of the chair with a tow ratchet around her waist. Over time, he would crank the ratchet ever tighter until it became impossible for her to expand her diaphragm. She would still be able to inhale by expanding her chest, but it would never be quite enough to fully catch her breath.

"Please, Erik."

"Do you really think I owe anything to you?"

Simone blinked tears from her eyes. "You told me you have a question you ask all your victims. Has anyone ever answered right?"

Erik's smiled faded. "No. Not one."

"Have you ever considered that torture might not be the way to get the right answer?"

"Here's the thing, Simone. It's kinda a trick question. I want to hear the answers you people give not because they're right, but because you think you believe them. You can't pass my test, Simone, cause it ain't a test. It's more like an experiment. Like a dissection, really. I use knives, dig up organs and shit like that. Good times."

She shook her head. "You're looking for something. I know you are. I studied you like you study us. And you didn't try to hide anything."

"Thing is, tubby, you're not like me. I have a perfect fucking memory. Anything I notice stays with me forever. And I have lifetimes of experience telling me what I should be noticing. What have you got? Enough brains to impress the other cockroaches? A shit ton of memorized religious verses? You don't know shit."

"I know that in your heart you're serving something greater than yourself. You are loyal, Erik. You have rules for yourself. You break all human rules, but not the ones you set for yourself."

"Actually, it turns out I have been the Creator all along. Part of the Creator, at least. I'm still processing the news, but I'm pretty sure I don't have to follow any rules anymore."

Simone wept quietly as Erik set his instruments up. A kitchen grater, screwdrivers, a drill, an old leather belt, a welding torch, sandpaper, and more. He could have prepared his tools before starting, but it was more fun to let his victims watch a review of the implements.

"Cheer up, sunshine. Since I'm the Creator, that means your answer was delivered. The Creator will continue to create. Happy ending, right?"

"You begged when they hurt you," she said.

"Course I did. Getting hurt hurts."

"What do you think you'll gain from my pain?"

Erik frowned. "Well, I really wanted to know how hard you would fight for life. And to hear your answer. But you knew about the game, so all that's left is causing pain."

"Why?"

"Well, everyone needs a hobby. And I can't crochet worth shit."

She continued to stare at him, hope in her eyes. Hope that he would kill her. Erik sighed. "Fine. I'll make you a deal. I will ask you the question. If you give a good answer, then you get a quick finish. No torture."

"Is there an answer?"

He shrugged. "Not a right one. But give me the truth as you see it and I will make things easy."

Simone swallowed. "OK."

"Here is the million dollar question. Why do your people hate the world?"

She opened her mouth and Erik raised a finger. "Take some time to think it over. I want a considered response."

"I've been asking the same question for almost a year," she said. "And I think I know the answer."

Erik spread his hands. "Really? Enlighten me."

"They're afraid," Simone said. "All of us are. We look at the world and we realize how insignificant we are. Any sane person recognizes that we cannot control our own lives. Deispite preaches living with dignity, but that is only possible under controlled circumstances.

"Events outside our control happen all the time. Earthquakes, tsunamis, forest fires, auto collisions, diseases, other people. You think we want our lives to be perfect, but that's not it. We just want to feel safe. But that's impossible for us. You just laugh because you know nothing can ever leave a mark on you. We can't do that. The world is so much greater than we are and it can crush us in a moment.

"We are afraid of the world. That's what drags Deispite down. We have this religion with dignity at its core, but the only message people take away from it is that we should blame someone else for our misfortunes. It's such a tangled mess. Deispite is its own worst enemy."

"All your institutions are shit," Erik said. "I never saw a religion that didn't undermine itself in some way."

"Was my answer good enough for you?"

Erik folded his arms in front of his chest. "To be honest, chica, you got me a bit intrigued. Not enough for a clean finish, but maybe you could earn a reduced sentence. Only an hour or so in the chair if you keep my interest. Go ahead and elaborate on your ideas."

After a minute, she began to speak again. "I told you why people hate the world. It's just fear. But you want me to explain, so I will tell you why you are wrong about us.

"We don't want to die and we don't want the world to stop existing. We want to live. And the proof of that is in our fear. If we were as nihilistic as you believe us, what would we have to fear? The only reason to feel concern over losing something is if it has value to you. You can twist us so that we are so terrified of the world that we choose to die, but that doesn't change the fact that at one point we did value our lives."

Simone looked at him, swallowed, and kept speaking.

"You think Deispite is about hating the Creator. It's not. At least it shouldn't be. People fixate on blaming someone else, but the central message is dignity. That is the important part. Everything that contradicts that message has to be removed.

"We are autonomous beings. We have choices every moment about how to live our lives. People ignore the possibilities their lives hold because it is easier to blame someone else. They are afraid to take advantage of the choices life offers. They cower behind traditions and rules instead of living their lives.

"The Book of Grievances says 'Damn the Creator'. I think that's a good start. It doesn't go far enough, though. Damn the Church. Damn the Government. Damn anyone who takes away my dignity by telling me I'm not responsible for my own life.

"We have no obvious purpose in this world. The Creator left out the instruction manual. Each of us gets to decide our own purpose. *That* is dignity. The ability to define ourselves and succeed or fail on our own."

Erik stared at her.

"Those are my honest thoughts, Erik. Please kill me now."

He picked up a knife, looked at Simone, then back to the knife. "I got to be honest, Simone. That was one hell of an answer. Maybe there's something to Reverse Polish Interrogation after all."

"You promised to kill me fast if I gave you a good answer."

Erik hefted the knife, feeling its solid weight in his hand. "I know what I promised, but I've had a change of heart." He studied the knife.

Simone squeezed her eyes shut.

Erik sighed. "This sets a terrible precedent."

CHAPTER TWENTY-EIGHT
Hess
Iteration 145

Jerome packed food and equipment while Hess prepared their bugout car. The EMP from *Demiurge's Dick* had scrambled any circuits within the city, so their collection of emergency vehicles consisted of dilapidated vehicles whose manufacture predated micro-electronics. He topped off the fluids, swapped out the battery, filled the gas tank, and verified the engine would turn over.

Then Erik reappeared. Jerome and Hess exchanged a wary glance before Hess took the lead. "What do you want, Erik?"

"Hey, easy on the hating, blue balls. I came back as a favor."

Hess felt his eyebrows climb his forehead. "A favor?"

"Wanted to give you some advance warning. I released my latest project not far from here."

"Is 'released' a euphemism?"

Erik rolled his eyes. "Why, yes, as a matter of fact, *released* is a euphemism for *probably bringing a fucking army this way*. Seriously, Hess, learn the language."

"You let someone go?" Jerome's voice screeched. "What did he say? What was his reason?"

"Now, Jerome, that's none of your business." Erik nodded to Hess. "You might want to get a sense of urgency."

"Erik," Hess said. "Why did you let the guy go?"

Erik hesitated. "Actually, it was a woman, you sexist pigs. And she said some things that blew my fucking mind."

"What did she say?"

"Well, Hess, that's my little secret. Don't worry though, I doubt the two of us have been looking for the same answer all this time." Erik walked through the door without looking back.

Hess turned to Jerome. "That's the last time we will ever see him. For some insane reason, I think I might almost miss him." He looked wistfully around the garage. "We might as well get started on our farewell tour."

CHAPTER TWENTY-NINE
Erik
Iteration 2

Several miles from where Erik attacked Geron, Hess and Elza had a camp set up on an exposed hill that overlooked six villages in the distance. In one of those villages, the people swarmed like ants to fight a fire consuming nearly a quarter of its buildings.

The three of them stood in silence. "Are meetings between Observers always this awkward, or are the two of you just sore I ruined your little adventure?"

"Adventure?" Hess said.

"You were going to catch a killer," Erik said. "I ruined your fun."

Hess and Elza exchanged a glance.

"I don't want to hear any more about me participating," Hess said.

"This is not the time for jokes. *Handle* him."

"What exactly do you expect me to do? He's an Observer!"

Elza clenched her jaw, but didn't say anything further. Her man folded his arms and fixed a steady gaze on Erik. "What kind of Observer are you?"

An interesting question. "You tell first, Hess."

"I'm not the one who goes from village to village setting fires and cutting people into pieces. I want an explanation, Erik."

He smiled. "Do you think the Creator wants to see the same things happen all the time? How many times have I seen men work a field and women pound Taro into dough? It is tedious. You ask me, I think the Creator appreciates a little novelty, even if I have to manufacture the circumstances."

"You think killing the people serves the Creator?"

"Not the killing. That's just how I clean up once I finish my work." Erik's brows shot up. "Do you want to hear about my discoveries?"

"Probably not. But go on and tell us."

"They hate themselves." Erik enunciated each word. "These creatures don't want to live. They despise the Creator."

Tension grew in Hess' shoulders. "They don't know the Creator."

"Oh, I let them in on the big secret when things get started. I tell them about the Great One who made the world and sent me into it. Then I start with the cutting."

"You can't believe the Creator wants you to do that."

"Why not? What I do is just a more aggressive way to chit-chat with the locals. They beg for their lives, they offer to give me things, they threaten me, they tell me people are coming to find them, they tell me sad stories and happy ones in the hope that I will start to like them. But in the end, they all break. They beg me to kill them."

Hess shook his head. "What you're doing is wrong."

Erik laughed. "Wrong? You think their rules about right and wrong apply to us? These creatures know nothing. They're not even real. They exist for the Creator's amusement. They don't even value their lives. Why is it so wrong for me to cut the truth from their flesh?"

"Why did the Creator make people if He doesn't value them?"

"*He?* You think the Creator has a giant body somewhere, complete with a third leg? The Creator is no more similar to the people than It is to a turtle or a tree. As an Observer, you should be able to appreciate that fact. We serve something far greater than the pathetic creatures of this world."

"You are participating. That violates the Divine Command," Elza said.

Erik waved a hand dismissively at the woman. "I decide my own limits. And I have never done anything to undermine my service."

"You disrupt lives in a drastic fashion," Elza began.

Erik spoke over her. "You think I do wrong, Hess?"

"I do."

"Then I say *you* are in the wrong. We serve only the Creator. The people are nothing. Even we are nothing compared to the Creator."

"The Creator doesn't want you hurting people."

"Now, Hess, be realistic. You don't got a clue what the Creator wants. Could be that painful deaths are the best thing ever. Or maybe we're sent here to collect jokes about chamber pots. We each have to use our best judgment."

For a moment, tension hung between them. Elza faded into the background until there was just the two of them. Then Hess turned away and the spell broke. "I don't approve," he said.

Erik shrugged. "Well, good for you."

"I don't have anything else to say to you."

"Are you telling me to leave?" He squeezed the haft of his walking stick.

"I'm telling you that we are leaving. I can't forbid you from doing what you think right, so I am going to put a lot of distance between us and do my best to forget about you."

"You'll remember me. We don't forget anything, Hess."

"Do you have any questions before I go?"

Erik glanced at Elza. "What's happening with you two?"

"That's not your concern. Last chance to ask questions."

"Is there a particular question you think I should be asking?"

Hess turned to face him again. "Aren't you curious how many Observers there are? That is the first question from everyone else."

"There can't be many of us or I would have found another before now," Erik said.

"Well, in case you want to know, you are the sixth I know of. Elza, Hess, Mel, San, Drake, and Erik. The Observers of the Creator."

Hess and Elza didn't speak to him again. They packed up their camp while he watched, then strode away as dawn broke. They looked back a few times, furtive glances to make sure they were not followed.

They didn't like him. But they knew he existed. No matter how much Hess might wish it, he would not be able to forget their meeting. *Elza, Hess, Mel, San, Drake, and Erik. The Creator's Observers.*

CHAPTER THIRTY
Hess
Iteration 145

They packed a car with the essentials. Food, water, fuel, weapons, clothing. Not that they truly needed any of it. They could survive anything the world decided to throw at them – starvation, dehydration, injury, exposure. The only true threat was the inevitable outcome of the vote they conducted.

Once Jerome opened her mouth to say something, but then she opted to maintain the silence instead. When their vehicle was prepped, Hess poured the remainder of the fuel throughout the garage that had served as a home to their group the past several months. The place went up in flames as he drove away.

They went along the outer rim of damage from the explosion, periodically passing through black smoke rising from the smoldering remains of buildings or vehicles. Neither Hess nor Jerome spoke as they found an intact expressway and joined a line of vehicles evacuating the city.

After an hour of stop and go driving, they reached the front of the line, where figures in paramilitary uniforms searched each vehicle in turn. Jerome stared at him for a moment with her too large eyes before hunching down into her seat. Hess rolled to a stop when a soldier stepped in front of his vehicle, rifle slung from his shoulders to hang in his hands at the ready.

There were two more soldiers performing over-watch from the sidelines, though one was drinking from his canteen and the other was rummaging through his pockets. It was many hours into what probably felt like an unending shift for those men. The leader of the group approached the driver side door.

Hess found himself looking into the face of Inspector Monterey.

The Inspector's only reaction upon recognizing Hess was to seize the pistol holstered at his side. In a flash, Hess surged through the open window to seize the Inspector. He pulled the man half into the car's cab, moving the half-pointed handgun past him before it could fire. Then Hess hooked an arm around the man's neck.

Inspector Monterey froze, panting. The soldiers outside exchanged horrified looks. "There are days," Hess said, "when I wonder if you people are worth the effort."

He slammed his foot down on the gas pedal, steering his car into the soldier blocking the lane. That man dove to the side in time to save his life. Monterey's feet skidded along the ground and he slipped back out the window. As the man's head began to pass the border of the window, Hess slammed his elbow down savagely into the back of his head, then watched him flop awkwardly in the rear view mirror. Judging by the way the body failed to curl to protect its head, Inspector Monterey was dead. Shots rang out behind them.

Hess switched roads at the first interchange and continued to put distance behind them. At his side, Jerome slowly untensed as evidence of pursuit failed to appear. Finally, she cleared her throat. "Hess?"

"What?"

"I need to know what happened last Iteration. After I left."

Hess grunted. "The usual. Maybe that's the problem."

"I'm sorry."

"Every love story ends in tragedy. Why should mine be any different?"

CHAPTER THIRTY-ONE
Elza
Iteration 145

The driver's door of the pickup opened with a squeal to admit San. "Elz, you look worse than the time I made you try a fermented egg."

Elza forced a smile. "Your food always disappoints."

San sighed. "Don't do this, Elz. He's miserable. You're miserable. Hell of a way to spend your final days."

"You know," Elza said, "all of us stalled in our development. Fixated on things. Fetishes. Cognitive biases. As much experience as we have, we still missed things. Obvious things."

San shook her head. "You know this isn't right."

"Tell me the truth of something."

"Course, hon. I'm a fan of the truth."

"Did you befriend me just to annoy Hess?"

"No." San placed a hand on Elza's cheek. "I only ever picked on Hess because it was so easy. The truth of our friendship is far sadder. We are kindred spirits, you and I, sad saps doing our best to forget the pain of lives that refuse to end."

Elza squeezed her eyes shut. "The only thing that made it tolerable was knowing I served something greater than myself. But that was a lie. We *are* the Creator. The endless Iterations of creation and destruction are the cosmic equivalent of masturbation . . . ." A bitter laugh bubbled free of Elza. "My entire life, I prided myself on being the most impartial of the Observers. Even after I stopped following the rules, I was impartial, San. I watched the people without the slightest judgment. But none of that really mattered. I've been a passionless servant of an amoral Creator. An Agent of the Demiurge in truth."

"Hon, just go back to him."

"No, San. He's realizing the woman he loved all that time only existed in his mind. He cares so much for the people, San. We watched a world kill itself with nuclear weapons. Every moment was torture for him. It hurt me to see his pain. He noticed when I winced at bad news. And you know what he thought, San? He thought the grand tragedy of Iteration one four four bothered me. That I cared about the people. Maybe I should have. Maybe I'm as much of a monster as Erik."

Elza grimaced. "After all this time, Hess still has no idea who I am. He thinks I've joined his causes out of some altruistic impulse when in truth I've been humoring him. I'm not who he thinks I am. And we are one serious conversation away from him realizing the fact. If I leave, we lose our future. But if I stay, we lose our past. So I leave." She tossed the key to San. "Could you drive the first shift?"

San remained silent until they were free of the shattered city. "Last Iteration, they had these coffee beans that had been swallowed and passed by an elephant. Supposedly the digestion process brought out interesting flavors. The sky opened before I could get my hands on some, but I think if we head south, we might be able to find coffee beans and some willing elephants. You in?"

CHAPTER THIRTY-TWO
Erik
Iteration 2

He took the name Rex as he entered the village. Rex. A false name to wear while he posed as one of the pathetic creatures. As usual, he'd taken the name from someone he had encountered in the past. This time, from a man he met once in passing. There was no significance to it. It was only a label he would wear while in this particular village. He was *not* Rex. He was the Creator's Observer, one of several, and his name was Erik.

Full Vessels

Book 3 of the
Participants Trilogy

CHAPTER ONE
Hess

A flicker of nothingness, followed by garish yellow walls, brass lamps, knotty oak stained mahogany, and nautical paintings: a chintzy hotel conference room with delusions of resort-hood. Hess stood a single step into the room, frozen mid-stride.

Where every other Iteration began with a download of fake memories from his current identity, this time there was only the realization that he still existed followed by the cacophony of a world crashing into motion from its freeze-frame beginning.

Hess gasped in air reminiscent of lemon-scented furniture polish, salt water, and fried food. His heart thundered in his chest as he considered the wall paneling. This world appeared post-industrial and pre-electric. Of course, as Elza always pointed out, technological developments didn't always follow the typical sequence.

Elza.

Shaking palms smeared sweat across his clammy forehead. He shouldn't be alive after the end of last Iteration, but here he was. Hess squeezed his eyes shut. Did Elza live too? Or had the Creator respected their individual wishes, ending her while preserving him?

Hess reached out a hand to steady himself on the wall, then took a knee. He lived. That should be enough. It *had* to be enough.

Before he could regain control of his trembling limbs, a violent spasm seized his abdomen, catapulting a volley of bile forth to splatter across the floor boards. For a moment, his forehead rested on the hard floor. Then Hess rolled over to stare up.

Up into the too-bright eyes of a dark-skinned man holding an uncapped pen like a dagger. "Fucking fantastic. The Creator made my death-day wish come true. I get to properly express my disappointment."

237

A memory fluttered to the surface of his mind. Hess squinted at the dark man above him, recalling the reverse of their current situation, with him standing above the other during the second Iteration. "*Erik?*"

The maniacal smile warped into a scowl. "Hess? You are literally the only Observer not on my shit list. I've got so many feelings I want to talk over with my coworkers." Erik made stabbing motions with his pen. "It's gonna be a fucking *wunderbar* conversation. Those suiciding pigs are gonna hurt so bad, Hess."

He pushed himself to his feet. "What makes you think the other Observers are here? We're the only two who wanted to live."

"Aw, did your tummy ache distwact you? Do you need me to read the literal writing on the wall? You know, the big fucking sign that says 'Executive retreat: discuss your observations for one week'? This right here is the perfect opportunity to fulfill my dying wish. I ever tell you that torture parties are my fave? Never got into sex or music or any of that shit, but hurting people gets me off every time."

Hess squared his shoulders. "You don't touch Elza."

Cold calculation registered on Erik's face for a moment. "Fine. Bitch built me a nuke, after all. The others are mine, so stay away unless you want to join in the festivities. I sympathize with your properly self-preserving ways and wouldn't begrudge you some vengeance."

"What about discussing our observations?"

Sudden cheer lit up Erik's features. "Oh, there will be so much discussion over the next week. These pathetic creatures are gonna positively *gush*. I mean that figuratively and literally, Hess-a-roni. They will apologize, and explain themselves, and squirt blood everywhere. Only thing that could ever top the fun we're gonna have is if I didn't have to die at the end."

Hess grunted, then shrugged. "You don't want to die? Then stay behind when the world ends."

"Don't be ridiculous. That's just a different way to die. Might even be that losing one of us hurts the Creator, which is the only thing I'm not willing to do at this point. Show must go on or some shit."

"A world can't end until the last Observer leaves. I've stayed behind twice." He took a deep breath. "And I'm doing it again in a week."

Erik's uneven squint grew more lopsided. "You fucking with me?"

"No."

"Then why would the Creator make us believe going AWOL was a death sentence? Either you're fucking with me or the Creator lied."

"The dangers of staying behind were only ever implied. If I had to guess, I would say it was for our own good."

Erik's upper lip began to twitch.

"You know how the others voted," Hess said. "Imagine if they had been staying extra in each Iteration. The group suicide would have happened a lot sooner. By making us leave on time, the Creator extended the lives of the Observers who wanted to keep going."

Like sunlight burning away shadow, reason displaced rage. Erik blinked several times, nodded, and cracked a broad smile. "The Creator suspected some of us would be rejects. Fucking brilliant. How long do you think a world can support life? A million years? I could be content with a million. 'Spose you could ask your ex for a sciency estimate?"

Hess blew out a hard breath. "I don't think we're speaking at the moment."

"Don't sweat it too much, lover-boy. I have it on good authority half the population possesses a vagina."

Before Hess could respond, the door to the conference room creaked open to admit a petite dark-skinned woman who stomped up to them radiating reckless indifference. He recognized body and attitude in an instant. It was San, looking exactly as she had the first time he met her in Iteration two; back then he had been wandering the world alone in search of Elza. They had identified each other as Observers when he passed through her village.

Hess turned to study Erik. Both San and Erik looked the same as they had in Iteration two. "Am I wearing the same body as Iteration two?"

Erik laughed. "Fuck no. You ain't that pasty albino."

"The two of you look exactly the same as the first time I saw you."

San shrugged. "More important, where's the booze? If we're ending it with an executive retreat at an island resort, I'm getting hammered."

"Suicidin' San. You're lucky, bitch, a minute ago I was ready to show you my game face."

"Did it look like this?" San screwed her face up into a parody of mental derangement.

Erik's eyes lit up. "How cute. You think you're a big girl."

San heaved a sigh. "I'll definitely need booze for this."

Hess interrupted their posturing. "Where are the others?"

"They're here. Starting an Iteration in a room full of Observers is an odd experience. Just as we start recognizing each other, the hotelier reads us an instruction letter from our 'company chairman' about how we are supposed to discuss our observations for a week. Not too subtle, that Creator of ours."

"Are the other cowards too afwaid to face me?"

San snorted. "I always thought the baby talk appropriate for your development level."

"Nothing 'bout me's appropriate. For example, I got this special technique I like to do. Burn every fucking millimeter of skin on a body.

Then you smear them in shit and give them free reign of a basement with running water. They always try to clean themselves up at first. But something makes them stop before long. Never could decide if it was the pain or seeing their skin wash down the drain."

San rolled her eyes. "You don't say. Well, once while sailing through shark infested waters I saw a frenzy. It looked like someone replaced all the water with fins and teeth. Terrifying. So, me being me, I jumped in. I can't even guess how many times they ripped me to pieces. They didn't stop for almost a whole day. I developed an actual phobia from the experience. Two years later, I went back to chase that adrenaline high."

Erik sneered. "What, you saying I can't break you?"

"I'm already broken. But yes, I think you overestimate your skills."

"Wanna test that theory?"

Hess stepped between the two. "Where exactly are the others?"

"Listening to the hotelier give a speech about the island. Industries and exports, that kind of thing. He's a sixth generation islander and oh so proud of his home. I'm not interested. I stopped observing the moment I cast my vote."

The next arrival stepped into the room. "Hey San, they got a bar in the restaurant. I put a couple bottles of gin on our boss's tab. Never thought the Creator would buy me a drink."

Hess identified the newcomer in an instant. Drake, wearing his Iteration two body and brandishing a bottle in each hand like a frat boy. As Drake approached, his eyes fixed on Erik and bulged. "Oh shit." He tossed a bottle towards San and retreated back through the door.

Gleeful cackles erupted from Erik. Hess rolled his eyes and followed Drake's path back into the hotel proper. As he walked, the layout became clear to him. The hotel was a multistory affair with a conference room attached to one side and a restaurant to the other, with a long hall on the first floor connecting the two. At the halfway point of the hall sat a double-door entrance overlooking a circular drive composed of faded paving stones, a check-in desk directly opposite the doors next to a public stair.

From the echoing sounds of retreating voices, his group had just ascended. He hesitated there, unsure of himself until the front desk staff offered him a room key with a flourish. "You neglected to take your room key when you checked in, Mr. Hess. I trust the conference room passed your inspection? It is separated from the hotel proper by the breezeway, so there should be no danger of people overhearing confidential matters."

"So I'm already checked in?"

"The porters took your things up already, and the rest of your party arrived on the second coach. The kitchens will deliver a welcome meal to the conference room in an hour. Until then, you are free to freshen up and unpack your things. We apologize for the inconvenience, but hot water is limited to after six o'clock due to a coal shortage. The barrier reef snagged the last barge and they refuse to send another until someone pays for what was lost at sea."

Hess studied the key on his way up the stairs. It bore a stamp indicating room 204, which sat conveniently close to the stair. He glanced each way down the hall but saw no one else. With a sigh, he entered to inspect his room.

Cramped, hot, and yellow described the space. Hess didn't waste any further time inside. As he turned from re-locking his door, he noticed a woman frozen in the act of descending the stairs. He slowly straightened.

She spoke first. "Everyone embodies the form they first encountered another Observer. That means Iteration one for us."

"Makes sense."

Elza nodded. "I'll see you at the meeting."

He watched her resume her trip downstairs, then re-opened the door and went to sit on the bed, head in his hands.

CHAPTER TWO
Hess

After fifteen minutes, he went downstairs. Elza sat in the conference room with San, Jerome, and Greg, which sent him retreating to the restaurant's bar where Drake, Griff, Kerzon, and Ingrid were availing themselves of the abundant merchandise. Kerzon smacked him on the back as he went to order. "Hey, last time all of us were together, we were watching Erik torture the shit out of you."

"I wasn't there," Ingrid said.

Kerzon waved that away. "Ya, but we thought you were."

Ingrid scowled. "We punished Hess in Iteration one four three for conquering most of a world. That was the end of it. You failed to justify your vendetta past that."

"Relax, Ingrid, we're all friends now." Kerzon slammed an open bottle down in front of Hess. "See? I'll even share my whiskey. If Hess winks the right way, I might even take him to bed. You're damn easy on the eyes in that body, you know. I can see why you got the girl. Elza getting you, on the other hand . . . . Well, I guess that's a lesson in personal taste. No accounting, right?"

Hess took a sip of the whiskey before passing it back. "Was that whiskey or kerosene?"

"Right? It's all shit, everything I've sampled so far. Guess the Creator didn't spring for top shelf liquor." Kerzon moved away to speak with Griff.

Hess ordered a dry red wine, whose cardboard flavor revealed the bottle to be corked. He drank it anyway, standing beside Drake, neither of them speaking. *This is going to be one hell of a week.*

Sometime before the hour was up, Natalia arrived and ordered a drink of rum with a wedge each of lemon and ginger. She saw his attention and raised her glass in toast. "All of this is quite unexpected." Wrinkled skin

242

hung from her twig-like bones, but she moved with a lithe grace that belied her appearance.

Soon after, they followed a line of wait staff carrying tureens full of steaming food to the conference room. The entire group present, they piled plates full of fried fish, boiled potatoes, crab bread, and vegetable medley. Forks scraped plates and throats gulped.

The noises of dining gave way to the sounds of gruff conversation. Kerzon and Griff, already drunk, competed in some game that involved coin flips and guzzling straight from bottles. Erik was busy terrorizing Drake. San spun a tale of skydiving without a parachute. All of them seeking to project their voice above the others. Hess settled back in his seat and waited for time to pass.

Greg interrupted the party by climbing onto the table, moving with the casual efficiency of a sober man. He turned in slow circles, hands waving in a bid for attention. "Everyone, please let me speak. This is a conference, not a drinking contest. We can't expect to provide any value to the Creator if we treat this week as some sort of house party. I suggest we establish some ground rules to make this process more productive."

Kerzon belched. "Want me to stop drinking? Too bad."

Greg squinted down at him. "Let's meet in the mornings. Then you can have the evenings to fill any way you want. Does that sound fair?"

No one responded. Greg spoke to Mel. "We'll start at nine in the morning."

Mel nodded. "Agreed. Are you leading our discussions?"

"I would rather not," Greg said. "My idea was to take turns presenting. If two of us go each day, we'll finish at the end of the week. The current state of intoxication leads me to believe that today will not be a productive meeting. So everyone should be prepared to present in the morning."

Griff squinted up at Greg. "Present what?"

"Your most significant observations, whatever those might be."

Ingrid stood, speaking as she walked to the door. "I think that's an excellent suggestion. The last thing I want to do during my last week is participate in another Observer party. I'll see everyone at nine."

Hess followed her out and returned to his yellow room.

CHAPTER THREE
Hess

The complimentary breakfast consisted of bread, butter, and fruit preserves. Hess refueled his body in solitude, watching the people and other Observers from his corner of the room. After a tedious night, he felt the urge to escape the resort and explore the surrounding island. *I'll look around after the meeting is over. I need to get the lay of the land if I'm going to spend time here after the others leave.*

After his meal, he found his way to the conference room and sat in a seat that presented a good view of the door. Greg, the only other occupant, sat near him. "Good morning, Hess."

"I wish it was, Greg."

"Can I depend on your cooperation?"

Hess shrugged. "I'll speak when it's my turn."

"Would you keep some of our more reactive elements in line?"

He snorted. "I would if I could."

Greg lowered his voice. "You are the only one who has ever been able to influence Erik. Given the circumstances of the previous Iteration, I believe his opinions of us have only been exacerbated."

"Erik will behave," Hess said.

"Apparently not. Last night, Drake discovered the severed head of a young man in his room. Before our conference even begins, he is murdering the locals and framing the rest of us for the crime."

Hess sighed. "Does Drake need help disposing of it?"

"That was handled. What we need is for you to distract Erik."

"I can't promise anything."

"Just try."

"Sure. I'll try."

As nine o'clock arrived, the other Observers filed into the room, bringing with them a sullen silence. They sat around the table with arms folded or reclined to watch the ceiling or hunched over in apathetic study of their own hands. Greg cleared his throat. "Shall we begin?"

Drake pushed to his feet. "Screw that. I got something to say. We need to do something about Erik."

"Oh, do we now?" Erik bared his teeth in a predator's smile. "Pray tell, tit-sucker. What you got planned?"

"You put that fucking head on my night stand."

Erik raised his hands in mock surprise. "A head? On your night stand? Oh my lucky stars. I am just beside myself. Who would do such a thing? My guess is *Twelve*. All we know about that guy is he's deceptive as fuck."

"Everyone knows it was you," Drake said. "You better watch yourself, Erik, we're not happy with you."

"Oh, cupcake, you hurt my feelings. I can't believe you don't like my presents. Why, you didn't even mention the hand." Erik held his wrist up to his mouth so his fingers projected out before his face. "I put a fucking hand inside the mouth to wave hello. Better than flowers, I thought."

Erik's smile continued to meet Drake's glare, growing more intense as his opponent's ire morphed into discomfort. Drake sat with a huff, crossing his arms and turning his gaze away.

Greg spoke quickly. "So who wants to go first?"

"You go," Griff said. "This was your idea."

"This is the Creator's idea." Greg fidgeted in his seat. "I only suggested adding some structure. Should we go in alphabetical order?"

In response, Drake fixed a glare on Greg.

"Fine. Then someone else decide the order of presentation. I'm tired of being the responsible party."

Griff grunted. "You're not any kind of party."

Natalia stood. With all eyes on her, she glided to the cupboard like a gray-haired ghost and withdrew paper, pencil, and an envelope. Her knobby hands folded the sheet of paper into regular sections and tore it on the lines with rapid precision. She scribbled numbers down onto twelve scraps, folded each in half, and swept them into the envelope.

Without a word, she went around the table, holding the envelope for each of them to draw a number. As Hess drew, he noticed Natalia had trapped a slip of paper between her fingers and the side of the envelope. It was a clumsy bit of sleight of hand, but he didn't think anyone else noticed. Even had he cared to point out her deception, he had drawn number eleven.

After Natalia returned to her seat, she folded her hands in her lap and nodded to Greg in a gesture that made clear she intended to do no more. The attention of everyone drifted back to Greg. He shrugged. "Who has number one?" Griff tossed his scrap of paper onto the table.

Greg continued to count off the numbers. Mel was second, Drake third, Ingrid fourth, then Elza, Erik, Greg, Kerzon, San, Jerome, Hess, and finally Natalia. "Then that is our order of presentation. Are you ready to speak, Griff? Or do you need a short break to prepare?"

"Don't matter either way."

"Then everyone please give Griff your full attention."

CHAPTER FOUR
Hess

Griff sat with hands folded on the table before him, brows shading shifty eyes that scanned back and forth as if reading from invisible note cards. For over two minutes, Griff kept them waiting in silence. When he finally spoke, he did so in a deliberative monotone, pausing often in mid-sentence to select his words.

"I don't know that my opinion on existence is particularly deep or . . . insightful or . . . worthy or anything like that. Most of you are smarter than I ever claimed to be. So maybe my ideas are like Observation one-oh-one and the rest of y'all got doctorates in Observation-ology. I'll try not to . . . belabor the points too much, but I can't go too quick on account of . . . me never thinking I would have to explain my thoughts . . . and having to go first and so on and so forth."

Griff licked his lips, glared at the patch of table in front of him, and continued in a softer voice. "Thing is, all the while I've been watching the people and the world and all that, I've been thinking in the back of my head 'all this hullabaloo is fake,' you know? I mean, worlds pop into being thinking they've always been. Same with us, right? How do we know we actually lived a hundred forty-five Iterations? Maybe this resort is the first real world and we just think we have histories like the people."

Griff rapped his knuckles on the table. "And what *is* this? Really, what is stuff made out of? Creator took nothing and turned it into something. You ever really think about that? Call it matter or particles or strings or whatever you want, but I think it's still nothing. Little pieces of nothing the Creator tricked into thinking they were something.

"Or maybe this is all a grand play happening inside the Creator's mind and there isn't any stuff to speak of, just the *idea* of stuff that we all treat like the real deal cause we don't know any better. Whole worlds come and go, but none of them were ever really here, if you know what I'm saying."

For a minute, Griff went silent, brow scrunched in deep thought. When he continued, his voice came louder, deeper. "There's . . . *ramifications* . . . to ideas like that. Everything is made from nothing and everything goes back to nothing when we're done with it. Even us. Maybe even the Creator, for all we know. All of us are little pieces of nothing waiting to unravel.

"Think about it. If matter's made out of nothing, then maybe nothing matters. I mean, every world ends up the same as every other, collapsing back into . . . non-existence. They all start the same way, too, as nothing whipped up into the appearance of something.

"Really think about all of this. Every world is . . . fundamentally . . . identical. Start as nothing, end as nothing. Made out of nothing. Any differences are illusion."

Griff shook his head. "Now if you've followed me this far, then you see the big problem . . . the conundrum. Or maybe I'm just not smart enough to figure my way out of this maze." He cleared his throat. "Anyway, if you buy that everything is nothing and every world is pretty much the same, then you got to ask yourself: why are we observing anything?

"Think about it, guys. Really think about it. Matter's nothing and nothing matters. And our whole purpose is what? To care about nothing? Maybe our purpose is nothing. We are nothing, right? Maybe the Creator is a lie that something exists. Just this concept floating in emptiness that thinks, and thinking makes these illusions happen."

Griff shrugged his shoulders. "However it all works, the fact is that, in the end, everything ends and is forgotten, us included. Nothing we ever observed or did actually mattered. Maybe I'm not a very good Observer, cause quite frankly I never worked too hard at it. I never sought out anything that wasn't right in front of me or ran little experiments like the rest of y'all. I just watched things happen and . . . doubted the significance.

"So . . . that's my take on existence."

No one spoke until Greg cleared his throat. "Thank you, Griff. I appreciate your willingness to not only go first, but to so unreservedly state your opinion. Does anyone care to start the discussion?"

"I would," Hess said. All eyes turned to him. "If you believe nothing matters, then why join the conspiracy against me twice? You helped bury me alive in Iteration one forty three, then tried to do the same in one forty four. It doesn't seem like you buy into your own philosophy."

Erik chuckled. "Looks like Griff don't like the smell of his own shit."

"Well?" Hess demanded. "Don't you have anything to say?"

"I was bored," Griff said. "Going after you was something to occupy the time. I never cared about Ingrid's reasons. Your misbehavior was an opportunity to do something."

Hess leaned forward. "Then I'll have a little fun at your expense. As someone much smarter than you, let me educate you a little. Your insightful idea is called nihilism. It's a concept that depressive personalities routinely invent to justify their existential grief."

"When I mentioned people smarter than me, I wasn't talking about you, Hess." Griff's eyes darted to Erik. "You neither. Both of you run around the worlds obsessed with doing things. You might as well be people."

Greg pointed imperiously at Hess. "This is not a forum for you to service your grudges. You are being asked to maintain your decorum for a single week. If civility proves too difficult for you, then perhaps you should remain silent in these meetings."

"What about me, Greggie?" Erik exposed his teeth in a smile-like expression. "You wanna read me my rights? Lay down the law a little? Come on, big boy, pull out your cock so we can measure how much of a man you are. You had a tiny little pecker back in Iteration five. You let me play with it before I brought a cheese grater to bed. Remember that? You cried like a baby while I ground your nub off again and again."

Erik held a hand to his mouth as he chortled. "I decided I wouldn't stop till you quit with the begging. Itty bitty Greggie didn't know the rules, so his tiny tinkler got trimmed for hours. You ever figure out why I did it, shit licker? Did you ever work out why I quit with the humping and moved on to the kinky shit?"

Greg shrank back into his seat, shame and fear warring on his face.

"Let me enlighten ya a bit, Greggie. Sex never did it for me with the people. Didn't do it for me with an Observer, either. But then I had the idea to make the genital play interesting. And sure as shit, mutilating your tiddly bits was great fun. Things only got better when I made the condition of your release that you had to eat some feces.

"I convinced you to show so much enthusiasm for your foray into fecophelia that over the years I found myself wondering if your convincing act had some basis in reality. I'm dying to know your thoughts, Greggie. Did I turn you onto a new food group? Or are you just that fucking terrified of *moi*?"

"Easy now," Drake said. "There's eleven of us and only one of you. If things get crazy, you're going down. We don't have to worry about you coming after us in future Iterations."

"Drake, did you just grow a pair? Should we throw you a fucking party or something? Or are you just posturing like a twat because you think you're safe from me?"

"It's over, Erik," Drake said.

"The fuck it is!" Erik shot to his feet. "You cowards voted to kill us, but at this moment I'm as alive as ever. And I'm pissed as hell that shitheads like you are dragging me down with you. The Creator has all of us gathered together under a white flag and I respect the rules of the Big

Boss. But if you break the truce, you're going to discover a level of violence you can't conceive. Your imagination can't go to the place I live."

"Your scary imagination doesn't matter if we lock you up."

Erik jerked his thumb in the direction of Hess. "Then my boy breaks me out and we go to work on the lot of you. Remember, me and Hess are BFF's now – Best Fucking Friends. And if you try messing with Hess, then the wrath of Elza comes down on you."

A piercing whistle from the other end of the table interrupted Erik. San pulled her fingers from her mouth. "Nobody is going to break the peace. So why don't all of you turn the hostility down a few notches? I think everyone here knows that nobody would follow Drake on a shopping trip, let alone into a fight. The most oblivious Observer imaginable couldn't help but notice that you've emasculated Greg . . . again.

"But we're on duty at the moment. The Creator wants our opinions to cross pollinate. So we need to have heated discussions without the threat of taking the arguments physical. I think we're all more or less loyal to the Creator. We can agree on that, can't we?"

Erik, every eye glued to him, chewed her words for a minute before turning to face Griff. "Making something from nothing is a fucking miracle. Existence isn't meaningless nothing. It is meaning-filled everything. Every spec of matter contains its own rules for interacting with other specs. Those specifications are meaning. Physics is meaning.

"The fact that everything ends makes what we observe infinitely more precious. Actions happen in a single moment of time and are lost forever if one of us isn't there to record it. Uncountable trillions of actions happen every second. This isn't some game of deterministic cause and effect, cupcake. We're talking a probabilistic model where the Creator Itself can't predict the outcome of a given universe. Existence is wonder and awe and terrible beauty.

"If you truly doubt that, then spend the rest of this week in my room. I will definitively, viscerally prove that actions positively radiate meaning."

Griff folded his arms. "I'm talking about the long view, not how a body feels in a moment."

"There's your mistake. You got a false dichotomy. Eternity ain't nothing but a shit ton of moments crammed together. When your brain rebels and says otherwise, that's a limitation of your psychology."

"Actually," Elza said, "infinite numbers are not the same as mundane quantities, even if we assume time is quantized to reduce eternity from an uncountable infinity to a countable infinity. But the mathematical treatment of an infinite set is still different."

Erik spread his hands. "Seriously, Elza? Everyone here is thinking WTF right now. I mean, are you a fucking robot whose purpose is to give technical definitions to people who don't give a shit? What does mathematical treatments of infinity have to do with the topic of Griff being a self-hating delusional asshole?"

"I'll try to explain using little words." Elza spoke with cold precision. "Infinity is fundamentally different from normal quantities. As creatures whose experiences are based on non-infinite spans of time, all of us lack the mental capacity to intuitively understand eternity. An educated individual could talk about eternity in the abstract using mathematical terminology, but neither of you are qualified to be part of such a discussion."

"In summary, everyone but you's an idiot?" Erik squinted at her. "Then tell us the answer, oh great and wise Elza. Does everything mean nothing or something mean everything?"

"Griff's argument is riddled with unfounded assumptions," Elza said. "First, we don't know what exists between worlds. Divine knowledge seems to imply that there is no physical matter, but that doesn't prove a literal void. The fact that every world has so much in common suggests to me that there exists some fundamental order that limits what can be created.

"But even if matter possesses no true corporeal component – whatever that means – that does not imply anything about the meaning of existence. Neither does the fact that everything might be forgotten. Griff assumes that memory is a prerequisite for meaning without ever providing a convincing rationale for that belief. All of this metaphysical chest beating falls apart upon rational examination.

"Not that you need to bother. The whole thing dissolves as soon as you try to define meaning. You could replace it with any number of synonyms and still not have a working definition. Significance? Importance? Interpretation? Meaning is a hazy concept, but I think if you boil it down to its bare essentials, what you have is social utility. The significance of anything could be considered an opinion.

"You could very easily get sucked into a moral relativism issue here, but fortunately for us we work for the Creator and She provides an absolute for us to measure against. So I would venture that by virtue of the fact that the worlds keep coming, they have meaning."

When it was clear that Elza was done, Erik returned to his seat. Everyone sat in silence until Greg cleared his throat. "While polite debate is welcome, I don't necessarily think this is supposed to be an exercise in proving opposing viewpoints wrong. There are twelve Observers and there are going to be twelve equally valid opinions. No one should be attacked for contributing a unique perspective."

No one responded to Greg, so he turned to face Mel. "Let's adjourn for a fifteen minute break before you begin."

CHAPTER FIVE
Griff
Iteration 1

"Stupid people," he grumbled as he squeezed deeper into the dense vegetation. The susurrations of nervous whispers from behind spurred him to redouble his flight through the brambles. This was what he got for climbing a tree to search for eggs.

Ironically, the people's reaction to seeing a man's crushed skull reassemble itself had been to crush it again. Then again. And again. They had been arguing over whether fire or burial in a deep grave would provide a permanent fix to their problem when he escaped. In the hours since then, Griff had snuck eastward, pushing and crawling his way through thick jungle growth bordering the river.

So far snakes, crocodiles, stinging insects, and poisonous plants had only slowed his pursuers. They sought him with dogged persistence, determined to rid the world of an immortal man. *Why do they care so much*, he wondered. They hadn't seemed angry the three times they killed him. If anything, they had been terrified by what was happening.

Maybe they do this because they're afraid of me? I am like a snake that has been on their sleeping mat. They must kill me to feel safe again. Stupid people.

Griff pushed against a stiff screen of green growth and plunged through it to land head first in the slow-moving river. He started to scramble back out of the water, but impaled his back on a row of sharpened sticks hammered into the shore. With a muffled groan of frustration, Griff pulled himself free. He spat out water the flavor of feet as he studied the river.

The still brown liquid obscured everything beneath its surface except the stench of decay. Both banks were lined with spears preventing anyone unlucky enough to be in the water from escaping. After a moment's hesitation, Griff began wading downstream.

His destination was the Lake of Death, and the river would get him there faster than the jungle. The only question was how many times it would kill him on his journey. Some forty years before, shortly after the world jumped into motion, Griff had been swept out to sea while on a fishing expedition. In a terrifying ordeal, he had drowned to death a dozen times before washing ashore. Memories of ineffectual flailing and desperate gasping still haunted him in restless dreams.

Surely the Lake of Death could not be as bad as drowning in the sea. Most locations people named as places of death had to do with diseases, which never bothered him. Of course, the further into the forests he had gone, the more deadly animals he had discovered. So far he had managed not to encounter a crocodile up close. *Today has been a bad luck day for me. I'll probably walk myself straight into their feeding grounds before long. Might be sorry the people didn't get me first.*

Griff sloshed down the river, eyes roaming the banks for a safe place to depart the water. The muck stole his moccasins one at a time, sucking them beneath the surface when he dared take a step forward. He picked leeches from his legs and threw the things far from him. Critters beneath the opaque waters darted their slimy bodies past him at random intervals.

Stupid people, Griff thought. *They should have run away from me if I was so scary. Instead they chased me into the stupid river. Something is going to eat me now because of those people.*

His silent complaints faded into wary attentiveness at the sound of growls in the distance. Jaguars, judging by the throaty wails. Another animal to kill him. Griff studied the shore, wondering if the cats would dare enter the water. The spears lining the bank did not hinder entry, only escape.

Griff moved quicker, eager to put the horribleness of the day behind him. If he had survived the sea, then he would survive whatever the Lake of Death did to him.

So complete was his focus on the shore that he did not notice the river had widened until something splashed in the distance. An abrupt turn sent him tumbling beneath dirty water. Griff emerged thrashing, head darting about to take in his surroundings. In the distance, what could be logs floated in stately grace. He glanced at the spear-lined bank and gritted his teeth. *Stupid people making traps for other people. What is the point? Nobody would ever want to live in the stupid Lake of Death anyway.*

After a moment, his eyes spied a bridge of sorts leading from the jungle and over the water to an island with a large building on top made from pieces of rock. The bridge looked to be made of woven vine fiber with bunches of sticks spaced apart as steps.

Where the bridge met the bank of the island, there were no spears. He would need to climb a steep cliff, but then he would be free to run across the bridge and escape this nightmare. His decision made, Griff ran for the island. He made good time, at first spurred by his determination to escape, then further motivated by the realization that the logs in the water were in fact swimming towards him.

He reached the island after the crocodiles, but they held back for some reason. Griff dragged himself from the water and up the slope as fast as his breathless body would move. The bridge grew closer. When Griff crested the cliff, he beamed with exultation, feeling his freedom.

A throaty growl tore the smile from his face. Only a body length from him, a jaguar crouched on the bridge, glaring at him with menacing intensity. Below, crocs swarmed in anticipation of a meal. *Bad luck day, Griff. Bad luck day.*

"Did you let one of the people sneak past you, Shadow?" The voice, high and brittle, belonged to an old crone who sat cross-legged atop a stone wall. She smiled at him through her tangled gray mane, looking every bit as wild as the beasts that surrounded her. "Shadow doesn't like people coming into our home. Do you, Shadow?"

Griff stared at the insane woman, trying to fit her into his understanding of the world. He couldn't. People did not live close to crocodiles. They did not live *with* jaguars. The odd woman flashed a small smile as she watched him. Her eyes twinkled in amusement. "What is your name, Observer?"

"What?"

"I asked your name."

"Right, yes, I'm Griff. But what did you call me?"

"Observer," she said.

"Why'd you call me that?"

"Because that's what you are, Mister Griff."

His mouth worked for a moment.

"You were sent to watch the world by the Creator."

"How do you know that?"

The old woman leaned forward. "Because I have magic!"

Griff's eyes widened. "Magic is real?"

"Of course not."

"But . . . how do you know?"

The woman turned to the cat. "Easy, Shadow. Go hunt for mama. Go on, go hunt." For a moment, the animal stared at the woman, no doubt confused. Then, the jaguar *obeyed*, turning to run back across the bridge and disappear into the jungle.

"It's a pleasure to meet a fellow Observer. My name is Natalia." She gestured towards the stone building. "Would you care to get out of the elements? I don't have much to offer in the way of hospitality, but you are welcome to join me inside."

Griff looked towards the building, which had been constructed from rocks much as people sometimes made walls – though never had he heard of anyone making a roof from them. A soft glow came from inside. "Observer? You're an Observer like me?"

"An Observer, yes. Though I would say a bit brighter than you, friend."

"How do you make jaguars listen to you?"

Natalia raised her brow. "Magic."

His heart began to pound. "Really?"

"No. Though it might as well be for someone with the brains you display. What I do is called selective breeding. I take the least aggressive cats and mate them together. There haven't been many generations since the start of this world, but I've made rapid progress domesticating my pets. Because I raise them, they are very loyal to me. The rest is just consistent positive reinforcement."

Griff followed Natalia inside, where he discovered another insanity. Tiny fires glowed all over the room from fiber braids in shallow bowls of liquid. "How is this?"

"Magic," she said.

Griff contemplated her words. "You don't mean that."

"There may be hope for you after all," Natalia said.

"I don't understand any of this," Griff said.

"I'll admit it's a bit anachronistic for our present circumstances, but I am certain you will see far more impressive wonders in future worlds. You won't be staying here with me long enough for an explanation of the arts of lamp making and masonry, so how about we stick to pleasantries?" The woman settled on the floor and folded her hands.

Griff's eyes drifted to the floor, where bone remnants mingled with shed fur. "If you're an Observer, why do you live away from the people?"

"I'm not watching people," Natalia said.

"But that's what we're supposed to do."

"We're supposed to observe. I don't see our mission as being restricted to people. In my opinion, animals are far less trying companions than the primitive tribesmen of this world. I wouldn't bother speaking with you at all if you weren't an Observer."

"How many Observers are there?"

"Twelve."

"Who are the others?"

"I couldn't say. I've only met you." Natalia glanced past him to the door and he turned to see what had caught her attention. Three cats stood there, eyes fixed on him. "Well, Griff, it appears our visit is over. I will walk you to the bridge and make sure my friends don't follow."

Griff was too concerned with the presence of the predators to do anything other than escape across to the mainland and run through the forests.

He never encountered any of the people hunting him. Later, when thinking back on the odd meeting with Natalia, one question about the strange Observer stood out above all others. *Why would an old woman prefer the company of animals to that of people?* Whatever the reason, Griff was certain it was scandalous.

CHAPTER SIX
Hess

Mel sat at the head of the table, one ankle across the opposite knee, hands folded in his lap, trademark half-smirk in place. He radiated expectation into the extended silence.

"Just spew out your artsy nonsense already," Drake muttered.

Mel's smirk grew broader as he arched a single brow. "Thank you for the vote of confidence, Drake. I'll be sure to return the favor tomorrow when it's your turn." He turned his attention to Greg and began to speak, his typical mannerisms amped up to maximum effect.

"No doubt the eleven of you expect a lesson in art appreciation. While I could indeed provide a marvelous introduction to the subject, I'm afraid that I must disappoint. Firstly, the lot of you possess neither the temperament nor the time required for proper study. My second, more pertinent, reason is that my study of high culture has always been secondary to my chosen subject – understanding each world through the lens of the indigenous population.

"While each of you slogged through the gutters of various societies in brute force campaigns to collect intelligence of questionable value for the Creator, I became a metaphorical spymaster, employing painters and sculptors and poets and musicians to deliver their most sincere insights of life and existence to me. Their assistance often cost no more than the price of a ticket to the local museum. How could I pass up such a bargain?

"I am certain that all of you are doubting the quality of these second-hand observations at this moment. More often than not, your misgivings would be well founded. All art says something, presumably about the experience of life. However, much of the time, the message proves unworthy of contemplation. Any of you who have joined me at a show know how much I detest themed works. In my opinion, the deliberate inclusion of a motif is cheap artifice. Rather, the heart of a work should be in subtle conflict. Despair hidden behind a smile. Joy on a battlefield. A neglected monument.

"These worlds possess a complexity no individual could ever encompass. In the space of a few hours, I can sample the insights an artist has obtained over an entire lifetime. The dross and the gold are easy enough to discern with some experience. Over the worlds, I have collected a wealth of reflections.

"Though none of these gems are what I choose to share with you. Rather, my most profound observation of the world is related not to what the world of art has presented to me, but instead to a quality that the common people lack. You see, what is most remarkable about art is that its producer must be aware of the world in order to reproduce some facet of it in the chosen medium.

"Most people drift through life reacting to the situations they find themselves in, unable or unwilling to contemplate their own context. Their lives start in motion. Either the motion granted them by the Creator at the first moment of a world or the motion imparted through upbringing – the effect is the same either way.

"They inherit their every idea and never realize their intellectual borrowings. Instead, they cling to their arbitrary indoctrination with a simple-minded tenacity, resisting new ideas with the full might of their ignorance. Confirmation bias filters experiences as they occur, granting significance to events that agree with their worldview and dismissing any that could challenge their assumptions.

"Their memories, faulty to begin with, are subject to cognitive dissonance. I once met a man who hated a certain painter while holding another in the highest esteem. Both produced gloomy surreal landscapes and their works were often confused. So this man I met explained to me why one was superior to the other in great detail, pointing to pieces from a private collection as examples.

"'Jenzee has greater depths in his shadows as you can easily see here. Jenzee's works have superior perspective – just look at it! Jenzee makes better use of color.' At some point, the host of the soiree arrived to speak with us and bragged about his landscape by Jenzee – which happened to be the one the man had assumed painted by the hated Erwood. When our host left to mingle with the other guests, my confused companion repeated the exact same opinions to me as before. 'Jenzee has greater depths in his shadows as you can easily see here. Jenzee's works have superior perspective – just look at it! Jenzee makes better use of color.' The only difference was the painting at which he pointed. When I pointed out his contradictory opinions of the two paintings, the man mocked me for a fool and departed.

"How common is the common man. He doesn't choose his own beliefs – he accepts them before he has his own mind. He doesn't consider new ideas he encounters – he rejects them as different from his own. He doesn't even apply his ideas to his own life – more often than not, he exists as a product of incompatible beliefs and habits.

"The primary fault isn't a lack of intelligence but rather an unconscious aversion to change. An unconscious aversion that could easily be over-ridden with a modicum of contemplation. I have never encountered a person who could be said to be incapable of conscious thought. Yet rare is the one willing to engage in the practice.

"The observation I present today for all of you is that most people cannot be said to be truly conscious. They are automatons, wound up with an arbitrary set of ideas and released upon the world to interact in a limited fashion. They stumble about in mechanical obedience to faulty internal wiring, refusing to see past the filters on their eyes. Unwilling to sort through the jumble of contradictions living within their minds.

"I believe the biggest difference between us and them is not our long and perfect memories, but our obedience to the Divine Command. We observe. We contemplate. We are consciously aware, sometimes painfully so, of the worlds that are our context."

Mel sat straighter, steepling his hands on the table before him. "That is the crown jewel of my collection. If you care to debate its merit, I am ready."

Greg nodded his head in tribute. "A fascinating observation. I have noticed the same phenomenon, though I never stated it so eloquently."

"You ruined the drinking game," Erik said. "We were supposed to do a shot every time you named a movement."

"As always, Erik, I am thrilled you opened your mouth," Mel said. "Does anyone else care to enlighten us? Elza, perhaps? Would you like to itemize the flaws of my argument?"

Elza shrugged. "There was no argument, Mel. You shared an opinion."

"There is the blunt literalism I expect from you. Do you object to my opinion?"

"No," she said.

Ingrid sighed loudly. "Seems the brainy trio have a truce. Did you reach an agreement or is this a case of professional courtesy?"

Griff turned a scowl on Elza. "Hey, why should Mel get a pass?"

"Fine," Elza said. "I'll object, since everyone wants it." She locked her eyes on Mel. "Your opinion is nothing special. I'm sure every one of us has cracked a psychology textbook at least once. Cognitive dissonance and confirmation bias are common. The failure to ever have what you term 'conscious thought' is not.

"Have you ever considered that your anecdote of the soiree could have an alternate explanation? I expect the man you met was not as knowledgeable as he claimed about Jenzee. No doubt he was parroting the words of someone else and became embarrassed when he realized his mistake. By pretending the mis-identification never happened, the man may have been requesting you to participate in a social fiction to help him save face. Instead, you acted like the smug asshole you are and the man became upset.

"More troubling is your use of nebulous terminology. Could you clarify for us whether people lack awareness or simply fail to think critically on a regular basis? The former is unbelievable and the latter trivial."

Mel collapsed his steepled fingers into fists. "The greatest objection you can marshal is word choice?"

"Semantics," Elza corrected. "Your grand thesis is that people fail to put enough mental effort into their lives. Then you use sloppy terminology to present your case. Given a perfect memory, even an idiot should be able to find the right words."

"Well, I can see I'm not the only asshole present." Mel waved the criticisms away with a dismissive gesture. "Anyone else?"

Erik laughed. "Like Elza left enough of your little notion for us to discuss. Your idea's been nuked, art boy."

Drake smacked the table. "Demiurge's Dick strikes again!"

"We are not here to bicker and tell crude jokes!" Greg split his spiteful glances between Elza and Drake. "This is as close as we will ever come to presenting our insights to the Creator. We are acting as stand-ins for the One we serve. Quit behaving like unruly children."

CHAPTER SEVEN
Mel
Iteration 8

Deliberate movements. Steady hands applying silicone caulking to the interior of a humble mausoleum. Unfaced concrete block composed the four walls and supported the concrete slab ceiling. Mel paused, adjusted the angle of his electric lamp, and resumed his task.

The sole entrance to his lowly abode stretched before him, a tight crawl way of block with a door on either end of the passage. From outside, the structure appeared a stoically square igloo. From inside, a claustrophobic box scarcely larger than a man. There was no art to it, but his purpose precluded any meaningful expression.

This was the opposite of art. There was no striving here, only morbidly competent workmanship. True art meant something. It did more than mean something. More than said something. It pointed, with the clarity of abstraction, towards a particular perspective on reality. This world tended towards abstraction. Sculptures of skewed geometric figures. Paintings of distorted scenes. Music of clever discordances. Stories of senseless happenings. All of it kaleidoscopes of randomness hinting at something greater.

In his estimation, the art of Iteration eight surpassed the shallow beauty-obsession from the prior worlds in every way. It did not offer its secrets casually like a lady of the night. It had class. Mystery. Depth.

Unfortunately, the passion for mystery no longer lived within him. No matter the complexity of the medium, art could only say so many things. Human thought roamed within narrow bounds and could be predicted so very simply. And art simply for the sake of art was not truly art.

Mel applied the final bit of silicone sealant to the plastic sheet covering the diminutive plywood door and sat back to scrutinize his work. After a moment, he nodded in satisfaction. It appeared air tight.

Again with meditative deliberateness, he removed glassware from a hiking pack, placing each piece in turn on the cold floor, tensing at the too-loud clinking. When everything sat before him, Mel removed the tops from two bottles and poured first one, then the other into a large beaker, filling it halfway with a mixture of formic and sulfuric acids.

He pushed his electric lamp onto its back so that it shone at the gray ceiling and settled the beaker into place on its flat surface. As the heat of the bulbs warmed the solution, bubbles began to form. Mel reclined back into a classic funeral pose; hands folded peacefully atop his abdomen, eyes closed as if in sleep.

No thoughts troubled Mel as he breathed in the carbon monoxide vapors. He had situated his mausoleum far from civilization. No one should be able to locate him before this world ended. Each inhalation brought poisonous gas into his lungs, where the hemoglobin of his blood bonded tightly to the deadly carbon monoxide.

Once formed, that bond endured. Each blood cell poisoned with carbon monoxide was forever prevented from carrying oxygen. The scientists of this world claimed one percent concentrations of the gas were sufficient to kill a man within minutes. Mel had mixed enough solution to make much more gas than one percent concentration. He had not actually done any of the calculations, instead relying upon an editorial written in layman's terms about the dangers of the substance. To be certain of its efficacy, he had tripled the amount of acid and halved the size of the room.

As planned, Mel slipped into a slumber which deepened into death.

Mel woke in the dark, dull and weak. He awaited a return to sleep that did not come. Instead, his memory grew clearer, bringing with it clarity that burned cold. With steely determination, Mel fumbled his way free of his crypt. Outside, he stumbled his way to where his truck waited at the end of a long trail used only by animals prior to his arrival.

When he yanked the door to his vehicle open, the glare of the dome light struck him. Mel stared at the glowing bulb, a snarl rising to his face. *There should be no light.* Car batteries lasted weeks or months at most. *There should be no light!* He seized extra glass bottles of acid and extra lamp batteries, then returned to his mausoleum.

Mel mixed chemicals and died.

He woke. Outside again, the truck's overhead light came on when the door opened. Mel swore. He beat his fists against the hard metal of the truck. He pulled the final bottles of acid free and hurled them at the useless block wall before him. Their crash brought no satisfaction.

"Why?" He raised both arms to the sky, shouted at it like a melodramatic stage actor. "Why can't I have this? Why? Damn you, Creator, tell me why!"

Last Iteration, he had anchored his clothing with rocks and stepped into a deep cistern. The water had vanished after only days, leaving him to crawl back to civilization and resume his duties.

The one before that, he had stayed behind when the world ended, daring the Creator to destroy him. Days passed before Mel accepted that entire worlds lingered past their expirations to prevent his freedom.

No escape existed. There would never be an end. Not even a temporary respite. Mel's breath bubbled oddly within him, not quite laughter, not quite sobbing, not quite rage. Some of each, but not firmly enough in any category to afford him relief.

Mel climbed onto the bed of the truck and began to dig through his tools. "Every day is too much," he said calmly, rationally. "Day upon day. It stretches into eternity. How many days have I lived? How many more must I face?"

His hands closed on the metal gasoline canister. "You know what I want." He twisted free the cap. "But you won't let me have it." Mel hefted the can above his head. "So I must assume that this is what you want."

With vigorous motions, Mel emptied the entire canister onto himself, soaking hair and clothing and flesh in liquid that stung eyes and offended nose and mouth. He threw the can aside and raised his face to the sky once more. "Is *this* is what you want from me? Is it?"

Mel lifted the matchbook.

CHAPTER EIGHT
Hess

Following Greg's lecture, they scattered from the conference room.

Hess didn't get three paces before Erik appeared at his side. "You think you're hot shit. I gotta admit you've got some marksmanship skill, but when it comes to killing, I'm the fucking king. Whaddaya say?"

"I couldn't care less, Erik."

"I'm sorry, I didn't hear anything after 'I'm scared of Erik'."

Hess continued walking. "Go bother someone else."

"Come on, Hess, you don't want me causing trouble. Your give-a-shit ain't gonna let you stand by while I do hi-jinx. So how 'bout you humor me a little? I got a competition in mind. We can finally see who's top man of our dysfunctional tribe."

At the door, Hess paused. "What do you want and how long will it take?"

"Not long. I acquired two sabers last night. Figured a game of swords might be called for. Three rounds to the death. Winner gets the title of *hombre de hombres*." Erik spread his hands. "Or you can forfeit the title. No biggie. Though I will have to find something else to occupy my time. Probably something associated with my hobby."

"You want to sword fight?"

"Fuck yeah. I love me some swashbuckling."

Hess smiled. "Sure, Erik. I would love to."

"Oh ho, you're getting cocky! This will be an edu-mi-cation for ya. Everything is set up downstairs. The hotel's got a huge coal room just going to waste."

With all the eagerness of a child, Erik preceded him down the servant's stair and into the basement. They passed the boiler room and entered a space littered with black grit and the odd lump of coal. Erik retrieved two sabers from a corner and passed one off to Hess.

Then Erik assumed a classic fencing pose and launched into a flurry of vicious swipes. Bouncing on the soles of his feet, he raised his brows. "Ready for this, fuck face?"

Without speaking, Hess hefted the saber, assumed a rudimentary two-handed position, and waited. Erik attacked in a rush; stab, stab, slash, stab, slash, slash, slash. Hess responded without thought, parrying and side-stepping and retreating to keep Erik's blade out of reach.

Erik fell back, breathing hard. He feinted a face strike, then lunged, driving his sword for Hess's abdomen. Hess bound their blades, sending Erik's strike to one side and sliding his own saber into position to deftly pierce Erik's sword arm at the bicep. In a blink, he closed the distance, elbowed Erik's nose, seized his opponent's sword hand in his, then twisted the tip of his blade to destroy the pierced muscle.

Hess fell back, maintaining proper form. Erik swore under his breath, switched sword hands, and came in hacking. Hess circled back from the strikes, refusing to engage until Erik spun about. In an instant, Hess ducked beneath the blade and drove his own home in Erik's gut.

As Erik stumbled back, Hess took the fight to him. He showered his opponent with blows, most of which drew shallow lines across exposed flesh due to deft last-minute flicks of his wrist. When Erik flinched back with a fresh gash on his cheekbone, Hess lunged, driving his saber into the upper chest. Then he stepped back.

His opponent collapsed to his knees, blood foaming from his mortal wound. Hess studied his work. It looked too high to have pierced the heart, but, judging by the effect, he had sliced through the aorta, which finished the job as thoroughly as his intended strike.

Hess stood back while Erik died and resurrected. "Erik, what was that spin? Did you learn how to use a sword from television shows? Rule number one is you never turn your back on an opponent."

"Go ahead and run your mouth." Erik stood and brushed soot from his clothes. "I underestimated you and it cost me that time."

Erik lunged in an instant, driving his saber deep into Hess's stomach.

Hess used his fist to plug the hole as Erik danced back, chortling gleefully. Thinking quickly, Hess sank to his knees, placing one hand on a crunchy pile of coal-dust to support himself. The other hand held his saber up and outward, point held towards his opponent.

Erik smacked his blade hard enough to knock it from Hess's hands and stepped forward for the killing stroke. Hess swept his hand on the floor up and out, flinging grit into Erik's face. He followed that up by sweeping Erik's legs. Knowing he didn't have much time before his injury robbed him of mobility, Hess pressed his momentary advantage.

Ignoring the slashes coming at his side, hoping the leverage wasn't there to do serious damage, Hess scraped his fingers across his opponent's eyes.

That triggered the instinctual flinch Hess desired, giving him the opportunity to wrest the sword from Erik's hands.

He sawed the blade across the only critical target he could reach given his awkward position, the front and inner side of Erik's thighs. Before Hess could ascertain the success of his cut, Erik drove his forehead into Hess's nose. Hess collapsed onto his back, eyes reflexively shutting and hands involuntarily cradling his face.

When Hess forced his eyes open, he saw Erik above him. The exultation on Erik's face faded as he noticed the blood spurting from his severed femoral artery. Erik shrugged. "Guess this one's a tie." He drove the sword into each side of Hess's chest, then stepped back to watch Hess drown to death from the blood pooling in his lungs.

Hess resurrected thirty seconds before Erik, who giggled as he stood. "Aw, Hessie, you *do* fight dirty. I'm so proud." And another lunge.

He accepted it into his body while swinging a counter across Erik's throat. When they separated, Erik scowled at the twin trails of red weeping from either side of his trachea: proof that his carotid arteries had been severed. Hess glanced down at his punctured abdomen. "It won't kill me in five minutes, so I guess I win two and tie once."

Erik's voice did no more than gurgle, so he flashed his middle finger in defiance before dropping to the ground. Five minutes later, a filthy Erik confronted him. "We got one more bout. Ties don't count."

"Well, I wouldn't want there to be any doubt that I am the man of men," Hess said.

They faced each other a final time, this time in solemn stillness. Hess moved first, a feinted lunge that sent Erik into retreat. Then Erik swung his saber in a series of slashes that Hess avoided without ever bringing their blades into contact.

As Erik broke off his attack, Hess dipped past Erik, scoring first blood with a slash across the shoulder that Erik blocked a moment late. They fell into circling each other, watching one another for attacks that failed to materialize.

The cement floor shifted beneath them. Erik startled at the unexpected development and Hess used that distraction to lunge deep, placing his saber into Erik's side. Too slow, Erik attempted to parry with a harsh swing. The blades collided at an odd angle and Hess's saber snapped, leaving the top third of its blade inside Erik.

Around them, soot rained from every surface as the room continued to rumble. Erik sliced Hess's wrist hard enough that he lost the remnant of his blade. They stared at one another as the earthquake subsided. Then Hess stood up straight and presented his neck. "You won that exchange."

"I did," Erik said. "But much as I like stabbing, right now I wanna know what the fuck is going on."

Hess straightened his grimy shirt. "Let's go see."

CHAPTER NINE
Hess

They emerged from the servant's stair back into the main hall of the hotel to find the staff glued to the windows. Hess squeezed between them to scan the courtyard for whatever held their interest. He saw nothing unusual. The circular drive sat empty, the unpaved road radiated rustic charm, trees luxuriated in the sunlight.

"What are we looking at?"

One of the desk staff noticed Hess and pulled away from his soot-stained clothing. "The mountain."

Hess stared at the distant peaks. "Why?"

"To make sure it's still dormant."

Behind him, Erik grunted. "Well, ain't this a fucking pickle."

Hess ignored him. "Is the ship that brought us here still in port?"

The man nodded. "Not that it does you any good. It snagged the reef pretty good on the way into harbor. They're going to scuttle it soon as they strip everything of value."

Hess and Erik stepped away from the windows by unspoken agreement. "I give it ten to one odds that fucking mountain blows at the end of our week. Creator's sending the Observers out with a bang."

"Seems likely," Hess said. "Which means we need a ship."

Erik nudged him in the ribs. "Look at us conspiratin' together. We're totally BFF's. Wanna go ship shopping together, buddy?"

"Let's clean up first." Hess didn't wait for a reply before marching to the baths, stopping only to grab a change of clothing from his room. He scrubbed for ten minutes with cold water before judging himself presentable, then dressed and hurried outside to where Erik waited.

They rented horses from the stable and set out for the main port along the harbor road. An hour at a canter brought them from the town on the scenic ridge hosting their resort down to the sea level harbor. The winding road, adhering to a religious observation of the path of least resistance, caused their travel time to be thrice what it should have been. Hess suspected the trip could be made on foot in the same time if one were to go off road.

Of the several available piers, only one held anything larger than a catamaran. A two-masted schooner, a steamship tug, and a yacht docked to that pier. "Not much of a selection," Erik mumbled.

"Not really. Unless you fancy crossing an ocean in a dinghy or a rowboat." Hess noticed a guard post at the entry to the pier. His eyes scanned the line of buildings facing the water. "Looks like there is a fish market. We can start asking questions there."

They proceeded to the market building, secured their horses, and separated to mingle with the locals. Hess chose a direct approach. He asked the proprietors of individual booths if they knew of any boats departing for the mainland. Time and again, the answer was no.

Apparently, the incompetent governor of the island had ignored complaints from shipping companies and locals alike that the channel markers had drifted and needed re-positioned. After a number of ships had dragged their bellies across the barrier reef, the flow of visitors had slowed to a trickle. The island's economy had stagnated. And in the wake of the governor refusing to pay for the loss of the last coal barge, they couldn't even hire out a vessel for supply runs.

The arrival of a passenger ship full of tourists would have been cause for hope if it hadn't snagged the reef on its way in. As it was, the port was all but empty. The only ocean-worthy vessels were the governor's private ship and the schooner that a local corporation used to trawl beyond the harbor. Neither ship rented passenger space.

Each person dismissed his mention of the tug with the same objection: "out of coal." The saltpeter refinery's insatiable appetite had driven the price of fuel too high to waste it on a mere steamship tug.

Finally, Hess asked several people if they were concerned about the earthquake. The responses were all negative, but Hess detected a hint of concern beneath the gruff bravado. The mountain had been inactive for hundreds of years, they told him. Once every few decades it snored in its sleep – no big deal, their husband or wife did the same thing.

When he met Erik back at the entrance, Hess shrugged. "The owners don't rent out their ships."

"Guess we got to steal one."

"The yacht would be more manageable for the two of us," Hess said.

"Always liked yachts. This one time, I went shark fishing with human bait. Too hard to reel them in before they bled to death, so I only did it the one time. Fun, though."

Hess fixed Erik with a level look. "Enough of that. We need to decide when we leave."

"Right, we got business." Erik scrunched up his face in thought. Finally, he clucked his tongue. "Volcano's gonna behave for a few more days. We give the Creator a full week of conferencing and sail out of here at the last minute. Everyone wins."

Hess nodded. "I agree. Give me a night to think. Tomorrow we'll figure out our plan for stealing the yacht."

CHAPTER TEN
Hess

The next morning, he arrived early to the conference room. He sat with Greg in the empty room until nine o'clock, when the others converged from various directions to take their seats. Greg waited until everyone settled before beginning. "By popular vote, we have decided to enact a courtesy rule. No one should interrupt our speaker. Further, insults and personal attacks are forbidden. We're here to serve the Creator, not our egos."

A near-unanimous rolling of eyes was the only response to his declaration. Greg cleared his throat. "You're up, Drake."

Drake reclined back in his seat, the hint of a smile evident by a tightness in his cheeks. "*Fear.* That's what's behind everything the people do. I been around a lot of different types. Some of them pretty hairy, y'know? But they're all afraid of something.

"Fear is the source of all emotion. Think you love something? No, you're just afraid it won't be there some day. Think you hate something? You actually fear its potential. Think you are curious? You're just afraid that everything's going to stay the same. Everything comes back to fear.

"Ever watch a baby? They only got two modes: afraid and not-afraid. People like to call not-afraid 'happy'. It makes them feel better about life to think that fear is the exception, because they're afraid of fear. Kinda funny, right? The people get confused as they get smarter, start believing their different emotions are distinct. Makes them feel better about themselves.

"Adult emotions are all twisted up on themselves. Too much repressing and controlling and thinking. They can't untangle the mess to figure out what they're feeling. You have to start by observing babies, then toddlers, then kids, then teens, then adults. When you finally get to the elderly, dementia cuts down on the thinking part and, all of a sudden, the fear's front and center again. Fear is biology. All the other emotions are abstract. Think of them as fancier ways to interpret fear."

His self-satisfied smirk faded as he glanced at his audience. "What? All of you think I'm wrong? Is that it? I'm not." He pointed at Mel. "Afraid of eternity." San. "Afraid of boredom." Ingrid. "Afraid of pain." Greg. "Afraid of Erik." He smirked at them. "You're all afraid of something."

"Hold on a sec," Erik said. "Not everyone's got a case of scaredy pants syndrome. Yours truly ain't scared of nothing. Anyone remember last Iteration? I had to take my own medicine for years and I never let it bother me much. Hell, those punishers were more afraid of me than I was of them. When the posse came by to save my ass, I smack-talked 'em so bad they almost left me behind. So you see, shit-for-brains, I'm not scared."

Drake's shoulders drooped and he licked his lips. "Actually, that's not true, Erik. You're afraid to die."

For a moment, Erik froze, his face eerily empty. Then he threw a snarl at Drake. "That's not fear. I'm *pissed off*, you idiot."

Natalia perked up, spinning in her chair to look Erik in the eye. "You're not afraid of death?"

"Course not, you dumb twat."

A look of pure condescension touched Natalia's face before her features fell back into the absent-minded bemusement that was their custom. "Very well, then."

"*Very well, then*," Erik mimicked.

Elza interjected herself into the conversation before Erik could continue. "A couple of flaws. First, you're generalizing from a sample of one. While the rest of us take into account to some extent how our perspective skews our interpretation of others' mental states, you don't appear to be making that effort. You can't assume that other people's minds work the same as yours. Second, the fact that everyone has fear does not prove fear is the fundamental emotion. Without evidence of a causal relationship, you are committing a non sequitur."

Drake shook his head. "You just don't want to believe that your thing with Hess isn't special. Lasting so long together just means both of you are crazy insecure. What do you think love is? How do you describe your relationship?"

"As none of your business," Elza said.

Erik chuckled to himself, but kept silent.

"Anyone can answer," Drake said. "I don't have all that much to say, really. But if everyone's so sure I'm wrong, then try to tell me what love is besides fear."

Chairs creaked as faces unanimously reoriented towards Hess. He sighed. "I suppose I've been nominated. What is love? Honestly, I have no idea. But I can tell you that it sure as hell isn't an escape from fear.

Loving someone is the most terrifying thing you can do. It leaves you vulnerable in ways I doubt any of you could imagine. It's deciding to live for someone else and putting their happiness above your own. It's tangling up your identities to the point where you don't even know who you are without referencing the other."

"That's all bull," Drake said. "You're thinking about it wrong. Just because you're scared of doing something doesn't mean you're not more scared not to do it. You might even do the thing that scares you more by mistake. It's all twisted up, remember."

Hess shook his head. "It sounds like your theory has a built-in defense mechanism. Any dissenting opinion is wrong because our minds are too twisted to understand our own emotions. I learned the hard way over the years that any idea that cherry picks its evidence is most likely a folly with delusions of grandeur."

Drake scowled at Hess. "You think it's my fault you can't disprove my idea?"

"Of course he doesn't," Elza snapped. "You presented us a tidy little tautology dressed up as philosophy and now you are being evasive when questioned. The burden of proof is on you. And referencing your theory as evidence of your theory doesn't count."

"Why do you get to make the rules? This is my presentation."

"I didn't make the rules of logic. I don't think even the Creator has the ability to change how causality works. You'll have to resign yourself to playing by the rules of reality."

Drake folded his arms in silent protest.

"I suppose that ends this session," Greg said. "Let's take a half-hour break."

CHAPTER ELEVEN
Drake
Iteration 1

The intruders picked through his possessions as he watched them from his hiding place. They took everything of value, including the ramshackle tent that held the rest, then departed.

He climbed down from the tree to inventory what remained. Not much. The supply of acorns, pine nuts, and tubers he had stockpiled for winter were gone. As were the blankets, the fire-bow, and even his collection of pretty rocks. All that remained to him were the frame of his tent and a stack of firewood.

It was forty summers since the start of the world, and he had not aged a single day. His body still presented itself as the child of fifteen summers it had been on the first day. A malnourished and stunted fifteen summers that people often mistook for even younger.

His original tribe had driven him away when he failed to mature. They had apologized one moment and threatened retribution should he ever return the next. He hadn't tested their goodwill, instead hiking away from their lands.

The first tribe he encountered killed him as a foreigner. He learned his lesson and avoided people after that. He figured he had observed enough already. The Creator could send him into a nicer world if watching people was so important.

He died many more times on his own. Once from wolves. Three times from the weather. At least ten times from accidents.

The second tribe he encountered took him captive, cut off his manhood, and made him work for them. They made him do both men's work and women's work since they thought he was neither. He hid the fact that his flesh had regrown. For seven summers, he stayed with that tribe.

They worked him to exhaustion and taunted him daily, but at least he had food.

Then a man took him to bed and discovered he was whole. They cut him apart again, then checked him the next morning. Amazed, the tribe butchered him to consume his healing properties. He escaped before they realized he didn't stay dead.

The third tribe he encountered killed him in passing. The fourth tribe he encountered only threw rocks at him until he ran away. The fifth tribe he encountered stole his possessions while he watched.

He did not want to encounter a sixth tribe. With no worthwhile possessions left to him and his campsite discovered, he chose a direction and walked. Starting over was hard, but he could do it. He would need to live in a lean-to of sticks stacked against a tree until he collected enough hides for a tent. The forests produced plenty of food in warm weather, so he would be fine once the cold departed. He could build his camp in a thicket again so people had trouble sneaking up on him.

He just wished the people had not stolen his pretty rocks. A lot of them were regular smooth river rocks, but there had been a blue one streaked through with sparkling yellow that he really liked. And another with bands of purple and red. Maybe he would find another one of those blue rocks. If not, the Creator would probably make more of them in the next world.

CHAPTER TWELVE
Hess

Ingrid sat erect as they reclaimed their seats. She waited until everyone gave her their attention before speaking. "I intend to take the conversation in a different direction than what we've heard so far. No offense intended to Griff, Mel, or Drake, but their presentations reeked of complaints. Weariness of life informed my vote to die, but I generally approve of the Creator's work. I have no problem with the worlds themselves. My only objection is to immortality.

"I stopped being an effective Observer tens of Iterations past. Making myself care grew into a labor beyond my strength. When I started to seek out comfort instead of insight, I became unfit for duty. It's a simple case of wear and tear. I imagine a torn O-ring appreciates the dignity of being retired and replaced so that the host mechanism may continue.

"Before my usefulness lapsed, I studied a wide array of things. One in particular represents the soul of my work. I approach every world as a battleground of ideologies. Iteration one gave us primitive tribes. Iteration two showed us communistic villages. The city-states of Iteration three surprised everyone. Then the islands of four. Five introduced us to machines and large-scale agriculture. Six had desert nomads. Seven was our first diversely-featured world, featuring elements from every world before it. Eight gave us the internet for the first time.

"I could continue for hours. My point is that each world presented something new, or a new combination of old things. The interactions drew my attention. Every time two things come into conflict, the potential for discovery exists. Sometimes you can only learn about something through contrast with other things.

"How many of us loved the second Iteration the first years? Its beauty lay in the contrast with the previous world. Once the horrors of our past were more distant, we all came to despise the monotony of life in villages

276

where nothing serious ever happened. The juxtaposition taught us more than the experiences in isolation ever could.

"The greatest conflict happens not within our minds, but between the people of a world. All of you know I love warfare. I've waxed poetic on many occasions about the contest of wit, strength, endurance, determination, and skill. No doubt everyone is tired of hearing about military strategy. Should that not be the case, feel free to let me know later."

Ingrid almost smiled before resuming her remarks. "Warfare remains my favorite form of contest to observe, but all forms of cultural conflict provide valuable insights. Possibly the most profound of these is the struggle between cultures primarily practicing virtue ethics and cultures primarily practicing consequentialist ethics.

"For the benefit of anyone not familiar with the terminology, virtue ethics emphasize individual character while consequentialist systems hold that the ends justify the means. I have a particular fondness for virtue ethics, but these systems are less enduring than the alternatives. My eventual conclusion was that virtues were too rigid. They couldn't adapt to innovations as easily.

"Of course, others would argue – probably will, knowing Elza – that adhering to strict morals is a tactical weakness. My counter is that the strategic advantage outweighs the tactical disadvantage. Cultures with higher trust waste less effort, which allows members of society to further cultivate their better traits.

"The problematic innovations are things like sabotage, terrorism, and guerrilla warfare. The most effective response to such distasteful methods is disproportionate retribution, especially when the targets are innocent members of the enemy population.

"Thus, the best part of the people dies or is abandoned in favor of the worst. There is a lesson there. Either the people choose the wrong virtues. Or survival – of the person or the ideal – isn't the ultimate good. Which took me entirely too long to realize, considering the fact that I regularly witness the end of universes."

Ingrid folded both hands on the table. "That's all I have to present."

Kerzon leaned forward, face dead serious. "I'm going to beat Drake to it. You're obviously afraid of Elza."

Across the table, Drake erupted into a staccato squirrel giggle. "Screw you, Kerzon."

Kerzon winked. "You'll have to buy me a drink first."

When Drake's expression became contemplative, Jerome turned to Elza. "What are your criticisms this time?"

"Ingrid gave a coherent presentation free of obvious fallacies. I see no reason to belittle the only person who hasn't wasted my time."

Griff snorted. "After the way you ripped me yesterday, you better criticize something."

"Go ahead," Ingrid said, "I'm actually curious about what you might say."

"If you are going to insist, then I suppose there is one thing. I question the significance of your observations. You investigated a minor intersection of ethics and sociology. That seems worthy of a conversation over a bottle of wine, but hardly something worthy of presentation as your ultimate contribution."

Ingrid sank back into her chair.

"Any other questions?" Greg waited a full minute. "Then I will see all of you tomorrow."

CHAPTER THIRTEEN
Ingrid
Iteration 1

She ground the seeds with two rocks, her back to the group of raucous men and subdued women. Lude lounged among the hunters, pride beaming from his broad face, no doubt reflecting upon his conquests of the day. First he had killed a dozen unarmed men. Then he had received a public reward in the form of an amorous Ingrid throwing herself at the new top man.

Ingrid knew a lot about pleasing men. She knew how to tease their expectations prior to the act. She knew how to control the tempo to bring them close to completion, then bring them back from the edge, to approach and hold back until a single squeeze of her insides caused them to explode. She knew how to flatter their egos with words and expressions.

Lude was well pleased as he reclined in the soft grass.

No doubt he had expected a less enthusiastic reception from the women after ambushing their men at a peace meeting. Instead, he had been courted and bedded as a hero and now relaxed as his new woman cooked a meal for him, apparently eager for the status of being owned by the top man of the tribe.

When the seeds were finely ground, she swept them into the mixture of water and acorn flour and stirred. She poured thin patties onto hot rocks pre-greased with the fat of a doe. Then she returned her attention to the meat being smoked above the fire in a wicker basket. She had cut the meat as thin as possible with a flint blade, then pre-cooked it closer to the flames using green wood skewers. Now it smoked while wrapped around a mash of starchy root vegetable that would bring a hint of sweetness to it.

To Ingrid's mind, even more impressive than cooking an entire meal herself was coordinating everything to finish at the same time. The men would be able to eat bread and meat and squash all at once in a great feast.

Bree, one of the other women, approached the fire, her sullen eyes fixed upon Ingrid.

"Leave," Ingrid said.

"My son is hungry."

"Your son is a boy. These mighty hunters eat first."

Bree's discontented gaze drifted to the pile of cooking discards hidden beneath the doe's hide. She bent to touch the remnants of a green plant, her fingers stroking the hairy stalk. Bree's eyes flashed up to Ingrid's, her jaw going slack.

"This food is not for your son," Ingrid said. And Bree nodded, a kaleidoscope of fear and hope rising to her face. The woman may not be the most competent at the fires, but she knew enough to distinguish poison hemlock from carrot.

When the food was done, Ingrid portioned it out on rough wooden planks and presented it to the men – Lude first and then the other men in order of decreasing size. Each of the men took the offered plate and devoured sweet and savory meat, cubed squash, and crisp bread. Ingrid brought forth an obsequious smile as she watched them eat meat sweetened by hemlock root, squash cooked with leaves of hemlock, and bread filled with hemlock seeds.

A single mouthful should be sufficient to kill a man. Each of the men consumed more than a single bite of their feast. Ingrid studied the various men as she wore her false smile and shifted her grip on the flint blade's handle. She recognized most of the hunters in the group. They had eaten among this tribe in the past as honored guests and hosted hunters from Ingrid's tribe in turn. Those she didn't recognize were young, except for one. That lone stranger crouched among the others, studying everything around him with a vicious intensity, occasionally joining in the revelry of his peers to make some comment or other that drew forth bursts of laughter.

Killers, all of them. She would have permitted their actions to go unpunished if they had done the killing in an honorable manner. Instead, they used trickery to take down unarmed men – men who considered them brothers.

Ingrid's smile-lines deepened as the men began to show symptoms, falling down or cradling their heads. Dizziness came first. Then weakness. Then the breath stopped. She observed the first stages, bending over the men to look them in the eyes and slice their throats before the poison could complete its job.

She saved Lude for last. His breath already came shallow when she met his eyes. "You are killed by a woman," she whispered as the sawed his neck open. "This is what happens to kin-slayers and backstabbers."

Around the perimeter of the camp, the other woman stared at her in silence. They could not be happy at the deaths of the men when that meant their tribe no longer had any hunters. Nor could they be sad at the deaths of those who had killed their lovers. Emptiness, she decided. That was what she read in their expressions.

As she watched, the women startled, their eyes looking past Ingrid. She turned to see one of the men sitting up. It was the one she had not recognized before. He looked around at the corpses of his comrades and laughed. He winked at Ingrid. "Now that was something else. I've been watching people a long time and never saw something like that happen. What did you feed us, woman?"

Ingrid studied the unbroken flesh of his neck. She remembered slicing it, freeing rivers of red to stain his beard and chest. No blood lingered anywhere on him. She blinked. "Observer."

His smirk melted into perplexity. "You too?"

"Did you encourage Lude's attack?" She hefted the blade in her hand.

"You're the one causing trouble. I just watch the people."

Ingrid studied him a minute, unable to read past the bored apathy he projected. "Watch the people somewhere else. This is my tribe."

"I'm the man here. I'll stay if I want. Might make you my woman too."

She squinted at him, head tilting to the side. He looked like he knew how to fight. Of course, so did she. "Try."

For a moment, his eyes weighed her. Then he shrugged. "I've got more interesting things to watch." He got to his feet and backed away from her. "What is your name, woman?"

"I'm called Ingrid in this tribe."

He continued backing away. "I'm Kerzon. Maybe we'll meet again some day."

CHAPTER FOURTEEN
Hess

As they exited the conference room, they encountered a press of bodies against the windows once more. Hess slipped past the crowd to exit the hotel's main doors and turned his face upward to stare with everyone else. The light of day shone clear and bright everywhere but for the plume of gray rising from the mountain and stretching downwind like a hazy streak of dust on the heavens.

"We might wanna check on our boat," Erik said.

Rather than wait for the stables to saddle a horse for them, they went by foot, skipping the zigzagging roads to jog along steep animal trails. Their haste ended after Hess broke a leg in a concealed hole. Erik continued forward more cautiously, leaving Hess to catch up after he healed.

They rejoined the road when it became obvious whatever their shortcut saved them in distance it cost them in time. Over an hour after their departure, they came into view of the harbor and stumbled to a halt. The schooner and yacht were gone. More, half the fishing boats from the day before were missing.

Erik scowled at the sight before them. "Now what?"

"We take the steamship."

"You talkin 'bout the one fresh outta coal?"

Hess shrugged. "We'll have to fix that. Until then, at least we know no one else will be stealing our ship."

"You expect us to row a fucking tugboat?"

"Don't be an ass. We'll burn wood. Or steal coal." Hess turned in a slow circle. "We'll need to stage our fuel somewhere."

"Leave that to me," Erik said.

"It needs to be -"

"Fuck, Hess, you think you know better than me how to hide shit? Maybe we're tied with swords, but no one's got smuggling on me. I've been hiding all sorta nefarious doings from the people for as long as I've been alive. Storing some wood ain't nothing compared to concealing a room full of screaming school kids."

"Don't hurt anyone."

"Whole island's doomed, dip-shit."

"Erik . . . ."

"I ain't risking my skin for the sake of giving one of the pathetic creatures a few extra days. So I'm gonna do what I gotta do. If it makes you feel better, there ain't time for the usual games. Now while I acquire us a hidey hole, what you gonna do for the good of the cause?"

"I'll scout some targets." Hess nodded towards the tugboat. "After I swim out to do an inventory."

They separated. Hess jogged towards one of the public access piers while Erik sauntered in the opposite direction. At the end of the pier, Hess stowed his shirt and shoes in an unoccupied rowboat before diving into the water. He dolphin kicked several times to get some distance before surfacing, then transitioned into a sidestroke, left side down. He added a scissor kick and lost himself in the repetitive movement.

His path looped out into the harbor a considerable distance before turning back in to approach the steamship from an angle that concealed him from the shore. The swim took close to half an hour. At its end, he climbed the hemp netting that served as a bumper and rolled over the side to squat on the deck.

After a quick scan of his surroundings, he slipped down the stair to the engine room. It was of a simple single-cylinder design. Hess identified the controls, checked that everything was properly greased, and moved on to the boiler room. He snorted at what his inventory revealed. Rolled iron and rivets. While well maintained, the entire apparatus lacked even the pretense of efficiency.

He studied the size of the firebox and the pile of leftover coal. Enough probably remained to bring the ship up to temperature, but it would never get anywhere without additional fuel. Hess checked the water level by opening the three valves. The lowest of them released a stream of water. That was good. If the water was below the bottom valve, that would indicate a critically low level of water in the boiler. The middle valve did nothing when he opened it. The tank needed water added until the water level rose above the second valve. The third valve was there to indicate when there was too much water in the system for safe operation.

The replenishment pump used hand power and had a length of heavy rubber tubing extending from it. Hess tasted some of the water still in the pump mechanism. Mingled with the tang of metal was a blast of salt. Excellent. They wouldn't have to waste time figuring out how to get fresh water to the ship; they could just pump straight from the sea. It was the sole advantage the primitive steam engine design had offered so far.

Back top side, Hess squatted in the door frame and studied the guard shack at the base of the pier. It held one guard who sat with his feet up while a second guard stood nearby. He watched long enough to see them rotate positions. They each carried a musket and wore a saber at the hip.

Then Hess dove back into the water and swam back to where he had left his clothes. After dressing, he walked back up the harbor road to tour the streets of the town, noting locations with stacked wood as he went. He returned to his room that evening to sketch out his plans. He intended to hit the targets first who were least likely to notice their losses. There were several houses on the outskirts of town that aged their wood in backyard lean-tos. He should be able to raid those without causing a stir among the locals.

He had also noticed that the saltpeter refinery spewed black clouds from corroded iron stacks, which meant at least one business still had coal to burn. Robbing the refinery of a bulky raw product might be more trouble than it was worth, depending on how successful their wood collection was.

Before he worried about any of that, he needed to figure out how he was going to transport tons of solid fuel. While the hotel stable rented horses and even coaches, they didn't have any freight wagons available.

A knock interrupted his thoughts. Hess cracked open the door on a smiling Erik. "Got us a nice deal on a vacation home, honey. Just cost us one old recluse. Guy was nice enough to contribute a house, a barn, and a lot of pre-split wood. A real sweetheart. Shame someone put an axe in his melon. Anyway, we're off to a good start."

Hess opened his door further to allow Erik in. "Our major unsolved problem is transportation. We need to move lots of fuel."

"Chillax, amigo, we scored probably half a ton of wood already. When we're ready to make our big move, we steal a wagon and steam out of that harbor. While carefully avoiding the infamous reef, of course."

"Half a ton of wood doesn't get us out of the harbor. I'm estimating we'd need between five and ten tons of coal to get us to a safe distance. If we substitute wood for coal, that doubles the fuel requirements."

"What's with the negativity, Hessie? Things go south, we steal a fucking rowboat. So what if we die of exposure a few times?"

"And where do you think we'll wash up when the boat inevitably capsizes? I'm thinking the answer to that is some place covered with molten lava."

Erik scowled. "Then we find some wheels. I'll check the stables."

"They don't have wagons."

"Then build a fucking travois! A horse can carry over two hundred pounds without a problem; lash together a couple poles and you up that to half a ton. Then on game day we acquire a freight wagon to move things from our hidey hole to the ship all speedy like. This ain't rocket science."

Hess sat straighter. "That could work. Of course, we'd be leaving ruts in the road to guide the people directly to our staging area."

"So what if a few nosy Nellies need stabbing. I got my saber."

"Better idea," Hess said. "We make a sign to advertise we have wood for sale."

"Uh, that sounds like a *worse* idea. We're collecting, not selling."

"No one will buy at our prices. Even if they did, we'll make it profitable enough that we could turn around and purchase an equal amount of coal. Everyone will assume we're clueless businessmen dragging the same load of wood around town. When we become a joke, no one will take us serious."

Erik shrugged. "Whatever. Just keep your fucking nerve. I don't got the patience to manage your feelings."

"Can you arrange to rent two horses for tomorrow afternoon? I'll rig up the hardware. We'll do four trips each the first day, then I need to identify additional targets."

Hess slipped outside and procured poles, planks, rope, and canvas tarp from the unguarded warehouse of the general store and made a sign using materials from the conference room. Then he assembled everything and hid it behind a road-side hedge. He ate a late dinner, collapsed into bed, and woke early the next day to plan the order of their robberies.

At nine o'clock, he entered the conference room to hear Elza's presentation.

CHAPTER FIFTEEN
Hess

Elza spoke with the calm precision that was her hallmark. "No doubt you expect something profound from me. Maybe something pretentious or esoteric. I would say that I hate to disappoint, but in truth I'm not overly concerned with your opinions.

"For the majority of my existence, I discharged my duties through intellectual studies. I have a talent for analysis and I put it to use on every topic of study I encountered. On occasion, I have even managed to advance beyond what the people have discovered.

"I always rationalized that while the Creator almost certainly did not send me into the worlds to practice the scientific method, my studies were useful in determining the limit of what the people were capable of learning about the created universe. Then Jerome revealed our semi-divine natures and I realized that, far from being an ideal Observer, I was horribly deficient.

"My most profound insight is not so much about the worlds as it is about our place in it. We were never meant to be apathetic watchers. We entered into Our creation to interact with it. When feeling less charitable, I liken this to cosmic masturbation. We create, play, destroy, and start the cycle over again.

"Observer is the wrong title for us. We should be called *Experiencers*. Because that is our purpose. To be people for a time. All the times I followed my sense of duty I failed at my true mission. Conversely, all the times I violated the divine command were justified."

Elza drummed her fingers on the table. "And now I suppose I must criticize the flaws of my own argument or risk being accused of unfairness. There were no informal logical fallacies, because I know better. However, I did make assumptions.

"My most questionable assumption: generalizing from my mind to that of the Creator's. I skirt the edges of arguing from personal incredulity, saved by the fact that there are no viable alternative hypotheses. Some evidence that the Creator intends us to experience rather than observe exists in the circumstances of our incarnations. Hess has never been a woman. Given his strict heterosexual orientation, it becomes obvious that the Creator intended to humor that preference.

"And Drake. Sometime after Iteration ten, he became a perpetual outcast in the social order. Whatever group occupied the position of most disadvantaged within the social structure became his by default. Once I decided it could not be coincidence, I suspected the Creator used Drake to study a particular phenomenon. Until last Iteration, when I overheard him telling Jerome that being a part of the out group brought with it the advantage of community. In all the times I have heard Drake complain about his circumstances, I never heard something as authentic as that one off-hand admission.

"Another piece of evidence is the existence of the Church of the Demiurge. I am convinced that the schism among us caused competing desires that the Creator could not resolve. Several of you desired to punish rogue Observers. Another questioned the inherent moral quality of the Creator. The result was the perverse religion that Ingrid and Erik learned to hate."

"The fuck," Erik said. "Rich people got better community than anyone. Why wouldn't Drake be sent into the country club class if he wants friends so bad?"

Heads turned to Drake. He shrank in on himself.

"I think I understand," Jerome said. "The upper class compete. Sometimes it is friendly; often it is only a veneer of civility that makes it appear that way. Those on the outside form tight-knit communities where people don't judge one another so quickly. If any of you have been listening during these meetings, what conversation we have tends to be combative. We, the privileged Observers living among the people, are snobs by virtue of our positions. The downtrodden stick together."

Erik rolled his eyes. "Aw, baby need a blankie? Grow the fuck up, Drake. You're a disgrace to the rest of us."

Drake slammed a fist onto the table. "I never said any of that! All of you stop putting words in my mouth! You know why I got the shit jobs so many times? Cause I can handle it! I been through more than any of you know."

"Please, cupcake. I've faced inquisitions."

"No insults," Greg muttered.

Drake glared at Elza. "Leave me out of this."

"Let's talk about you instead," Griff said. "We get Hess don't like cock, but what's your reason for being a woman?"

Elza hesitated. "Because I would do anything for Hess."

"Except, you know, *live*," Erik said.

Ingrid leaned forward. "I refuse to believe the Creator has frivolous goals. While I agree with your low opinion of some of our coworkers, that doesn't provide us any additional insights. The Creator is not just the twelve of us. We are more than employees but less than the sum total."

In the silence that followed, Drake stood. "Are we done? Good."

Greg cleared his throat as the door slammed shut behind their departed colleague. "If there are no other questions, then we appear to be taking a fifteen minute break. It is my sincere hope the Creator finds more value in our meetings than I do."

CHAPTER SIXTEEN
Elza
Iteration 1

Her father gestured and Elza approached. As she took his hand, she noticed his skin felt cool even in the heat of the day – a fact that seemed even more ominous than his inability to stand these past few days.

"My Elza," he said.

"Yes, papa."

"I am sorry."

Her brow wrinkled. "For what?"

A coughing fit interrupted whatever he was about to say. When it passed, her father had to recline on the hammock she had constructed for him. "I die soon."

Elza nodded. Age had robbed all vitality from him.

"I worry. You need a man."

"Of all the women who have ever lived, I need a man the least."

A pleased smile lit his face. "Clever Elza. Strong Elza. *Still* . . . ."

"I don't need a man, papa. And I don't want one giving me orders."

His smile faded. "Yes, yes. But it's not good to be alone. Not a woman, not a man, not anyone." The speech winded him, and he had to stop. Elza caressed the back of his hand.

"I'll be fine, papa. You were the only man I ever needed in my life."

His eyes grew sad. "I loved you too much. No love left for other men."

"That's not how the world works, papa."

"Maybe."

"Trust me, papa. I have been watching for many years now."

He closed his eyes. "Tell me about the giants of the sea."

Elza smiled down at her father. "There are no giants of the sea making waves when they jump to grab the moon. It is a silly idea. The waves come all the time, not just when the moon is in the sky. The giants don't cause

289

the tides either. That is the moon pulling on the water. I don't know how it works, but it does. That's the only thing that makes any sense."

She paused, then placed her fingers alongside his neck to search for a heartbeat that was no longer there. Elza bent over to kiss his forehead. "You don't have to worry about me. I serve the Creator of the world and nothing can harm me. I promise to remember you. Goodbye, papa."

Elza arranged her father's body for the next person to find it, picked up the pack she kept prepared for this moment, and abandoned the tribe of her youth. There was an entire world for her to study.

CHAPTER SEVENTEEN
Hess

During the recess someone had found and convinced Drake to return to the meeting. He sat away from the table, arms folded and a dour expression on his face. Like everyone else, he looked to the man sitting tall at the table.

Erik wore a smile that threatened to curl into a snarl as he made eye contact with each of them in turn. "None of y'all got a clue what I'm about. You have notions that I'm nutty in the noggin. That I struggle with anger issues and shit like that.

"*Wrong.* I got mountains of self-control. I'm cool as snow, yo. My actions are a hundred and eleven percent justified, and I'll prove it. Look around. Boring ass conference room, right? What's beyond that? Old-timey hotel still bragging about running water. An island sitting around an angry fucking volcano. A sea. A whole world. A whole fucking universe.

"You see, dumb asses, the Creator don't do half measures. This place exists a single week. There's hardly any reason to try. Yet we find ourselves in a complex, self-consistent universe. That's beauty. Every moment is a miracle. A real deal miracle.

"The pathetic creatures don't get that. Suicides were the thing that opened my eyes. I couldn't fathom why anything would want to punch the clock. I mean, I used to feel sorry for the bastards' short lives and I didn't even like 'em. So anyways, people were looking at their options and voting no on proposition existence.

"I'll admit, I went a teensy bit extreme at first. Then I got the idea of a lifetime. Started on a methodology I kept up until last Iteration. I abduct someone and do the torture bit until they ask me, without prompting, to kill them. Badabing, badaboom, I'm done. Just gotta ask one question and I'm dumping a body somewhere.

"The things I learned were grade A observation. Pampered people put up less of a fight than the downtrodden. What the fuck, right? I mean, you'd expect them to have more to live for and all that. Nope. And age does weird shit. If you graph out quickness to embrace oblivion, with age as the independent variable, it looks like a sine wave. Kids are fighters. Teenagers got a death wish. Adults wanna live. Old fucks are ready to go.

"Course, that's averaging out a lot of distinct individuals. I seen some interesting shit. *Caused* a lot of interesting shit, to tell it straight. That graph, though, really got me thinking. It's not a straight line up or down. So the big factor's gotta be life stage. Here's how I reckon the facts.

"Children are going off of what the Creator programmed into their biology. Body says live, so they live. Teenagers got more brains, so they can override the program when their shorts give them a wedgie. But then adults get a jolt of self-preservation hormones when they have cum-stains running around. Then the inconvenience of getting all decrepit makes them ready to give up. Deep shit, right?"

Ingrid slapped the table. "Do we really have to listen to this? Your insights aren't deep Erik. They're sick. They're twisted. They're *simple-minded.*"

"Aw, honey, are you ragging it? Cause if you are, *I still do not give a shit.* I will start doing things if anyone interrupts me again. Try to get some objectivity! You're Observers, not people.

"Anyway, here's some fascinating factoids. Men last longer than women. Soldiers do fantastic as a segment. Malnourished or diseased people got no will to live, but that's mostly biology, I think. Hoodlums probably win. They're survivors. Mostly, that is. They never survive some quality time with *moi.*

"So the moral of the story is that creation despises existence. Which, I suppose, the lot of you suiciding turd-suckers already knew. But wait, there's more!

"See, before I killed anyone, I asked a question. *Why do you hate Creation?* They told me some bullshit, I gave em a quick finish. Then, last Iteration, I made a friend while the Church of the Demiurge kept me in their lovely torture hotel. Made lots of friends, actually, but this one was a friend friend. Not a real friend – I'm still being ironic. But not like a gonna-hurt-you-so-bad friend. More like a wanna-see-how-you-react friend.

"Anyway, bitch was quite the conversationalist. I told her all about my routine. Then my main man Hess broke me out of the slammer. So I reconnected with my friend friend from the inside. And before I even got started with my thing, she blows my fucking mind.

"Said some stuff about fear taking over people. Then the big reveal. *The people don't have a purpose.*" Erik brandished his hands as if he had performed a magic trick. His eyes darted from face to face. "Did you fucking hear me? The people don't have a purpose."

Hess put a hand to his forehead. "Erik, I'm certain none of us are following your line of reasoning. Unless you're telling us that you have yet another excuse to hurt the people."

"Not at all." Erik slumped in his seat. "You're all fucking morons. Let me lay it out for you. The Creator made animals as creatures of instinct. Made us with the mental power to ignore instinct but gave us the divine command. What about the people? Too much brains to go along with the instinct programming. No divine command to guide them.

"They are the closest thing to a blank slate you can get with a conscious creature. People have no purpose. That's why they're always suiciding. No purpose means no reason to live. But no purpose isn't the end, cause they can adopt a purpose.

"*That's* what we need to be studying. Much as I enjoyed my old job, a new way has presented itself. I need to study the people who make a new purpose for their lives. Like dictators or innovators or gladiators. Only problem is I can't use my usual methods if I want to get a good understanding of their *raison d'être*.

"But that's cool, cause I realized that since I'm part of the Creator, I deserve a hobby. And my new hobby is – you guessed it – torturing! Even though it was my job all those years, I never lost the passion for it, which I think is the true sign of a good torturer.

"That's my spiel, y'all. Bring on the debate."

Hess sighed. "I know I'm probably going to regret this, but why do you like torture?"

Erik pointed a finger at Hess. "Good question, you brown noser. I like torture for many reasons. First, it's hard not to enjoy something you're good at. And I am like the gold fucking medalist of torturing. Second, it brings out all the legit emotions, cuts through all the fakey shit. Another reason is that people deserve it. Choosing not to embrace life is insulting to the Creator." Erik turned to Elza. "Come on, lazy-eye, hit me up with a question."

"I have no questions for you," she said.

"Then maybe you have a comment? Criticism? Sick burn? Don't hold back, *Fraulein*, the two of us are tight as protons and neutrons."

Elza pursed her lips in thought. "You never made anything close to a logical argument, so there isn't anything concrete to attack. But I can criticize your experimental design. More accurately, your lack of one. I have observed in your recitations that your chosen methods are commensurate with your estimation of your victim. You put in extra effort to break challenging subjects and move slowly to stretch out your time with those you consider more delicate. There is no objectivity – not even the illusion of it. All your data is useless."

Erik shrugged. "We'll agree to disagree. We done, shitheads?"

CHAPTER EIGHTEEN
Erik
Iteration 1

Before anything else, there was knowledge. A collection of simple, profound facts. The first formed the absolute bedrock of an identity: *I am an Observer.* The second provided context: *It is my duty to observe this world on behalf of the Creator who made it.* The third gave a sense of the future: *Before the world is destroyed, the sky will open so I can give my report.* And the final fact promised more: *There will be other worlds.* Those four facts and the minimal context necessary to understand them were everything.

Then came sensation. Sight, scent, and touch erupted into existence. Smell of salty sea air and smoke. Feel of coarse clothing and smothering heat and sandy soil. Sight of a breathtaking expanse of sky meeting glimmering green-blue water at the horizon. The world. Nothing moved, and there was an intuitive understanding that this moment existed outside of time in the realm of creation.

And the moment was glorious. The Creator's Observer studied the scene, content to exist and marvel at the display. How far did the world extend into the distance? Did it even have an end? What would change when things began to move?

Memories poured forth, dim in comparison to the brilliant experience of the present, detailing a life lived in this world. A complete history arrived within the mind of the Creator's Observer, providing a meticulously prepared identity.

The name of the identity was Ressi. She had lived among a tribe of fishermen for all sixteen years of her life, playing on the beach with the other children, cooking fish over smoldering flames with the grown women, stitching together the skins of animals with sinew to make clothing, swimming in the warm waters at every free moment.

Ressi's prize possession was a crude doll fashioned by her deceased mother. Her favorite food was soup made from squid and seaweed. Her best friend was a girl named Annit. The men of the tribe often watched Ressi with desire, appreciating the grace of her body and the beauty of her face. So far, her father Kenja had refused to allow any man to take her, but the day would come soon when a man would do more than ask.

The Creator's Observer devoured the memories. So many experiences awaited her in this world. She would collect every observation possible for the Creator. Learn everything about the people and their world.

"Ressi, get over here," Kenja barked. Her father projected a presence far grander than his slight frame. As the best spear fisher of the tribe, he commanded much respect. Though, given that the world had begun so recently, Kenja had never actually spear fished – a fact only she knew.

Ressi slipped into her clothes as she approached their hut, noting the way her father's eyes chastely avoided the contours of her body. She recalled that he had never taken a woman since her mother died. Yet it was known in the tribe that men's passions were as wild and uncontrollable as the flames of a fire. Had grief truly quenched the heat of his loins?

She noticed a tension in Kenja's jaw as she approached. Quick as the leap of a fish, his palm struck Ressi on the side of the head, sending her tumbling to the ground. She blinked away her startlement. "Get in the hut," Kenja said.

She moved to obey, then stopped. "Why did you hit me?"

Kenja scowled. "You like running around bare for all the men of the tribe? Do you not see the desire of their eyes? You are too young, Ressi."

The Creator's Observer remembered this man as a doting father still grieving for a woman he had lost more than five years past. He rarely struck her, but then again, swimming unclothed in the waters was something she had not done in years. She had swum nude today because in the thrill of her first day of existence, she had yearned to feel everything.

Kenja pointed at the hut. "Get in."

She ducked inside their home, glanced from the roof of layered broad-leaf above to the dirt floor below. Between the two surfaces was an empty room holding two sleeping mats. Along walls of loosely bound bamboo rested personal items. So strange, to see a place she remembered falsely. She wondered if all the experiences of the people were as dim as her memories from before the world began. If so, that would make them rather dull of mind.

"Go to sleep," Kenja said.

On her sleeping mat, Ressi listed to her father toss and turn. In the twilight of evening, she desired nothing less than sleep. The world called to her, promising to reveal wonders untold. She sat up, eliciting an angry grunt from Kenja. He would not allow his daughter, the remnant of a woman he loved in spite of death and time, roam the night.

She glanced at the door, then at her father. The man was not yet gray, so surely he still felt passion. Ressi slipped free of her clothing. The resemblance between her and her dead mother was said to be strong. Surely Kenja would appreciate the similarity. Incest was common enough despite the stigma.

Ressi rolled closer to her father, sliding a hand along his silhouette in the dark, touching knee, hip, side, belly, and chest. He lay silent. Ressi pressed herself against him, trying to piece together what she knew of sex. It was not much beyond the basic mechanics. Insert that into this. The women were divided over whether or not the act brought pleasure.

Lacking any practical knowledge, Ressi decided to simply touch his manhood. Her fingers discovered him already hard. As she traced his anatomy, Kenja moaned softly. She wrapped her hand around him and stroked with silky slow deliberateness. Her father's hips moved counter to her own motion.

"What are you doing?" His whisper came harsh in her ears.

"I want to try sex."

"This is wrong, Ressi. Your mother . . . ."

"Is dead," she said.

Kenja pulled away from her. "Why are you acting this way?" She stretched out her hand and he seized it. "Tell me why, Ressi. Why would you shame your mother's memory like this?"

"I don't care about her memory. I want to try sex."

His fist connected without warning, hidden by the darkness. Ressi blinked tears free of the battered eye. She never anticipated his reaction would be so strong. "Your loins still have fire. Do you lust for a memory?"

Whatever reaction she expected, it was not what happened. Kenja leaped on top of her and rained down his fists, growling in wordless fury. Ressi tried to block the strikes, but he effortlessly pinned her arms beneath his knees. As she lay gasping, heart racing, trying to flinch back into the ground to avoid each blow, Ressi began to scream.

Stone hard fingers seized her throat, squeezing hard enough to crumple her windpipe and make the blood rush in her head. Ressi began to buck, trying to dislodge the beast on top of her. She couldn't escape. She couldn't even free a hand to claw at her throat.

Her heart thundered. Ressi thrashed wildly. *I'm going to die! No, I am the Creator's Observer! No! No!* Her vision faded from the outsides to the sound of hollow ringing.

The Creator did not appear to save her. The world faded from her perception. An Observer meant to outlast entire worlds died on her first day of life. Bitterness faded into nothingness.

Ressi woke with a start, finding herself floating in the water. She got her footing in time to see her father disappear into his hut. For a few moments, her hands traced the lines of her unbruised throat, verifying she was unharmed. Then she left the water as quietly as possible and walked away from the huts of her tribe.

Of course I cannot die, she thought. *The people get old and die. And they are always taking injuries. If I am to live through whole worlds, then of course the Creator made me to survive.*

Her feet carried her around the bend and out of sight of her tribe. Ressi collapsed onto a rock and stared out at the quarter-moon rising over the crashing water. Despite everything, she had to admit that the world was beautiful. And if the experience with her father taught her nothing else, it taught her that she did not have to fear death.

Now she could walk away from the tribe to wander the world. Everyone would think her dead. Her father would probably tell the others of the tribe some lie. They would believe him because he had a reputation. Fiery pain shot up Ressi's jaw, the first she realized she had clenched it.

The things Kenja had done to her . . . . No one should be able to do those things to her. She was the Creator's Observer. She represented the one who had brought this majestic world into existence.

Her brow drew down. She could not die, but her father could. Ressi wandered back towards the hut of her father. She stopped outside to grasp at one of the spears he used for fishing, sending the others crashing to the ground in her haste.

"Who is that?"

Ressi began to back away as the flap to the hut swung open. The figure before her startled. For a moment she froze. Then the fiery rage within her flared. Ressi drove the spear into her father's gut, pulled it free, and slammed it home again.

Kenja stumbled back into his home and fell onto his back.

The Creator's Observer approached, placed both hands on the haft of the spear, and rocked it back and forth, eliciting a moan from the man it impaled. "You wouldn't put your stick in me, so I'll put my stick in you," she growled, wishing more hateful words existed to throw at him.

"Ressi, don't do this, I'm your father!"

"I am not Ressi!" She glared at him. "Do you really think a woman could come back to life? Do you think your daughter could shove a spear into your middle?"

She pulled the spear free and stabbed again. The man who had seemed so powerful before wept as she claimed her vengeance.

"Please," Kenja moaned, "please."

She sneered down at the pathetic creature before her. "I can't believe I feared you. Never again. The Creator's Observer fears nothing."

Later that night, she departed the lands of her tribe. As she left, her sole regret was that she hadn't caused enough pain to the man who dared try to harm her, the Creator's Observer.

CHAPTER NINETEEN
Hess

Following Erik's presentation, they rented horses and attached the travois Hess had constructed the previous night. With their advert for overpriced wood prominently displayed, they moved to their first target.

The house sat outside of town, its fenced back yard holding a large coop packed with chickens. Outside the fence sat a large silo spilling kernels of maize from its base, and beyond that a shed with split logs aging at its rear and along one side.

Hess led their horses a stone's throw into the forest, checked that the two travois were properly seated, and began liberating armfuls of aged oak. Erik matched his every move, slinking through the woods without a sound, hauling loads of ill-gotten boiler fuel.

Sweat soaked every inch of their bodies and clothing by the time their travois were loaded to capacity. Hess brushed away splinters of wood and peeled damp clothing off his body. A sour musk emanated from him to assault his nose.

Ignoring his discomfort, he led his horse along the road behind Erik. They passed through town and down the harbor road. It took an hour and a half walking their beasts of burden. They passed the piers, turned onto a windy private drive, and deposited their cargo in the main room of the shack Erik had procured for their use.

They reversed their trip and got a second load from the same house. After unloading that, their next haul came from a small cottage closer to their destination. A single raid emptied out all the wood at that cottage.

Following a much needed break, they swung by another of the targets Hess had identified. Due to the presence of children in the yard, they had to give it a pass. They returned to the first house and claimed the remainder of the wood there. It was enough for half a load each.

As they stood breathing hard, Hess studied the silo. Holding up a finger for silence, he snuck up to the structure and took a handful of maize. The kernels felt dry. He returned to Erik. "Better idea. Tomorrow we'll fill burlap sacks with corn. It burns about the same as wood."

"Sounds fan-fucking-tastic to me. I'm not a fan of the logs."

They unloaded the wood, hid the travois, returned the horses, and entered the hotel. Hess bathed, went to dinner, and passed out for the night seconds after his head touched the pillow. The next morning he woke late and had to skip breakfast to make it to the conference room on time.

CHAPTER TWENTY
Hess

Greg greeted each of them by name as they took their seats. When the last of them, Drake, appeared and slumped into a chair, Greg began his presentation. "Over the worlds, each of us drifted into a specialty. Mine was academia. I enjoy being around intelligent people and learning new things. Especially I enjoy historical analysis. And to head off the inevitable accusation, I also very much enjoy being safe and comfortable.

"My understanding of our mission has evolved over time. At first, anything was worthy of my attention. Later, I came to the conclusion that diversity was the key feature. Thank you for the dramatic eye rolls, everyone – those were right on cue. Before you stop listening, allow me a few moments to put my revelation into context.

"Piggy-backing off of Griff's ideas, I would like you to imagine nothingness. Ignore for the moment the impossibility of understanding non-existence, our limited imaginations should more than suffice for this illustration. There is a key defining feature of nothing. Have any of you pictured the concept as containing any contrast? I doubt it. The typical visualization is of blackness, which isn't quite right, but right enough.

"There is no diversity in nothing. The creation of something from nothing could be viewed as the differentiation of the undifferentiated. Perhaps a misguided analogy, but perhaps not. To offer a possible answer to the question posed by Griff, what matters is not the origin, nor the destination, nor the fundamental nature of existence. What matters is the contrast between those things that do exist.

"I also agree with Mel's point. Most people behave as faulty automatons. Not all of them, however. The subjects worth studying are different from the people around them. That fundamental diversity makes them interesting. It makes them matter.

"While I disagree with the premise that fear is the only emotion, Drake's presentation made me think. An individual emotion would be impossible to distinguish. There is no happiness without sadness. Diversity of feeling provides the contrast to interpret emotion.

"Ingrid's fascinating idea that the entire world is a stage to act out the conflict of ideas meshes with my theory. There is no meaningful conflict between the identical.

"I think the wildly different interpretations of reality provided yesterday by Elza and Erik represent a great diversity within ourselves. To me, this is an excellent demonstration of how the Observers exemplify the Creator's values. Everything that can be said to exist gains this status by virtue of differentiation. Diversity is everything and its absence is, literally, nothing."

Greg smiled around the table. "I prepared a longer presentation, but I distilled it down to its essence when it became obvious no one else planned on speaking longer than half an hour. I'm ready for questions now."

Kerzon grunted. "Can I take my turn now? I've got other things than this conference going on."

Greg's smile wilted. "*What?*"

"I'm running a gambling ring. And before anyone asks, Observers aren't welcome. This is my own thing."

CHAPTER TWENTY-ONE
Greg
Iteration 2

The strangers sat across the fire from him at the center of the village, unblinking gazes fixed on him as they fielded questions from the elders. While dark-skinned people occasionally found their way this far north, they seldom stayed for long. Far odder than their coloration, the man and woman claimed to travel the world collecting stories.

From the moment they entered the village, the two of them had stared at him as if he were the only person at the crowded evening feast. Somehow, they seemed to sense he was different from the other people. Greg studied the press of bodies around him, charting the quickest path to freedom. His eyes completed their scan and froze on the spot across the fire. The couple were no longer there.

"This man here is Greg," warbled the voice of elder Cane at his shoulder. "Smartest man of the village. Maybe smartest man of the world. He knows the answer to most any question you might ponder."

The man and woman, now standing directly beside him, exchanged a brief glance before turning bemused expressions on him. The woman spoke first. "The smartest man of the world? How quaint."

"Greetings, friend. My name is Hess. This beautiful woman is Elza."

Elder Cane scratched his head. "I must have misheard earlier. I thought your names were different."

"We have a lot of names," Elza said. "But for the smartest man alive, we are Elza and Hess. I hope you like the name Greg, friend, because it just became permanent."

He blinked. "Uh, yes . . ."

"Tell us some words of wisdom."

Greg glanced to Hess, who watched in silence. "Well, I told the villagers just the other day that the flesh of animals can be eaten."

304

Elza's brows rose. "The flesh of animals, you say. I suppose the corpse would need to be skinned and then hung to drain the blood before roasting over a fire."

He blinked at the dark-skinned woman. "That would make sense."

"Give us another brilliant observation," she said.

Observation? "As travelers, perhaps you are aware there are lakes of water too great for a man to swim across?"

"We are."

"Then you will be shocked to learn that it is possible to build wooden platforms to float across its surface."

"You mean a *boat*?"

Greg flinched. He hadn't realized that word existed in this world. "That's right. You seem very knowledgeable."

She tilted her head in shallow agreement. "It is only natural to expect the world's smartest woman to know more than the world's smartest man."

He forced a laugh. "You think much of yourself."

"An accurate opinion, in my experience."

"Then you tell me some wise words."

Elza lifted a finger. "People who pick all the insects out of their food get the wasting disease." She raised a second finger. "If you store rotting fruit in clay jars, the juice will make those who drink it happy." Another finger. "Injured backs can be repaired by pushing the bones back to their proper places." A fourth finger. "The villages resist violence even after someone kills." The thumb. "Elza, Hess, Mel, San, Drake, Erik, Ingrid, Kerzon, and Greg."

"What? None of that makes any sense."

Hess smirked at him. "Just give up. She's almost never wrong."

"Really? Think about what she said. Not eating insects causes the wasting disease? That's ridiculous."

"Observe what the people eat," Elza said. "The ones who pick out insects get sick. Flesh needs to consume flesh to survive."

"You're wrong. About that and the rest of it, too."

"Rotten fruit juice is the best invention ever," Hess said.

Greg shook his head. "Ridiculous. And the last thing you said didn't mean anything. It was just a list of names."

"A very important list." Elza folded her arms. "Each of those names belongs to an Observer. You're not the only one, Greg."

Hess raised both hands in an exaggerated shrug. "That is why you don't argue with Elza. Now, try not to look too disappointed. We're going to make up for your humiliation by teaching you how to rot fruit."

CHAPTER TWENTY-TWO
Hess

Kerzon shrugged at the attention on him. "Well, I'll just get started then. Hi, my name is Kerzon, and I have just about every type of addiction known to man. Woops, wrong kind of meeting.

"Seriously, though, I'm messed up. See, from the first days of my life, I was only ever able to want something that belonged to someone else. Because of my Observer status, I took pretty much whatever I wanted. The Creator needed my input, so I took things in the hedonistic direction. Lots of sex, drugs, and rock 'n' roll. Side note: methadone is the hardest drug to kick. Don't do drugs, kids.

"Anyway, I used to think my pleasure sense was broke. Then I realized no one wants what they have. They just aren't entitled pricks like me, so they learn to be content with what they got. Wish I could do the same. I'm always wanting something but never happy when I get it.

"I guess people are designed to always want more. And Observers are inserted into people-bodies, so same deal with us. Makes sense, in a way. What would everyone do if they had enough? Nothing interesting, that's for sure. So desire makes the world go round.

"I know none of that was particularly profound, and I feel a little guilty for running, so here's another nugget of wisdom. There's no such thing as a need. When someone says they need something, that just means they want you to give it to them out of guilt. I hate that. When I want something, I take it. That's dynamic, right there. Take what you want. Whining till someone takes pity on you is just a bitch move.

"And . . . that's it. I don't pretend to be a genius like others around here, so someone shout out a question or tell me I'm full of shit so I can get out of here."

Griff perked up as if coming awake. "What kind of gambling?"

"Kittens versus rats is the headliner. Don't tell any of the wait staff, but those kittens are rat food. I still have to round up some critters for the opening acts. Tell you what, I have another lesson for the group. Gambling is the best. I really, truly mean that. The randomness, the wins, the losses, the excitement." Kerzon glanced to Elza. "And I am dead serious about this being my thing."

Greg threw up his hands. "Let's just quit for the day."

"Fine by me," Kerzon said.

CHAPTER TWENTY-THREE
Kerzon
Iteration 1

He swung his spear with all the torque he could generate and crashed the haft against the skull of the man walking before him. Gill collapsed to the ground unconscious. Kerzon dragged his brother to the edge of the pond and submerged his head. Gill woke too late to do more than thrash his limbs in uncoordinated protest. The deed done, Kerzon posed the corpse as if it had tripped and struck its head, then returned to camp.

It took two days before another of the hunters discovered Gill. Kerzon wept convincingly at the burial, dedicated his contribution to the next feast – a moose, no less – to Gill's memory, regaled everyone with tales of posthumous glory, and only then proceeded to claim his inheritance: Emma.

Kerzon moved her into his tent six days after Gill's discovery. Long enough to show respect for the dead but not long enough for any of the other men to claim her. He resisted the urge to bed her the first night to heighten his anticipation. The second night they rutted like animals.

Though not a beauty, Emma exuded passion in everything she did. In speech, her entire body participated. In the drudgery of women's work, her expressive eyes danced free. In the dark of night, she moaned soft sighs of encouragement and surprise and approval. As she had with Gill, Emma cooed and gasped and giggled, coaxing him to glorious completion. The swap of mates appeared to have gone unnoticed by her.

Night after night, he claimed the sex that had been denied him while Gill lived. For a month or two, the midnight heat bedazzled him. Kerzon imagined the Creator would be quite pleased with the sensations he had experienced.

And then he noticed how much more attractive Meran was than Emma. Meran was woman to his uncle, top man of the tribe. Her curvy figure flared outward from a tight waist in both directions, wrapped in unblemished skin and crowned with golden hair. She drew the eyes of more men every year as if gaining the beauty other women lost to age.

In an instant, Emma's spell shattered. That night, her noises reminded him of the deranged hooting made by a simple-minded child the tribe had abandoned two winters past. It grated on him until he commanded her silent, whereupon she withdrew her affections for the night.

The next day, he followed his uncle to the privy pit. While the older man squatted, Kerzon chose a rock as large as two fists and approached. His uncle had just begun to stand when the rock connected with his temple. His uncle collapsed into the pit. Kerzon hefted a spear and drove it down in vicious movements until blood and shit coated the body.

Immediately upon his return to camp, he announced that his uncle had confessed to killing his brother out of fear of being usurped. When the men warned him that he would have to face the wrath of his uncle for making such a claim, he took them to the privy to look upon the corpse of their top man. A tense hour followed, at the conclusion of which one of his cousins became the new top man and Kerzon received Meran as his woman.

Kerzon evicted Emma and bedded Meran while the sun still shone. For days, he did little else but rut with his woman. After the passage of a few hours, the sight of her would stir to life the fire of his loins and he would take her again. His manhood ached with overuse, a sensation akin to being bruised from his abdomen to his thighs, but he still hardened and still managed to finish.

The bliss lasted, again, no more than a few months. This time, his disappointment arose from the declining condition of his life. Tarps had come loose on his tent, his clothing remained unwashed, food came to him cold, the stench of menstrual blood clung to their blankets, and the other men ogled his woman without respect for him.

His subsequent attempts to improve Meran's work failed. Everything she did reeked of laziness. Kerzon became so disgusted by the way she collapsed on her back as if sleeping during sex that he lost all interest in her. Eventually, he evicted her from his tent.

While trying to decide which woman to take next, the other men accused him of murdering his brother and uncle, then crushed in his skull with stones. Their violence ended abruptly when he returned to life in their midst. As the men stumbled back from him in horror, Kerzon decided that what he wanted next was not a new woman.

He wanted to kill his cousin and claim the position of top man.

CHAPTER TWENTY-FOUR
Hess

Hess took advantage of the short meeting by consuming a late breakfast. As he sat down with a generous helping of complimentary bread and jam, the other Observers entered the room. Kerzon split from the group to join Hess, spinning a chair to straddle it backwards.

"What's the deal with you and Erik? Ingrid saw the two of you taking out horses yesterday."

"We're getting off this island before the volcano blows." Hess glanced at the line of Observers loading plates. "Have the rest of you formed a breakfast club? And what about your urgent business with the gambling ring?"

Kerzon shrugged. "We're all struggling with the early mornings."

"Nine is an early morning?"

"That depends entirely on the hours you're keeping." Kerzon's eyes darted down Hess's figure and back up. "You should have run off with me two Iterations ago. I was gonna fuck you silly before Erik and the rest barged in to catch us. Instead you finished your shift at a gas station and had to go straight to the torture without any of the pleasure."

"Did you really think I would believe you were Elza?"

Kerzon twisted his face into an odd expression. "Erik thought it would work. Ingrid – Jerome, I mean – told us that your time underground messed with your mind. It was worth a shot. I had you collared, so you weren't getting away from us either way. I'm telling you, Hess, I was hot in one four four. Everything hung just right."

"This conversation isn't going anywhere I want to be," Hess said.

"Shit, man, you never bedded down with any of us except for Elza. Aren't you curious? Even Elza did San once. You ought to give it a try. Do it with another man and you can check two firsts off your list at the same time."

Hess finished his meal and stood. "Sorry, Kerzon, it doesn't matter what my relationship status is with Elza. I'm a man on a mission and you're not remotely tempting as a distraction."

As he walked away, Kerzon called after him. "You know, it's pathetic how much penises freak you out." The occupants of the room turned to stare at Kerzon, who met their gazes with casual hostility.

By the time Hess emerged from the hotel, Erik looked ready to kill. He handed over the reins to one of the horses without comment. They retrieved the travois, then Erik led the horses while Hess scaled the general store's fence to liberate extra-large burlap sacks and a flat shovel from the warehouse.

For most of the day, they snuck onto private property, loaded sacks with silage, and hauled them back to their staging area. They managed to do six loads before it grew dark. Then they returned the horses and sat down to a large meal at the hotel's restaurant.

"Hessie, we got one more day to get shit squared away. No late breakfasts tomorrow. I decided I'm gonna be generous and forgive your tardiness this morning. I'll see to getting us a freight wagon and a couple of draft horses for the day after tomorrow."

Hess leaned forward. "Watch yourself, Erik. You would be braving the ocean in a rowboat if not for me. No, worse than that, you wouldn't even know to stay behind at the end of the world. You owe me."

"Just told you, all's forgiven. Pull your tighty whiteys out of your ass."

They finished the meal in silence. On their way up the stairs, Hess spoke. "I'll need to collect a few things before we leave. Food, fish hooks, a salt water still for drinking water."

Erik nodded. "Then soon as the last presentation ends, we split to get our shit in order. Shouldn't take too long the last day, it's just you and Natalia. We'll meet at the hidey hole before stealing our ship."

Fifteen minutes later, after a brief scrub in the bath, Hess dove into his bed. The next morning, he woke late once more and rushed to get downstairs on time.

CHAPTER TWENTY-FIVE
Hess

When he arrived at the meeting room, a luxurious buffet awaited him. Hess hesitated, then noticed Elza seemed to be enjoying the food. "Did San make any of this?"

San laughed. "It's safe, Hess. I know a lot of recipes that work in a traditional way. The time for experimentation has passed, so I won't be serving any more bleach-tinis. This is just good food and adequate company."

"Thanks for complimenting my adequacy."

"Oh, Hess, you're one of my favorites. In the top twelve for sure."

Hess glanced at the contents of the closest tureen, at what looked like a jumble of autumn color. San looped her arm through his. "Honestly, I'm not playing any tricks on you today. This is me proving to everyone that I'm more than the one who eats weird things. I discovered some phenomenal combinations while walking the worlds."

"What is this one?"

"I call it kitchen sink stew. It has three types of meat: duck, pork, and horse. Plus assorted vegetables: carrots, celery, peppers, peas, and ginger. Half the broth is made from caramelized onions and garlic. The other half is based on lemongrass and mushrooms. After I combined everything, I seasoned it up to perfection. The thing beside it is noodles in a creamy wine sauce that you will not believe. Whatever you do, don't leave without trying the pickled salad."

Hess glanced around the room. "Is this your presentation?"

"I'll do the talking thing too. This is mostly me showing off."

When San left to speak with a newly arrived Ingrid, Hess glanced to Elza, who without looking up from her plate signaled back with a thumbs up. Hess placed a single spoonful from each tureen onto a plate and sat one seat away from Elza. As the room slowly filled, Hess took a tentative bite of the kitchen sink stew.

"You have to admit it's good," Elza said.

He smiled. "I admit nothing."

"I hear that nothing is pretty popular these days."

"Only if it's differentiated."

"So they tell me." Elza took a sip of a dark liquid. "You would hate this one. It's too bitter, too sour, and too sweet all at once. The lighter one is more your style. I think it's sassafras mixed with wheat beer. Somehow she made it spicy, so don't drink too fast."

Hess studied his plate. "You're spending a lot of time with San."

"I'm still keeping my promise from Iteration five. What is your plan to escape the island?"

"We're stealing a steamship."

"Sounds promising."

Hess sighed. "It's low on coal. I'm not sure if it will be able to get up to operating temperature, let alone make it out of harbor."

"And you can't get more coal?"

"There's an island-wide shortage. What's left is under guard. We could get it, but transporting it to the ship unnoticed would be a challenge. We're using wood as our fuel."

Elza turned to him. "You should make rocket candy. This island has a saltpeter factory and the kitchen seems to have plenty of sugar on hand. Be careful not to add too much at a time. Excessive heat will make your boiler explode. And even if you avoid that problem, you still have to worry about your firebox melting. Speaking of fireboxes, copper or steel?"

"Cast iron," Hess said.

"What gauge?"

"Thick."

"Hmm. Should work. I'll let you know if I think of anything else."

"Thanks." Hess looked down at his empty plate. "She's going to think I like the food if I go back for seconds."

"If you must have something to complain about, try the dark drink."

He returned from filling his plate and grabbing a drink just as San began her formal presentation. "Feel free to keep eating while I talk. The food is in no way related to anything I'm about to say, by the way. I worked quite hard on this meal. My speech, on the other hand, is unlikely to impress."

San rubbed her hands together. "My contribution to the discussion is boredom. I have been bored since the first world. Some of you seem content to live the same day through eternity, but I can't do it. I yearn for novelty or, lacking that, oblivion.

"I suspect that the Creator is as bored as me. Maybe that's the reason to make universes. You do your creation-thing, then you stop existing until your Observers come back, then you get to ponder over the new data for a millisecond or two. Rinse and repeat. Sounds boring to me, but then again, *everything* sounds boring to me.

"That's it, the grand total of my reflections on existence. To riff off of Greg's presentation, there should be more diversity." San turned and presented her palm to him. "High five?"

Greg folded his arms. "Just two minutes?"

"In my defense, I spent twelve hours preparing this meal. So I put in more time than anyone, just in a different way. Enjoy the food."

CHAPTER TWENTY-SIX
San
Iteration 4

Another world. Another thousand years or so watching people do the things people do. This latest world seemed to be all islands. A shame, as he'd never cared for sea food.

At least he was a man this time. He hadn't been the rugged sex since the first world. Iteration two was a fine world to be a woman, but three had treated anyone lacking a penis as a frail blossom in need of constant protection. San didn't do delicate very well. He liked to go where he pleased and do his job without interference from the quaint notions of the people.

Maybe one of these worlds would do some interesting role reversals. He would like to see women lording it over men for once. Of course, that was hardly a stable social order. Men were, on average, larger, stronger, and more aggressive. So far the Creator had not deviated in matters of basic biology between worlds, but he could still hope.

San settled into life on one of the larger islands, watching the people do the usual song and dance. They ate and shat and procreated and accumulated possessions and gossiped incessantly. Little things changed, but the core of human life never did. People were depressingly simple subjects. They hardly merited eleven Observers. Maybe Natalia has the right idea studying animals. Of course, if you listen to Griff, Natalia beds down with the beasts she studies.

But San could not believe his purpose was anything other than the study of people. Which meant that he spent several years in Iteration four cataloging the myriad details of life on an island. The locals obsessed over fish, eating it with every meal. Indeed, their word for meal meant fish. They ate big fish cooked whole so that their scales had to be flaked off between bites. They ate little fish grilled over coals. They ate sea creatures with shells. They ate water snakes. They ate insects found beneath the water. They ate gelatinous sea animals. And for side dishes of vegetables or grains, they used garum as their primary seasoning.

Garum: fermented fish guts. As in the organs removed from a freshly killed fish and placed into a barrel with salt to rot, whereupon the potent, thick liquid was placed in jars to be relished by deranged villagers.

Garum: a substance capable of spoiling a bowl of grilled squash with just a drop. An unpalatable addition to every dish the people made. The only condiment provided in public eateries. The secret ingredient in every specialty dish ever offered to him by one of the locals.

Garum: the bane of San's existence.

He had endured horrible foods before. The tubers used as a famine food in Iteration three had been one – the unpleasantness of their blandness exceeded only by their horrible mushy texture. Another had been the bitter plants used as a medicinal supplement in Iteration two and consumed every spring by entire villages. The meat of the bobcat his tribe had killed in Iteration one. Each time he had dutifully chewed and swallowed the offered fare to avoid attracting any undesired attention.

Not in this world. Not with garum. The substance offended him on every level. He hated the thought that the stuff came from rotten offal. He despised the taste of it. He objected to its undeserved popularity.

As a consequence of his unique opinion, San made most of his own food. He avoided the street vendors popular among the people of this Iteration and ate a monotonous diet of grains, vegetables, fruits, and birds – until the day he realized that he had become a recluse.

A ten-day without human interaction sparked this realization. Gardening, hunting, preserving, and cooking were all time-consuming activities, which placed them in conflict with his mission. So San took action. He abandoned his hut, moved into town, got a job heaving nets on a boat, and committed to partaking in local customs.

His first meal was breakfast on the street. He dutifully bought a bowl of egg-white soup that reeked of garum. By slurping quickly, he minimized the horror of the experience.

His second meal was a light lunch provided on the ship. It consisted of flat bread, pickled fish, and a small sweet onion. He forced it down with a hearty dose of self-pity.

His third meal was a buffet inside a pay-to-enter food tent. With an almost perverse pleasure, San consumed an array of disgusting food choices. Smoked fish. Crabs. Squid. Bitter greens. Raw egg-yolk over fried insects. Every garum-laden bite affirmed his low opinion of the local food.

The following day, he broke his fast with raw porpoise blubber. After the standard fare of his ship-lunch, he dined that night on offal pie. Inside the shell of the pie was a wild menagerie of undesirable leftover fish organs: liver, tongue, skin, bladder, heart, and roe. Plus garum. Lots of garum. San emptied his stomach after his first bite.

Day after day, San sought out the most horrific culinary disasters. He grew inured to the sense of disgust. After his first month, he had gained a reputation among the people as someone with an iron stomach and a defective tongue. He continued his meal-time adventures partly in perversely ironic protest of their food traditions, but also because – more and more as time passed – he enjoyed the intensity of his reactions.

Over several thousand years of life, he had learned what he liked and disliked. The inevitable consequence had been that his diet in previous Iterations had consisted largely of figs, almonds, grains, and land animals. Foods, even his favorites, had become bland. In the midst of his current disgust, he had discovered an odd pleasure in novelty.

One day, several months after his change in diet, he found himself at a buffet lacking any suitably entertaining options. San contemplated the open table for several minutes, despairing at the thought of eating food that no longer excited him in some way. Then he resolved to remedy the situation.

San dipped fried finger-fish into a bowl of garum to intensify their flavor. When that failed to provide the desired reaction, he began to concoct a more provocative combination. He used an edible flatfish scale plate as the base, placed bitter greens on top, then added pickled beets, onions, and a ridiculous amount of garum.

San eyed his hideous creation with pride. It should be simultaneously too fishy, too salty, too sour, too bitter, and horribly textured. In short, he had designed the most revolting food item he had ever encountered. San took several moments to appreciate what he had done – and also to steel his stomach for the upcoming ordeal.

He folded the fish scale over on itself and took a bite. Scales crunched, juices squirted, beets smooshed. A riot of intense flavors struck him. San chewed, swallowed, licked garum from his lips, and studied the thing in his hands. It was every bit as powerful as he had imagined. But it was *not* unpleasant.

San took another bite and chewed thoughtfully. It wasn't unpleasant at all. Another bite. It was actually quite good. Excellent, even. He swallowed the last of his invention and returned to the buffet table. The next one he made had more of everything, but especially more garum. This food called for lots and lots of garum.

CHAPTER TWENTY-SEVEN
Hess

When the meal concluded, Jerome tapped the side of his glass with a fork. "This shared meal makes a convenient segue to what I want to talk about." He paused before continuing. "A long time ago, during the first Iteration, I decided that I would fulfill my purpose best by remaining unknown to the rest of you.

"I based that decision upon what I witnessed among the tribes. The people did horrible things to one another, had such vicious vendettas. I witnessed a woman jealous that her child died while another's lived convince an entire tribe that her nemesis was cheating on her man. The end result was another dead child. Such spite seemed endemic, so I resolved to hide myself.

"By the time I thought to question my reasoning, it was too late. The eleven of you were a cohesive group. Showing up at that point, no matter how much I might wish to, would have been awkward at best. I resolved to live with the consequences of my decision, and that is what I did.

"Until Iteration one forty three. While conducting research on what I believed to be fascinating world leaders from history, I discovered rumors that the unusual couple had survived gruesome assassination attempts in miraculous fashion. You can imagine my initial horror at the idea that Observers had conquered over half the known world.

"Then I learned that after their disappearance, the remains of several palace guards were discovered – each bearing the signs of horrific, yet undeniably creative, deaths. By this point, I suspected something untoward had happened. I broke my cover to contact Ingrid by letter, posing as San. The response indicated that the guilty party would be entombed in darkness until the sky opened. So I immediately opened the sky.

"One forty four had the internet. I watched the online forums as Elza sent out message after increasingly frantic message. When no response came, I went to find Hess in person. He was working in a gas station, broken. I moved closer to watch over him.

"And then the unthinkable happened. Hess became newsworthy. Knowing that Ingrid was out of circulation in a backwater nation, I posed as her and reached out to the other Observers, some of whom were already on their way. I made arrangements for everyone to meet on my property, hoping that Hess would come to his senses and flee while I delayed the manhunt.

"He did not. Instead, he walked right into the inept trap set for him. I freed him. He came back the next day to surrender himself. Unable to resolve the situation, I opened the sky once more after revealing myself to Hess and Elza.

"The greatest irony in all of this was how much I enjoyed being part of the team. Even faking another's identity every moment, even while sabotaging the goals of the group. I loved interacting with my own kind. It was the community denied to me my entire existence.

"During one forty five, I was tasked with conducting the vote. In the process, I joined a team to liberate Ingrid and Erik, an experience that I unhesitatingly rank as the most meaningful of my life. After, Hess chaperoned me on my travels.

"The great lesson of my life is that no one can exist in a vacuum. Human connection is the most important thing any of us can ever have. We need community. And I regret with all my heart that I waited so long to join mine."

"Fuck you, *Twelve.* You're not welcome in my community."

"Hey," Griff said, "you realize none of us actually like each other, right?"

"I have no illusions. Every encounter seems to fizzle out due to lack of interest. I sincerely doubt you could understand the value of what you have without having experienced its absence as I did."

Drake chortled a bitter laugh. "What do you think you got now that you didn't before? Not friends. None of us much care for you, Jerome. Guess you could say the same about any of the rest of us, but at least we got history. You crashed this party."

Jerome flinched. "Well, if it's any consolation, you only have to endure my presence one more day."

CHAPTER TWENTY-EIGHT
Jerome
Iteration 8

He sat cross-legged on his hotel bed and watched the eleven on his computer screen. Their party had become boisterous enough to warrant an eviction from the hotelier. In response, Erik had corralled Griff, Drake, and Ingrid to one side, where they were plotting who knew what brutality. When they broke apart to enact their plan, Elza informed the room that she had purchased the official's goodwill. Across the room from her, Hess surreptitiously slid a knife from the serving line up his sleeve. The two of them made eye contact for a brief moment. They were protecting the people again.

He smiled. This was the first time he had ever been in the same building as his comrades. Their first full gathering was the last place he should be, but that hadn't been sufficient motivation to keep him away. He was one of them, whether or not they knew he existed.

San handed a drink to Elza, the latest abomination she had concocted from the stores of the well-stocked liquor cabinet. As always, Elza tried it. Like everyone else who had braved San's failed experiments that night, she spewed it out of her mouth in a spray of mist. Having watched the entire evening from hidden cameras, he knew that the secret ingredient of every drink that night had been detergent from the cleaning closet.

Natalia drifted in and out of random conversations, more interested in kissing the snout of the dog she carried in her purse than anything happening around her. She left soon without telling anyone.

Greg and Mel sat together in a corner, politely alternating whose turn it was to pontificate on subjects the other feigned interest in. The microphones had long since ceased reporting intelligible speech due to the rising sound level, but earlier they had lectured on the semi-satirical movement and the cumulative impact of tariffs on the world economy.

Drake approached Kerzon to show yet another person his state-of-the-art SlickSlate tablet computer. Drake had given each of the Observers an identical demonstration, one at a time, repeating word for word the same fan-boy pitch.

A drunken Kerzon made a pass at Hess, either forgetting that Hess was strictly heterosexual or having fun with the fact. Mel disappeared with Ingrid. San walked out with Kerzon even as her eyes lingered on Elza. Greg left by himself.

Everyone trickled away until only Hess and Elza remained. Half a room apart, they smiled at the same moment, their eyes meeting half a second later. Seconds later, the banquet hall stood empty.

He watched the space from his computer, remembering the second-hand sights. San and Ingrid spontaneously break-dancing. Erik sawing through chair legs so that Griff crashed to the floor when he sat after returning from the restroom. Ingrid spinning some epic tale while standing on a table. Kerzon leaving a trail of laughter behind unheard punchlines. It appeared to have been a good party, no matter the awkward moments or the times violence threatened. And now it was over.

The others had not opted to book rooms in the hotel. He didn't think it wise to remain there himself. The threat of discovery loomed over the entire city. If there was a lesson to be gleaned from the lives of the other Observers, it was that they recognized one another on first meetings with all the ease of lifelong friends. For all their differences, the similarities of origin and purpose were greater still.

He packed the electronics into his bag and departed his room. As the main entrance neared, he slowed, then stopped. The banquet hall's doors stood a stone's throw away. With quiet steps, he approached.

The room stood empty. He studied it for a time, imagining himself there. The cup San had offered to Elza still sat at the center of the space. He drifting inside, lifted the half-full cup, and took a sip. Then spit with all the speed of an autonomic reaction. The substance burned with malicious astringency. He looked down at the liquid and almost-smiled.

On his way back out, he noticed a figure standing in the shadows and his heart began to race. Hess had spotted him. Feigning ignorance of his surveillance, he slunk towards the hotel's exit, digging into one nostril with a pinky as if oblivious.

No one followed him once he was outside. His feet felt light as they navigated him towards the train station.

CHAPTER TWENTY-NINE
Hess

He approached Elza as the others left the room. "So I need saltpeter?"

"And sugar." She went to the cupboard to get paper and pencil. "Two parts oxidizer to one part fuel. Mix it together in water. Bring the solution to a boil. Once it becomes a thick paste, remove it from the heat and shape the material into lumps the size of a finger."

He cleared his throat. "Which is the oxidizer? The sugar?"

"The *saltpeter*, Hess. It's potassium nitrate – nitrate means one nitrogen to three oxygen. You're making rocket fuel, so be careful. Make it in small batches. Don't let the mixture overheat. And when you feed them into the furnace, do it only a few at a time."

Erik sidled up to them. "Rocket fuel, eh? I have some experience with oxyhydrogen gas. Burns nice and hot, but you gotta be extra-extra-*extra*-careful about explosions."

"As I was saying, Hess, be careful. This is a solid fuel, so there will be an explosion hazard if too much ignites at once in an enclosed space. You'll have to watch the steam engine, too. Bring it fully up to temperature using coal. Too hot too fast –"

"And the boiler explodes. I'm familiar with the process."

Elza pushed the hand-written instructions at him. "I know you are. Just be safe."

They stood silent for another moment before separating. As he walked out the door, Erik nudged him. "So are we done stealing corn?"

"I'm not sure how much rocket fuel we can make. Why don't you do a load of maize? I'll get a few bags of bulk sugar and figure out how we're going to get inside the refinery."

After Erik departed with the horses, Hess climbed the general store's fence once more. He searched the warehouse for half an hour before determining consumables weren't kept there. Then, he used two nails from

322

the warehouse to pick the rear door of the store. The lock sprung open with hardly any effort, a combination of its poor craftsmanship and the fact that it only had two pins.

With abundant care, Hess eased the door open and slipped inside, closing up behind himself. He stood among shelving on the clerk's side of the counter. The clerk, a middle-aged woman, sat oblivious on a tall stool, penning something. Judging by the pile of paper, she wrote something consequential; a memoir or novel or perhaps even a treatise on a subject dear to her heart.

Hess ghosted along the shelving until he located the sugar. There were several sizes, ranging from one pound bags to fifty pound sacks. He tested the floor boards for give along his path, making a mental map of where not to step. Then he shifted the largest sack onto his shoulder and waltzed around potentially squeaky boards on his way to the door.

Checking that the clerk sat undisturbed, he opened the door, exited, and placed the sugar near the fence. Then he returned three more times to repeat the maneuver. After the final trip, he staged the sacks of sugar on a corner of the roof before climbing over the fence. He carried the sacks two at a time away from the store to stash them behind a rock.

Satisfied with himself, Hess moved on to study the saltpeter refinery. The complex of buildings sat in the center of town, patrolled by a guard enamored of catcalling women through gaps in the sturdy gate. His lewd comments drew a variety of responses. Some women ignored him, others called back insults, a few laughed at the attention, one even bent over to shake her rear in his direction – an action the guard very much appreciated.

Hess scouted the entire perimeter of the refinery, but the only place it didn't abut another adjacent property was along the street where a guard currently manned the gate to the yard. He identified his ideal route of bypassing the fence, which involved climbing the lintels along the main building's front to descend from the roof into the open yard, as well as a backup route, which would be to lasso a crenelation atop the fence and use heavy gloves to pass over the barbed wire.

Retracing his steps, Hess waited for Erik along the main street. Together, they loaded the sugar and rode to their staging area. Hess put aside a large skillet and made sure the wood stove was stocked and ready to light. Then they planned for their trip into the refinery that night.

CHAPTER THIRTY
Hess

Two guards sat on rickety stools by the gate, rolling cigarettes and complaining about their domestic lives loud enough for the echoes to reach Hess and Erik. Isolated phrases like "won't cook anymore", "alcoholic", and "man on the side" reached their ears, lacking the context they didn't need.

Erik leaned close. "Sure you don't want some stabby?"

Hess shook his head. Riding the edges of shadows, he reached the far side of the refinery's main building. Hess gauged the distance to the first window ledge, crouched with hands extended down to each side, and launched himself straight up. His palms smacked down on the lintel, fingers clenched and held.

He shimmied to one side, legs swinging like pendulums; pressed his weight onto toes and knees to stabilize his position; reached one hand to grasp the corner of the building, which he seized between his thumb on one side and the strength of his combined fingers on the other. The rough surface of the brick stung beneath his solid grip.

Hess worked his hand up the corner, re-positioned his toes to take advantage of the different angle, then pivoted the hand on the lintel to face palm down. Then he worked himself as high on the corner as possible while pushing himself up with the other hand. When he was as high as he could go in that position, he paused to gather courage.

Two quick breaths.

He pulled against his grip on the corner, pushed down with the other hand, and moved a foot onto the lintel. Continuing the dynamic movement before he could fall, Hess extended the planted leg to press himself up. His weight thrown off, he started to swing off the wall as if his hand on the corner were a hinge.

At the last moment, his hand from the lintel seized the side of the window casing, grasping with frantic strength. His momentum slowed, slowed, and stopped. Releasing an unsteady breath, Hess worked his other foot over so both were on the lintel.

Hess looked down and mouthed *only two windows to go.*

Erik mimed smacking his head.

At least I have friends who believe in me. Oh, crap, did I just think of Erik as a friend? That's a problem for later. I can't stay on the side of this building for long.

The distance between windows was less than the distance from the ground to the first one, so Hess was able to grab the next lintel by hopping instead of leaping. Using the same method, he worked his hands up, placed a foot, nearly fell, and caught himself.

He had to rest his hands a moment, so he wedged his head into the top of the window casing until the rough facing of the brick cut into the skin of his forehead. Using the tension of his spine, anchored by his feet and his head, Hess maintained his position while he shook out his cramped and bleeding hands.

After weighing the need for speed against his desire to heal his hands before continuing, Hess decided he couldn't afford five minutes. So he continued with only a two minutes break. His method barely got him onto the third lintel.

Breath ragged, Hess paused for another break. Now not only his hands were shaking, but his legs as well. His breaks might be good for his grip strength, but they were hell on his calves. Not good. Someone inexperienced might think of climbing in terms of upper body strength, but a skilled climber knew legs were every bit as critical as arms.

Before the shaking became too bad, Hess resumed his climb.

He reached one hand up and over the lip of the roof to feel at the slate shingles. The pitch was shallow, so he placed both hands on the lip. Then he hopped, pulled with both arms, swung his legs to one side, hooked a heel over the edge, and curled his leg to bring his lower body up. He harnessed his upward momentum to roll over onto his back, laying on the edge of the sloping roof.

Hess gave himself several minutes to relax. Sitting up, he nearly fell off the roof and had to use his core muscles to redistribute his weight. At a snail's pace, he inched further up the slope of the slate tiles before transitioning to his side, then this knees, and finally onto his feet.

He waved in case Erik was watching, then padded across the roof to look down on the guards. They had moved on from discussing wives. The current topic of conversation was the prospect of better work on the mainland. Apparently, besides nitrate-rich soil and abundant sea life, the island had little to offer ambitious young men.

Hess moved past the guards, down the gated receiving yard to where the main building abutted a shorter one. He climbed down to the other roof, went to its edge, took a knee with his rear end and feet hanging out over empty air, and dropped to dangle by his hands. He fell to the loading dock two body lengths below, rolling as he hit. It left him winded and sore but uninjured.

After waiting to see if the guards would react, he slipped off the loading dock to search for an improvised weapon. The area was bare, so he contented himself with pulling free a loose cobblestone.

As the guards discussed how the governor's stubborn refusal to pay damages was costing the entire island the coal it needed to operate – coal the saltpeter refinery needed – Hess slunk up behind them. When he was in range, he lifted the cobblestone high and to one side, then brought it down with a mighty twist of his frame and all the force of his arms. The blunt instrument struck hard, sending the guard tumbling from his seat.

In a blink, the other guard jumped up and sunk a short dagger hilt-deep in Hess's eye socket. Hess stumbled back from the strike, tripped and fell. His hands hovered around the protruding hilt, afraid to touch it.

The guard opened his mouth to shout, then gasped as Erik's sword slipped into his side. Strong hands reached through the gate's slats and pulled the guard close. Erik seized the exposed throat and crushed it like cardboard. The hapless guard broke free and screamed a high-pitched fluting noise through his broken trachea.

He screamed and screamed, till he had to take a breath, whereupon he discovered the air only went one way in his throat. The guard sank to his knees beside Hess. In a final act of defiance, he aimed his collapse to hammer the knife deeper into Hess with his forehead.

Even as Hess swore at the renewed pain, he felt admiration for the man's grit.

"Open the gate, dagger-face."

Hess fumbled at the pockets of the guards until he found a key. He stumbled to the gate and fitted key to lock. With a twist, the gate opened to admit Erik. "Pull that fucking thing out of your eye."

Hess backed away from Erik. "The blade will vanish when I heal."

"Whatever. Give me the keys."

Erik opened the door to the loading dock and went inside the building.

They bumbled through the darkness, scattering haphazardly stacked pans, stepping into boxes of dirt, and colliding with industrial stoves. Finally, Erik located a lantern that he lit with a flint and steel.

Holding the lantern aloft, Erik led Hess deeper into the three-story building he had scaled earlier. The immense first floor held hundreds of desks with oversized mortars and pestles. Prominent signage in every direction read "ABSOLUTELY NO FIRE".

They halted their tour of the desks to return to the original room by the loading docks. Erik kicked in a locked door to reveal bags filled with saltpeter. He hefted one. "Five pounds a piece, I think. How many do we need?"

"Four hundred pounds."

"Please say you're fucking kidding me."

"I wish I could." Hess noticed light from outside and went to the nearest window. In the receiving yard, a handful of people stood around the corpses of the guards. Hess thought he saw a musket and at least two swords in the group. "While we're making wishes, I'd like those witnesses to not be here."

Erik scowled out the window. "To state the obvious, this ain't good, Hessie. Way to go, Mr. Screamy Guard. The whole fucking town's coming out to check on their precious refinery. What the hell even makes this operation a refinery? It looks like a dirty bakery."

"Let's go out one of the windows," Hess said.

"You get started on that. I'm going to disobey some signage. The fire brigade will have to earn their keep tonight."

Hess loaded a cart with bags and pushed it to a row of windows facing the yards of houses abutting the refinery. He shattered the glass and began dropping bags one at a time, counting as he did so.

When he returned to refill the cart, a frantic Erik ran into him. "We got to go. This saltpeter shit turns wooden desks into fucking matchsticks."

"More bags first," Hess shouted. Together they piled the cart high and then raced the smoke filling the room all the way to the window. They tossed bags by twos and threes, not bothering to count, not caring that a man ran towards them through the yard with a fire iron in his hands.

Hess jumped to the ground, twisting an ankle as he landed on a shifting pile of five pound saltpeter bags. The man raised the fire iron above his head and glared down at Hess.

And Erik crashed into him, burying a shard of glass into the man's neck mid-air. The man and Erik found their feet at the same time. The man noticed gushing blood and fell back with a look of horror on his face. Erik slapped blood-slicked hands to his cheeks and screwed his face up into the mirror expression of the man's. "Oh no, I cut your neck!"

Erik punted the toe of his foot into the man's testicles, then slammed the man head-first into the brick of the refinery. He flashed a big smile at Hess. "We should do this more often."

They moved the bags to the front of the dead man's property, doing their best to balance speed and stealth. A bucket brigade was storming the refinery while an unheeded man shouted at no one in particular that water couldn't put out a saltpeter-fed fire and they were throwing away their lives.

In the confusion, Erik took a hand-drawn wagon from an old woman under the pretext of hauling back water to fight the blaze. She had sent her two sons with Erik to assist in loading "a dozen full rain barrels from the hotel" but the boys had vanished by the time the wagon pulled up in front of Hess. He pointedly avoided asking Erik about them.

After piling the wagon full, they dragged it down the main street and turned down the harbor road. The gloom painted the world in shades of gray, darker at the tree line, somewhat less so along their path. At one point, their wagon overturned in a rut they had doubtless carved themselves in previous trips with their travois. It took fifteen minutes to collect and reload as many of the sacks as they could find.

Hess ran ahead when they were close to start a fire and bring water to a simmer. It wasn't until then that he realized his blunder. "We need a scale," he told Erik in greeting.

"Well, too fucking bad. We ain't got time for shopping."

"Chemistry is done by weight, not volume. Help me rig up a scale. We can calibrate with the five pound bags."

"There ain't time for perfection. This is the eleventh hour. Guesstimate."

Hess snatched a bag from Erik, dumped it into the waiting water, then eye-balled approximately half the volume of sugar and added it to the solution. He did the same for a second pot, then alternated stirring each pan while Erik retrieved more water in a bucket, setting it close to the fire to preheat it.

When the mixture thickened, Hess removed it from the heat, rolled it into snakes, and pinched off lengths. Then he put fresh ingredients in each pan and put them on the stove again. They moved at a rapid pace, their process limited solely by the time it took water to boil. Batch after batch of solid state rocket fuel came out of the crude shack, to be placed in the emptied five pound sacks on a freight wagon already loaded with a portion of their conventional fuel.

Not long before dawn, they stopped their production. They had processed somewhere around forty of the five-pound bags. Both of them sagged with exhaustion as they loaded the freight wagon and watered their draft horses. They would need to make at least two trips to the pier to load the steamship's fuel.

"I still need to get the rest of the supplies from the hotel," Hess said.

Erik sighed. "Leaving me to load the rest of the damn logs."

Hess began the trek back to the hotel. Pushing hard, he managed to reach the town just past dawn. As he trudged past the solemn town, sucking down gasps of stale smoke, angry shouts sounded. Hess looked up to see a group of five angry townies charging at him.

He shuffled back the way he'd come. At the first alley, he slipped down the gap between the houses and huffed towards the tree line, his pursuers hard on his heels. A sword flashed past his face, bare inches from flesh. Hess reached out a hand and seized the smooth trunk of a tree in passing, turning his momentum and sending his opponent past him.

Hess paused to catch his breath as the second man in line reached him. With a snarl on his face, the man executed a sloppy lunge. Hess stepped to the side of the blade, letting it rush past him. He seized the wrist and used his opposite hand to backfist the nose. Then the saber was his.

At the same time, the other men arrived. Three approached from the front while the one who had raced past him came from behind. Hess glanced to the man sitting on his behind with a bloody nose. He couldn't afford to leave behind potential enemies. With a practiced lunge, Hess pierced the neck, driving his blade from one side of the trachea all the way through the neck to pierce the vertebrate.

While his first victim collapsed, Hess moved to place one of the men between himself and the rest of the group. The first rule of fighting multiple opponents was to *not* fight multiple opponents. Serial single engagements were much more survivable than a single parallel battle. He closed the distance, holding his blade at the ready. The man struck first. Parried. The man struck again. Parried hard. The man struck a third time. Hess dipped his point below his opponent's blade, brought it up, established a clear line, and lunged to place steel through the upper rib cage. This time he got the heart.

Hess pulled his blade free, moved to place his next target between him and the two other men, and watched his previous opponent collapse. When they hesitated, Hess feinted a slash to the face and then opened the man's middle. Now they couldn't retreat without abandoning a friend. He approached a different man and pointed his blade at his face. When the man swung at his blade, Hess jumped in to kick the side of the knee. The third man turned to run and received a stab in his back.

"I'm sorry this was necessary," Hess said. "None of you deserve to die. But I'm committed to my survival." He finished off the two wounded men as humanely as possible. He avoided people for the remainder of his journey to the hotel, skirting the tree line for part of it, then slinking through alleys and jogging down empty streets.

Back in his room, he disassembled a lamp to dump the oil and scrubbed out some of the residue with a pillow case. Briefly, he considered washing it with soap and water. A quick sniff deterred him. A little olive oil in their water wouldn't hurt them.

Hess went to the communal bath and lifted a mirror off the wall hook. Before the other man present in the room could complain, he took one of the lamps and returned to his room. He cleaned up the second lamp, then tinkered with the metal brackets until he was able to attach the two lamp bases together.

One of the lamp bases would hold saltwater and sit on top of the mirror. Water vapor would rise to condense along the glass of the upper portion of his still, where it would roll down the sides to be absorbed into rags placed around the perimeter for that purpose. They would be drinking small amounts of water wrung from rags, but at least it wouldn't be saltwater.

He raided the linen closet, using two nails to pick the lock. All of it went onto his bed, where he wrapped the breakables, then made a sling to carry everything. When he finished, he went to the first floor to check the time piece. It read a quarter past nine.

CHAPTER THIRTY-ONE
Hess

He jogged into the conference room, transitioning to a quick walk at the threshold. To Erik's silent query, he returned a somber nod.

"How nice of you to show up," Greg said. "It's nice to know you can be counted on to out-do the rest of us, even when the competition is demonstrating complete disregard for our mission."

Hess placed a hand on the man's shoulder as he passed. "Shut your jaw, Greg, or I will break it."

All eyes on him, he spoke as he sank into the last available seat. "I apologize for being late. For anyone who hasn't heard, Erik and I are escaping the island tonight so we don't have to die when Jerome opens the sky. There is a lot of prep work involved, some of which has me avoiding the authorities."

Hess caught his breath before continuing. "I would like to share two observations with the group. The first I had at the very beginning. The great flaw in the worlds is the inability of the people to work in their own best interests. They are so short-sighted that they cannot understand how less for them today can translate into more for everyone tomorrow. They treat life like a zero sum game, scrabbling after pieces of the pie when they could be playing a positive sum game and making more pie than everyone together can eat.

"To my way of thinking, the people are their own greatest problem. I saw them in Iteration after Iteration and thought that their lives were not worth living. I blamed the Creator for bringing into existence flawed beings who could never be happy. It seemed perverse to me.

"Then several of you decided to throw me in a crypt for a few hundred years. Between begging to die and trying to escape the inescapable, I went crazy. At the start of Iteration one forty four, I became Zack Vernon, the most pathetically miserable person I have ever had the displeasure of knowing.

"His greatest desire was to stop existing. Every moment of life brought pain and relief refused to come. With all of my past suppressed, I couldn't understand how other people could be happy. I obsessed over the question. I considered the possibility that they were too stupid to grasp the tragedy of their lives, but I could never commit to it. So I watched them. Constantly, I watched them, trying to figure out the key to the puzzle."

"If he starts talking love, I'm out of here," Griff muttered.

"You can relax," Hess said, "this isn't what you expect from me. When I came back to myself, I wasn't depressed anymore. To be honest, I have trouble remembering what being Zack Vernon felt like. Which should be impossible, considering we have perfect memories, but it's true. The pain isn't the same when I'm not him.

"One thing did have a permanent impact on me. I never noticed it before because I was so fixated on the flaws of the worlds. Most people are happy most of the time. Perhaps that fact struck me as profound only because I spent so long assuming it was not the case.

"The people are happy, more or less. Which means the worlds are not as flawed as I once believed. Except possibly the disaster last Iteration."

"I set off a nuke," Erik said. "That was a fucking kumbaya moment right there."

Hess glanced to the clock. "That's all I have to report."

CHAPTER THIRTY-TWO
Hess
Iteration 1

He stumbled through mountainous terrain in the company of a hunting party, breath rasping with every step. The other men traded jokes and ignored the scrawny Observer struggling to match their pace.

When the world sprang into motion, the Observer had assumed the identity of Hess the fatherless, who had been graciously included in a group hunt by men who usually mocked him. His role, both before and after the world's start, had been to drive game with the young men towards where the real hunters waited. Essentially, he had walked up and down mountains the entire day in an attempt to move deer.

Two of the men carried the benefit of his hard work between them – the meat of three animals wrapped in valuable skins. Very little of that meat would go to Hess. Only what the lead men chose to share with him. *If* they chose to share with him. It hardly seemed fair that those who did the most work on the expedition received the least, but the tribe rewarded skill above all else, including effort.

The Observer smiled when he saw the tents appear in the distance. Though he had never actually been to the camp he remembered leaving that morning, coming home represented something very special to him: an opportunity to stop walking.

So far, his experience of the world consisted of making tiresome hikes on an empty stomach. His feet ached inside his moccasins, sweat plastered his garments to his flesh, every muscle in his body demanded rest, and the dull pain of his middle reminded him that he had, in fact, never eaten. Filling his stomach was an observation he would gladly make for the Creator.

Women and children met the returning party, swarming them to see what prizes they carried. The Observer watched the grand presentation of their future feast, listened to the dramatized tale of its acquisition, and wished the day was over. He wondered briefly if his attitude might not be appropriate for his position, but he was too exhausted from the day's labors to care.

Had the Creator placed him into the identity of a better hunter, things might be different. Instead, he was Hess the fatherless, a man who had never been taught how to be a man. A clumsy outcast unable to hunt or fight or claim a woman.

The hunters settled around the fire to watch the women prepare the feast. Hess collapsed to the ground some distance from the others. *I do not know if I care for this world,* he thought. Perhaps the Creator was as poor at creating as Hess was at hunting. That would explain why an Observer was necessary. His complaints would presumably inform the creation of the next world. Why else would the Creator need input?

Things are too far apart, Hess thought to himself, starting a list for the Creator to address in the future. *The next world should have less walking. Maybe make the deer live closer to the people. And everyone in the tribe should get a fair share of the food. All the children should have fathers to teach them hunting. And definitely less mountains.*

"And do we share with Hess?"

The Observer perked up at the sound of his name.

"Not one scrap," said Ron, the man who had brought down two of the three deer. "His stomping scared away all the animals. I bring down four or five on a good day. Only reason I did bad today was that boy." Ron turned to fix a sinister look on Hess. "You have to earn food in this tribe. If you're not man enough to hunt, then you should try to earn it on your back. Let me know when you are hungry enough to be a woman, Hess." The other men barked rough laughter in response.

Hess glared back at the brute. *I can learn to hunt on my own. When he grows old and weak, I will bring back meat enough for the entire tribe and forbid it only to him.* How long would a world last before the sky opened? Surely longer than it would take a grown man to become frail. Otherwise how could he see what this world had to offer?

He looked down at his hands. Hess the fatherless didn't know how to do much beyond tending fires and gathering plants. But he *wasn't* Hess the fatherless. He was Hess the Observer, sent to watch this world for the maker of worlds.

All he had to do was learn the things every father taught his sons. It would take longer without a teacher, but he had more than enough time and motivation to learn. In fact, there was no reason he couldn't become better than the men of his tribe.

So what skill do I learn first? Hess frowned. His identity truly did not have much talent to build upon. Twenty years of children's chores and begging for scraps of meat. He would need to start at the beginning, mimic what the older children did. Learn to navigate the wilderness on his own away from the camp. Spear fish in creeks far from their home. Track animals on the land. Take down prey.

Actually a smaller list than what a woman would be expected to know. A man's duties were few in the tribe, but those few were vital. Ironically, in order to be successful at procuring food, one needed the benefits of eating well, namely strength and stamina.

Fishing would require less exertion than hunting, so he would begin his journey of self-improvement with that. The biggest problem would be the hike from the tents to the streams, but he could endure it. After all, his feet had already healed from this day's exertions.

While the rest of the tribe feasted, Hess located the women's stock of roasted tubers and helped himself to one. He ate alone, planning his future. Some day, he would reverse roles with the great hunters of the tribe. And if their old age didn't come fast enough, he could always arrange a crippling injury. Or would that type of action conflict with his duty to observe?

He still mulled the issue when his sister Cora approached. Hess studied the girl, recalling that she had made every effort to disassociate herself from him in the past year, ashamed to be known as sister to a non-man. Cora squatted beside him, pressing her back to the same tree so that their shoulders touched. Her hands unclasped from before her to reveal a prize. She held the back straps from one of the deer. The best cut of meat.

Hess slowly reached out to accept the gift. "Why?"

Cora shrugged her shoulders. "Ron gave me the back straps because he said I was pretty. And I thought about you helping him all day and not getting to eat dinner. It's just not fair, Hess." Inexplicably, glimmering tears began to flow down her cheeks. "And I thought about how I never do anything nice for you. You're my brother, Hess, and I think you might die soon for want of food. Why haven't I ever done something about that?"

Awkwardly, he patted her shoulder, his eyes fixed on the gift held in his other hand. The cure to the pain in his stomach. An investment in his future as an expert fisher and hunter. The start of his journey towards becoming a man the tribe would admire.

"It's not your fault," Hess said, eyes still on the food.

"Yes it is," Cora said. "There is enough food to go around. Everyone eats well except you. Because the men want you to die for being another man's son. Anyone in the tribe could split their share with you, but no one ever does. All of us are killing you, Hess. Why would we do that? What kind of tribe are we?"

They were the kind of tribe the Creator had made them to be. Hess turned his eyes to his sister. Watched as she silently wept under the weight of transgressions made in a past that never happened. And he realized this girl was not what the Creator had made her to be. A single day had passed and she was someone different. Someone better.

Hess wrapped his arm around her shoulder and pulled her into an embrace. "You are a good person, Cora. Maybe our tribe will be kinder when you are a mother and I am the best hunter."

She laughed through her tears. "Promise me you won't give up, Hess. Don't let them kill you."

"I promise." He kissed the crown of her head. "Now help me eat our meal before it grows cold."

CHAPTER THIRTY-THREE
Hess

Natalia watched them over steepled fingers, the ghost of a smirk upon her thin, aged lips. "I suppose," she rasped, "I should begin."

Drake leaned forward. "We're dying to know if you really had sex with tigers like Griff says."

Natalia's nose lifted higher. "The lot of you are positively primitive."

"So," Drake said, "you're denying you had sex with tigers?"

"Jaguars," Griff muttered.

"Of course I didn't," Natalia said.

"Smart," San said. "Cats and bestiality mix badly."

Drake shifted his attention to the other woman. "Is that a fact?"

San clawed at the air. "There's very little I haven't done, big boy."

Natalia cleared her throat. "I would appreciate it if you would provide me the same courtesy I extended to each of you in turn. If you're an attentive audience, I promise to show you a magic trick at the end."

Erik snorted. "Like what? How to pull a specific number out of a hat? Your sleight of hand is fucking atrocious."

"Nevertheless," Natalia said, "I insist upon respect while I provide my testimony." She met each of their eyes in turn, then nodded.

"Very well. My tale begins in what we naively termed the First Experiment. When the Creator finished winding the mechanism and set things into motion, I inhabited the form of a sturdy lass in her first year of medical school."

"Um," Griff said, "*bullshit.*"

Greg cleared his throat. "Natalia, I don't want to offend, but this is meant to be a serious affair. We are here to discuss truths and not fictions."

For a moment, no one spoke. Natalia took obvious care in choosing her next words. "All I ask is for the courtesy provided everyone else.

Whether you think my words fabrications or metaphors or delusions, trust that I speak in service to the Creator."

Erik snickered, but there were no other reactions.

Natalia's gaze drifted into the distance. "It was a marvelous place, that First Experiment. Our method of inquiry was natural philosophy, which was not the combative and artificial science Elza follows. Indeed, that entire planet celebrated civilization – ironic, how often the etymological relationship between civilization and civility is overlooked.

"But not by the civilization of that Experiment. Or Iteration, if you prefer the intellectually pretentious terminology foisted on us by Elza. Anyway, I studied medicine for a few years before deciding that the mind interested me more than anatomy. I became a clinical psychologist. Quite a good one, I say without exaggeration. I helped a lot of people in exchange for the opportunity to plumb the depths of the human mind.

"Then came a day when I met an enigmatic anthropologist at one of those social functions where everyone pretends they are enjoying themselves far in excess of reality. We both homed in on the most fascinating character at that event, a man who unintentionally crashed the party because the host had attempted to invite a famous composer of the same name. This man, a wig-maker by trade, thought quite a lot of himself and assumed he belonged in the esteemed company he found himself.

"This wig-maker would ask a second question before his target had answered the first, interleaving his hasty interrogations with self-aggrandizing anecdotes, off-color humor, and ignorant assumptions meant to seem profound observations. This man may have been a blight on the party, but he was a gold mine of mental disorders to a young psychologist. I never had a chance to properly diagnose him, but I would wager pathological narcissism co-morbid with hyperactivity and oppositional defiant disorder.

"As I was doing my best to observe this fascinating individual, I found myself sharing an orbit with the aforementioned anthropologist. Time and again, she got between me and the witless wig-maker. This would not have particularly bothered me if she had engaged the man in a meaningful fashion. Yet she only watched from the background, invisible to everyone but myself as I found my view obstructed by her more often than not.

"Finally, I made an ironic comment that we both seemed intent on studying the same fool. To which my new friend replied that she was more interested in how the other guests were responding to him. We exchanged brief biographical blurbs that identified her as an anthropologist and myself as a psychologist. Our snooping became easier to disguise as we effortlessly used each as cover.

"My companion made a passing remark that I seemed perfectly suited for observing. I replied that the entire world was a grand experiment and I was there to observe it all. No doubt all of you can tell where this is leading. This anthropologist, remarkably inscrutable all evening, turned pale and stared at me. Oblivious, I moved to follow the wig-maker, but my companion seized my arm and exclaimed 'you are an Observer'. The way she said it, the capital O clear in her voice, was a revelation.

"We left the party to have what remains one of the most energizing conversations of my long life at a nearby beer garden. From then on, we met up once a week. Neither of us could have been more pleased to have company. Yezzen was her name. Dear Yezzen. My best friend throughout my entire existence. And lest one of you savages feel the need to put your crude curiosity into words, we were never physically intimate. Our mutual attraction was unadulterated by lust.

"A few years later, Damien stopped by to introduce himself. He was a true gentleman and explained that he had knowledge of our identities and the ability to open the sky at a time he felt appropriate. So naturally, the twelve of us eventually met up for a week of stimulating conversation and mutual encouragement.

"Ours was a good group. We lasted seventeen Experiments. Then Damien got us all together, as he was wont to do. But this time, he conducted a vote. One by one my friends elected to cease their existence. I . . . I remained silent until Damien begged me for a response. To them, I said that I did not wish my life to be over, but that I would cast my vote in solidarity with them."

Natalia's lips compressed to a line. "I was saved from my bitterness by Koji. Always the most distant of my friends, Koji took me in his arms and told me that I would live to see another Experiment. As many as I wanted. He told me that there are two Observers in every batch who serve a special function. One opens the sky and serves as a check on the others. The second carries the memory of every Observer who ever existed and even the thoughts of the Creator who ceases to be at the genesis of every universe.

"For the First Experiment had *not* been the first. There was a Cycle before my series of Experiments, which Koji had survived. He surrendered his special position to me so that I could live on while he became no more than a series of memories.

"And so one Cycle ended and another began. All my friends died and were replaced by brutal creatures forged in a primitive dystopia. You each bear the indelible stamp of your origin. To be blunt, your feral natures disgust me. You may make fascinating studies, but none of you meet my minimum criteria for friendship. I avoided you and did my best to make certain none of you had reason to seek me out in turn."

Natalia sighed. "Truthfully, I have done very little observing this Cycle. You see, I carry all of these memories in me. If my entire life experience could be represented as a single drop of water, then there is an entire ocean available for me to relive. It is impossible to navigate. I can live an entire day of another Observer's life, then never manage to find a single bit of that individual again. It is a jumble, an ocean frenzied by a hurricane.

"For as long as any of you have been alive, I have been sipping from eternity. I have tried with limited success to seek out particular types of memories. Never have I found any of Yezzen, but I have some success picking out happy ones, or exciting ones, or any type of mood I prefer in the moment. And there are other memories I can identify. Memories too incomprehensibly vast for a mere Observer to ever have had.

"Within me lives the memories of the Creator, a fact which segues right into my magic trick. As you could imagine, the Creator remembers the details of creating. And some portion of those details can be understood by the likes of us." She sat up straight. "Now give me your full attention. I likely will not be able to repeat this trick in the limited time available to us."

A smug smile on her face, Natalia's frail old-woman form flickered into that of a chubby middle-aged man with a patchy beard. She, now a he, pointed a finger at Griff. "For the record, not a single syllable was false, you uncivilized cretin."

Erik jumped to his feet and leaned forward, resting his knuckles on the table. "Excellent trick. Now, let's talk about you giving me your job."

Natalia studied his new body. "I never know what I'm going to become when I do that. This ability does not come with a preview option."

"I want," Erik said, "to live next Iteration, next Cycle, next Experiment, whatever the fuck you want to call it."

"Slight problem with your request." Natalia scratched at his semi-bearded face. "I nominated Jerome already."

Erik decked the table hard, a thud wrapped around a brittle snap. His face contorted as he turned his attention to Jerome. "*Twelve*. I will . . . fuck! Fuck, fuck, fuck!" Face red, eyes bulging, spittle flying, Erik brandished his shattered hand.

"Of course," Natalia said in a contemplative tone, as if speaking to himself, "that was a deal struck in a different universe. Given our extenuating circumstances, I am willing to reconsider my choice."

Erik's insane eyes fixed on Natalia. "That's right, tubby."

"None of that," Natalia snapped. "You have no power over me, Erik. If you engage in your trademark shenanigans, Jerome opens the sky and you lose. I make the rules, Erik, and you follow them with unfailing obedience if you have any hope whatsoever of continuing your twisted existence. I am in charge. You understand?"

"...yes."

"Fantastic. Hess, are you also interested in the opportunity to become my successor?"

Hess shot a glance to Elza, who stared at her lap impassively. "I am."

"Very well," Natalia said. "After the meeting, I will journey with Jerome, Erik, and Hess to discuss who gets to see the next Cycle. For the moment, however, we are participating in an unprecedented conference. I took this opportunity for my grand reveal, but I would be remiss if I didn't present my findings for the group's contemplation."

Natalia scratched at his protruding abdomen. "By virtue of the memories I carry within me, I can tell you that there has been a remarkable diversity among our kind. Sinners, saints, and everything in between. As near as I can tell, the early Experiments of every Cycle tend toward mono-cultural. I imagine that phenomena to function as a mold for each generation of Observers. We are cast in specific circumstances, then exposed to a variety of worlds.

"Based on these insights, I long ago concluded that the ultimate goal of our inscrutable employer must be to manufacture every consistent world from the infinite sea of possibility. Before we travel too far down the path presented by my data, I want to elucidate what I am not saying. Under no circumstances do I believe the Creator is bored. Nor would I claim that diversity per se is the goal.

"What I believe is that the entity we serve creates with a passion beyond mere obsession. With the utmost sincerity, I confess my suspicion that the Creator does not conform to our concept of sanity. While a post-vote conference is something I never encountered in my other memories, I *have* witnessed many erratic worlds like the previous Experiment. On occasion, the Creator . . . malfunctions. As if two potential worlds were merged into an inconsistent jumble."

Natalia smiled. "Having unveiled my great secret and spoken blasphemy, you might expect my contributions to be complete. However, I have yet to pass judgment on existence itself, so bear with me a moment or two longer.

"I am, to put it mildly, an unabashed fan of creation. My esteem for particular worlds varies to a great extent, but I find the overall experience to be downright amazing. If the twelve of us spent a thousand years at this table, we would get no closer to the truth than we are at this moment. Words are utterly inadequate to express the richness of reality. Our minds are insufficient to grasp the vastness of existence. We have each strained to the utmost to grasp even a single drop of water and the vastness of the ocean is forever beyond us."

Natalia looked around the room, meeting eyes. "To be blunt, I'm not interested in a passive-aggressive Q and A. I move to adjourn our conference. Anyone who feels a pressing need to discuss my revelations can do so without me. Hess and Erik, please be sure to include myself and

Jerome in your plans to escape the island." He leaned forward. "Would someone like to second my motion?"

Greg cleared his throat. "Seconded."

"Thank you, Greg. All in favor?"

A scattering of hands rose.

"All opposed?"

Silence.

"Then the motion is carried. Conference adjourned. Everyone try to enjoy the rest of your lives."

CHAPTER THIRTY-FOUR
Hess

Observers no more, their final duty to the Creator discharged, they dispersed in a hush of chair scrapes, footfalls, and door clicks. Hess avoided eye contact with all of them. The profound purpose that bound them had vanished, taking with it whatever comradery existed in their sad group.

Jerome hooked his arm around that of Hess the way he had done a hundred times the last Iteration when he was a woman. "It doesn't seem right, everyone going their own way without parting words."

Hess shrugged. "It's always been that way with us."

"Sorry I didn't tell you about the deal Natalia made with me."

"I would have kept it from you if our situations were reversed." He pulled his arm free.

Jerome stepped in front of him. "So I'm not even allowed to touch you now that I'm a man? Nothing has changed about me. I didn't try to seduce you last world, so why distrust me this one?"

"Don't take it personal, Jerome. He's never been affectionate with men."

Jerome startled at Elza's words, then stepped back. "I'll go on ahead of you."

The two of them spent a few moments not looking at each other. Elza broke the silence first. "I wanted to wish you luck. I hope Natalia picks you and that you have a fulfilling life in the next Cycle. You deserve it, Hess."

He studied the floor between them. "I appreciate that. I'm glad you're getting what you want. Well, no, not glad. Horrible word choice. Let's just say I will be comforted knowing that you are no longer unhappy."

She spoke again, her voice soft. "Then goodbye."

He took a breath. "I really wish you were saying the other thing."

"Then one last time, for the sake of tradition." Her voice was thick almost to the point of incoherence. "Find me fast, Hess." And she left.

He collected the stolen items from his room and carried them in a sling made from linens. In the stables, he encountered the corpse of the stable boy when he attempted to hire a horse. He saddled an animal himself and trotted it through town, one hand on the reigns and the other cradling the glassware hanging from his neck.

The few townies he saw were more interested in staring at the smoking mountain than a man on a horse. He kept to a walk for fear of shattering his homemade still. When he arrived at the harbor, the others were waiting for him in an overloaded freight wagon. Hess handed up his cargo and took the buggy whip from Jerome's hand.

He locked eyes with Erik. "Be ready with your saber. I'll take out one of the guards."

"With a whip?"

"I've never seen someone keep fighting after losing an eye."

Erik giggled. "Give me ten minutes to get in place." He jogged away with one hand steadying his scabbard.

Natalia frowned at him. "Do you do this type of thing often?"

"That depends on your definition of often." Hess uncoiled the whip and snapped it a couple of times to get a feel for it.

"Interesting. I look forward to the show."

Ten minutes later he drew reign before two guards standing at the pier's entrance, one of whom held a rifle at the front chest carry position. The senior guard twirled his finger in the air. "Get your ass out of here."

Hess pointed back towards the town. "Someone's been hurt. Real bad. They told me to let the guard on duty at the pier know so he can pay his last respects." He slapped his forehead. "I can't remember the name of the man I'm supposed to find."

The senior guard hesitated, then his gaze hardened. "This is private property. Ernie, put a hole in him if he ain't gone in sixty seconds."

As Ernie snapped his weapon into position, Hess threw his whip hand into the air and snapped his wrist. The musket's sights aligned, creating a direct path from the guard's eye to the rear sight post to the front sight post to Hess's chest. The tip of the whip intersected that direct path at its far end, connecting with the squinting eye.

The guard screamed, jerked, and discharged his weapon into the air. The senior guard ran to the guard shack. As he yanked open the door, light glinted off a slashing saber. The man tumbled back, hands hugging his chest even as he hit the ground. Erik emerged from behind the guard shack and drove his blade absentmindedly into the throat of the man.

"Nice whip work, Hessie." Erik drove his blade down into Ernie's chest. "Reminds me of that time I sliced your eyes out two Iterations ago. Good times."

Hess waved both hands over his head to summon Jerome and Natalia, then inspected the pier. It was possibly wide enough for the freight wagon, but they would never be able to get it turned around. "I don't suppose you brought the travois with you," he said.

"Of course, ya horse. I'm a fucking pro at this shit."

Jerome and Hess rapidly unloaded the wagon. Rocket fuel came off first, then sacks of maize kernels, then wood. Meanwhile, Erik attached travois and horses. When they moved the first load from the base of the pier to the steamship, Hess pointed to the wagon. "Someone needs to get another load. I'll warm up the firebox and pump water into the boiler. Whoever is left can haul fuel up the pier. Make sure none of the locals gets too curious about our activities."

Erik jabbed a finger at Jerome. "You heard him, Twelve, go reload the wagon. Me and Natalia have the pier under control."

Their voices faded as Hess climbed into the heart of the vessel. He turned at the sound of footsteps behind and found Natalia following him.

"Are you sure this thing is seaworthy?"

"It's designed to tow ships in crowded harbors," Hess said. "I'm guessing the locals use it to rescue and salvage ships that get torn up on the reef. It should be able to handle deep ocean with no problems. The real question is how far it can take us before we run out of fuel. Which is why you should be hauling wood."

Natalia waved at his obese form. "I could haul more wood as an old woman than I can like this."

"Fine. You're running the hand pump."

"You know, I have the power of life and death over you," Natalia said.

"I'll be sure to kiss your ass once the crisis is over." Hess checked that the rubber tube reached all the way to water, then demonstrated its operation: Lever up, lever down.

While Natalia labored at the pump, Hess threw open the door to the firebox and loaded it with some coal. On top of that, he built a structure from wood kindling and lit it with scrap paper and a magnesium striker.

Then Hess began moving wood from the deck of the ship into the coal room. After a while, he checked the water level using the three valve system. They were still low, so he kicked Natalia off the pump and labored at it himself, taking occasional breaks to feed more coal into the firebox.

Getting up to steam would take two hours, which was twice as fast he would try if there wasn't a volcano to worry about. Cold boilers tended to react poorly to rapid increases in temperature.

When Hess next checked the water, it was at an acceptable level. He resumed loading wood into the coal room. Outside, Jerome had returned with the freight wagon and was helping Erik move wood. When they finished, everyone climbed onto the deck of the ship.

Erik glanced back at the mountain. "We ready to go?"

"Let's give it another half hour," Hess said.

"Look Hess, I know it would be cool as fuck to outrace a tidal wave of lava in a steamship . . . but I'd rather not."

Hess raised a brow. "Spoken like someone who has never seen a boiler explosion." He turned to Jerome. "When are you opening the sky?"

Jerome glanced to the mountain. "I'm letting the Creator dictate the time-line."

They studied the smoke until Natalia broke the silence. "We might as well use the time. I plan to decide my choice of successor by plumbing the depths of your minds to discover your underlying motives. Rest assured that I don't intend to judge you by my personal standards of conduct, which would favor none of you, but instead by your commitment to the truth."

Natalia scratched his bulging abdomen. "Dishonesty and disqualification walk hand in hand. I'm not keen on laziness, either. Each of you should do your utmost to offer sincere reflections. Erik, I'm going to start with you. You have the advantage and disadvantage of being the most disgustingly fascinating subject. My first question: why do you enjoy hurting the people?"

"I'm doing research."

Natalia made a rude buzzing noise. "Sincere answers, Erik. Only honesty can preserve your life."

The false cheer faded from Erik's face, allowing something cold and reptilian to emerge like jagged rocks rising from the sea at low tide. "Because," he said. "I hate them."

"Why do you hate the people, Erik?"

"They don't appreciate existence."

Natalia shook his head. "Not justifications, Erik, reasons. You value your life more than anyone, so prove it. Give me your reasons."

Erik cleared his throat. "Can't we do this in private?"

"No."

Erik's face contorted into a pained expression. "Why do I hate the people? *Why do I hate the people?* Why do I hate the pathetic creatures? Why *wouldn't* I hate them? They are weak and soft and stupid and cowardly. They are fucking pathetic. They deserve everything I have ever done to them. Every fucking poke. Every fucking prod."

"Why do you hate the people, Erik?"

Erik turned his glare on Natalia. "I just told you. They are pathetic!"

"A reason to pity, perhaps. Why do you hate them?"

Erik's lips clamped together.

"Come now, Erik, you don't value your ego over your life. Would you not do anything to ensure your survival? Tell me the truth. Why do you hate the people?"

"Because." Erik turned away from them. "Because I once feared those pathetic creatures."

Natalia patted flabby hands together in subdued applause. "Well done, Erik. I'm quite pleased with your progress. Now, Jerome, I have a different question for you. Namely, why should I choose you?"

Jerome frowned. "What do you mean?"

"My meaning should be quite evident, Jerome."

"Well, for one, I'm not a sociopath. Also, I'm not going to waste the next Cycle pining for a lost love – sorry, Hess."

Natalia tsked. "I didn't ask about your competition. Why do *you* deserve to live?"

Jerome hunched his shoulders. "I never got the chance to be one of them."

"Of course you did," Natalia said. "You didn't take it. There is a tremendous difference. Try again."

"Because I have been an obedient Observer."

"Not compelling."

"Because I want to start over again. I want to live a different life."

Natalia chewed on the answer a moment. "I'll accept the answer. It would be unfair to handicap you for lack of drama. Hess, I must confess that you bore me. I of course respect you as a man of honor, but the action hero persona never impressed me. While well-intentioned, you remain a primitive reactionary. Tell me why I should find you interesting."

Hess blinked. Interesting? "Why should that matter? The only reason we ever considered you interesting was because of the rumor Griff started about you having sex with animals."

"Hess, my preferences are of supreme importance in this matter. Convince me that you are worth my time."

He sucked in his cheek. "Fine." He pointed behind him. "Do you know how to operate a steam engine? I do. I could even rebuild it given the proper tools. In case you weren't aware, I'm not Elza's idiot sidekick. The perception that I'm dependent on her for technical support is ridiculous. I can thrive on a boat, in the desert, within the arctic circle, in the wilderness, at court, or even an electronics repair shop. I am capable."

Natalia nodded. "I suppose it would be remiss of me not to grant you credit for our timely escape. Providing we do escape in time. Back to Erik. Assuming you are chosen, what would you do at the start of the next world?"

A portion of Erik's cheer returned. "I always like to start things off by hurting someone."

"Why?"

He sighed. "This again? I hate them because they . . . scared me . . . once upon a time. Ta-fucking-da."

"Why does torture bring you pleasure? Do you relish the sense of power? Does it reinforce your superiority? Does the sight of their weakness ease your lingering shame?"

Erik chewed his lip as the questions came at him. He flinched at the expectation on Natalia's face. "Maybe?"

Natalia's brows rose. "Are you asking me?"

"I don't know."

"You don't know if you're asking me a question?"

"I don't know why I like hurting people. Why don't you ask Hess why he likes sex so much?"

"We'll give you some time to ponder the question, Erik. I would put the same question to Jerome. What would you do at the start of a new world?"

Jerome raised his chin. "I would find the other Observers."

"And?"

"Talk to them. Tell them everything. No secrets."

"Dear Sir, I'm almost too disinterested to ask, but why?"

"Because I want the next Cycle to be better than this one."

Natalia rolled his eyes. "Hess?"

He stood looking at the volcano in the distance.

"Same question, Hess. New world. What do you do and why?"

The gentle rocking of the boat, the creaking of wood and crashing of waves, the taste of salt on the air all fell away. What did he do when a world began? He found Elza.

"Hess?"

For over a hundred Iterations – close to a hundred and forty thousand years – he had sought his woman with single-minded tenacity until she stood at his side. Though their tradition had grown ever more elaborate, its core had remained unchanged. She awaited him at the largest city she could find; assumed the name of an in-world state or province; worked at an intellectual trade or profession; frequented quaint watering holes where she would wait patiently for the right man to approach. He lived for that moment, that giddy anticipation, the thundering pulse and jittery legs as their eyes made contact. It brought him back to Iteration two every time. The weary walk that had threatened to never end. The endless wash of unremarkable faces. And then his name on her lips.

"Hess?"

He turned back to face them. "Feed more coal every twenty minutes, but don't let the pressure rise above the first tick before two hours are up.

Then start sprinkling the rocket fuel. You should be able to figure out the engine room easily enough."

Natalia raised a finger. "If you leave, you forfeit the contest."

"I should never have been in it."

Erik seized his arm. "The fuck, Hess? You giving up? Suiciding?"

"The opposite of giving up. I'm going to find her one last time."

As Hess pulled his arm free of Erik, Jerome wrapped him in a firm embrace. Hess shoved the man away. "Enough of that, Jerome."

"Sorry," Jerome said. "I know the Ron thing still bothers you, but you can't say goodbye to your best friend without a hug."

Erik scowled at them. "Fucking pathetic, Hess."

"As much as I'd love to continue this conversation, I've got a woman to find. Good luck everyone." All three stared at him, cataloging his actions with the alien, attentive gazes of Observers. He turned away to begin his hunt, his mind taking up the new puzzle. *Where on this island would Elza go to await the end of her last world?*

CHAPTER THIRTY-FIVE
Hess

He found her on the roof of the resort, reclining against sun-warmed brick to face the rumbling mountain's outline against the setting sun. She didn't move at his approach other than to touch a wine bottle to her lips. "How did you find me?"

Hess slid down the wall to sit at her side, leaving a finger's width of space between them. He gestured at the view before them. "You always preferred to watch from a distance. How did you know it was me?"

Elza shrugged. "An unfounded assumption. I've spent so much time waiting for you." She touched the full wine bottle to her lips once more. Several more, unopened, rested by her feet. "Who won immortality?"

"I had to leave before that was decided."

Her eyes flashed to his. "Hess, *no*. What are you doing here?"

"Finding you. Did you know that a good woman is worth a whole tent?" He took the wine bottle from her hands, inspected the label, and took a large swallow.

"Don't do this for me, Hess. Please don't."

"Do you know why I hate Zack Vernon so much?" Hess pressed the bottle back into her hands. "Zack despised existence. He was a miserable bastard who couldn't find a single reason to live his own life."

"Then fight for your life, Hess."

"The rest of them think I'm romantic by nature because of the circumstances they met me under, but you should know better. Hess of Kallig's tribe was an angry man who despised his own existence. He treated his women well while they were his, then discarded them when they showed signs of age – ignoring the plight of a childless older woman because he *did not care*. Hess of Kallig's tribe was not a happy man and not even a good man. He was an ignorant savage who blamed the Creator for everything.

The best that could be said of him was that he had enough empathy to imagine a better world.

"I remember that man, Elza, even if you pretend not to. And I can tell you from first-hand experience that the distance between him and Zack wasn't as great as you think." Hess stared at the setting sun. "For most of my life I've been someone very different, but only because I had you by my side."

For a moment, the rooftop was silent. Then Elza took a swig from the bottle. "I may have glossed over a tiny sliver of your history, but I know who you are, Hess. You don't understand me at all."

"That's ridiculous. I guessed where on the entire island you would be in five seconds." Hess gestured. "And here you are."

"Two Iterations ago, you thought I cared for the people."

"*What?*"

She pointed a finger at him. "You thought I was upset because the people were dying!"

Hess blinked. "You really think I'm that naive?"

Her finger drooped. "But . . . you kept trying to shield me from news."

Hess cocked his head. "Because you kept getting upset."

"I was responding to you. You are the one who loves the people."

"No, it wasn't the people. It was *science*. Science was bad, Elza."

For a moment, she stared at him, then Elza pushed the wine bottle into his hands. "Science is an experimental methodology, Hess. It's fundamentally amoral. It *can't* be bad."

"It destroyed an entire world, Elza. That's pretty bad."

"People destroyed their world," she said. "And they didn't use science to do it. They used technology."

"Technology made by science."

"Science doesn't make technology. People do."

"They can't make tech without science."

"Of course they can. They do it all the time, Hess. Science isn't the only way to innovate technology."

Hess raised a brow. "So you are claiming that the people could build a nuclear weapon without science?"

"Maybe not a *nuclear* weapon," she said.

He drank and passed the bottle back. "This conversation clearly isn't going anywhere productive."

Elza nodded. "You've never been good at abstract."

"I never said you were right. Science was clearly a bad thing. But you like it, so you'll never admit it."

She opened her mouth, then paused. After a moment she shook her head. "You never thought I was empathizing with the people?"

"Of course not. Don't you remember Iteration one four three? You only agreed to help me build an empire after I started bringing up all the technical challenges. You care about ideas and I care about people. The only thing we ever really had in common was we hate being apart."

Elza took a violent swig and dropped an empty bottle. "Then I'm an idiot."

"Sometimes." Hess picked up an unopened bottle and read the label. "But at least you make a passable *sommelier*."

A throaty giggle bubbled free of Elza, then turned fragile as she leaned into him. "I'm so sorry, Hess. I don't know why I keep messing up. I'm the rational one."

"How about you promise not to do it again?"

Elza locked eyes with him. "Do you want to make a run for it? We might be able to escape the island. We could spend a few centuries here until we're ready to go."

"I'm ready now," Hess said.

"Are you sure?"

He shrugged. "It's too late to escape now. We would just waste our last moments running around this damn island. Besides, it might be that chasing eternity misses the point. Maybe we can't appreciate something until it ends."

"The economics of immortality," Elza said. "Would you care to discuss the marginal utility of life?"

"While I hate to disappoint you . . . ." Hess shrugged.

They drank in silence, watching the sunset darken with time and smoke, hip to hip and shoulder to shoulder. Periodic shudders provided unsubtle reminders of their limited time.

"You know, I still don't understand what you ever saw in me." Elza stared into the distance. "I did everything I could to drive you away."

Hess pecked a kiss on her cheek. "Nice try, but you can't saddle me with the blame for all of this. You started it."

Elza smiled. "I couldn't stand you, Hess. You wouldn't relent until I loved you back."

"Sure, your words said you didn't like me."

"Come now, Hess, you were the one who gallantly rushed in to save me from my attackers."

Hess shook his head. "I would have done that for any Observer. I told you there was no reason for you to experience that."

"And I was quite clear that I was willing to endure anything in service to the Creator."

"I was able to tell the Creator everything He needed to know about what the men did."

"But you couldn't report how it *felt*."

Hess turned his face away. "I knew enough."

"Witnessing and experiencing are two different -"

"I *knew*, Elza. No one else had to go through that for the Creator's curiosity."

"You . . . . Oh." She blinked. "You mean . . . ."

"We aren't discussing it."

Elza cleared her throat. "Well, this actually makes our story more pathetic. I was a fat, unattractive woman with a lazy eye who threw my heart at the feet of a beautiful man because I mistakenly believed he liked me. Everything between us started with mixed signals."

"You were beautiful."

"Please, Hess. Your fondness for curves came later."

"About the same time, as I recall."

Elza took the bottle back and emptied it. "The important thing is that, contrary to everything I ever believed about our past, I loved first."

"Well, if we're clarifying our time-line, let's do it properly." Hess opened another bottle. "I liked you first, because you were so delightfully different. Then you like-liked me back even though you sorta hated my guts. Then . . . somewhere between leaving Kallig's tribe and the winter freeze I decided I would never willingly leave your side."

"So perhaps you were slightly more pathetic."

Hess pressed the bottle into her hands. "You wrote me a love letter. You dumped me in it, but I still think that cements your status as the romantic one."

"I've lost track. Am I the pathetic one?"

"No. Mel is. And San. Greg, Griff, Erik, Drake, Ingrid, Kerzon, and Jerome. They are the pathetic ones who never managed to make a real connection with someone else."

Elza stared at the red haze in the distance. "You forgot Natalia. Unless you think she connected with her friends from the last Cycle?"

A tight smile stretched across his face. "I know she connected with that little dog in Iteration eight."

Her befuddled expression gave way to a grin. "She kept kissing that damn purse dog at the party! Do you think the animal thing was really all just an act?"

"Elza, you can't fake true love."

She settled more firmly against him. In the distance, the dark smog emanating from the mountain lit up with a demonic backlight that quickly increased in intensity. Elza sought his hand and squeezed it. "Thank you for finding me all those times. It meant everything."

"I would do it all again." Hess held his woman as the land rocked in ponderous preparation. "Every last moment."

ABOUT THE AUTHOR

Brian Blose is an Army Veteran, husband, father, software developer, and writer. In his spare time, he pursues interests such as rock climbing, skiing, kayaking, sampling ethnic cuisine, and reading. He likes flawed characters, unreliable narration, and moral ambiguity.

Visit his author website at www.brianblose.com for bonus content.

Made in the USA
Charleston, SC
03 August 2016